PIERRE
BOULEZ
A SYMPOSIUM

PIERRE BOULEZ
A SYMPOSIUM

Edited by
William Glock

EULENBURG BOOKS · LONDON
DA CAPO PRESS · NEW YORK

First published 1986 by
Ernst Eulenburg Ltd
48 Great Marlborough Street, London W1V 2BN

ISBN 0 903873 12 5

© 1986 Ernst Eulenburg Ltd

Peter Heyworth's *The first fifty years*
© 1973 The New Yorker Magazine, Inc.

Phototypeset by Tradespools Ltd, Frome, Somerset
Music examples drawn by Susan Bradshaw
Printed and Bound in Great Britain by
Whitstable Litho Ltd, Whitstable, Kent

Contents

Our age is one of persistent, relentless, almost unbearable enquiry. In its exaltation it cuts off all retreats and bans all sanctuaries; its passion is contagious, its thirst for the unknown projects it forcefully, violently into the future; it compels us to redefine ourselves, no longer in relation to our individual functions, but to our collective necessity.

Pierre Boulez on IRCAM, 1974

Foreword

The hazards that threaten any Symposium have certainly accompanied the preparation of this present volume. It is a considerable time since some of its chapters were finished – though the authors concerned have been free to revise their original contributions if they wished. Other parts of the book have been added recently or else brought up to date, where fresh material made that essential.

No present-day composer has been more intensely self-critical than Pierre Boulez in realizing down to the finest detail the projects that his imagination dictated. One might assume that he would then abandon these projects as tasks that have been fulfilled. Yet it is deeply characteristic of him that he should sustain sometimes for years on end a cross-examination of certain past works of his that to others seem convincing as they stand, but that he will not finally relinquish until they have yielded everything that his capacious mind can conjure up for them. Perhaps one could speak in these cases of an amalgamation of precision and prodigality.

However that may be, those who are closely drawn to his music feel certain enough that in each of the last four decades he has produced masterpieces, of which *Le marteau sans maître*, *Pli selon pli*, *Rituel* and the present work in progress, *Répons*, are only the most celebrated. And to add to all this, he has also been tireless in his general advocacy of twentieth-century music, and in recent years in advancing its frontiers at IRCAM.

The present Symposium does not claim to encompass all that this great man has achieved. It does attempt, though, to delve as thoroughly as possible into his works and the principles underlying them, and at the same time to reflect some of the inspired activities which together with his compositions have left a giant imprint on music in this second half of the century.

William Glock
Editor

The first fifty years

Pierre Boulez was born on 26 March 1925 in Montbrison, a town of some seven thousand inhabitants about fifty-five miles southwest of Lyons. It would be hard to find a background less calculated to nourish creative talent. Neither parent was in the least musical, and the area boasted no cultural life nearer than Lyons. That the Boulez children were taught piano was merely a matter of convention. The family was reasonably prosperous (Boulez's father was technical director of a local steel factory) and at that time bourgeois offspring were still tormented with lessons, even if they were not expected to touch a keyboard for the remainder of their lives. For young Pierre, however, these lessons were no burden. Within a short time he had overhauled his elder sister, Jeanne, and even their teacher, so that a new one had to be found. Indeed, his devotion to the piano was such that his mother's most effective means of bringing him to heel was to threaten him with missing a lesson.

But his precocious talent was not confined to music. At high school, in the nearby town of Saint-Étienne, he was from the start one of those children who seem gifted with an extraordinary ability to learn, irrespective of whether it is Latin and Greek or mathematics and music. It was Pierre's talent for mathematics that particularly pleased his father. The elder Boulez was an austere, authoritarian paterfamilias of the old school. A Jesuit upbringing had implanted in him a severity, at once moral and intellectual, that Pierre Boulez has inherited. Like many self-made men, the father took it for granted that his first-born son would follow the path he himself had laboured so assiduously to clear. Music was not something that a boy could make a career of – a hobby, maybe, but not a means of earning his living, particularly when a talent for mathematics clearly cut him out for training as an engineer. The stage was set for a classic contest between father and son, with Pierre's mother – whose appearance he has inherited, together with her liveliness and humour – cast in the traditional role of peacemaker. But his real champion in those years was his sister Jeanne. His love for her has remained the deepest emotional tie in his life.

In 1942, the Boulez family, who lived in what was then unoccupied France, went for a holiday at a nearby hotel. There by chance they encountered Ninon Vallin, one of the outstanding French sopranos of her

3

day and a singer of unusual culture. Her career as a performer was nearly over, but she was on the staff of the conservatory in Lyons. Since the young Boulez boy could play the piano, she asked him to accompany her while she practised arias from *Aida*, *La Damnation de Faust*, and Respighi's *Maria Egiziaca*. It is an event that Boulez looks back on with mixed feelings. Even then, both the plot and the characters of *Aida* struck him as crudely melodramatic and to this day he has remained curiously allergic to Verdi. But these occasions provided his first encounter with the music of Berlioz, a composer for whom he has developed a passion rare among French musicians, and whose career and character have striking parallels with his own. Ninon Vallin was enchanted by the boy's manifest musicality and intelligence. She intervened with Boulez *père* and persuaded him that Pierre should sit for the entrance examination of the Lyons Conservatoire. Here the story departs from the classic pattern, for, to the family's consternation, he failed. Jeanne Boulez and Mme Vallin went to beard the examiner, but he merely shrugged off their protests; and, since Boulez was subsequently turned down for piano classes at the Paris Conservatoire, who can say whether he was unjustly rejected? Boulez himself regards both episodes with detachment; beyond setting the style in which he wants his keyboard works performed, he has never claimed to be a pianist. But it is, to say the least of it, odd that a man who, in the words of Messiaen, 'has totally transformed the sonority of the piano' should not have been found worthy of studying the instrument at either institution.

The effect at home was calamitous. Boulez's father felt that his opposition to a musical career had been vindicated, and he dispatched the boy to Lyons for a year's advanced mathematics as a preliminary to matriculation in one of the *grandes écoles*. But at the end of that year Pierre Boulez revolted, and announced his intention to go to Paris and study music. It was not a sudden decision; even as a small boy he had always believed that he would be a musician. Here again, however, the actors in the drama fail to follow the classic script, for the father unexpectedly relented. Far from showing his son the door, he accompanied him to Paris, arranged for him to enter the Conservatoire, found, through friends, two simple garret rooms at the top of an old house in the Marais (Pierre was to occupy them for the next fourteen years), and subsidized him until he could support himself. Subsequently, when Boulez had started to compose, the engineer's eye of his father was fascinated by the precision and clarity of his manuscripts, and he would stare at them without comment. Nevertheless, it was a long time before he lost his scepticism. Many years later, when his son had become famous, he went to visit him at Baden-Baden, where he had settled. During a walk with Heinrich Strobel, who had done more than any man to launch Boulez as a composer, the father suddenly asked, 'Now, tell me. Do you really mean to say that my son has talent?' 'Monsieur, he is a genius', Strobel replied. The old man shook his head incredulously. Yet thereafter, until his death in 1969, his attitude was more respectful. The fact that he had no understanding of music made it hard for father and son to talk. Boulez, however, has a characteristically Latin attachment to his family and, though his relations with his father were sometimes tense and never close, he at no time excluded him from his affections.

Even by provincial French standards, Boulez's knowledge of music when he arrived in Paris at the age of eighteen was extraordinarily limited. As a choirboy, he had sung a certain amount of religious music, including a little Bach and a few of Handel's most familiar pieces. In modest chamber-music evenings at Montbrison, he had occasionally taken part in performances of works by classical composers and Saint-Saëns. He did not hear a live symphony orchestra until he was sixteen, and he only attended his first opera, *Boris Godunov*, a year later in Lyons. The Boulez household boasted no gramophone, but occasionally Pierre listened to the radio, and in this way he first consciously heard a piece of 'modern' music. It was a performance, relayed from Geneva, of Stravinsky's *Le Chant du Rossignol*, conducted by Ernest Ansermet, and Boulez still vividly recalls how strange the 'out-of-tune' harmonies sounded to his untutored ear. But he believes that his unfamiliarity as a boy with the ritual of concert halls and opera houses gave him a keen sense of its irrelevance to the twentieth century, and hence a desire to reform the conditions under which music is traditionally heard.

In France, it is decreed that counterpoint should be studied only after harmony. But Boulez was in a hurry (he usually is) and refused to be held up by regulations he found meaningless. At the Conservatoire, he got to know a niece of Arthur Honegger, and through her he met the composer, who arranged for him to be taught counterpoint by his wife, Andrée Vaurabourg. Mme Vaurabourg lived in a small apartment high up on Montmartre, just off the Place Pigalle, and it was here that Boulez started his lessons. Twenty-five years later she remained a woman of precision. Consulting a piece of paper on the table before her, she was able to declare, 'Pierre Boulez first came here on Wednesday 19 April 1944, at 3 pm. He continued to come weekly until 2 May 1946. He never missed a lesson and he was never late.' She recalled him, a shade wistfully, as a pupil such as she had had neither before nor since. 'He always seemed capable of anything.' Once the principles of fugal writing had been explained, he had needed virtually no further instruction. His exactitude, his memory, and the quantities of homework he produced were phenomenal, and that tiny, meticulous handwriting, which, like his signature, has been widely imitated by a generation of younger French composers, was already formed. Until the end of her teaching career more than thirty years later, she continued to use her former pupil's exercises as models in advanced counterpoint.

It was while he was studying with Mme Vaurabourg that Pierre Boulez
first shouldered his way into history. In the winter of 1944/5, as Paris
was beginning to recover from four years of humiliating German
occupation, the city was eager to take up the threads of its musical life,
and how could that be better achieved than with a grand retrospective of
Igor Stravinsky's music, which the Nazis had blacklisted as 'decadent'?
Although Stravinsky had been born in Russia and in September 1939 had
crossed the Atlantic (he later made his home in Los Angeles), in Paris he
was still regarded as an essential part of French music. He had lived in
France for two decades – indeed, he was a French citizen – and the neo-
classical works he had written during that period had not only served
virtually an entire generation of French composers as a model but had
provided the basis of a new French academicism. One of a series of
concerts of his music included the first European performance of a work
he had composed in America – *Danses concertantes*. To the astonishment
of the audience at the Salle Gaveau, it was greeted with sustained booing
from the gallery. The protesters were a group of young students from the
harmony class of Olivier Messiaen at the Paris Conservatoire, and their
leader was Boulez. This upheaval was merely the first of a number that he
was to cause in Paris.

Student protest has become such an accepted part of life that there may
seem nothing very unusual in that uproar at a concert twenty-eight years
ago. What was significant, however, was that Boulez and his colleagues
had chosen to protest not against some figurehead of the establishment
but against one of the heroes of twentieth-century music. Nor was it just
a perfunctory gesture of revolt. It was an announcement that the musical
life of Paris could not return to its pre-war ways, that the neo-classicism
which had been its hallmark was over, that the future would move in a
quite different direction – and that it would do so under the leadership of
Boulez himself. Though few in that audience could have been aware of it,
the door had opened on a new period of musical history. Within a few
years, Boulez was to become the undisputed leader of the European
avant-garde, his supremacy resting almost as much on his dazzling
intellect and forcefulness of character as on his purely musical gifts.

Stravinsky's reputation was only the first to be led to the scaffold and
formally executed. For Boulez and his young Jacobins, that was merely
the first step in a general process of demolition. Systematically, they
examined the music of their predecessors, retained the few components
that seemed serviceable, and contemptuously kicked the rest aside.
Schoenberg and Berg followed Stravinsky, and even Messiaen was not
spared. 'Brothel music' was his pupil's description of a few fragments of
Messiaen's *Turangalîla* when it was first heard in public, and another
work was dismissed as 'a débris of entirely unnecessary chords'. Brahms,

naturally, was 'a bore', Tchaikovsky 'abominable'; the whole of Italian opera was written off as 'a delirium of bel canto'; as for the traditional French virtues of lucidity and elegance, so much prized before the war, they were no more than 'a mixture of Descartes and *haute couture*'.

Boulez's intransigence, his rages, the harsh yet accurately aimed abuse that he hurled at the heads of his unfortunate victims, made him famous and feared in Paris long before his music was known to more than a handful of initiates. 'He was against everything', Messiaen later recalled. His assaults were, of course, a manifestation of a struggle for creative identity. But Boulez carried revolt to the length of open war against what he regarded as the obscurantism of French musical life, and in his struggle he seized the weapons most immediately available – caustic mockery and plain abuse. The Pierre Boulez his friends knew was another man. To them he appeared formidably intelligent but simple and unaffected and, in his withdrawn way, affectionate. And behind this affability they sensed an almost morbid sensitivity – a tenderness too proud to reveal itself.

Except for professional contacts, Boulez did not mix much. Nor did he show much appetite for the conventional bohemian life of Paris students. He preferred the company of three or four close friends and contemporaries, among them Armand Gatti, the dramatist, Pierre Joffroy (who later wrote *A Spy for God* – a remarkable book on Kurt Gerstein, the Christian SS man), and Bernard Saby, a painter. His friends would discuss their problems, their successes and failures, with the frankness of young men who know each other well. But Boulez exchanged no intimacies, gave no confidences. His reticence bordered on secrecy, and the only time Joffroy recalls his momentarily losing his self-containment was when, in 1949, he burst into his friend's room to announce that Heugel had decided to publish his Piano Sonata No. 2. He inspired affection, yet even to his closest friends he remained an enigma.

Fundamentally, Boulez's life was – and still is – solitary. He lived at the top of five flights of stairs, in two tiny, primitive mansard rooms on a street that lies between the Place de la Bastille and the river – a street that Baudelaire and Cézanne had once inhabited. Here a devoted concierge attended to his needs. There was no running water in the garret (he had to use a bathroom on the floor below), and in winter his rooms were icy. But they were always immaculate. Though the piano, an ancient upright, might be covered with books, the desk at which Boulez worked was invariably clear. Robert Craft, who visited him in this retreat in 1956, noted in his diary that the young composer's manuscripts were 'rolled like diplomas and piled on the floor like logs'. Among the few pictures, a framed photograph of Kafka and a reproduction of Klee's portrait of Stravinsky were prominent. There was a copy of *Finnegans Wake* in English. For a brief period, a sign warned visitors 'Don't step on the turtle'. Alas, its life was short, and Boulez has had no pets since. In appearance, he was far from a monkish recluse. Under black hair, large brown eyes sparkled with warmth as well as intelligence. Only when trouble was afoot did a glint give warning of danger. The lips were full and sensual, the jaw announced the presence of uncommon will-power, and a compact Latin build and quick decisive movements gave an impression of immense energy. Pierre Souvtchinsky, an old and close friend of Stravinsky's, who was probably the first person to be fully aware of the young man's genius, remarked that he bore uncanny resemblance to portraits of Pushkin at a similar age.

During his first two years in Paris, Boulez did occasional odd jobs (one took him to the *Folies Bergère*), but in 1946 the Honeggers found him a permanent post, which enabled him to support himself. Jean-Louis Barrault and Madeleine Renaud had recently left the Comédie-Française and established an independent company at the Marigny Theatre. Their first production was *Hamlet*, in a new translation by André Gide, and Honegger had written incidental music for brass, percussion and ondes martenot. A musician was needed to conduct and to play that siren-like electronic instrument, of which Messiaen, to Boulez's disgust, later made such indulgent use in *Turangalîla*. Boulez thus made his professional début on an instrument that he came to dislike and in music that was certainly not to his taste. Within a year, he had become Barrault's musical director – a position he occupied for over a decade. The title was grander than the work it involved. Among other chores that can hardly have appealed to him, Boulez had to arrange snippets of Tchaikovsky for a production of Chekhov's *The Cherry Orchard*. But the job gave scope to his marked practical gifts. It provided his first opportunities to conduct, it brought him into contact with instrumentalists, taught him – though not without difficulty – how to control his temper and, as he himself has put it, 'how to manage a group of human beings'. As a result, when he later started a series of concerts of contemporary music, he had a pool of devoted instrumentalists at his disposal. The work also gave the raw young provincial a chance to travel extensively on tour and brought him into contact with a wider world than he had encountered at the Conservatoire.

The Barraults at once took Boulez to their hearts. A deep sympathy developed between the childless couple and their young musical director, and for a while he was virtually an adopted child. 'When he first arrived, he lived with his claws out', Barrault later recalled. 'He was like a young cat, at once bristling and charming. He was sharp, aggressive, sometimes irritating.' But behind this savagery the Barraults perceived 'an extreme bashfulness, a quivering sensibility, even a secret sentimentality'. They realised that 'his blood-thirsty assaults were really a form of defence'. 'We felt that strongly and loved him the more because of it.' Many influential people in Paris, however, did not, and that fact was more than once to have a crucial effect on his career.

The most important event of Boulez's first year in Paris was his encounter with Olivier Messiaen. In post-war France, Messiaen was still an outsider, whose main point of contact with orthodox French musical life was the organ tradition of César Franck, for since 1931 he had been organist at the great Paris church of La Trinité. In the early stages of the war, he had been held in a prisoner-of-war camp, but after his repatriation in 1942, a small job had been found for him at the Conservatoire as a teacher of harmony. (Not, be it noted, of composition, and not as anything more august than a member of the staff. One of Boulez's youthful activities was to organize a petition that Messiaen be given a full professorship in composition.) No doubt to the surprise of his colleagues, Messiaen's classes began to attract some exceptionally promising students, including a number whose names have since become well known. One was the pianist Yvonne Loriod, his future wife and a noted interpreter of his music. Another was Pierre Boulez, who joined in October 1944. Like Mme Vaurabourg, Messiaen has said that Boulez's perceptions were so quick that he hardly needed a teacher – and in fact he remained Messiaen's pupil for only a year, after which he graduated from the Conservatoire with a first prize in harmony. What proved more valuable to Boulez than Messiaen's official course in harmony were extramural sessions of analysis, in which teacher and pupils examined works such as Bartók's sonatas for violin and piano, Berg's *Lyric Suite*, Schoenberg's *Pierrot Lunaire*, and, most significantly, Stravinsky's *The Rite of Spring*. These sessions, for which Messiaen accepted no fees, would begin in the afternoon and continue until the analysis was complete – sometimes deep into the night. To Boulez they opened a new realm, virtually unrepresented in the concerts of Paris. For the first time, he perceived where his musical ancestry lay.

Above all, Boulez was seized by what he has described as the 'rhythmic unrest' in Messiaen's own music. Through his study of Hindu rhythms and the pre-1914 Russian music of Stravinsky, Messiaen had come to see that rhythm, which had traditionally played a supporting role in Western music, might be subjected to rational discipline, instead of just being left to instinct, in such a way that it would become a primary, even an autonomous, element in composition. Indeed, in his analysis of *The Rite of Spring* he revealed that Stravinsky had already achieved something of the kind. That insight was the first essential contribution to Boulez's development as a composer. Though the relationship between Messiaen and his one-time pupil has had its ups and downs, Boulez has never failed to express gratitude for what he learnt from him. A man who forgets a good deed no more readily than a bad one, he has described his period of study with him as 'an irreplaceable event' in his life. Yet he was far from enthusiastic about Messiaen's own music. Although he shared his teacher's absorption in oriental rhythms and oriental instruments, Messiaen's style was too narrow a base to serve him as a model. His nonretrograde rhythms seemed a gratuitous constraint, his use of harmony largely precluded counterpoint and was in any case too lush and selfindulgent to appeal to the astringent ear and mind of his pupil. Often the music seemed to consist of contrasting blocks of sound, crudely stuck together; as Boulez put it with his customary asperity, 'Messiaen doesn't compose, he juxtaposes'. In particular, its daring rhythmic complexities were allied to harmonic rigidity. In this respect, at least, it bore a resemblance to the very characteristics that his analysis had revealed in *The Rite of Spring*. To Boulez, Stravinsky's masterpiece was a crucial landmark in twentieth-century music. Yet its non-rhythmical elements were no more adequate to his purpose than the same elements in Messiaen's music.

It was at this point that Boulez first encountered Arnold Schoenberg's dodecaphonic music. Neither Schoenberg nor his pupils nor his technique had made any headway in Paris before the Second World War. In the French capital it was generally assumed that back in the early '20s he had lost himself in some characteristically abstract Central European theory, whereby music was made out of rows of the twelve notes of the chromatic scale, all of which had to be heard before any one of them might be repeated. With few exceptions, French musicians of the '40s knew little of the works Schoenberg had written before 1914. Consequently they were unaware of the crisis that had arisen when in these scores he first moved up against and finally breached the frontiers of tonality. In Paris Schoenberg's dodecaphonic technique was still widely regarded as an intellectual conceit, rather than an attempt to replace the laws he himself had shattered. For Boulez, that technique was 'not a decree but a constatation'. But before awareness of it had spread across the Rhine, the Nazis had come to power, and as 'cultural Bolshevists' Schoenberg and his school had been scattered to all points of the compass.

One evening in 1945, Boulez heard a private performance of Schoenberg's Wind Quintet, the first major work in which he consistently deployed his tone-rows. Today, its complexity can sound stiff and contrived, but to Boulez it came as a revelation. First, it obeyed no tonal laws, and long before he heard of the existence of tone-rows he had known that his own music could not be tonal. Second, he found in it a harmonic and contrapuntal richness and a consequent ability not merely to generate ideas but to develop, extend, and vary them that he had missed in the music of Messiaen and Stravinsky. Schoenberg himself was a frail old man, living in distant Los Angeles. The only person Boulez knew of in Paris who had studied with him was an obscure composer and conductor called René Leibowitz. Boulez swiftly organized a group of Messiaen's pupils to study each Saturday morning with Leibowitz, who, though he was poor, charged nothing for those sessions.

Boulez now started to compose the first work that he still recognizes as in some degree his own. This is the Sonatine for Flute and Piano, in which he made a bold attempt to match Schoenberg's tone-rows to Messiaen's rhythmic structures. But beneath this lay a more fundamental attraction: that of the Central European tradition of thematic metamorphosis, which Schoenberg had inherited from Bach and the Viennese classics. Among the first people to hear it – also at a private performance – was Virgil Thomson. To his ears (though to few others), it sounded like 'slightly out-of-tune Ravel'. In the *New York Herald Tribune*, he gave Boulez the first review he received, describing him as 'the most brilliant, in my opinion, of all the Paris under-25s'. Not for the first time, a critic proved right for the wrong reasons.

Boulez was, however, far from happy about the dogmatic manner in which Leibowitz expounded dodecaphonic technique. Worse still, he began to have doubts about the use that Schoenberg himself had made of it. He noticed that from the moment that Schoenberg had adopted it as his basic means of composition he had reverted to classical forms – and what, Boulez asked himself, had devices such as sonata form, which originated in the harmonic tensions implicit in tonality, to do with a technique that had been brought into existence precisely because those tensions did not function as they once had? Indeed, was there not here a certain parallel with Stravinsky, customarily regarded as Schoenberg's antithesis? Had not he also, and at more or less the same moment in history, reverted to classical forms instead of allowing new forms to emerge from new material and new ways of using it? Could it be that the two arch-revolutionaries of pre-1914 music had both, on different pretexts, subsequently begun to play reactionary roles in the evolution of music? In 1946, that was in itself a revolutionary notion.

Through Schoenberg, Boulez naturally came to the music of Schoenberg's pupil, Webern, and it was in Webern, who before the war had been widely dismissed as an eccentric miniaturist, that he finally found what he had been seeking. As he analysed those exquisitely-fashioned scores, he saw that, whereas for Schoenberg tone-rows were an intrinsic part of thematic invention, Webern had regarded them essentially as a series of intervals, which in his later works he had manipulated without trying to fashion them into themes. In this way, the distinction between the vertical and the horizontal dimensions of music – in particular, the notion of a horizontal theme accompanied by vertical harmony – which had dominated Western music since the eighteenth century, was effectively abolished. Schoenberg had described the tone-row as a hat that could be squeezed into any number of shapes, but it was left to Webern to put the concept into practice. His substitution of cells, based on 'privileged' intervals, for themes was a step as momentous as any in musical history. Indeed, it was directly comparable to the beginnings of abstract art, for what are themes if not the equivalent of objects and human figures? With his discovery of Webern, Boulez found himself, as he later wrote, 'on the threshold of modern music'. In a long essay, entitled 'Eventuellement . . .' and published in 1952, he surveyed the ground he had covered up to that date, and arrogantly proclaimed, 'I assert that any musician who has not experienced . . . the necessity for the dodecaphonic language is USELESS. His whole work is irrelevant to the needs of his epoch.' Henceforth it would not be Schoenberg and Stravinsky, pope and antipope between the two wars, who dominated the evolution of music, but a withdrawn figure who had rarely left his native Vienna. Within ten years, the wheel was to come full circle, with Stravinsky himself paying public homage to Webern's achievement. But Boulez was the first to perceive its implications for the future.

Liberated from the need to construct themes, Boulez now had what he had been looking for; by matching Webern's use of tone-rows to the vastly increased rhythmic resources brought into being by Messiaen, he had a means of integrating, to a degree never before attempted, the two principal components of music – pitch and rhythm. The result of this synthesis was his Piano Sonata No. 2, which not only breaks with dodecaphonic technique as Schoenberg had practised it, but with any reference to classical form. Instead, the rows are here divided into cells, each with its characteristic intervals, and on these pitch-cells rhythmic cells act as what André Hodeir has called 'chemical reagents', to produce a kaleidoscopic sense of constant variation as one dimension transforms the other. Out of this interaction the music erupts like a huge head of water under pressure and envelops the entire keyboard, which is exploited to a degree at that time unprecedented in the literature of piano music. After more than twenty years, the Beethovenian vehemence of this sonata still astounds the ear, and in its rage can be heard echoes of its young composer's volcanic temperament. Yet it is not all savagery and fury. The brief scherzo has an elusive mercurial brilliance, and in the long slow movement there is a lyricism that harks back to the last works of Debussy. Boulez completed his Second Piano Sonata in 1948. It was an astounding achievement for a man of twenty-three, and, though few ears were aware of it at the time (it was not heard in public until 1950), it announced the arrival of a new force in twentieth-century music.

Boulez's intensely rationalistic mind was still not satisfied. If pitch and rhythm could be intellectually integrated, then why not timbre and dynamics? In 1950, while he was wrestling with this problem, a vital clue arrived from an unexpected source, in the form of a new piano study by Messiaen, called *Mode de valeurs et d'intensités*. Boulez had long since abandoned his teacher's world and, not surprisingly, his scathing remarks about Messiaen's music had led to a personal breach. But a friend drew his attention to the study, which had just been published. Boulez bought it, and was electrified by the little piece of music before him. 'As soon as I saw it, I jumped at it.' He realised, to his amazement, that Messiaen had been working on much the same problem that had been occupying him. In what Boulez has described as 'a stroke of genius', Messiaen had taken Schoenberg's conception of a row and applied it not just to pitch and durations (that is, rhythms) but to dynamics as well. It remained only for Boulez to add a row of timbres (and he thought he could perceive a foreshadowing of this in some of Webern's later works and in Schoenberg's notion of a *Klangfarbenmelodie*), and he would be able to control and integrate all four elements of music with a precision that had until then been applied only to pitch. Music was on the brink of total serialism.

Messiaen either did not see the implications of his own study or drew back from them. But Boulez, who has an implacable need to demonstrate the logical necessity of every step he takes, was enthralled by the possibility that the work had opened up of determining rationally the exact characteristics of each note consigned to paper. It was not, however, only a passion for control that drove him towards the goal of a totally rationalized music. He was aware that his own idiom, as far as it had then developed, had been a synthesis. That, of course, might be said of any composer who has ever walked the earth. But Boulez was dissatisfied with a state of affairs in which he looked in one direction for the rhythmic characteristics of his music and in another for his organization of pitch. For him that could be only an intermediate step towards his goal. He felt that his idiom must be purged of all remnants of the past, and he therefore prepared to embark on an unprecedented attempt to construct a new method of composition from first principles.

A generation is often obsessed with the sins of its fathers, and in Boulez's opinion the two greatest composers of his own past, Schoenberg and Stravinsky, had both, at a crucial moment in their development, sold out to tradition, so that there was a fatal discrepancy between what they were trying to say and how they said it. That was a mistake that *he* was resolved not to make, and to avoid it he decided to strip musical language down to its fundamental elements, so that he could determine what was essential to him. It was a heroic deed, comparable to Freud's self-analysis. 'With exaltation and fear', as he later recalled, and without pausing to consider whether the result could be played by existing instruments, he threw himself into the composition of music in which every detail would follow of logical necessity from a few basic decisions. For him, 'it was like Descartes's *Cogito, ergo sum*'. 'I momentarily suppressed inheritance. I started off from the fact that I was thinking, and went on to see how one might construct a musical language from scratch.'

An early result of this attempt to lift himself by his intellectual boot-straps was *Polyphonie X*, a work for chamber ensemble, which was given its first performance in October 1951 at Donaueschingen. There it occasioned an unprecedented uproar. Boulez was detained in London with Barrault's company, so he could not attend the concert, but a tape of the Donaueschingen performance was enough to convince him that the work was virtually impossible to play. Later, he admitted that it was 'a theoretical exaggeration in which his intellectual preoccupations had caused him to overlook instrumental practicalities'. There was, as he put it, 'a dichotomy between the mental project and the result'.

However, nothing that Boulez undertakes is a mere shot in the dark and one failure was not enough to deter him. He turned next to a studio that the engineer and composer Pierre Schaeffer had set up in Paris for producing *musique concrète*. Perhaps machines could achieve what was beyond the capacity of human instrumentalists. But the equipment was primitive; two studies that Boulez produced with it were unsatisfactory, and he marched out of what he scornfully dismissed as 'a sonic flea-market'. Electronic music, for which he was subconsciously searching, did not yet exist.

In fact, before composing *Polyphonie X*, he had, in a single night, written a work that was to prove more durable. He chose to compose it for two pianos, as 'the instruments that rebel least'; and, as a means of eliminating any element of personal choice that might sully the new work's pristine logic and also as an expression of his debt to Messiaen, he selected a series used in the *Mode de valeurs et d'intensités*. In 1952, the two composers, now reconciled, gave the first performance of the first section of the new work. *Structures*, as it is called, proved a milestone in post-war music.

In the United States Milton Babbitt had also composed scores in which durations, dynamics, rhythms and intervals were all derived from an initial series as early as 1948. But these were still unknown outside America. In Europe in the early '50s Boulez's breakthrough pointed the way for a whole generation of rising musicians, headed by figures such as Stockhausen and Nono, who were seeking a manner of composition that would be entirely free of what they regarded as alien elements and stylistic reminiscences. The more vehemently the outer world mocked, the more resolutely these pioneers set their faces towards what they were convinced would be the future, and manuscript copies of Boulez's 'Eventuellement . . .' were handed round like a revolutionary manifesto.

Serialism produced a rash of unperformable monstrosities. If *Structures* falls acceptably on the ear today, that is because Boulez, being vastly more musical than most of those who had begun to regard him as a new Messiah, remained the master of his machine. In fact, only the first part of its first 'book' – a section that lasts hardly more than five minutes – is rigidly serial. Once Boulez had made his initial experiments, he started to manipulate the series so as to give direction to the shapes that it assumed. Indeed, no one has written more scathingly than Boulez himself of 'the cauldron of figures' into which he plunged his generation. 'Having been preceded by a generation in large part illiterate, are we to become a generation of technocrats?' he asked rhetorically in another extensive essay – '. . . Auprès et au loin', published in 1954. He mercilessly mocked 'the timetables of trains that never leave' – works that existed on paper but were unable to take off as aural experiences – and 'the exasperating monotony' of perpetual variation. Disdainfully, he pointed out several truths he himself might well have perceived earlier: that all the elements of music are not of equal importance, that some can be more precisely heard than others, that the mere fact that there are twelve notes in the chromatic scale does not make that figure equally applicable to all the elements of music, that some instruments are of their nature louder than others. With a fine sense of the obvious, he proclaimed that one of the functions of a composer is to choose between a number of possibilities, and then, in a phrase that had implications wider than he perhaps realised at the time, he declared that the results of a system that relieves a composer of much of his responsibility (and by this he meant the serialism he had himself devised) must be largely fortuitous.

Yet for Boulez the serial experience, which in his case lasted barely a year, was a period of purification, and as such it served its purpose, if only because it abolished once and for all the concept of music as necessarily thematic. That he was able to drive his flock through an experience that he has referred to as 'self-mutilation' is a telling tribute to the spellbinding influence he then exercised. Once he himself had emerged on the other shore he was, however, prepared to admit that 'it is necessary to imagine the revolution as well as to construct it'. Serial 'laws' should be regarded not as a system but as a manner of musical thought, with all the flexibility that the phrase implies. In another essay, 'Recherches maintenant' (1954), he even went so far as to proclaim the necessity of invention, and the result was immediately apparent in his next work. *Le marteau sans maître* is a brilliant, lyrical, even charming work for alto voice and instrumental ensemble, based on poems by René Char, to which he was drawn by their air of violence and concentration (not too many words). Stravinsky described it in 1960 as 'one of the few significant works of the post-war period of exploration'.

Yet the first performance of a work that today sounds almost decorative did not come about without a struggle. Boulez might be a hero in Darmstadt, but in Paris he was still widely regarded as a fanatic, and his talent for invective had made him powerful enemies. As late as 1960, feeling against him was so strong that the musical director of the French Radio, an organ of the state, formally forbade a critic to interview him on

15

the air. In 1955, *Le marteau sans maître* was entered for the annual festival of the International Society for Contemporary Music. Fortunately for Boulez, the festival was to take place that year in Baden-Baden, the seat of the South-West German Radio, whose musical director was Heinrich Strobel. Strobel had sought out Boulez on a visit to Paris in 1950 and had been impressed by his talent and character, and it was due to him and the conductor Hans Rosbaud that *Polyphonie X* had been performed at Donaueschingen in 1951. When the French members of the ISCM jury refused to include *Le marteau sans maître* among the French works to be considered for performance, Strobel, who, as musical head of the host radio-station, was in a position of power and was not shy about using it, decided to include the composition in a concert in which the hosts traditionally have the right to present a programme of their own choice. The French protested furiously at this deliberate circumvention of their wishes, but there was little they could do about it, and they looked sillier still when, after forty-four rehearsals under Rosbaud, *Le marteau sans maître* proved an overwhelming success and transformed Boulez's position overnight. In short, he had arrived.

He is, however, irritated by suggestions that that success was due merely to the fact that he had greatly relaxed the rigour of his serialism. On the contrary, he maintains it was precisely the serial experience of *Structures* that enabled him to turn at once to the composition of what has proved his first fully mature (and still his best-known) work. 'People say it "sounds well", but that is not merely because I have a good nose for sound – it is also because the textures and harmonies are absolutely controlled . . . Serialism provided me with a syntax. In *Le marteau*, I used it to formulate thoughts.'

Inevitably, the excesses of serialism soon gave rise to a fierce reaction, and once again the commanding intelligence of Pierre Boulez for a while appeared to be in the van. As early as 1951 he had let fall a remark that must have seemed meaningless at the time: 'We shall eventually have to restore its potential to what Mallarmé called chance.' On the face of it, nothing could be more remote from the rigidly determined world of serialism. But Boulez's mind was already playing on distant perspectives. Even in 'Eventuellement . . .' he had reminded his readers that 'the unexpected cannot be excluded from art'.

Still earlier, in 1949, Boulez had been in correspondence with John Cage, and they had met later that year, when Cage came to Paris to give concerts and to take part in dance recitals with Merce Cunningham. Though he and Cage shared a contempt for neo-classicism, no two minds could be more unalike, and today Boulez is opposed to almost everything Cage stands for. ('I like his mind, but not the way it thinks.') But at that time several of Cage's ideas caught his interest. One was the perception that instruments devised to play tonal music inevitably restricted the evolution of music in which the octave was no longer of the first importance. (In this, Cage himself was the follower of another Frenchman, Edgard Varèse, who lived still largely unrecognized in New York and whose ideas were to prove a crucial influence on the development of music in the '60s.) Boulez recognized that Cage's prepared piano was a significant step toward breaking down the frontiers, until then regarded as inviolable, between music and noise; and Cage's device in *Imaginary Landscape No. 4* (1951) of manipulating a dozen radios according to a precise schedule of durations and dynamics fascinated him, not for the result, but as an experiment in combining exactitude and chance. Above all, he was intrigued by Cage's practice of spinning coins in accordance with rules laid down in the *I Ching* as a means of introducing 'chance operations' into music. All this was far from Boulez's creative concerns in the early '50s, and when Cage moved into the world of Happenings their ways parted for good. Yet a seed had been planted in Boulez's mind which was to bear fruit several years later.

Though serialism had given Boulez the means he had sought of controlling his material, by 1954 certain deficiencies in the system had become apparent. One was that in the absence of themes, which had served as dramatis personae prior to Webern, it was difficult to articulate development so that a work's overall shape would be readily apparent. Where every element was in a constant state of variation, there was a paradoxical lack of variety. Boulez, who has always been keenly responsive to the visual arts (from an early age he had been particularly drawn to Klee, Kandinsky and Mondrian), saw the problem as akin to that of reintroducing perspective into abstract painting. But there was another element missing from serial structures – what he called 'a momentary submission to free will'. How, he asked himself, could the wilfulness of the imagination be squared with logical necessity? Cage's device of spinning coins was perhaps too arbitrary. But the operation recalled Mallarmé's observation that 'each thought is a throw of the dice', and Mallarmé, Boulez was shortly to discover, had put his epigram into practice in a book, *Le livre*, in which the reader could choose for himself the order in which he would read the pages. Might not a piece of music also be conceived as a series of compartments to be visited at will? In any case, was the traditional notion of a work as a closed circuit – an object determined once and for all by the composer – applicable to the relativity implicit in a serial world, where each score generated its own form? These are some of the considerations that led Boulez to the brink of aleatory music.

He was, however, only one of several composers to reach comparable conclusions at approximately the same moment in time. In 1953, Karlheinz Stockhausen, whom Boulez once described as 'the only man I can talk to about music', was studying the physical nature of sound at

Bonn University with Werner Meyer-Eppler. There he perceived, in the vibrations that form its raw material, certain indeterminate elements of chance, which seemed to him to offer a parallel to the principle of relativity in twentieth-century physics. Like Cage, he was also fascinated by the possibility of finding a musical equivalent for the drip techniques used by Jackson Pollock, and here, too, aleatory devices seemed to offer fruitful possibilities. For Stockhausen, as for Boulez, the basic motive was to 'bring relativity into music', and in 1954 he composed some short piano pieces in which details were left to chance.

In the serial adventure, Boulez had been the pioneer and Stockhausen, three crucial years his junior, a follower; indeed, Boulez is said to have had a good deal to do with the final shape of *Kontrapunkte Nr. 1*, the score with which Stockhausen first made his mark, in 1953. Four years later, the situation had changed. In 1957, the two composers were in close contact while each worked on his first important aleatory score, and the pieces were presented to the world within a few weeks of each other. On 28 July 1957, in Darmstadt, Paul Jacobs gave the first performance of Stockhausen's *Klavierstück XI*, and Boulez was sufficiently impressed by it to play it to Stravinsky the following month in Paris. Then, that September, Boulez gave the first performance of his own Piano Sonata No. 3, also in Darmstadt. In both works, shape and content might be varied at each performance. But, because Stockhausen's commitment to the aleatory principle had from the start been more far-reaching and wholehearted than Boulez's, the resemblance remained superficial. Stockhausen had accepted the full implications of chance; Boulez, in contrast, had tried to confine its implications to choice. The evolution of post-war music had arrived at a critical bifurcation, which was eventually to leave Boulez an isolated, even a lonely figure.

Klavierstück XI consists of nineteen fragments – or 'groups' as Stockhausen prefers to call them – each of which is followed by playing instructions. The pianist is specifically instructed to approach the work without any preconceived idea of its eventual shape. He starts with any group that happens to catch his eye and plays it at any speed, at any degree of loudness, and with any mode of attack (staccato or legato, and so on) he chooses. Thereafter, however, he has to take the instructions that follow the group he has played and apply them to whatever group he plays next. Indeed, infinite variants are possible, so that not even the composer could foresee the juxtapositions that might arise. To Boulez's mind, *Klavierstück XI* thus reintroduced the gratuitousness that had been a defect of serialism. At first sight, serial determinism and the wilder shores of aleatory music appear as far apart as any two things can be. But both, when carried to their logical conclusion, seemed to him to relieve the composer of much of his responsibility.

Boulez's conception of the role of chance was from the start far more precisely circumscribed. Whereas for Stockhausen the stimulus had been scientific, Boulez has said that at this moment literature was a stronger influence on his ideas than music itself – a reference to Mallarmé's *Le livre*, which was published only in 1957, while Boulez was at work on his sonata. Mallarmé was already dear to Boulez for his attitude to language: his willingness to take it to bits and reassemble it is indeed somewhat comparable to what Boulez had attempted in *Structures*. Now, in *Le livre*, he found a conception of a work of art that would be 'like a map of a city in which you choose your own way' – but, of course, each road would have to have been explored in detail by the mapmaker. In his Piano Sonata No. 3 he aimed to produce a work capable of assuming more than one shape. As he pointed out, a score is in any case only a code that is never realized twice in exactly the same way. Here, the modifications were, as it were, built-in and more far-reaching so that both the interpreter and the listener would encounter new situations at each performance. As the third and last movement has, however, never been completed, the work has yet to be heard in its entirety.

Boulez was too deeply concerned with intellectual coherence ever to admit anything as potentially destructive as mere inadvertence into his carefully controlled structures. He was never, as he put it, 'a great friend of chance'. What he sought was 'a dialectic between order and choice', and to that end he built into his sonata a series of alternate circuits, to be entered at the choice of the performer, who at a given moment would take one route rather than another. The larger the element of choice, the more important it seemed to Boulez to foresee and provide for all the possibilities it offered. As he caustically put it, 'if you have no rules, you have no chance', because chance is, by definition, an event that does not happen according to rules. What he had in mind was a work that at each performance would reveal a different aspect of itself, like a familiar view seen from different positions. If serialism had opened the door to relativity in music, in the sense that each work generated its own structure instead of relying on a preconceived form, then perhaps the moment had come to introduce relativity into performance.

But it is clear that Boulez and Stockhausen understand very different things by relativity – a word they both use liberally. Stockhausen has said, 'Boulez's goal remains the work, mine is the impact . . . That is why he strives to make his work self-contained and autonomous, whereas what concerns me is the model character of a work and not how that model is subsequently exploited'. For Boulez, chance was never more than an element in a work of art, not the work itself, and in an essay called 'Aléa', published only a month after he had presented his Third Sonata, he revealed how aware he was of the dangers involved. In a remark that today has a prophetic ring, he observed, 'if chance is to be interpreted as nothing more than inadvertence, why not also leave the context in which it appears to inadvertence?' And that is precisely what happened. The sluice-gates were opened, and the waters of Dada rose so rapidly that within a couple of years large areas of the musical landscape were submerged as the order that is implicit in the simplest tune was abandoned.

In 1958, Iannis Xenakis based a score on his design for a pavilion at the Brussels World Fair by treating its contours as though they were of musical significance. Twenty years earlier, it is true, Villa-Lobos had plotted the New York skyline on music paper and treated selected points as pitched notes, but Xenakis's experiment was the beginning of a general movement toward 'graphics', whereby a piece of music derived its shape from a purely visual pattern. From there it was only a short step to a point where a work might be derived from what the performer happened to read in the evening paper or from any other arbitrary, non-musical factor. In 1963 in Palermo, in a hall surrounded by rat-infested streets where children rifled rubbish dumps for a crust of bread, an invited festival audience was entertained by a mock-spastic cellist, who for fifteen minutes laboured unsuccessfully to draw his bow across the strings of his instrument. By the later '60s, Stockhausen had extended the boundaries of chance to a point where his 'scores' were mere texts for group improvisation.

Such antics were not for Boulez. Aleatory music he still regarded as a necessary antidote to the rigidity of serialism, but 'idiotic and vulgar exhibitionism' like that of the cellist in Palermo was inadmissible. Oblivious of his warnings that pure chance could produce a satisfactory piece of music only by pure chance, that instrumentalists left to their own devices would almost inevitably regurgitate the clichés of the music they had already absorbed (something that Stockhausen subsequently discovered to his cost), that shock was of its nature a device that could work only once, that an attempt to make performance a quasi-dramatic end in itself overlooked the fact that few musicians are good actors ('I'm for specialized workers'), the Gadarene herd hurled themselves down the aleatory slopes into a sea of chaos. Boulez turned in the late '50s to the composition of *Pli selon pli*, one of the few indisputable high points of post-war music, which combined aleatory and serial techniques, and which now, less than two decades after its first performance, appears a monument from a bygone age. Entitled 'a portrait of Mallarmé', whose poems here serve purposes of construction as well as of inspiration, it remains the most extensive score he has completed to date. Ostensibly, this brought him a new degree of eminence. But by the time he had finished it most of the other leaders of his generation had in varying degrees made their peace with the new aleatory order, and he had become a middle-aged composer on the brink of isolation. It was almost exactly at this moment that a new chapter in his career began: he became a conductor.

This development was not in fact as new as it seemed when Boulez first made his mark on the international scene in the early '60s. Quite apart from his early activities as musical director of the Marigny Theatre, he had already accumulated a fair amount of conducting experience in Paris and elsewhere, though this had come about through force of circumstances rather than through any deliberate intent on his part.

In 1953, Boulez, as he later wrote, decided that the time was ripe for his generation 'to prove itself in action' with a series of chamber concerts that would serve as 'a means of communication between the composers of our time and the public that is interested in its time'. Accordingly, he persuaded the Barraults to launch a modest series of four concerts at the Petit Marigny – a series that soon expanded and became known as the Domaine Musical. At first, he had no intention of conducting himself, and indeed it was not until 1956, when Hans Rosbaud was not available, that he took over a programme that included the first performance in Paris of his own *Le marteau sans maître*. After that he conducted most of the concerts, but in the early years of the Domaine Musical his chief contribution was as mainspring and organizer, and it was during that period that he first revealed an unsuspected talent for administration. He chose the musicians, selected the programmes, edited the programme notes, dealt with subscriptions, and generally functioned as artistic director, accountant and errand boy. The programmes were made up of contemporary classics (the first included Stravinsky's *Renard*, with Barrault in a mimed role, and Webern's Concerto for nine instruments), new works (by Karlheinz Stockhausen and Luigi Nono), and masterpieces of the past that for one reason or another seemed particularly apposite but were rarely heard in ordinary concerts, such as Bach's *Musikalisches Opfer* and Debussy's *Études*. What was of prime importance to Boulez was that, as he later put it when discussing the presentation of experimental works in New York, 'if the music itself is to be controversial, there must be no controversy about the performance it receives'.

The Petit Marigny was tiny, the wooden seats were hard, the heat was sometimes extreme, the programmes long, and in the audience painters and writers were more conspicuous than musicians. But the concerts were an instantaneous success, attracting from the beginning that peculiar blend of the far-out and the fashionable which is essential to the success of any avant-garde project in the French capital. There was only one snag: they cost far more than had been envisaged. The Barraults, whose support had from the beginning been unstinting, nobly shouldered the deficit for the first season. Public subsidies were out of the question. (The Domaine Musical began to receive state support – and then on a very modest scale – only in 1959, when it followed Barrault's company to the Odéon, which is a state theatre.) Nor was any help forthcoming from the

French Radio, which did not broadcast a single Domaine concert during the first five seasons. Private support was therefore essential and it was provided by Suzanne Tézenas, a woman in the venerable tradition of Paris hostesses who are also patrons of advanced art. Mme Tézenas not only contributed money herself but worked hard to raise it from others. After each concert, she gave a lavish reception, and if some of the supporters she gathered were attracted more by her hospitality than by the music itself, that did not trouble Boulez. On the contrary, the young bear began to reveal an unsuspected ability to charm the rich and fashionable. Years later, he said that he still felt 'an extreme repugnance at the idea of a composer's giving himself up to all the work involved in running a series of concerts'. But it was a repugnance he learnt to overcome in Paris in the '50s. Today, Boulez likes to quote a remark attributed to Lenin that 'not every compromise is a concession', and it was during the period he served as impresario of the Domaine Musical that his once intransigent character began to accept the need for tactics.

The Domaine Musical was to provide the basis for the first real association between Boulez and Stravinsky, sole survivor among those composers who had their roots in the pre-1914 world and to whom Boulez looked as his musical ancestors. They already had met at a party in Virgil Thomson's apartment in New York in December 1952, when Boulez first visited the United States with Barrault's company. The great man cared greatly for his reputation among the young and it may seem inconceivable that he should have been unaware of Boulez's notorious assaults on his neo-classical scores, but Robert Craft claims that he was. He had, however, heard a performance of *Polyphonie X* conducted by Craft and been so impressed that he later made an analysis of the score. There is some discrepancy in the accounts of what took place at this first encounter. Virgil Thomson has written that Stravinsky and Boulez seated themselves on a sofa and chatted happily for a couple of hours, oblivious of the milling throng around them. Boulez says that Stravinsky simply asked him to dine alone with him later, at which time they talked at length. It was, however, only after Stravinsky had supervised recordings for the Domaine Musical of two of his own works that a warm relationship sprang into existence between them. There is little doubt that, of all the composers who emerged since the war, Boulez, both as a man and as a musician, was for a while the closest to Stravinsky. In early 1957, when Boulez came to Los Angeles to conduct *Le marteau sans maître*, he frequently visited the Stravinskys and, as Robert Craft has recalled, 'soon captivated the older composer with new musical ideas, and an extraordinary intelligence, quickness, and humour'. Craft has stated that an inadequately-prepared performance of *Threni*, which Stravinsky himself conducted in 1958 under the banner of the Domaine Musical, brought about a cooling of the friendship. However, the two men appeared to be on friendly terms at a small party given for Boulez by Lawrence Morton the day before Boulez conducted the world première of *Éclat* in Los Angeles on 26 March 1965. But after 1967 there was no further contact between them. Stravinsky criticized Boulez's recording of *The Rite of Spring* (for the un-Boulezian quality of 'sloppiness') and publicly withdrew what he referred to as his earlier 'extravagant advocacy' of Boulez's music. Boulez riposted by accusing Craft of putting words into his master's mouth. By the summer of 1970, the last of Stravinsky's life, relations had become so bad that Stravinsky referred in print to Boulez as an 'arch-careerist'. But what perhaps cut most cruelly was the posthumous publication of a description – uttered only three weeks before Stravinsky's death – of Boulez's *Pli selon pli* as 'pretty monotonous and monotonously pretty'.

The Domaine Musical gave Boulez a position in Paris musical life. But performances of his own music were too few to provide an income (he has consistently refused to use conducting as a means of promoting his compositions) and after a decade as the Barraults' musical director he felt a need to move on to new fields. Consequently, when his old champion Heinrich Strobel persuaded the Baden-Baden Radio to offer him an allowance in return for the right of first performance of his new works, he accepted, and decided to move to Germany for a while. Like Berlioz a century earlier, he found there a warmer appreciation of his genius than at home, and he admired the vigour and enterprise of German musical life. The horrors of recent German history provided no hindrance to his move, not because he is oblivious of political issues, but because he regards as naïve the notion that, given similar circumstances, other peoples might not behave as atrociously. He crossed the Rhine in January 1959 with the intention of remaining only a year or two and at first lived in modest rooms in an apartment directly above that of Strobel and his wife. A close friendship sprang up between him and the childless Strobels, and he soon found himself in a relationship curiously similar to the one that existed between him and the Barraults. Baden-Baden, a nineteenth-century spa cradled in the slopes of the Black Forest, proved an unexpectedly agreeable domicile, and on two occasions in the '60s, when it appeared likely that he would return to live in Paris, events there prevented it. As a result, though today he has a flat in the French capital, he still lives in Baden-Baden, in a large, solid late-nineteenth-century villa, set back from a side road and remote from the bustle of the town. Originally, Boulez occupied only a single floor. Today, he rents the entire house. Furnished in a stringently contemporary style, it is both still and spacious. There are no aleatory effects here, no trace of the knick-knacks that most people assemble haphazardly over the years. In the living room are some of Mies van der Rohe's famous Barcelona chairs and a television set that enables one to see four programmes simultaneously.

On the walls are paintings by Miró and Klee, and a Giacometti drawing of Stravinsky. The effect is deliberately cool. It is a house quite without nostalgia.

It has frequently been stated that Boulez went to Baden-Baden to succeed Rosbaud as conductor of the South-West German Radio Orchestra. The fact is that Rosbaud remained the orchestra's principal conductor until his death in 1962. Moreover, in 1959 Boulez's conducting experience was too limited for him to have been considered for the post, even if it had been open. But during that year, when Rosbaud was in poor health, Strobel asked Boulez to deputize for him. At Rosbaud's wish, Boulez also took over a number of the sick conductor's engagements with various other orchestras. Thus his career in this field began by chance rather than by design.

Up to that point, Boulez's experience as a conductor had been limited largely to chamber ensembles. But though he had no formal training, he had learned much from close contact with two expert practitioners, who had championed his music and whom he respected as men and musicians. The first was Roger Désormière, the finest French conductor of his generation, whose career was brought to a tragic end in 1952 by a stroke. In 1950, Désormière had conducted the first performance of Boulez's cantata *Le soleil des eaux* (this was his first large-scale piece to be performed in public) and Boulez had admired the sobriety and functionalism of his gestures. Boulez had also had long talks with Rosbaud about conducting and had been impressed by his respect for the composer's intentions. It was, however, in the relative seclusion of Baden-Baden that he learned to handle a full-scale symphony orchestra. Today, he radiates calm authority in rehearsal. At first, he tended to be impatient and uncertain in his relationship with the players, but with experience his natural talent soon began to reveal itself. Today only conducting his own music makes him nervous. ('It's like looking at your spots in a mirror.') The precision of his ear is legendary. 'Boulez can hear a pin drop and tell you what key it's in' is how one New York Philharmonic musician put it. Almost to a fault, he is devoid of that exhibitionism which orchestral players find so hard to endure, because they, of all people, know how extraneous it usually is to the matter in hand. Above all, his analytical powers give him a phenomenal ability to reveal the structure of a score, so that, at their best, his performances stem from a profound inner understanding of the music.

Boulez himself makes light of his achievements as a conductor. 'Any decent, scrupulous musician could do it just as well', he has said. In his view, an ability to conduct is simply an ability to read a score and then make the music sound the way one's inner ear has heard it. The idea of 'interpretation' as something a conductor is there to impose on a work is foreign to his approach, and so is the notion of an interpretative tradition,

24

which he has mockingly compared to the party-game in which a phrase is whispered by one person to another until it finally returns to its originator, generally in an unrecognizable form. There is nothing arrogant about this lack of concern with tradition. On the contrary, Boulez was quick to see when he had something to learn. In 1965, when George Szell first brought him to Cleveland, he was well aware that he was standing before an orchestra that had acquired an authoritative classical style. 'I learned how to conduct the classics with that orchestra . . . As far as the strings were concerned, I was watching as much as conducting.' Not everyone, however, would agree that he has ever learnt how to handle the classics from Bach to Schumann.

In general, Boulez's technique is devoid of self-consciousness. Indeed, apart from one or two procedures he has introduced to deal with polyrhythms and aleatory music, he is hardly aware of having one, and this, no doubt, helps explain why his podium appearance is so unlike that of any of his colleagues. Yet orchestral players unanimously agree that, technically, he is a highly accomplished conductor. He uses no baton but indicates time with the forefinger and thumb of his right hand. In legato music he also makes sweeping, karate-like movements of that hand with the fingers pressed together, so that it resembles a penguin's flipper. His left hand, which is used sparingly and rarely imitates the movements of his right, is slowly raised for a crescendo. The eyes are intensely watchful. But there is no trace of theatre – not even the rather theatrical sort of economy that was practised by Richard Strauss. Boulez's perfunctory bow at the end of a work is an acknowledgment of the applause received, not a request for more. Though he can achieve it, he is not much concerned with virtuosity for its own sake.

With time a certain modification in his stern objectivity as a conductor has become apparent. Earlier in his career he remarked, 'C'est le document qui m'intéresse', and he would, of course, still insist that wrong notes cannot give rise to the 'right' emotions. If they are correctly perceived and accurately played, they will, he implies, realize the emotional world of a score more faithfully than any 'interpretation' a conductor may impose on them. In the classical repertory, this approach can lead to performances that are plain and impersonal, even schoolmasterly. There are no flourishes in his Haydn, no rosy streaks of a romantic dawn in his Mozart, no Promethean drama in his Beethoven, and his phrasing is frequently unyielding. Yet precisely because his conducting is so free of stylistic preconceptions and personal mannerisms, classical scores sometimes come across with the freshness of a newly-cleaned picture. Still, notes are, of course, no more than approximate symbols and no conductor, however 'objective' he may be, can avoid a degree of interpretation. In music that makes little instinctive appeal to him, Boulez is apt to reveal the limitations of an intellectual approach. In a Mahler

Ländler, for instance, the rhythmic accents elude him and the result is unidiomatic. And when, on occasion, he finds himself conducting something he actively dislikes, he makes no attempt to disguise his aversion but bolts through the music like a child downing a draught of medicine.

Boulez is certainly not a conductor who approaches music in terms of emotional thrills. Yet over the years he has come to reject 'objectivity' as an interpretative end, and this is not surprising from a musician who has also been more drawn to pre-1914 Expressionism than to the *neue Sachlichkeit* of the inter-war years. If he still seems as a conductor more concerned with light than heat, he has his own means of making the sparks fly. The precision of his ear produces a lean, athletic quality of sound, and this, underpinned by an uncanny rhythmic exactitude, can generate an electric sense of excitement, even in romantic music that might be thought remote from his Gallic sensibility. Similarly, he never leans on a line to emphasize its emotional content but draws it with a clarity and elegance that carry their own eloquence. His ability to realize elaborate textures can also produce poetry; no conductor has more precisely caught the melancholy of Debussy's *Ibéria*.

What sets him apart from the practitioners who have increasingly come to dominate the concert scene in recent years is his sense of musical structure. Boulez is one of those rare musicians who do not merely reveal detail, like a conjuror producing a rabbit out of a hat, but point its relevance to an emerging whole. It is a quality that makes him a true successor to the vanishing breed of conductors who put cause before effect. Even when Boulez is at his most nonchalant, his performances are rarely less than illuminating. At their best, they have a distinction and a depth of understanding equalled by no other conductor of his generation. No musician can hope to be equally at home in music of all periods and places, but Boulez has come as near as any to fulfilling Alban Berg's injunction: play new music as though it were classical, classical music as though it were new.

As success snowballed – and its rapidity seems to have surprised no one more than Boulez himself – larger prospects began to open up. In 1962, Georges Auric took over the direction of the Paris Opéra and one of his first moves was to invite Boulez to conduct an entirely new production of *Wozzeck*. In Boulez's younger days, when the least trace of romanticism had aggravated him, Berg, unlike Webern, had seemed to have one foot in a rejected past. With the years, the richness of his music had become more apparent, and in 1960 Boulez had analysed *Wozzeck* with students at the Basle conservatory. Instead of the usual handful of orchestral rehearsals, Boulez demanded thirty – and got them. The first night was a triumph, and after it the orchestra – not a body of men given to intemperate enthusiasm – spontaneously rose to applaud him. Not all orchestral musicians have since responded equally warmly, but rapport with them is doubly precious to him, because no group is more remote from or hostile to contemporary music. Though not given to boasting, he has claimed, 'I have shown that a composer of new music can conquer the reputedly closed world of orchestral musicians'.

After a four-year absence from Paris, Boulez suddenly found himself a hero. 'Le succès donne bonne mine', and he himself seemed to have changed. The hair-line had receded, the face had grown fuller, and the sturdy frame had broadened into middle-aged squatness. Unlike Stockhausen, who today sports a mildly hippie appearance, Boulez in his middle years has remained as neat and impersonal in appearance as a bank manager. Indeed, his almost wilfully conventional appearance in public seems to bespeak a contempt for conventions of any sort.

Yet today, he appears more at ease with the world. Once a near-recluse, he is now occasionally charged with being *mondain*. With strangers or chance acquaintances he is courteous, laughs readily, and is rarely at a loss for a smooth answer to an awkward question. But it would be an error to take a polite drawing-room manner for hunger for social success. Boulez accepts the fact that conducting inevitably brought him into circles that he would not otherwise frequent, and, in particular, he was worldly enough to be aware that good relations with rich dilettantes might well contribute to his success in New York, as they did to the success of the Domaine Musical. In any case, neither by nature nor by upbringing is he boorish. In private, he will still unloose devastating comments – notably on other composers. (Boulez has a characteristically French inability to resist a witticism.) But in public he has become more of a tactician. 'I find one catches more flies with honey than with vinegar', he remarked recently. That is not an observation he would have made twenty years ago.

The suave bonhomie Boulez has learned to present to the world is more than a veneer. When not angered, he is a far more kindly man than his severe public persona might indicate. Indeed, to people he likes, respects or feels he can help, he manifestly finds it hard to say no, and as a result, he often succumbs to time-consuming commitments that a packed schedule can ill accommodate. In rehearsal, he can be negligent of those tiny courtesies to orchestral players which ease a relationship that is inevitably full of tension. But when he is off-duty his manner is frank and easy: the wide grin, the jovial good humour and the Rabelaisian comments that give a pungent flavour to the torrent of conversation he pours forth when he finds himself in congenial company are hard to relate to the austere, Jansenist image he presents to the world as a conductor, composer, theorist, and polemicist. Perhaps the two sides of his character represent his inheritance from his very different parents. Only occasionally, when some enemy is mentioned or half-hidden wound inadvertently touched, are claws suddenly bared, so that, looking across a dining table, one is abruptly aware of a powerful cat who might, if he were so disposed, put out a paw and remove a side of one's face. Boulez still has his rages, when, as he told a friend, 'I could really kill'. There is still music he loathes so deeply that it makes him (and in this he resembles Berlioz) literally want to vomit. But with the years he has increasingly become a domestic animal, and no doubt it was partly because on his return to Paris he proved personally more amenable that his drastic conception of the musical reforms necessary in France began to seem more palatable than they had done only a few years earlier.

The Ministry of Cultural Affairs, presided over by André Malraux, had in the early '60s already made an inconclusive attempt to investigate the manifest deficiencies of French musical life and in 1964 an inter-ministerial commission was set up to consider the situation afresh. Many musicians were consulted, but in the view of Gaëton Picon, a writer who was then director-general of the Department of Arts and Letters, in whose province the project of reform fell, 'Pierre Boulez's conceptions were by far the most imaginative, precise, and practical'. As a result, Boulez gained the ear of Picon's department. One of his principal ideas was that the plethora of indifferent Paris orchestras, whose personnel were virtually interchangeable, should be merged into two large and flexible bodies – one to be maintained by the state, the other by the city. It was a plan that menaced a host of vested interests, and at that stage Boulez took a step that well illustrates his grasp of the realities: in 1965 he became honorary president of the Paris musicians' union. That he accepted was not due only to his sympathy for its members; he was well aware that 'they react like peasants defending their land' and were thus in many ways the most conservative factor in the whole situation. But their consent was essential if the reforms were to be effected, and as president he would be well placed to obtain it.

As news of Boulez's new influence spread round Paris, opposition began to gather. There were old grudges to be paid off and positions to be preserved, and intrigues focused on the personal staff of Malraux. The composers André Jolivet and Henri Sauguet emerged as the pivots of opposition, which was centred on an organization called the Comité National de la Musique, of which Darius Milhaud became president and figurehead in 1966, shortly before the opposing armies joined battle. Thoroughly alarmed by what was afoot, Picon warned Boulez that the reforms, which were just about to be presented to the Minister, were endangered, and urged him to write directly to Malraux. Boulez did so. Malraux ignored his letter and, two weeks later, announced a series of administrative measures that ran directly counter to those that had already been worked out in his own Ministry. Picon resigned in disgust, and Boulez considered that he had been betrayed. In an article in *Le*

Nouvel Observateur titled 'Pourquoi je dis non à Malraux', he denounced the minister's action as 'thoughtless, irresponsible, and inconsequential'. He formally announced, 'I am on strike with regard to everything remotely connected with the official organization of music in France'. That meant cutting his links with the Opéra, the radio, and all French orchestras. It also meant refusing a public subsidy for the Domaine Musical. In 1967 he conducted a special appeal concert that raised more money than the state had provided in a year, and resigned from the organization which he had founded fourteen years earlier and which had, in any case, largely fulfilled its function. Accompanied by a volley of press abuse, he returned to Germany. Later, implacable as ever, he forbade the newly-founded Orchestre de Paris, which had been set up on lines that were a mere parody of his original proposals, to play his music.

Like many intellectuals, particularly in France, Boulez had grown up with a contempt for opera, and what little experience he had of it before he accepted Auric's invitation to conduct *Wozzeck* had only confirmed his prejudice. *Wozzeck*, however, made him aware of the immense potential of music drama in its broadest sense, and he began to nurse a project of his own. Traditional opera might be a dinosaur, but in Jean Genet he thought he saw a possible collaborator in a new sort of music theatre, for Genet's plays afforded what Boulez has described as 'a sense of space that leaves room for music'. He accordingly induced Genet to set foot in an opera-house for the first time in his life to see *Wozzeck*. In fact, Genet went twice and was enthralled by the work. Long discussion about the possibility of a collaboration took place, and a subject – treason – was agreed on. But to this day the text has not arrived and, though Boulez returned to the assault when Genet unexpectedly turned up in Baden-Baden a few years ago, it seems unlikely that it ever will, as Genet has declared that he has abandoned creative writing for political engagement.

Wozzeck brought other contacts, among them Wieland Wagner, the director of his grandfather's Festspielhaus at Bayreuth, who first invited Boulez to do the same opera with him at Frankfurt, and then, after the death of Hans Knappertsbusch, in October 1965, persuaded him to conduct *Parsifal* in the following year at Bayreuth. For the iconoclastic champion of the avant-garde to conduct Wagner's most solemn music drama in the sacred precincts of his own temple of the arts was not such a bizarre notion as might at first appear, for *Parsifal* had had a deep influence on Debussy, with whom Boulez has always felt a kinship, and was thus in some degree part of Boulez's own inheritance. Even so, he hesitated, and it was only on Wieland Wagner's insistence that he finally agreed. In spite of these doubts, his impact was such that after the first rehearsal at Bayreuth he was invited to conduct *Tristan* the following spring, during the Bayreuth company's tour of Japan. His *Parsifal* knocked no less than twenty-one minutes off Knappertsbusch's reading of the first act alone. But it was a tautly-phrased and luminous performance, marked by an unerring grasp of the proportons of each of the work's vast acts.

At Frankfurt, Boulez and Wieland Wagner had acquired a deep mutual regard. In their partnership, it seemed, Bayreuth had at last gained the team it so desperately needed if the spirit of Wieland Wagner's productions was to find its counterpart in the orchestral pit. But by the time Boulez arrived in Bayreuth for rehearsals in the summer of 1966 Wieland Wagner was in a hospital in Munich, where he died the following October, at the age of only forty-nine. His death was a heavy blow to Boulez, for, as he wrote in the Bayreuth festival programme of the following year, it was Wieland Wagner who 'drew my attention above all to the world of opera, the importance and topicality of which I had not previously been prepared to recognize'. They had planned to collaborate on a series of projects. Boulez at once withdrew from all but one – a production of *Pelléas et Mélisande* at Covent Garden in 1969. Stylistically, his interpretation stood many accepted notions of Debussy's masterpiece on their head, and approval was far from unanimous. Boulez's approach is well illustrated by his comment, in an essay on the opera, 'I don't like the French tradition of sweetness and gentleness . . . [The work] is not gentle at all, but cruel and mysterious'. On another occasion he said, 'I like to burn the mist off Debussy', and indeed his *Pelléas* was less dreamy, sharper in outline, and more urgently dramatic than usual. And once again his pacing of the music seemed uncannily right. Boulez was less successful, however, in imposing his ideas on his cast. Both in London and the following year at Bayreuth, where he returned to conduct and record *Parsifal*, some of the singing lacked character. In the crucial roles of Golaud in *Pelléas* and Gurnemanz in *Parsifal* he seemed to be content with fine voices that could sing the notes, and to be relatively unconcerned with interpretation. In the recording he subsequently made of *Wozzeck* the singing conspicuously lacks the accuracy he exacts from orchestras.

If opera fascinates Boulez, its condition fills him with revulsion, as he made abundantly plain in a long interview published in the German weekly *Der Spiegel* in September 1967, in which he attacked savagely a number of opera composers ranging from Henze to Kagel and urged that the opera-houses of the world be burnt down as a first step towards reform. Basically, his intention was to attack a widespread belief that Rolf Liebermann, then *Intendant* of the Hamburg State Opera, had transformed his house into a centre of living music theatre. But the uproar occasioned by the interview obscured the fact that much of what Boulez had said was basically justified – that Hamburg, for years regarded as the Mecca of modern opera, had under Liebermann done little more than apply a modernistic veneer to traditional forms of an art which could hope for revival only on the basis of a new fusion of music and theatre.

As it happened, Boulez got an opportunity to put his ideas into practice far sooner than he could have imagined. In the same month as he gave that interview, he was approached by Jean Vilar, founder and director of the Théâtre National Populaire. Would he collaborate with Maurice Béjart, who would be responsible for ballet, and with Vilar himself, on a thorough-going reform of the Paris Opéra, with a view to subsequently becoming its musical director? The prospect was tempting. The institution had long been legendary for artistic and administrative malpractice. For Boulez it was 'a place where only tourists go, because it's part of the circuit, like the *Folies Bergère* and the Invalides'. But he had to think of his 'strike', for what could be a more integral part of the French musical establishment than the Opéra? Vilar assured him, however, that, administratively, it did not come under the musical directorate of Malraux's Ministry, and that, in any case, Malraux regretted the role he had played the previous year. Thus, for a second time Boulez found himself involved in a project to reform an important segment of French musical life. For much of that winter, he laboured with Vilar and Béjart on a scheme that would put the Opéra on its feet after decades of neglect.

By May of 1968, a drastic but carefully considered programme of reform was ready. The Opéra-Comique ('a completely absurd place') was to be shut for good. The Opéra itself ('I could easily console myself if a bomb hit it') was to give nothing but concerts and concert performances of opera for a year, so that the orchestras and choruses of the two houses could be amalgamated and their standards raised. All singers' contracts were to be ended. (Some singers on permanent engagement had for years performed only once or twice a season, so that, as Boulez pointed out, their appearances were rather more expensive than those of Birgit Nilsson.) When the Opéra re-opened, it would offer a smaller but less flimsy repertoire, and, to ensure adequate rehearsal, only a limited number of works would be performed during any given season. The enlarged orchestra would function as a pool, serving both the main house and a small mobile company. These reforms were only a beginning. A workshop was to be set up to give composers an opportunity to experiment with new methods of combining music and drama, so that fresh air might be introduced into an art that had so long been insulated against change. Finally, it was hoped that, as a longer-term project, an entirely new theatre would be built. Boulez acidly remarked in reference to the huge fresco that Malraux had commissioned from Chagall, 'You can't renew an opera house by painting the ceiling'. It would not be enough merely to construct in concrete a shape that (apart from Wagner's innovations at Bayreuth) had remained essentially unchanged since the eighteenth century, when it had served a social order and musical demands quite different from those of the present day. What Boulez had in mind was a theatre whose architecture would not merely permit but demand new uses and possibilities. These were bold ideas indeed. But, as Vilar ruefully admitted, 'every time Boulez takes up what at first seems an extreme position, it later proves to be justified'.

Once again, extraneous affairs intervened. The *évènements* of May 1968 shook the structure of French society to its foundations, and when de Gaulle issued a call to resist the revolutionary situation that had emerged, Vilar, who was a man of the left and already in poor health, chose to regard it as a move towards Fascism and sufficient cause to resign, which he proceeded to do without warning either Boulez or Béjart. But the recommendations were published the following month, in the form of a bulky report. Several of them have since been put into effect. Ironically, the principal beneficiary proved to be Rolf Liebermann, who took over as the new director of the Opéra in 1973.

Feeling that he had no alternative, Boulez followed Vilar's example and resigned. But in his own reaction to the events of 1968, he revealed a deeper political insight. Like many young Frenchmen in the immediate post-war years, Boulez had been a communist in his youth ('it was our substitute for churchgoing'), but the rape of Prague in 1948 and Zhdanov's humiliation of Dmitri Shostakovich and other Russian composers in the same year had brought about an early disenchantment. Boulez still sees the world in Marxist-Leninist terms, yet he is too coolly realistic and too mistrustful of dilettantism to attach much importance to the busy activity of 'engaged' artists. 'Governments aren't frightened of artists', he has observed, 'they're frightened of active revolutionaries who might take their place.' On another occasion he commented, 'I can't change society. I haven't the technique for it'. If he had, he undoubtedly would. But he scorns political attitudinizing, and the only manifesto he had put his name to prior to 1968 (and he was the only musician to do so) was that of the 121 intellectuals who in September 1960 supported the refusal of French citizens to bear arms against the Algerians in their struggle for independence. He was therefore profoundly sceptical of the students' revolution in 1968. Some acquaintances took this response as an indication of cynicism, as evidence of the corrupting power of the sizeable sums he had started to earn as a conductor. In truth, after nine years abroad he felt a certain remoteness from French internal affairs. But he was in France during *les évènements*, and he was shocked at the way the young had 'lost themselves in generosity', as he put it, for in their political anarchism he saw a direct parallel to the anarchism that the aleatory movement had unleashed in the field of music. That, he was sure, was not the way to make a revolution. Turning upside down a slogan that covered the walls of the Latin Quarter at that time, he sadly wrote to a friend, *L'imagination n'a PAS pris le pouvoir*. Except for his resignation from Vilar's committee, his only overtly political action during *les évènements* was to give up his position as president of the Paris musicians' union, when its parent organization, the Confédération Générale du Travail, threw its weight against the revolution. Then, after the government had regained control, he signed a manifesto of a group of young intellectuals deploring the notion of 'spontaneous' revolution and saluting Marxism-Leninism as 'the only valid revolutionary theory of our time'.

Boulez's most important action in May 1968 was essentially non-political. For the first time since his boyhood, he returned to Saint-Étienne, and there he delivered a long and searching survey of the contemporary musical scene. 'Où en est-on?' – as he called his talk – provides an unusually lucid compendium of his thinking on a broad range of subjects. Much of Boulez's writing gives the impression of having been hastily thrown together, for brilliant insights and vivid phrases often lie embedded in thickets of jargon that do less than justice to the clarity and coherence of his ideas. In 'Où en est-on?' the power and range of his thoughts – his ability to relate practical detail to distant developments in other fields of knowledge – are strikingly evident. Reading it, one comes to understand how by the age of forty-five this man had forced his musical generation through the dark night of serialism, had twice been called on to reform French musical life, and was already engaged in projects, not merely to conduct orchestras in New York and London, but to reactivate the musical life of these two largest cities of the West.

At the heart of what Boulez said lay the idea that music had reached a turning point as decisive as that which had confronted architecture more than fifty years earlier, when concrete first began to take the place of stone and brick. An old world had lost momentum and direction; a new world was yet to be born. Signs of the present crisis were to be found in all aspects of musical life. The orchestra, which had evolved in the eighteenth century in response to certain harmonic innovations, was obsolescent. Insofar as concert life had been reduced to interpreting a repertory that lacked the power to renew itself, it was dying. Both concert-halls and opera-houses were increasingly ill-suited to the needs of new music. Instruments were related to the requirements of the past. Electronics, once the hope of the future, had failed to evolve. Too many composers, having lost touch with the general musical public, had withdrawn into enclaves in which they thrived on mutual esteem and little else. This, Boulez maintained, was a situation that could not be resolved by musicians alone. What was needed was a far-reaching collaboration of composers, performers, and scientists in a properly equipped research centre, which might play a role similar to that played by the Bauhaus in the emergence of modern architecture.

At the time of this discourse at Saint-Étienne such a notion must have seemed a pipe-dream. In any case, a new chapter of his career was about to open, which, at any rate for a few years, was to lead him away from such long-term considerations. Within a week of Boulez's resignation from the Paris Opéra in 1968, he was approached by Sir William Glock, the BBC's Controller of Music, with an invitation to become chief conductor of the BBC Symphony Orchestra in London. Glock, who is one of the most imaginative and courageous musical administrators of his time, had known Boulez for many years. As early as 1951, he had asked him to write an article on Schoenberg for *The Score*, a periodical he was then editing. The result was the notorious 'Schoenberg Is Dead', which caused a furore of resentment among Schoenberg's disciples, for this was the first time – at any rate, outside France – that the recessive implications of Schoenberg's dodecaphonic scores had been laid bare. In 1957, Glock had had a part in bringing the Domaine Musical to London and Boulez had conducted a concert – one of the first occasions on which he had done so outside Paris. Then, in 1963, Glock had invited him to conduct a series of concerts with the BBC Orchestra. Some critics found the performances 'cool', 'detached', and 'analytical'. But Otto Klemperer, the last survivor of a school of conducting that went back to Mahler, sat through a number of rehearsals, deeply impressed, and subsequently travelled, in his eighty-third year, to Bayreuth to hear Boulez conduct *Parsifal*.

Glock and Klemperer were by no means alone in their admiration for Boulez's gifts. In 1965, Lord Harewood, then the director of the Edinburgh Festival, had mounted the largest retrospective of Boulez's music that has yet been presented and Boulez had himself conducted *Pli selon pli* and *Le marteau sans maître*. In the same year he had conductd the BBC Orchestra during its tour of the United States, and George Szell, most exacting of perfectionists, had invited him to Cleveland where in 1969 he was appointed the orchestra's principal guest conductor. Gradually, his engagements multiplied, and each time he replied to a question about how many months of the year he proposed to devote to composition, the number shrank. On each occasion he emphasized that he was not really interested in conducting for its own sake. For him it was no more than a means of bringing together the creative and the executant sides of his character and of bridging the gulf that separates the general concert-going public and contemporary music. Yet the time he was prepared to devote to it steadily increased.

In 1966, Boulez had stated that he would on no account accept any permanent post as a conductor. But Glock's invitation seemed to offer a unique opportunity to put into practice his ideas for regenerating concert life. The resources of the BBC were immense, in Glock he had a sympathetic and trusted collaborator, and he had already established a good working relationship with the orchestra. Furthermore, London, which was not too remote from Baden-Baden, was large enough to contain the new, younger musical public he was determined to unearth. In every way, it looked like an ideal marriage. It would provide satisfying work, obviate the need for much travel (which he hates) and leave him about half the year free for composition.

In January 1969 Boulez's appointment was made public, and shortly afterward, with his future more precisely determined than at any earlier moment in his career, he left for the United States to conduct a series of concerts with the New York Philharmonic Orchestra. On his arrival, he was asked in an interview whether he was in the running to succeed Leonard Bernstein as the orchestra's musical director. His answer was unambiguous. Even if anyone had approached him – and nobody had – he would not consider a job in which one was 'a prisoner'. 'Nor', he continued, 'do I know enough about New York's musical life to bring about the necessary changes. To change bad habits, one must know them well.' To drive the point home, he added, 'London is the model of my conception of contemporary musical life ... Today London plays the role of Berlin in the '20s.' Nevertheless, his month at Philharmonic Hall so impressed the orchestra, its board and its management, who for two years had been searching for a successor to Bernstein, that they felt they had found their man and offered him the job. Boulez returned to London to discuss the matter with Glock – as he was bound to do, for a New York engagement would mean some reduction of his contractual commitments to the BBC. Not unnaturally, and by no means only on his own account, Glock was appalled at the prospect of Boulez assuming responsibility for two orchestras three thousand miles apart, especially as each of the jobs, as Boulez viewed them, amounted to an open-ended commitment to a far-reaching reform of concert life, and were thus vastly more taxing and time-consuming than the usual practice of gyrating between the two cities with a handful of specialities. And when was he going to find the time to compose? Boulez saw the force of these arguments, and in May 1969 Glock left for a holiday in France in the belief that the threat had been averted. On his return, however, Boulez told him that the 'problem' of the Philharmonic had 'come up again'. The Philharmonic would, he said, accept a short initial season if the BBC would agree to an equal division of his time (four months in London, four months in New York, and four months 'strictly for composition') in the second and third seasons. Furthermore, Carlos Moseley, the Philharmonic's managing director, would be arriving in London within a few days to negotiate such a deal. Realising that Boulez was now intent on New York, Glock concluded that the choice might well lie between having him for four months and not having him at all. In June 1969 it was announced that Boulez would become Musical Director of the New York Philharmonic for a term of three years and would assume his duties in

September 1971 – the very month in which he was due to take over the BBC Orchestra for a similar period. In New York, if not in London, the Philharmonic appointment was, on the whole, well received. Bernstein gave it his blessing, the Board expressed itself as delighted, and even the players spoke highly of their new chief in this honeymoon period. Boulez's impact on the orchestra was already apparent when he returned to conduct it for a month in the spring of 1971. David Hamilton, in *The Nation*, described the quality of its sound as 'lighter, thinner, decidedly more brilliant'. Today, there is general agreement that he left a better orchestra than he inherited.

Initially, only two groups were less than enchanted by his activities in New York. The first consisted of the more elderly subscribers, who adorn, in particular, the Friday-afternoon concerts. Of these occasions, Boulez has rather unkindly said, 'the audience seems to consist of widows who have five-o'clock tea appointments on Fifth Avenue', and whose decorous, gloved applause 'sounds like snow falling'. No snow fell, however, on a Friday afternoon in the spring of 1971, when he treated his audience to a concert of music by Schoenberg, Berg and Webern. Those are names still calculated to strike panic in the hearts of well-heeled matrons and many members of the audience on that occasion did not even wait to discover that all the pieces to be performed were such early works that they might almost have been written by Wagner, Mahler or even Brahms. After the interval Philharmonic Hall was, it seems, half empty.

In New York Boulez came to see that there was little point in exposing audiences to shock treatment and still less in alienating geese that laid golden eggs; the Philharmonic Orchestra is, after all, largely dependent on its subscribers. His policy of gradualism did, however, undoubtedly do a great deal to broaden the repertory, though his programmes remained on the whole more cautious than those he gave in London, where he had the resources of the BBC behind him and was thus less immediately dependent on box office returns. Symphonies by Beethoven, Brahms and Tchaikovsky, familiar concertos and often staples of concert fare figured far less prominently than in the past. In their place Boulez singled out supposedly familiar composers, such as Haydn, Schubert and Liszt, for special investigation. All the Mahler symphonies were done and special attention given to Ives. Performances of new works were relatively rare.

If Boulez was not a complete success in New York, that was in the final resort due less to unusual but far from revolutionary programmes than to the man himself. The orchestra admired his musicianship. But, accustomed to the highly-personalized, even theatrical, style of his predecessor, Leonard Bernstein, it found him a dry dog, who did not inspire excitement in performances, even if he markedly improved the standard of playing. For much of the same reason, audiences found him a remote figure, who never acted out the music before their eyes and thus deprived them of the emotional kick that is often sought by less musical concert-goers. If attendances held up remarkably well (at the end of Boulez's last season the concerts were 99 per cent sold out), that was in part due to the fact that in New York he was conductor of the city's sole permanent symphony orchestra. In London, by contrast, he was only chief conductor of one of five such orchestras (and by no means the best of them), so that his activities were more easily swallowed up in a torrent of events. In London Boulez achieved more than he did in New York, yet, paradoxically, the English capital was less aware of his reforming zeal.

Curiously, it was at the opposite end of the musical spectrum, among far-out American composers, that his New York appointment at first aroused most opposition, and for this Boulez himself was not blameless. In the 1969 interview in which he had ridiculed the notion that he might be Bernstein's successor, he had also delivered himself of some exceedingly unflattering comments on the American avant-garde. He dismissed its absorption in electronics as 'just a trick of fashion', adding, 'Next year, they'll discover the viola da gamba'. Playing Bach on a synthesizer revealed 'an appallingly low level of thinking'. He went on to describe that rigorously intellectual periodical *Perspectives of New Music* as having 'a cashier's point of view'. The situation in the universities he characterized as 'incestuous': 'the university musician is in a self-made ghetto and, what is worse, he likes it there.' The trouble with American music was that it lacked strong personalities. It had no one 'as good as Henze, and that is not setting your sights very high'. Given Boulez's already published view of his German contemporary, it was setting them very low indeed.

Needless to say, those comments rankled, and the following year there was an answering fusillade. In an open letter to Lawrence Morton, the director of the Ojai Festival, in California, where Boulez was to conduct nineteen works in the spring of 1970, a group of composers, including Morton Feldman, Terry Riley, La Monte Young, and Frederic Rzewski, complained that not one of the nineteen was by an American composer. They accused Boulez of 'imperialistic thinking', aimed at preserving 'the illusion of European superiority'. Boulez ridiculed that accusation, and, in truth, he is too deeply cosmopolitan to harbour prejudice of this sort. He pointed out that in literature and painting Europe had not been slow to accept American influences, and that Cage's music had by no means passed unnoticed there. The fact that today's far-out American music had made little impression across the Atlantic might, he implied, say more about its achievements than about European prejudices.

His critics also argued that it was not necessary for Boulez to come to the United States to present early-twentieth-century music as an introduction to more recent developments. Such music was, they asserted, 'taught and performed extensively ... in any good college or university'. Their claim was well founded, but it failed to meet Boulez's point that, at any rate in 1970, the classics of the century had yet to be accepted by the general concert-going public. It was precisely to drag such music out of the university that he entered the fray. 'To be an effective revolutionary, you have to enter organizations and change them', he said in a scornful reference to those who prefer purity to involvement. He has never claimed to be the only leading member of his profession able and willing to conduct the classics of twentieth-century music, but he has remained the only one of his stature to do so as part of a coherent, long-term policy. It is this, as much as his musical style, that distinguishes him from other conductors.

The composer-conductor is not a new phenomenon. Strauss and Mahler are only two outstanding twentieth-century specimens of a breed that was once common. But, for a man who still considers himself primarily a composer, Boulez saddled himself with a prodigious amount of conducting during the years that he occupied two positions as demanding as those in London and New York, not to mention a variety of other commitments. He also occasionally showed an incautious tendency to bite off more than he could chew, as when at the centenary celebrations of the Bayreuth Festival of 1976 he undertook to conduct the entire 'Ring' for the first time in his life and in conditions that exposed him to the full glare of publicity. Small wonder that during his period in London and New York he frequently looked tired, that there were reports of an uncharacteristic glumness at rehearsals, and on occasions the performances themselves suffered. Unfriendly voices began to ask whether it was Pierre Boulez changing concert life or concert life that was changing Pierre Boulez. Certainly in those years he put himself in a position that demanded superhuman mental and physical stamina.

But even before the period of his life that was to be devoted primarily to conducting had begun, an event had occurred that was to end it some years later. In 1969 Georges Pompidou succeeded de Gaulle as President of France. A man of wide perspectives, with a keen interest in modern painting, he at once launched a plan for the Beaubourg arts centre, which now houses France's gallery of modern art, a centre of industrial design, a reference library, and, France being a country in which food and wine are regarded as an integral part of culture, a variety of eating places. Music was also to have a place in the scheme, and it was at this point that Pompidou was made aware that France's greatest living musician was living in exile. At the time of the Malraux fracas Pompidou had been known to be unhappy about Boulez's hostile relations with French official life but had felt unable to intervene in a matter directly within his minister's competence. In the meantime Malraux had ceased to be minister, and, in 1969, the rebel was bidden to the Elysée, where he dined alone with Pompidou and his wife and was asked to return to Paris to direct the musical activities at the Centre Beaubourg. A copy of the musical plans as they were then formulated was sent to Boulez in America. These he dismissed outright. Instead, he outlined his own project of a research centre, such as he had so prophetically sketched the previous year in his discourse in Saint-Étienne. On these terms, he would, he indicated, be willing to return to France.

It says much for Pompidou's breadth of mind, as well as for Boulez's ability to argue his case, that the President accepted his conditions, although there was no room for such an institute in the centre as it had been planned. Accordingly, he agreed to the building of a quite separate underground construction at a cost that was in January 1973 already estimated at 12 million dollars. Not even Wagner succeeded in getting support on this scale from Ludwig II of Bavaria. But Boulez had other conditions, and they, too, were conceded. First, his institute was to be entirely international, so far as staffing and equipment were concerned. Secondly, it was to be financially independent of the Ministry of Cultural Affairs. Thirdly, it was to enjoy the status of an independent foundation, which at a stroke would not only free it of some of the administrative red-tape that proliferates in France, but enable it to accept money from outside sources, in addition to the annual subsidy of some four million dollars it receives from the State.

Pompidou's death in April 1974 and the economic repercussions of the oil crisis which had struck the industrialized world that winter produced a temporary hiatus and some plans were modified. But Pompidou's successor, Giscard d'Estaing, had been involved with the project since its early days and approval was soon given for the completion of the 'Institut de recherche et de co-ordination acoustique-musical', or IRCAM as it inevitably came to be called. With the opening of its central feature, the *Espace de Projection* in October 1978, the subterranean building, whose studios, laboratories and office plunge several storeys below a deceptively modest entrance, was finally complete.

Reprinted, by permission, from *The New Yorker*, 31 March 1973.

The early works

Gerald Bennett

Pierre Boulez's composition is the record of his attempt to impose strictly logical rules on the materials of composition. In his early works this seems to be achieved with relative ease. Later on the material begins to resist Boulez's attempts to impose ever more complex structuring upon it. A struggle of the highest drama – and of the greatest importance – is being enacted here. This chapter proposes to show in some detail how Boulez learned to control the compositional material he chose to work with as a young composer. Looking at later versions of certain early works will indicate in some degree how the material begins to assert itself and, ironically, how Boulez in fact begins to lose command over the material through the imposition of ever stricter control. Thus will the lines be drawn up for one of the most important confrontations in the music of our time – that of a composer determined to force the material to obey his complex structural demands on the one hand, on the other the musical material itself, increasingly reluctant to submit gracefully to these demands.

The earliest pieces by Boulez still to exist were written in 1942 and 1943. All of them are songs with piano accompaniment (on texts by Baudelaire and Rilke), except a *Berceuse* for violin and piano. The pieces are all quite modest, delicate and rather anonymous. They employ a certain number of standard elements of French salon music of the time – whole-tone scales, pentatonic scales, polytonality – which is not surprising, considering how little serious music Boulez had been exposed to before leaving for Paris in the autumn of 1943.

What is rather surprising in a person of Boulez's gifts is the lack of any strong expressive urge in the music – the pieces are quite content to repose in a sort of languorous contemplation so typical of mediocre French taste. A bit of one of the texts gives an idea of the mood: *Après une journée de vent / dans une paix infinie / le soir se réconcile / comme un docile amant.* These pieces are shy, gentle, and altogether passive. There is a great deal of repetition, the accompaniment often alternates between two chords for long stretches, the melodic line is simple, and the form is always quite straightforward. Here is an example of this earliest music of Pierre Boulez, the end of the *Berceuse*, probably written in the first part

41

of 1943, when Boulez was seventeen (Ex. 1):

Ex. 1

Attractive music, certainly, but much like that of any gifted seventeen-year-old; hardly what one would expect from the young man who barely three years later was to write the Sonatine for Flute and Piano.

When Pierre Boulez came to Paris he enrolled in a harmony class at the Conservatoire, where he spent a dreary and boring year. In April 1944 he began studying counterpoint with Andrée Vaurabourg, the wife of Arthur Honegger. In the autumn of 1944 he enrolled in Olivier Messiaen's class in harmony at the Conservatoire.

Mme Vaurabourg must have been a remarkable teacher, for Boulez remained her pupil until May 1946, when he had already finished the Flute Sonatine and was working on the First Piano Sonata. It is difficult to imagine how she kept Boulez occupied for more than two years, but whatever she did was eminently successful: not only did her pupil develop great mastery in academic fugal counterpoint, but the work with Mme Vaurabourg instilled in him a sense for contrapuntal writing which deeply influenced his growth as a composer and from the beginning distinguished his own music from Messiaen's almost exclusively homophonic style. Ex. 2, probably written towards the end of his studies with Mme Vaurabourg, shows the richness of Boulez's academic contrapuntal technique. It is the exposition of a fugue on a theme by Purcell.

These counterpoint lessons were certainly one of the strongest early influences on Boulez's compositional technique. They remained, however, a largely abstract influence, for their style did not interest their author in the least. It was not until his contact with Olivier Messiaen that the Pierre Boulez we recognize began to emerge.

Boulez studied with Messiaen until the summer of 1945, and there can be no question that during this time Messiaen succeeded in awakening and channelling Boulez's extraordinary gifts in a decisive way. It is impossible to re-create this process; there is too little material still remaining from this period, and in any case the important influences certainly did not come through the lessons in Conservatoire harmony.

Nor are the participants themselves very objective witnesses of precisely what happened during this year. Nevertheless, let us try to suggest some of the ways in which Messiaen may have influenced the young Boulez.

In the first place, the mere proximity of this strong and highly original personality must have been an intense stimulation for Boulez. Messiaen surely transmitted – largely unconsciously – something of the fascination and magic of the act of composition to his pupil. Boulez himself feels that Messiaen taught him to listen harmonically, to be aware aurally of the weights and values of both functional and non-functional harmonies. While it is strange to hear a man with such an acute ear say he learned to listen from anyone, there can be no question but that all Boulez's works possess a marvellous harmonic balance in the choice of pitches and chords, and it may well be that Messiaen focused his pupil's attention on this particular problem. It seems more likely, however, that Messiaen was the first person to make severe demands on Boulez's ear, and that these demands helped him to discover for himself an intensity of listening and an aural world of which he had not previously been aware.

But Boulez not only studied harmony with Messiaen, he also took part in the informal analysis classes that Messiaen conducted outside the official curriculum of the Conservatoire. It was here that he made his first intimate acquaintance with some of the most important works of the century: *Pierrot Lunaire*, the *Lyric Suite*, and *The Rite of Spring*; and it was probably here that Messiaen exercised his strongest and most pervasive influence, as he laid bare the structure of these complex and difficult pieces in his often rather eccentric analyses. For Boulez, this experience must have had enormous significance, for not only is he a magnificent analyst who can reduce an entire work to a tiny germ of an idea, but his development as a composer shows that he used analytical techniques to derive complex groups of structures from simple elements, in the same way as the analyst relates more and more distant structures through more and more abstract and general explanations – a kind of analysis in reverse. In fact, Messiaen's intense and fascinating analyses may have had an influence far beyond mere questions of technique. Messiaen introduced his students to some of the most important works of the century, but their acquaintance with the works consisted primarily of intellectual knowledge of the score and its analysis rather than the intimate and complex aural knowledge that comes when one has studied and performed a piece. One can easily imagine how a young composer without great experience of the technical and emotional complexity of the music of the eighteenth and nineteenth centuries meeting these works for the first time would see their significance mainly in the newness of their structure rather than in the newness of their forms of expression.

In the winter of the year during which Boulez studied with Messiaen (December 1944–January 1945), he wrote a set of piano pieces (*Prélude*,

Ex. 2

Ex. 3

molto

crescendo

Thème - Très lent

Piano
(m.g.)

doux
(Pédale)

expressif

sans arpéger

più f — molto cresc.

p subito

mat

Psalmodie, Toccata, Scherzo, and *Nocturne* – this last piece originally bore the legend 'Prière et incantation à la mystérieuse nuit'), in which we can begin to trace Messiaen's influence on his technique. Ex. 3 is from the *Toccata,* the most interesting piece of the group.

Here we meet a very different Pierre Boulez from the one we saw in the pre-Paris works. The music is much more aggressive, much less delicate and sensitive, polyphonic rather than homophonic, rhythmically more interesting, and much more expansive (the *Toccata* fills sixteen manuscript pages, the early songs three to four). Messiaen's direct influence can be seen in the rhapsodic development of the upper voice, as well as in the construction of the accompaniment. We are probably justified, too, in discerning evidence of a more general liberating influence, due to Messiaen, in the easy, relaxed expansiveness of the music, typical of all the pieces of the set. One can sense Boulez's exuberance while writing the music. Another example from later in the same piece (Ex. 4) illustrates Boulez's preoccupation with counterpoint.

Boulez's life at the time must have been quite active: he was studying harmony with Messiaen as well as preparing for analysis sessions, he was learning the ondes martenot, studying counterpoint, doing some odd piano-playing at night to earn money; and he even found time to compose. The music reflects something of this busy, outgoing life: it is garrulous and frequently a little awkward, like a boy who has suddenly grown very fast and has not quite learned how to co-ordinate things properly.

These were, however, the last pieces in which Boulez was to allow any trace of awkwardness to survive past the sketch stage. His next work, *Theme and Variations for the left hand,* written in June 1945, is a much more mature and elegant piece. Ex. 5 gives the theme in its entirety.

Boulez wrote this piece at the end of his studies with Messiaen, and the influence of his teacher is profound, particularly in the rhythmic structure of the music. Messiaen was concerned with giving his students a new insight into the role of rhythm in music. Since the middle of the sixteenth century at the latest, rhythmic structures in Western music have been determined by dividing large units of duration into a certain number – usually three or four – of notes of equal length. Messiaen was fascinated by the idea of constructing rhythmic phrases by adding together groups of a small common unit such as a semiquaver rather than by dividing a large unit such as a semibreve. Such rhythms have no clear unifying beat, but give an impression of great suppleness. Messiaen also devised systems of rhythmic augmentation and diminution in which the increases and decreases in note-value were irregular, rather than merely multiples of two, as in the classical tradition. The traditional augmentation of the rhythm ♩ ♩ was its double 𝅗𝅥 𝅝 . Messiaen suggested augmentation by a discrete small value, for example by a semiquaver: ♩♪♩♪ or by 𝄾♪ :

♩ ³ ♩ ♩ ³ ♪ ♪. In both cases the 1:2 relation between the notes in the original motif is obliterated. The result is a rhythm with a very special inner life, but without the easy-to-follow, large, metric division of the eighteenth and nineteenth centuries. One can see Boulez's use of this technique in the first five bars of the accompaniment in Ex. 6.

The theme itself shows something of the same sensitivity we saw in the early *Berceuse*, combined however with a much greater control over the material. A twelve-note row determines both the melody and the chords of the accompaniment and is used quite straightforwardly throughout the entire piece. Formally the theme is very simple:

```
     ┌──A──┐    ┌──B──┐      ┌─A─┐
                α  β  α      γ
bar:  1  2  3   4  5  6      7 8   9
```

Bar 7 seems not to fit into the mood of the rest of the theme, but in fact we shall see this sort of sudden eruption in every work of Boulez's from now on. The sensitivity of the pre-Paris music has matured, become more dangerous; it bears within it the possibility of violence, which makes an otherwise maudlin delicacy take on great interest and life.

Theme and Variations for the left hand was written in June 1945. In August and September Boulez wrote the first two movements of a Quartet for four ondes martenot. He did not get around to writing the final movement – a quite marvellous fugue – until March of the next year. (In the summer of 1948 he revised the last two movements of the Quartet, set them for two pianos, added a first movement written in February of the same year, and named the new piece Sonata for Two Pianos.)

The first movement of the Quartet dates from August 1945 and still shows the clear stylistic influence of Messiaen. As in the *Theme and Variations*, Boulez uses a twelve-note row, but only to ensure a sufficiently chromatic texture. It is traditional motivic development that is important here, not recondite manipulation of note-rows. The largely homophonic movement is devoted to presenting and elaborating a rhythmic theme according to techniques developed by Messiaen, but employed much more rigorously by Boulez than by his teacher. The theme of the movement itself reflects several variants of a basic long-short motif (♩♪) – see Ex. 7. Ex. 8 shows a texture typical for the movement. The melodic development is rhapsodic: expansion is achieved through varied but clearly audible repetition. Again we recognize the influence of Messiaen, and *The Rite of Spring* can be heard in the background.

The second movement consists of several expositions of a four-part canon with entrances at the octave and the quaver (Ex. 9). Here the theme uses a twelve-note row, first presenting all twelve notes, then successively ten, eight, six, and finally four notes, before repeating all twelve as at the beginning. The next two expositions are constructed similarly but are

Ex. 6

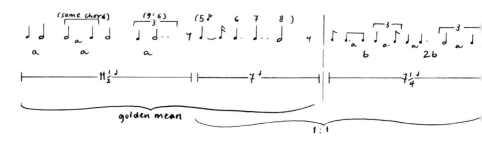

Ex. 8

Ex. 7

longer, and the final canon is the retrograde form of sections of preceding expositions. As introduction and coda, and as interludes between expositions, we find music which is very much in contrast to the hard canonic writing (Ex. 10).

The third movement, written six months after the second, is an elaborate and quite exciting fugue. We meet a much more mature composer handling his material in a much more subtle and differentiated way. Compare, for instance, an example of four-part counterpoint (Ex. 11) with Ex. 9. The counterpoint is freer and more supple; the part-writing is rhythmically more subtle and immensely more interesting than the canons of the second movement. The range of the individual parts has been expanded considerably, and their intervallic structure has changed, major 7ths and minor 9ths predominating over diatonic-sounding minor 2nds (Ex. 12).

The result of these changes is a much more chromatic texture, for although here a twelve-note row is used in the same simple, linear fashion as in the second movement, without any attempt to control the vertical structure of the music, it is the expanded range, the reduction in the number of minor 2nds, and the generous use of rests, that combine to make it impossible for the ear to latch on to a tonal centre of any sort. We sense clearly that between the second and third movements of the Quartet for four ondes martenot some far-reaching change took place in Boulez's contrapuntal language, a change that hastened his emancipation from the stylistic influence of Messiaen. This change was due to Boulez's becoming acquainted with the music of Anton Webern.

In the spring of 1945 Boulez had heard a private performance of

Ex. 9

Ex. 10

Arnold Schoenberg's Wind Quintet, Op. 26, Schoenberg's first large-scale work to use note rows in a systematic manner. The piece was a revelation to Boulez and, though he is no longer particularly fond of it, one can easily imagine how its severe counterpoint and wilfully harsh dissonance might have appealed to him then. Apart from any superficial attraction, however, it is clear that Boulez heard here, perhaps largely unconsciously, a new world which could offer him a solution to his own compositional difficulties.

The piano pieces of the winter of 1944/5 had given Boulez a chance to experiment both with the rhythmic techniques Messiaen had demonstrated and with contrapuntal techniques first practised on academic models. However, the harmonic question – how to organize the pitch structure – had not at all been solved, or even worked on meaningfully. Both the homophonic sections (Ex. 13) and the contrapuntal sections (Ex. 14) are unsatisfactory from a harmonic point of view. The disguised

Ex. 13

Ex. 14

diatonicism of the first example and the emphasized octaves of the second cannot long have been acceptable to Boulez's astringent ear. On the contrary, Messiaen's instruction was sharpening his harmonic sense, making it even more selective than it already had been. But at the same time that Boulez's ear was becoming more critical, Messiaen offered him no really satisfactory substitute for the embalmed academic harmony they studied in such detail (many of Boulez's harmony exercises still survive, at best in 'style Fauré', more often in the style of some master of French Conservatoire tradition: Gallon, Gaubert or Fauchet). Boulez must have imagined in the academic structures of the Schoenberg piece a way out of his own largly academic difficulties.

Paris had not been very sympathetic, to say the least, to the apodictic dogmas of Schoenberg in the 1920s. In the 1930s, when Schoenberg was heard less and less in Europe, France ignored him and his pupils almost entirely. In 1945 the only person Boulez could find in Paris to introduce him to Schoenberg's twelve-note music was René Leibowitz, a former pupil of Schoenberg's and at the time a not-very-well-known composer and conductor. In the autumn of 1945 Boulez organized a group of students from Messiaen's Conservatoire class to work each Saturday afternoon with Leibowitz. The Saturday sessions had a profound effect on Boulez's growth as a composer, for it was through Leibowitz that he became acquainted with Anton Webern; and, next to Messiaen, it was Webern who was to exercise the deepest influence on the young composer.

By December 1945 Boulez knew two scores by Webern, the Symphony, Op. 21, and the Concerto for Nine Instruments, Op. 24. He had not yet heard a work by Webern. These two pieces have a number of technical aspects in common. Both derive their pitch material exclusively from one twelve-note row each, and both are exemplary in achieving such varied but closely-related structures from this note-row. Both works employ rhythmic techniques not unlike those Messiaen had discussed with his students, and both of them, but especially the Concerto, substitute short motifs for the long melodic themes of Schoenberg. Each motif has a characteristic intervallic structure, and it is the interplay and development of these figures of three and four notes that give each work its own particular shape. From the technical point of view Webern's problem was twofold: to reduce the texture of each piece to a minimum so as to keep the short motifs audible, and to cast each motif into as clear and precise a form as possible so as to give the short figure the strength and weight it needed to fulfil the great structural demands made on it. Webern's solution to the second problem was to give all the intervals equal importance in strictly chromatic surroundings. In particular this meant stretching small intervals like major and minor seconds either to their complements or to their equivalents one or more octaves distant in order to avoid diatonic connotations which might emphasize specific pitches at the expense of the individuality of the intervals themselves. So the first theme of the Symphony consists of the notes A–F sharp–G–A flat, which are disposed as follows (Ex. 15):

The beginning of the Concerto uses the notes B–B flat–D, which Webern places like this (Ex. 16):

One result of the spreading of small intervals is the expansion of the range of each voice in a polyphonic complex as at the beginning of the Symphony, where the distribution of the four notes over two octaves avoids the diatonicism of Ex. 17.

Soon Boulez was to make more explicit use of certain techniques he discovered in Webern's twelve-note scores, and to develop them further. But his first reaction to his encounter with Webern was simpler and more direct, if nonetheless decisive for the future. Boulez began immediately to move away from the rhapsodic long-windedness he had inherited from Messiaen, to punctuate his music with rests, to choose the expanded form of an interval more and more often, and to increase the range of the individual parts, giving the impression of a more uniformly chromatic texture.

The third movement of the Quartet for four ondes martenot was not written until the spring of 1946. By then Boulez was quite well acquainted with Webern's music. We can see more clearly the immediate impact Webern made when we look at Boulez's first orchestral piece, *Onze Notations pour Orchestre*, eleven short orchestrations of a set of twelve pieces originally for piano, finished in January 1946, only a few months after Boulez began working with Leibowitz. The first striking thing about the pieces is their brevity, particularly compared with the chatty music Boulez had written until then. Phrases, themes, and motifs in each piece are correspondingly short. The articulation of each phrase is minutely prescribed, and the dynamics are differentiated to a degree we have not yet encountered in Boulez's work. Here we are certainly entitled to see Webern's influence. But perhaps the most important difference compared with earlier pieces is in the pitch-structure itself. Virtually diatonic passages alternate with others in a style more nearly resembling Webern's own jagged chromaticism. Compare the beginning of number 9 of the *Onze Notations* (Ex. 18) with the end of number 10 (Ex. 19), or with the melody from number 5 (Ex. 20). (Boulez liked number 9 well enough to use it for interludes in the first 'Improvisation sur Mallarmé' in *Pli selon pli*.) Examples 19 and 20 clearly show a change not merely in style, but in the very way of dealing with the musical material.

18

Lointain - Calme

Ex. 19

(Score is written in C)

Ex. 20

In the *Onze Notations* the influence of Webern co-exists more or less happily with that of Messiaen. In Boulez's next work, the Sonatine for flute and piano, written in January and February 1946, and the first piece still recognized by Boulez as his own, much of Webern's influence has superseded that of Messiaen, or more precisely, Boulez has chosen to work further on ideas he found in Webern, and it was this that necessarily moved him away from Messiaen's world. In the Sonatine we find the same details of musical language as in *Notations*, but also an extraordinarily imaginative development of these details into middle- and large-scale phrases, sections, and entire movements. The piece is absolutely bursting with energy, good humour, and with a tone new to Boulez's writing: a sharp, brittle violence juxtaposed against an extreme sensitivity and delicacy. The Sonatine is a marvellous work which has lost none of its excitement in the intervening years, and a remarkable achievement for a twenty-year-old who had only begun studying music seriously two-and-a-half years before. In its wealth of ideas and sureness of diction it announces a composer who has found the musical world he intends to explore – and to conquer.

The Sonatine employs both relatively straightforward thematic writing and athematic writing, where short motifs are developed. There are a few sections (the Introduction, for example) where free, quasi-improvisatory writing provides a contrast to the generally quite strict counterpoint of the rest of the piece.

The Introduction (bars 1–31) presents the twelve-note row on which sections of the Sonatine are based (see Ex. 21). The movement 'Rapide' – a sonata-allegro movement of sorts – develops a real theme (Ex. 22). The following section (bars 97–140) ornaments the note-row in a chain of

Ex. 21

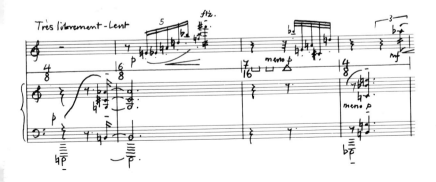

Ex. 23

Ex. 22

trills over which the theme from the previous movement appears in various forms. A long Scherzo follows (bars 140–341), in which a few short motifs are subjected to intense contrapuntal development. After a brief return of the first theme (bars 342–79), the concluding movement develops the motif of the repeated minor third, whose entry at the end of the Introduction was so surprising. A codetta repeats music already heard at the beginning of the piece.

In his essay 'Propositions' (1948), Boulez explains how the rhythmically most complicated section of the piece (beginning at bar 286) was constructed by forming rhythmic phrases using a 'rational' and an 'irrational' version of the ternary motif 2–1: ♫ and ♩♪ respectively. Boulez's explanation gives the interested reader all he needs to analyse the rhythmic structure of the passage himself. Nonetheless it might be of interest here to analyse a passage of some length, from the Scherzo (Ex. 23), to show how Boulez conceived of larger sections of his music.

The Scherzo has three sections, each conceived like a strophe of a poem. Boulez constructs the principal motif of the first strophe from two simple cells (Ex. 24):

Using this motif he forms three different rhythms (Ex. 25):

(Figure *b* is the beginning of *a*, figure *c* is related to *b*, as shown in Ex. 26.)

The passage is in three-part counterpoint, with the flute, the right hand and the left hand each being treated as a separate part. The structure of the parts for the first strophe (bars 222–53) is shown in Ex. 27.

The first strophe is followed by a second of the same texture and similar structure (anti-strophe), ending with a stretto of motif *b* from the first strophe (Ex. 28).

The Scherzo is concluded by a third strophe (epode) constructed as Boulez has explained in 'Propositions'. As the Scherzo has three sections, so the epode is clearly tripartite (the first two parts even close with the same flutter-tongue cadence-formula used to end the first two strophes of the movement). So Boulez moves from the smallest motivic element to an entire movement, nesting smaller structures within ever larger ones to form a unified whole.

The Sonatine was certainly an important work for Boulez. Stylistically the piece is by no means completely homogeneous: we have already remarked that there are large contrasts in the sort of material used, for instance between the athematic motivic development of the epode of the Scherzo and the clearly thematic writing of both the 'Rapide' movement at the beginning and the 'très rapide' at the end. The difference between these two styles is less in the manner of handling the material than in the audibility of the structural elements. Those elements which are either sufficiently simple or sufficiently distinctive to be recalled and recognized easily tend to work like themes in a traditional sense: one orientates oneself by them and by what happens to and around them. Where motifs are either too short or else appear in too varied a form to function as themes, the ear follows other aspects of the musical development. Boulez's attachment to themes – most extreme in the concluding movement of the piece ('très rapide'), where the repeated minor 3rd appears incessantly – is a remnant of the tradition which we sense today as a rather severe stylistic inconsistency in this otherwise marvellous piece. Apparently Boulez also heard it as such, for the Sonatine is the last work in which he makes use of clearly thematic writing.

In the Sonatine Boulez develops and deploys with great originality a number of techniques in which he seeks to bring together what he had learned from Messiaen on the one hand with what he had learned from Webern and Schoenberg on the other. The attempt to find a common structural root for rhythm and pitch was to occupy Boulez for a number of years to come. In the Sonatine the need for the co-ordination of pitch and rhythm at a deeper structural level is not yet pressing, because thematic development and repetition serve as unifying factors. But as soon as Boulez gave up these techniques – beginning in the First Piano Sonata – the central musical problem became to find means of creating and articulating large-scale works without having recourse to traditional conceptions of phrase and form.

Ex. 27

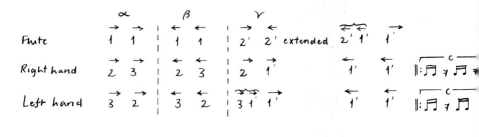

Ex. 28

The First Piano Sonata, written in May and June 1946, moves decisively away from thematic writing and towards new kinds of relationships between structures. To be sure, the beginning of the first movement does take on something of the function of a first theme (Ex. 29). However, these first bars are not a theme in the sense of a fixed,

Ex. 29

clearly-recognizable bit of music; they are a collection of intervals which usually appear in somewhat the same rhythmic garb, though never exactly the same (see Ex. 30). One can no longer speak of a theme here; this is a group of closely-related structures with no hierarchy between original and derived versions. Whereas traditional forms typically move from clarity of theme to relative obscurity and back to clarity, here no form is clearer or more obscure than another. The two-dimensional arch

Ex. 30
(a)

(b)

(c)

(Ex. 29)

(d)

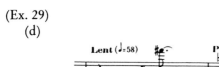

(e)

(f)

(g)

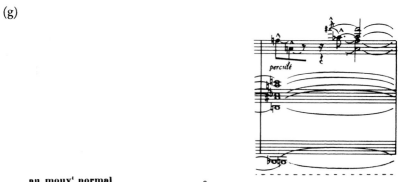

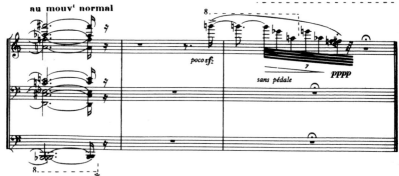

of classical tradition: clear–obscure–clear, preparation–tension–resolution, has been replaced by a three-dimensional space where all the related forms are equidistant from an imaginary centre. Webern's later music, of course, was quite athematic, but Webern was always very intent on moulding his music to traditional formal models; so that, while his musical vocabulary broke radically with the past, the formal movement of his pieces – their syntax – remained dependent on the linear classical movement we spoke of above. Boulez here is intent on moulding his music on no traditional models whatsoever, and this desire to invent a new musical syntax will remain one of his chief preoccupations.

Boulez's next work was *Le visage nuptial*, a setting of five texts by René Char. The published version of the piece (1950/1) is for large orchestra and women's voices. The original version, composed between September and November 1946, was for soprano solo, two ondes martenot, piano and percussion. By the autumn of 1946 the lessons of Webern had been digested, Messiaen's direct influence was as good as non-existent, and Boulez was busy evolving and realizing his own ideas. Analysis of one of the pieces from *Le visage nuptial* will give us an insight into some of these ideas.

'Post-Scriptum' is the last piece of *Le visage nuptial*. The original version is scored for soprano, both ondes martenot, timpani, cymbal, and tam-tam (Ex. 31). In the example the rhythmic phrases of the voice and the accompaniment are marked. These phrases are used to generate the entire piece. The following diagram will make the relationships between the phrases clear:

voice: a_1 a_2 a_3 a_4 a_1 a_2 a_1 a_2 a_4 a_3 a_2 (a_1 a_2)

ondes: b_1 b_2 $c_1 \times 2$ $c_1 \times \frac{1}{2}$ c_2 c_1

c_1 c_2 $b_1 \times 2$ $b_1 \times \frac{1}{2}$ b_2 b_1

Note in particular the retrograde symmetry between the first and third sections in both voice and accompaniment. Boulez clearly expects from these symmetrical relationships some sort of structural aid; they are a substitute for more traditional modes of musical development – thematic evolution, for example, or what we earlier called rhapsodic melodic evolution. In contrast to the use of the opening 'theme' of the first movement of the Piano Sonata, the repetition and manipulation of rhythmic themes here is at once far more rigorous and much less audible. The entire piece is derived from the opening bars in the strictest manner imaginable; the operations are abstract, simple, and are carried out on large groups and with absolute consistency, whereas the operations on the 'theme' in the First Piano Sonata were performed at a lower level with smaller groups, single notes, rests, or chords. At the same time, the 'theme' of the Sonata is always acoustically recognizable, thereby playing a part in the formal structure, whereas no one will hear the repetitions of these long rhythmic phrases in 'Post-Scriptum'. The result is rather strange: increasing rigour in the handling of the material at higher and higher levels, but diminishing effectiveness of the rigorous structures in the articulation of form. The sense of form here is communicated not by structural symmetries, but rather by more obvious factors: a three-part division is given clearly both by the phrasing of the voice and by the setting of the ondes in the three sections: low–high–low-and-high-together in range, with contrasting texture in the middle part; the fermata and the similarity of the voice part at *D* to the beginning give a two-part division (as do the two timpani phrases, in a different sense), in counterpoint to the three-part framework. This piece is formally clearer than, say, the first movement of the Piano Sonata, but the clarity comes not from the complicated symmetrical structures but from the care with which more superficial aspects of the music are treated. There is an irony here: the more refined Boulez's compositional techniques become, the more difficult it is to get larger-scale aspects of the music under control, and the more Boulez seeks to extend procedures used for one dimension of the music to other dimensions as well. This apparent discrepancy between intent and realization – highly structured symmetries which remain largely inaudible – is an important clue to a deeper understanding of the composer Pierre Boulez.

The score of the next piece Boulez composed – *Symphonie* – was lost on a trip in 1954. A miniscule fragment of the work is quoted in the article 'Propositions', but of course it is impossible to form any opinion from the quotation. Boulez himself considers *Symphonie* a very important work, for he feels it was here that he brought many of his ideas about the relation between pitch and rhythm to fruition.

The music of *Le soleil des eaux* exists in four quite different versions. The first piece to bear this name was a 32-minute orchestral work, which served as incidental music to the radio drama of the same name by René Char. This version was broadcast with the play on 29 April 1948. Much of the music of this radio score was written in February as a movement ('Passacaille-Variations') for two pianos (it was this movement that was combined with the two movements from the Quartet for four ondes martenot to form the Sonata for two pianos). For the incidental music to Char's drama, besides writing a good deal that was new, Boulez had used bits and pieces of the February 1948 movement quite out of context but in an order appropriate to the dramatic development of the play.

Post - Scriptum

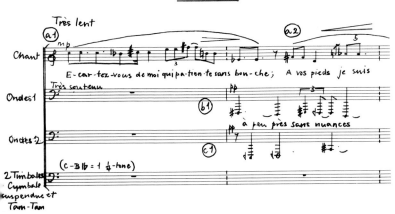

(Ex. 31)

31)

32 (a)

Ex. 32 (b)

x. 32 (c)

Ex. 32 (d)

(Ex. 32d)

(∗) Tous les trilles sont au demi-ton supérieur.

(Ex. 32d)

In October 1948 he revised the radio score, eliminating much of the newly-composed music and restoring most of the Passacaglia-Variations to something like their original shape. This October revision served as the basis for the two later published versions, the edition of 1959 and the edition of 1968. Both these versions set Char's poem *La Sorgue* for voices as their second movement (the 1959 version uses a chorus of soprano, tenor and bass, with one solo voice from each register; the 1968 version calls for soprano solo and four-part mixed chorus). This vocal music is a later addition and consists largely of a doubling of the orchestral music. The soprano solo in the first movement ('Complainte du lézard amoureux') is already present in the radio score, where it is sung – without accompaniment – in its entirety, without the later division into verses.

Let us examine briefly these four different versions, which span twenty years, in the hope of learning more about Boulez's growth as a composer. Ex. 32 gives a short passage from the present second movement of *Le soleil des eaux*, first in the version for two pianos of February 1948, then in the radio version of April 1948, then in the revision published in 1959, and finally in the version of 1968.

In the version for two pianos the polyphonic structure is very clear, and the voices are easy to distinguish because of their disposition (one high and one low voice to each piano). The radio version follows the piano version exactly, except that the instrumentation adds a certain articulation in the realm of timbre:

    (a)   woodwind – strings (woodwind doubling) ⎫
    (b)   brass – woodwind (strings doubling)   ⎭
    (c)   woodwind – strings   ⎫
    (d)   strings – woodwind   ⎭

The 1958 version is quite different. In the first place, the entire vocal part has been added. Comparison with the two-piano original will show the derivation of the soprano solo (Ex. 33). All the vocal parts in the second movement were obtained analogously. Secondly, the instrumentation has been changed altogether. In this passage the entire four-part counterpoint is entrusted to the strings. Apart from being limited to one instrumental colour, the orchestration is immeasurably more subtle than in the radio score, but the original polyphonic structure has been obscured considerably. Whereas in the radio score the change of instrument usually coincides with the beginning of a new motif, in the 1959 version most motifs are broken up and are often played with more than one colour (Ex. 34). The ear has considerable difficulty in following the polyphony, and here one's attention would probably be concentrated on the soprano line, itself a sort of composite of the polyphony. At the same time, in the 1959 version, Boulez uses the instrumentation to articulate the larger form in a way that he did not in the radio score. This short section is all strings for sixteen beats; the previous section,

Ex. 33

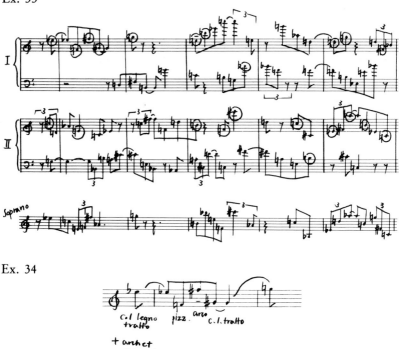

Ex. 34

seventeen beats long, was all for wind; and the following section of twenty beats uses both wind and strings and leads to a dramatic climax. This gives the following proportion:

	1		1		
	wind	/	strings	//	both
	17		16		20
		33		: :	20

golden mean

The wind and string sections are virtually the same length, and together they form the ratio of the golden mean with the third section.

The 1968 version of this passage is once again quite different, so different in fact that one has to look closely to be sure it is the same music. The vocal part has been considerably augmented, and the original polyphony seems at first glance to have been absorbed entirely into the legato chords of the strings. In fact, however, the polyphony of the piano version is present here in its original form, in the harps (a), vibraphone

76

(b), celli I and violas (c), and celesta (d), except that chords of varying density have been added to each part. Yet strangely enough, precisely because of this harmonization, and because of its relegation to instruments (harps, celesta) whose tone disappears very soon after the attack of each note, the polyphony here loses its structural function and becomes merely decorative. In terms of loudness, one hears first the voices, then the original polyphony. But the coherence and homogeneity of the string sound will cause these very soft chords to be heard as more important than the polyphony. This polyphony, which serves as the basis of all four versions, was virtually obliterated in the 1959 version. In the 1968 version it is restored in more than its entirety, but it is now only embellishment, like a half-timbered house, its own visible framework long since covered over by restoration, whose new owners have painted it to resemble a half-timbered house.

We have examined this passage in such detail because it demonstrates a process very typical of Boulez's thinking: the obscuring of the structure of the music, as though the music would lose its validity if the underlying structures became visible or audible. The work must be highly structured, but the structures must remain hidden. There is a contradiction here: Boulez needs to employ ever more complex procedures in order that originally well-organized structures become invisible.

The last work we shall speak of here is the Second Piano Sonata, written in 1948. This is an altogether remarkable piece for a young man of twenty-three, and it represents the end of a first period of development in Boulez's work. In this piece Boulez found a sort of balance between the techniques of ordering the pitch-structure of the music to which Webern had inspired him on the one hand, and the consistent rhythmic structuring of music for which Messiaen had been the model on the other. Two examples must suffice to show the degree of technical mastery Boulez achieves. The first example (Ex. 35) shows (a) the beginning of the second movement of the Sonata, together with (b) a rhythmic and motivic analysis of the counterpoint.

Both the rhythmic and the pitch material are divided into short motifs. The rhythmic motifs are generally figures of two, three, or four notes of equal length, the pitch material is derived from segmentation of a twelve-note row (two of whose forms can be found at the beginning of the first and third movements respectively). The example from the lost symphony in the essay 'Propositions' shows an early stage of this combination of pitch and rhythmic motifs, and we can assume that many of the procedures found in the Sonata had their genesis in the *Symphonie*.

The second example (Ex. 36) is taken from the same movement. This section has a clear tripartite form. The first part uses two different combinations of the intervals (*a*) and (*c*) from example 35(*b*):

Ex. 35

(a)

absolument sans pédale (observer rigoureusement les silences de chaque contrepoint)

avec pédale   sans pédale   avec pédale   sans pédale

(b)

Intervals: a) minor 2nd.   Rhythms:
          b) major 2nd.
          c) minor 3rd.
          d) tritone

(a) minor 2nd–minor 3rd–minor 2nd, and

(b) minor 3rd–minor 2nd–minor 3rd.

The structure is shown in Ex. 37. Here, motivic and rhythmic values

Ex.37

remain the same, but the density of the passage changes. The second part uses the two-note motifs we saw at the beginning of the movement, but fixes the octave in which each pitch appears. This vertical pitch structure is first as in Ex. 38,

then as in Ex. 39.

(D♮ does not appear)

Here, we see that even the order of the pitches in vertical space is predetermined. The concluding section takes up the idea of the first section again, using the same motif but with different note values.

In this passage we see the beginnings of a new direction of musical thought that was to occupy Boulez for some time. In the First Piano Sonata we saw his first attempts to break with traditional means of treating formal elements of music, and in *Le visage nuptial* the use of a highly-structured framework to provide a substitute for traditional means of development of phrase and form. In *Le visage nuptial* the experiment was not entirely successful, in the sense that the symmetrical structures exerted very little influence on the movement and shape of the piece. We saw that Boulez would need to develop more far-reaching procedures to gain control over the more general aspects of his music. In the Second Sonata he has created a whole battery of procedures that give him this control. The tripartite form of the example quoted above is articulated in several ways at once. Most evident is the difference in texture between both the outer sections on the one hand and the inner section on the other. But if we consider the technical procedures employed here, we can express the difference at a higher level of abstraction:

	outer parts	*inner part*
range:	varied	fixed (two versions)
motifs:	fixed (two versions)	varied

This sort of description is altogether unspecific and is not linked to one dimension of music more than to another. Its very abstraction would allow it to apply to pitch, rhythm, timbre, or to practically anything else. By moving to this level of generality in thinking about music, Boulez had come much closer to controlling several dimensions of music simultaneously and by the same basic structure.

We have followed in some detail Pierre Boulez's development as a composer from his arrival in Paris to the completion of the Second Piano Sonata. We have seen how first the influence of Messiaen, then of Webern, served and guided him in the forging of his own musical language. We have also seen how a similar treatment of rhythmic and pitch material allowed the formulation of certain musical problems at a higher level of abstraction than was possible before, a level of abstraction which led Boulez on to seek even greater control over a wider range of the materials of music. We have spoken at some length about technical details of Boulez's developing musical language. In conclusion, what can be said about the growth of his aesthetic vision?

The question has several aspects. In the first place, it is clear from the examples we have given that Boulez possessed, almost from the very beginning, a remarkably sure and consistent aesthetic judgement, in the sense that he seems not to have had the slightest hesitation about the stylistic direction his music should take. The pre-Paris pieces were quite derivative, though delicately and sensitively done, and the piano pieces from the winter of 1944/5 are rather surprising in their frequent roughness; but beginning with the *Theme and Variations for the left hand* we recognize the acoustical world of *Le marteau sans maître* and *Pli selon pli*. The sureness of this aesthetic judgement manifested itself primarily in a negative way: most chords, melodies, and rhythmic motifs were automatically excluded from Boulez's vocabulary, principally because of the associations with which the past had burdened them. There remained only a small number of intervallic combinations, and only a very limited selection of rhythmic figures even came into consideration, so that an ear of the subtlety and acuteness of Boulez's was necessary to endow this arid universe with such luxuriant growth as it brought forth. The maturity and consistency of Boulez's aesthetic vision, which seems to emerge full-blown in the spring of 1945, are largely responsible for the astounding rapidity with which his musical language grew (barely three years separate the *Variations for the left hand* from the Second Sonata). Had Boulez been forced to furnish his aesthetic world from scratch, his development would certainly have been slower.

Boulez's stylistic sense at the age of twenty was surer and more consistent, or to put it less kindly, more restrictive, than either Messiaen's or Webern's at that age (Webern was twenty-five when he wrote his *Passacaglia*, Op. 1). However, not only the superficial, cosmetic aesthetics of Boulez's music are important. What is the aesthetic intent behind the music?

Messiaen and Webern share a common wellspring for their music: both write out of a deeply emotional urge, which seeks musical expression. In Messiaen the spring becomes a huge river, flowing, one sometimes feels, only too unchecked and free; in Webern the flow is less copious, the pressure at the source all the greater. Messiaen and Webern both employ structural devices of varying complexity in their music, but they are quite differently disposed towards these devices. In Messiaen's music the structural elements used are likely to be so abstract or so abstruse – or both – that their effectiveness in structuring a piece at either a conscious or an unconscious level is minimal. In works like *Chronochromie*, *Oiseaux exotiques* or *Livre d'orgue*, where Messiaen has certainly taken care to build complex and differentiated rhythmic structures, the effect remains altogether decorative. The interest, excitement, fascination, and the development of the music do not arise from structural relationships.

In Webern's music, however, particularly in the works after Op. 21, the structures *become* the music. The movement, development, and expression of the music take place in the changing relationship of simple, clear structures to one another. Perhaps the most moving gesture of the first movement of the Symphony, Op. 21, to take just one example, is the change from the exposition's main canon with its subordinate, accompanying canon, to the development's single, four-part canon with long notes in common between the voices. This change cannot be explained without recourse to analysis of the twelve-note structures involved, but at the same time it is a moment of unspeakable poignancy. Here the structure, and the relationship between structures, *is* the music.

The contact with Messiaen started Boulez composing seriously, and it seems likely that Messiaen's analyses played an important role in determining Boulez's conception of what music can and should be. But there can be no question but that Webern's scores interested Boulez far more than Messiaen's. Not only was the severity and astringency of Webern's ear more to his liking, but Webern was forced to structure his music with infinitely more care and consistency than Messiaen, since the entire burden of its emotional charge had to be borne by this edifice. Boulez took over many of the constructive principles he found in Webern, extended them, enriched them, and gave them a breadth and generality they never had for Webern. But Boulez did not take over Webern's aesthetic intent: with Boulez, structure does not become music, or at least not as in Webern. In Webern's music the structure lies open, the frank and perhaps occasionally naïve bearer of the full significance of the music. In Boulez the structure is hidden, submerged, covered over, giving life to the music, but secretly, as if ashamed.

The history of Boulez's growth as a composer is the history of an ever-increasing sensitivity which caused him to eliminate from his music those features that had traditionally accounted for coherence: repetition, clarity of formulation in theme and motif, and readiness to communicate emotion, whether personal or not. The rejection of these easily-used and -understood features left Boulez to build a musical world of his own, and his character, upbringing and training convinced him that only a world logically structured and of complete inner consistency would serve his needs.

We are moved by the exuberance with which this young man sets out to remake music. But the examples from *Le soleil des eaux* are two windows into the future through which we can glimpse for an instant the consequences of this logical consistency. Structural differentiation leads to greater differentiation, abstraction to greater abstraction, but the material resists this one-sided ordering: out of complex but absolutely consistent structures new, unrelated, accidental structures emerge and begin to direct the course of the music. We saw this happening in the 1959 version of *Le soleil des eaux*: the foreground is occupied by the vocal part, which represents no logical necessity but is a sort of shadow of the underlying polyphony. In the 1968 version the accretions of 1959 have themselves begotten new structures, and even the reinstatement of the original polyphony cannot change the fact that below a certain general level it is impossible to speak meaningfully of structure in this music. Intricately delicate structure becomes shimmering surface, surface masquerades as structure. The two become indistinguishable, which means the ultimate abrogation and annulment of structure itself.

Boulez's composition represents one of the great adventures of music in this century: the restructuring of the language by imposing on it relations of absolute logical consistency. The task has shown itself to be more difficult than it seems in these early works: here the material yields with apparent graciousness to Boulez's attempts to form it; later, as Boulez's control grows and his vision matures, the material begins to resist this structuring in a deep and mysterious way.

It remains to be seen to what extent Boulez will succeed in the task he has set himself. Whatever his success in his own eyes, the record of this confrontation with the material will be of the greatest concern to everyone for whom music is important. Much more elementary, much more profound than any mere extension of the musical language by new scales, new instrumental techniques, or new modes of presentation, the adventure of Boulez's music is an examination of the very foundations of composition itself. As all adventures should be, this one is full of danger, and like any true adventure it will enter into the mythology of our future. Most of music's concerns today are of less importance than the drama being enacted here. Nonetheless, there is hardly one of these concerns that will remain untouched by the adventure of Pierre Boulez's composition.

Extracts from the following works have been reproduced by kind permission of the publishers: Sonatine for flute and piano (Amphion Editions Musicales, Paris); *Le visage nuptial, Le soleil des eaux*, Second Piano Sonata (Heugel et Cie, Paris).

The piano music

Charles Rosen

The Sonatas for piano Nos. 1 and 2, along with the Flute Sonatine, are the first items to be admitted to the canon of works acknowledged by Pierre Boulez. Music for keyboard is a traditional outlet for experimentation: it allows an immediate control over the musical idea. If the composer is even a modest pianist, it enables him to escape (momentarily) from the terror of being interpreted; and the limitation of tone-colour and range is a positive advantage even for composers for whom timbre is not a compositional element clearly subordinate to pitch – the limited timbre of the piano acts as a focus. Music for piano has therefore become, starting with Beethoven, a convenient form of announcing a revolution in style: Schumann, Liszt, Brahms, Debussy and Schoenberg are the most conspicuous examples of composers who used the piano for this purpose. In spite of later developments, the piano work which initiates a change of direction often indicates at once the nature of the revolution and suggests its limits.

The First Sonata treats the series as a nucleus to be exploded, its elements projected outwards; this particular spatial metaphor, indeed, remains present in most of Boulez's later works. The opening bars display this at once (Ex. 1).

The elements of these clusters are suspended in different parts of space: at the opening of bar 2, the cluster is, indeed, exploded. The effectiveness of this passage depends upon an unspoken acknowledgement of the module of the octave – in other words, of the inaudible presence of the cluster.

The consequences for the dynamics of this conception may be seen in the extreme case for the piano of the crescendo on a sustained note (Ex. 2).

The presence of the cluster, and the explosive force that projects the E flat outwards imply the crescendo – after the fact and through the *sforzando*.

The next bars force the issue (Ex. 3):

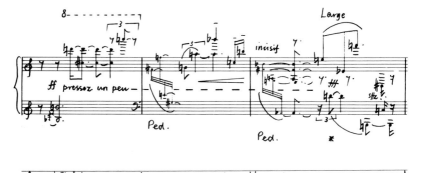

The condition of intelligibility is an understanding of the tension between the serried texture of the cluster, which provides an implied (inaudible) structure, and the wide spacing of the actual music. The dynamics are strictly determined by the point of intersection of these two textures: the *fff* arrives with the first minor 2nd of the piece (D–E flat) – not quite simultaneous, however – and the full simultaneity of the immediately following minor second (C–C sharp) is italicized by the *sffz* within the area still controlled by the triple *forte*.

This opening page solves some of the problems that had faced serial music (and naturally raises more pressing ones). The first is the ambiguous relation of the full chromatic space to the module of the octave within which the series is conceived. This relation becomes for Boulez a focus of the work.

Octave transposition, for Schoenberg and for Webern, is still a method of orchestration: the realization of the series is conceived not in terms of register or *tessitura* (which remain secondary matters) but in terms of the complementary intervals (3rds and 6ths, 4ths and 5ths, 2nds and 7ths); in other words the series is still almost always realized *within* the octave. The intervals within the octave must be emphasized by Schoenberg to create melodies, by Webern to create patterns of equilibrium. Boulez is preoccupied not at all with tunefulness, and only marginally with symmetrical balance – at least on the local level of the individual phrase. A 17th is not, for him, primarily a transposed 3rd, but a projection in musical space. The realizations of Schoenberg and Webern refer back to the intervals that can be contained within the octave, which give the *stable* form of the series. For Boulez, however, the realization within the octave is privileged but not stable. It is, in fact, almost never stated in its full form.

The relations of stability and tension in Boulez have been displaced, and realized in a different manner. The module of the octave privileges the cluster, but does not make it a point of rest: it is only an implied antithesis to the open texture in a continuous dialectical progression. The extreme point of stability in Boulez is difficult to illustrate from the First Sonata, as the end of each of its two movements relies too much on traditional gestures. The end of the Second Sonata gives a clue (Ex. 4).

Stability is not resolution here, as it still is for Schoenberg, but the *diffusion* of the several directional forces. This movement towards stability through diffusion can be found throughout the First Sonata, but never in so absolute a form as here.

An excuse may be offered for the constant recourse to spatial metaphor in this discussion: in the construction of an aesthetic, Boulez's music appeals constantly to our experience of space, and, in short, constitutes itself as a spatial metaphor. This becomes even more marked with the unfinished Piano Sonata No. 3.

The second problem of serialism dealt with by Boulez, if somewhat less radically, is the relation of the motif to the series. For Schoenberg, the series is a quarry for motifs, and it is the motifs that provide the energy for the piece, that have a generating force. They provide this energy by implying sequential motion or – Schoenberg's practice is both complex and occasionally contradictory – by a mimesis of the tonal functions of dissonance and consonance which therefore push towards resolution. By contrast, Boulez's motifs are neutral agents: the expressive content of his music is conveyed not through the motifs but through texture and dynamics (which are really a part of texture). Schoenberg's motifs, and Webern's as well, imply direction and movement, tension and resolution: Boulez's motifs are not emotionally charged, and imply spacing above all. They therefore become – at least in part – independent of the series, and the same motif can be realized with different elements of the series without losing its identity (Ex. 5):

In each of these cases, the identity is affirmed by the context.

The central role of spacing derives of course from Debussy, but Boulez from the first carried it further than anyone previously. The slow opening of the last movement of Sonata No. 1 may be compared with the beginning of the second section that immediately follows (Ex. 6):

The second example realizes the series almost within the octave – that is, as an arpeggiated cluster. The fact that in an earlier version the spacing of the first example was not nearly as wide as the published form only confirms the implicit presence of the serried form in the dispersed final version.

The energy is imposed rhythmically on the motif by Boulez, not derived harmonically from it. If the toccata-like rhythm seems to imply an exact measurement of time by a motorized impulsion, the treatment of the motif (and this is one of Boulez's most remarkable and original inventions) prevents any such strict measurement. Each phrase decomposes into its several motifs. Entrances of the motif (Ex. 7)

succeed each other so closely that the beat is obliterated,[1] and the rhythmic groupings define a continuously variable dynamic movement. At only one point, the climax of this second section, does this motif take on the classical character of generating the shape of the phrase (Ex. 8):

Here the *sforzandi* are grandly rhetorical as well as functional, and the barlines try in vain to obscure the fact that there are six regular beats between each note of the motif.

The large outlines of the form are related to this mosaic construction of the phrase. Denying a generative power to the motifs, yet still employing them as basic to his texture, Boulez is forced in this work to use a kind of passive form, a technique of juxtaposition that derives most obviously from Messiaen. The large structure of the first movement is not a sophisticated one: it sets up two textures, *Lent* and *Beaucoup plus allant*, and alternates them in an A-B-A-B-A sequence in which each A has the clear contour of a reprise – a symmetrical ordering. The metrical organization is, however, very sophisticated and evades any sense of symmetry: the slow sections have a floating beat which imposes a continuous *rubato*; the fast ones, with a regular pulse, have a continuously shifting accent.

The second movement puts the technique of juxtaposition to much more complex use, and in its last pages recalls Stravinsky's scissors-and-paste construction of the finale of *Orpheus*. Boulez uses three textures here: *Assez large* and *Rapide*, both quoted above (Ex. 6), and *Modéré sans lenteur*, an extraordinary section which looks like two-part counterpoint on paper, but which turns the piano into an immense vibraphone.

---

[1] This is a technique already elaborated in the extremely close canonic passage of the earlier Flute Sonatine. By the time of the Piano Sonata, however, Boulez has abandoned the reactionary forms of the strict canon.

This third section requires a heavy wash of pedal, as the lines of sound cross, lose their individuality and are suspended in a variable floating rhythm. The third texture is interrupted, after a time, by the other two in a pattern of collage.

The reappearance of fragments of the first section, in particular, when pieced together stands for a recapitulation. The concept of the interrupted recapitulation has remained with Boulez, and it was his intention – and may still be – to finish *Éclat* by a return of the opening piano cadenza, but with continuous interruptions from the orchestra which is gradually expanded during the course of the work. This is a method of reconstituting the late eighteenth- and nineteenth-century classical effects of symmetry by means of discontinuities and juxtapositions, and it still aims at the traditional form of synthesis and closed form. In the First Sonata, Boulez wishes to mark each fragment of the return of the opening section of the second movement by the tempo mark *Plus large*, so setting the recapitulatory function into relief.

There is a notational problem in this movement as Boulez has written the section *Rapide* first in quavers and then on its return in semiquavers, and finally in quavers again for the last three systems of the final page. This in itself creates no difficulties, as the identity of rhythm is evident, but the notational ambiguity has unfortunately contaminated the return of the opening section (*Assez large*). Its final appearance, marked *Rapide*, must actually be played twice as slow as the few bars of the toccata rhythm that follow, and the continuous movement from one texture to another here requires not a break in tempo but a swift *accelerando*. The paradox of Boulez's style is that the rhythms are to be interpreted strictly and the tempo very freely.

The isolation of motifs in a context which denies the power of generating movement through harmonic tension comes directly from Debussy. As in Debussy, this technique gives extraordinary relief to timbre – both of the intervals of the motif and of the *tessitura*. It is, in fact, less the exact pitches of the opening 6th of the Sonata (see Ex. 1) than its timbre that is immediately and directly active, and this enables Boulez to release the power of contrasting timbres through the structure of a long work as no composer for the piano, with the exception of Debussy, had been able to do before.

The exasperated fury and the extrovert virtuosity of the Second Sonata have often been remarked. Boulez's distaste for openly expressive gesture has here been sublimated in its collision with an openly expressive form and the grandiose implications of the traditional virtuoso piano texture. The concept of classical theme and motif, as Beethoven used them and as Boulez follows him, is necessarily expressive to the extent that expressive power can be equated with the drive that forces thematic development and impels it forward.

The explicit model of much of the Second Sonata is Beethoven, explicit in the music itself. The quotation from the *Hammerklavier* Fugue on the opening page is direct (Ex. 9):

The use of Op. 106 signifies an aspiration to the sublime in the academic sense (as in Brahms's Op. 1), and Boulez's Second Piano Sonata aims both to conquer and transcend the academy. The structure accordingly incorporates the most problematic elements of academic form. The first movement has a clearly defined exposition rounded off by a slight *ritenuto* and a short fermata, and this exposition contains easily recognizable first, second, and concluding themes. There is a development section, elements of recapitulation set in relief (with the themes in a new order and interrupted by new development as in Haydn) and a coda, which achieves a stretto of the now fragmented themes. There are other references to fugue form in the consistently imitative texture and the reappearances in the recapitulation of the inversion of part of the main themes.

The four movements follow the standard pattern. After the first, there is a slow movement which ends with a return to the opening measures (partly transformed by retrograde inversion). The third movement is a scherzo and trio, and the finale has – like the *Hammerklavier* – a fragmented introduction, but then develops a highly original form of its own, an immense stretto and a very slow, soft coda. Even the finale, however, has a conveniently rhapsodic grandeur.

The motifs are no longer neutral agents, but Beethovenian themes with generating power.[2] Their identities are affirmed not by timbre and texture but by imitation and sequence (Ex. 10):

The form insists upon our recognition of these themes as the vehicles of

---

[2] These procedures would seem to be a partial affirmation of Schoenberg's principles in contradiction with Boulez's inflammatory manifesto 'Schönberg est mort': but the rhetorical provocation of that article, directed as much at Leibowitz as at Schoenberg, is misunderstood today.

significance except in the finale.

The retrogressive aspects of the Second Sonata are apparent: its innovations are more subtle and more interesting. Perhaps the most important relate to rhythm. Two may be mentioned here. There is a dramatic use of certain rhythmic conflicts which temporarily annihilate a sense of metre. The most important of these (Ex. 11)

is used throughout the first movement, often with more complex combinations (Ex. 12):

Boulez's contention that the barlines are only visual points of reference can be maintained hazardously by his practice of placing them so that they appear to contain an extra beat, a technique derived from Messiaen. Much of the metre of this sonata is relatively regular, which makes both the superimposition of conflicting rhythms and the *rubato* demanded for an intelligible performance more telling.

The other innovation is the use of the rhythm of the release of notes as well as of their attack (there are precedents for this throughout music as well as in Messiaenic theory, but there are, as far as I am aware, no such large and consistent exploitations of the effect before the slow movement of this work). The use of the dispersed cluster formation, frequent in the slow movement, emphasizes the releases (Ex. 13):

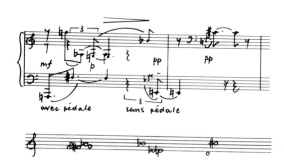

The entrance of the G, *p*, only a triplet semiquaver after the rest of the cluster's *mf* is almost imperceptible if dynamics and rhythm are strictly observed: the pitch of G is obliterated by the F sharp and A flat that precede it. It becomes clearly audible as the other notes are released.

It is evident that the exploitation of the release of sounds is a small-scale effect of retrograde motion. Large-scale examples of retrograde motion have been difficult to handle in music and, except in a very few instances, appear as a *jeu d'esprit*, because they entail too demanding a use of spatial metaphor – spatial, because they treat past and future as reversible by analogy with left and right, and metaphorical in the most elementary sense by implying a displacement of significance.

This disruption of the traditional sense of metre represented hesitantly by these innovations was to become a central concern of Boulez, above all in the attempt to reformulate the fundamental elements of music in the two books of *Structures* and the, as yet unfinished, Third Sonata. The opening piece of *Structures I* has become famous as a kind of manifesto, but of what? Of the composer's freedom from tradition or of his submission to a new self-imposed order? In fact, this opening is a piece that tests the limits of music, by displaying its elements under conditions where their traditional *expressive* interaction has been made impossible – less an experiment than a clearing-away of irrelevancies.

Boulez here adds a serialization of rhythm, attack and dynamics to the traditional serialization of pitch-class, still leaving free the actual register at which a given pitch is to be played. The four series are independent in that none of them is designed specifically to reinforce the rhythm or the attacks, but each series is there to interact with the others.

This 'independence' of the four series has been made a reproach to the work, largely out of a nostalgic sense of an aesthetics of the Organic, in which the total dependence of all details on a central idea is a guarantee of aesthetic unity. Whatever the merits of this theory in tonal music (and it is often absurdly abused even where it is relevant), it is out of place here, at least at the stage of the compositional process at which it is directed. Boulez himself adheres to some extent to this traditional aesthetic (there being no viable alternative as yet) and has written – specifically about the project of *Structures* – that 'il fallait absolument, et nécessairement, que chaque oeuvre crée sa forme à partir des possibilities virtuelles de sa morphologie, qu'il y ait unité à tous les niveaux de langage'.

The misunderstanding has arisen because the four independent series have been considered as the *form* – predetermined – of the piece, whereas they are only the elements of its morphology. The series is not conceived merely as an ordering of the elements, but as itself a fixed element; Boulez attempts to carry out what Webern had only started. The extreme nature of the work lies in this: that its form is minimal – not zero, but the absolute minimum of form that arises from the interaction of the morphological elements without (or almost without) the composer's intervention. The purpose of the piece is to expunge the presuppositions of a form that are traditionally embedded in the morphological elements, and thus to create the basis for a new language of music. Out of this experience came not only the rest of *Structures I* and *II* but other works, in particular the unfinished Third Sonata.

From this point of view, the evaluations frequently offered of this introductory work, analyses which oppose the composer's total and 'responsible' control of his material to the actions of chance, are largely irrelevant. The musical events created by the interaction of the series do not in fact constitute a musical form, if by 'form' we mean strictly a temporal order of events in which the order itself has an expressive significance. The order of events is fortuitous in the sense that it is neither foreseen nor alterable by the composer, but this fortuity has no interest. The structure of the piece is not aleatory (although the temporal order of musical events may be said to be determined by chance) because the structure is not conceived as temporal, and the realization in sound – the performance – does not reflect the structure *directly*. It would be best to say that the interaction of the morphological elements does not create a temporal form, but indicates and exposes the possibilities of new forms. This opening piece is both an introduction and a demolition. It erases the last traces of thematic form that still attached themselves to the elements of music.

Even here the composer intervenes to fix the register. This intervention is not completely free: the need to avoid a coincidence or close proximity of octaves limits the choice. Nevertheless, Boulez refuses to accept any unnecessary constraint here. That is, perhaps, because his use of register is more idiosyncratic than any other composer except Debussy, who has been an obvious influence and even a source in this regard. If he often exploits this use of register in the interests of spatial metaphor, this is only rarely an intrusion of extra-musical considerations, as the analogy with space may be said to have been built physically into musical elements.

Boulez's gift for spatial metaphor is perhaps the most remarkable in the history of music, and it is to the operation of this technique that some of the most striking of his innovations may be attributed. Retrograde motion is only the simplest form of spatial metaphor, but we may start with an example of this from the unfinished Third Sonata. *Parenthèse*, one of the sections of *Trope*, is written so that the second half is a very freely interpreted retrograde of the first. I give the moment of the reversal of direction (Ex. 14):

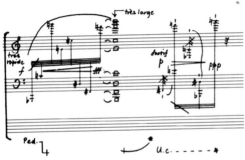

The beginning of the retrograde is conceived strictly in terms of the release of sound; what is ordinarily a visual trick, requiring an effort of memory to appreciate aurally, has been transformed into purely sonic terms with extraordinary effect, like the sudden reversal of direction of a tape.

This metaphorical imagination is at work throughout the Third Sonata: the metaphorical fusion is so complete that it is hard to pull the elements apart. One of the two movements so far published, *Trope*, has four sections: *Texte*, *Parenthèse*, *Glose*, and *Commentaire*. The performer may start with any one of these sections, and *Commentaire* may be played before or after *Glose*; otherwise the order is fixed. The form of the piece is therefore a double circle, and each performance represents only a cut from the total form.

The central movement, *Constellation*, is the metaphorical realization in sound of a poem which is itself already the realization of a spatial metaphor: Mallarmé's *Un coup de dés jamais n'abolira le hasard*. Mallarmé lays out the words on the page like a constellation, and the relations of words are revealed by the patterns, the movement of thought traced by the movement of lines on the plane surface. Mallarmé's poem concerns the play of chance which remains implicit in any creative ordering, the freedom of meaning essential to a form both defined and closed. He affirms as a delusion the classical ideal of the work of art that attempts to ignore chance and contains at its centre a definitive nucleus of meaning. *Un coup de dés* neither abolishes nor yields to the probabilities, but contains them by an essay in transcendence.

Boulez's use of aleatory principles differs sharply from that of his contemporaries. *Constellation* does not surrender to the probabilities (*l'ombre enfouie dans la profondeur par cette viole alternative*), but contains them – more simply, uses them. The work exists in two forms, *Constellation* and the retrograde *Constellation – Miroir*, only the second of which has been printed. It is made up of two kinds of fragments: points and blocks. The blocks, as Boulez has written, are 'structures based on ever-changing resonant aggregates, either struck together or decomposed horizontally in very rapid succession (in such a way that the

95

ear does not lose the identity of the aggregate)'. The points, by contrast, are suspended over a continuously-changing web of harmonies, created by depressing the piano keys silently so that their strings vibrate in sympathy with the notes actually played. The variety of sonorous effects is considerable: the most striking are the gradual release of notes one by one from thick chords, and the use of the pedal to catch the reduced but still vibrating sounds after the dampers have momentarily touched the strings. The structure is therefore determined as much by timbre as by pitch.

As in Mallarmé's poem, the fragments of music are laid out on the page like a constellation. The order is controlled but not fixed: each is to be followed by another chosen among a limited number (up to four); the direction chosen may imply a specific set of dynamic markings and tempo relationships. The real freedom of the performer – as in all music – lies in the imposition of continuity by the inflection of the phrase, and of dramatic clarity by articulation and spacing. The form of the work is not to be found in any single set of choices but in the total of all the possible permutations. Nevertheless, the creation of such a structure would be an uninteresting game if each individual realization or performance did not imply the existence of the total form.

This larger structure is implied by the decentralized concept of time in Boulez's later work, perhaps his most radical contribution to music. *Constellation* reveals certain aspects of this concept in an extreme form. It is the immovable, still centre of a larger work, which literally revolves around it. The stasis of *Constellation* depends on a concept of time in which the strict measurement of duration has been deposed from its central position. The metronomic indications must often be freely interpreted, and the rhythm controlled by the levels of sonority achieved. This technique was to reach its most important development in the first ten minutes of *Éclat*, where the rhythm is often entirely dependent on the decay of sound of a set of instruments whose decay cannot be strictly controlled in advance (piano, vibraphone, harp, bells, etc.), but it is already present in *Constellation*. In *Trope*, too, the alternation of a strict beat with a constantly varying one carries the seed of the later achievement of the most recent version of *Don* in *Pli selon pli*, where brief sections lasting a few seconds of completely free figures in one section of the orchestra (rhythms left to the discretion of the players) are superimposed upon strict uniform figures played by the others.

The intention is to disorder the sense of a single and central unit of temporal measurement while still keeping control over the temporal realization of the work. The music is conceived in terms of rhythmic structures which do not submit to the directed flow of tonal music, with its magnetic attraction to, and drive towards, the cadence. In this sense, rhythm has been the last bastion of tonality. Boulez's conception of non-directional rhythmic flow is the logical and responsible consequence of serialism.

The aleatory aspect of *Constellation* annuls the sense of direction in time without yielding an iota of the ideal of a fixed and defined form – the outlines are never blurred or fuzzy. If the choice of one set of tempi or dynamics remains free, the equilibrium of such choices is determined and achieved by the conditions of the piece, which enforce the equivalence of all possible choices. (This is not the case with *Trope*, where the choice of an order ending with the subsection *Commentaire* is, in concert performance, more dramatic and more effective than any other.)

The new structural importance of timbre – in particular the intensified employment of harmonics – is inseparable from the concept of a variable measurement of time. These overtones have rhythmic qualities peculiar to them – they sound when their fundamentals are struck, but they have no attack of their own. As the fundamental is damped, the overtones appear to swell, and their entrances are not measurable in any way compatible with classical rhythm. On the other hand, their releases give a more strictly definable rhythm. The pedal effects of *Constellation*, above all those of a gradual dampening of sounds, act in the same way, a-rhythmic by classical standards but defining a measurement that gives the illusion of accelerating as the sounds disappear. The scale of events according to which time is measured is turned from an absolute and abstract system into one in which the quality and the intensity of the sound directly affect the sense of movement. The forms of the Third Sonata are no longer (like those of the first two) traditional and simple structures imposed on an original sense of sound, but ones in which timbre, register and intensity immediately determine the larger scheme.

The convergence of two poetic systems

Célestin Deliège

The conjunction between Boulez and Mallarmé

What we shall be doing here is simply to recall various aspects of one of the most unexpected encounters of our age, between a composer whose essential creative activity is rooted in his reflexions on contemporary musical language and a writer who, a century earlier, underwent a parallel experience through the medium of verbal language. This encounter is all the more astounding in that it was lived through by the composer in the context of his global experience and because in the final analysis it appears to be no more than circumstantial – for example, where the relationship between music and text has been deliberately sought (*Pli selon pli*).

Paradoxically, it may well be that this relationship is most apparent when the composer is expressing himself in the most general way; for in *Pli selon pli* one must modify one's point of view and re-orientate oneself towards those things which become a transformation of Mallarmé, or rather a transformation that tends to confirm, through music, the most essential of the poet's attitudes to his art. Now, it is probably just this point that Mallarmé would have taken exception to, in the same way that he uttered such a severe judgement against Debussy's 'attentat' on *L'Après-midi d'un faune*,[1] the sole example he knew of a composer trying to get close to his work. But are Mallarmé's views on the autonomy of his own work very important when three first-rate musicians (Debussy, Ravel, Boulez) have measured themselves against it, moving it into new areas of expression into which it merges, yet losing none of their preponderance?

Before going any further, however, it would be as well to remind ourselves that we must distinguish between a convergence of approach in the most general sense and the relationship of the music of Boulez to the

[1] P. Valéry, *Oeuvres*, vol. I, Pléiade, p.670

99

writings of Mallarmé insofar as one can detect it: here there is more than unevenness; indeed, as already implied, there is virtually a contrast of perspective.

Is it historically interesting to elaborate on the two points of view? Is it essential, for instance, to know how the composer's approach could have met that of the poet's, when in fact it may well have been a matter of chance? Naturally, it is still possible to deprive oneself of certain evaluating factors, for fear, for example, of over-estimating their importance; but it is nonetheless most significant that a very secret link must exist between the two afore-mentioned aspects of the problem, and that an attempt to produce a relative appreciation of the first may perhaps lead to a deeper elucidation, albeit localized, of the second.

I

It is to 'the astonishing duration of resonance of Mallarmé's word in today's world'[2] that we owe this privileged encounter between Boulez and Mallarmé – an encounter that is anachronistic only in appearance. One century later it is still possible to transpose the poet's concerns to our own time.

Mallarmé's prophetic action is the first important factor here. By engaging in a kind of research which had language as its object, by feeling the necessity of basing his work on his own previously thought-out theory, the poet outstripped his age to an unbelievable degree, preparing, in isolation, our own – so to speak – already placing himself in the position of a scientific researcher (a description of the artist of today) who only accepts given data in order to transcend them, while being careful above all to avoid any kind of reproduction, even disguised, of systems and models.

Nevertheless, the dissimilarity of the historical conditions of the process of creation is a poor explanation of the convergence of approaches, of concerns and, above all, of research that have the same object of reflexion and expression – language and theory. Seen as a whole, these subjects of convergence seem more inescapable for Boulez in 1950 than for Mallarmé in 1867 when he was laying the foundations for his work. However, the hope of seeing the birth of a common style resulting from a collective effort on the part of post-Webernian musicians was only short-lived; and finally Boulez, like Mallarmé, remained rather isolated in his creative activity. Could it not be said, consequently, that it is their individual will that best defines the observable relationship between the

[2] P. Valéry, *Lettre sur Mallarmé*, op. cit., p.634

two creators? Perhaps one could even postulate that it is an obsession with the Mallarméan model which, within a combination of historical circumstances, has guided Boulez's behaviour.[3]

Like Mallarmé, Boulez very soon realised who his true masters were, and, as with Mallarmé – who was very attached during his whole life to the work of Baudelaire, Gautier and Banville – remained faithful to them. Starting from the rhythmic system of Messiaen and the grammar of Webern, he understood that his first task must be the construction of a new syntax: in this way, from the Second Sonata onwards, the rhythmic system opens out to combinations of irrational values, while the constraints sought by Messiaen – not rationally based – are eliminated. In the same way (starting mainly with *Structures II* and *Pli selon pli*), Webernian harmony was progressively replaced by a harmonic system based on limited groups of sounds, allowing a treatment of the note-row by areas – something that made the music less monotonous and more efficient.

In so doing, Boulez (following the example of Mallarmé, who preserved 'the words of the tribe') did not intend to destroy the morphological principles available in the serial pitch-system; he kept to equal temperament and, if he dreamt of going beyond it into micro-intervals, this would be done while still safeguarding the division of a module into equal parts. Besides, the extension of the serial principle to other parameters than that of pitch did not imply a reassessment of the 'values' used.

One cannot exclude the possibility that such similarities of approach may be fortuitous. They are still striking for all that, and one is rather more inclined to ascribe some significance to them when one knows in what esteem and admiration Boulez held Mallarmé from the time of his earliest works. Other poets (Char, Michaux, Cummings) have 'coloured' his work; other authors (Joyce, Pound, Eliot, Artaud) have on occasions deeply influenced the content. But, at the very moment when these writers are present in Boulez's work via the text or through another occurrence that is highly significant on the immanent level of aesthetic results (think, for example, of the influence of the *Théâtre de la cruauté* upon the most lyrical episodes of *Le marteau sans maître*), it is still the Mallarméan principle that is the most active.

Let us recall Boulez's allusion to parenthesis as early as 1954:[4] there has been much heart-searching as to what the equivalent of this could be in

---

[3] It is not denied – quite the contrary – that during this time research was going on into language, stemming principally from electro-acoustic discoveries. However, apart from a few well-known cases, this research was often diverted towards conformist forms or structures dictated by chance – something that Mallarmé, like Boulez, always strongly rejected. Is the use of the element of chance in recent aesthetics, then, anything more than the memory of an aberrant ethical option?

[4] P. Boulez, 'Recherches maintenant' in *Relevés d'Apprenti*, Seuil, 1966, p.32

musical terms. But is it not enough, really, to grasp the direction of Boulez's overall form in the various parts of *Le marteau*, for instance, and then progressively insert in the reading the multiple little groups that appear to be injected into this form from inside, in order to understand to what extent the technique is close to the Mallarméan form in which the principal clause is, as it were, dislocated by the integration of parenthetical clauses and subordinate clauses that vastly enrich the context? And, from an analogous point of view, one could also mention the spreading-out of phrase and period that is no less striking in the work of the composer than in that of the poet.[5] From the Second Piano Sonata and *Le visage nuptial* onwards, structures unfold in broad utterances that are confirmed by the later works as a whole. No doubt it would be very unfair to prefer to see Mallarmé rather than the Germanic music tradition here, but it is nonetheless significant that such a relationship contains no contradiction. This point of convergence in approaches was to become very important particularly in the way Mallarmé's verse was amplified through the 'vocalise' in *Une dentelle s'abolit* and *à la nuit accablante tu*.

These density factors (cutting-up and length of the Boulezian period, to which should be added its weight and its intensity) introduced a dramatization of content from the first works onwards – a dramatization that few works managed to escape. Now, one of Mallarmé's conscious struggles, he who never lost sight of the musicality of the verse, was the conquest 'of a new dramatic verse-form' whose 'divisions' should be 'servilely traced on gesture',[6] a kind of verse that should 'ravish the ear in the theatre'.[7]

Evidently, this new element of convergence of approaches has neither the same origin nor the same goals, but it is nevertheless notable that we encounter it through a desire to create a discourse strongly emphasized by structures that multiply the internal ramifications, unfolded on a canvas of vast forms. Yet, Mallarmé is not seen as an initiator in this field, as he found in nineteenth-century music – especially Wagner – a source of inspiration. Today, however, Boulez's work has determined a return towards music which finds its fulfilment in what Scherer described, referring to Mallarmé, as the 'depth' of the phrase[8] – in other words, in the multiplication of parenthetical clauses which disguise the main clause, a writing technique that we have seen re-evaluated and retransposed by

---

[5] Admittedly, one must be careful in assenting to the notion of 'phrase' in Boulez's case; even the acceptance of the metaphorical meaning calls for caution when the discourse veers very resolutely away from traditional phraseology. All the same, the quality – one might even say elegance – of the 'curve' in Boulez's large forms guarantees the presence of a *unity* of a similar type.

[6] Letter to Eugène Lefebure, July 1865, *Correspondance*, vol. I, Gallimard, p.169

[7] Letter to Henri Cazalis, ibid., p.168

[8] J. Scherer, *Expression littéraire dans l'oeuvre de Mallarmé*, Nizet, 1947, pp.181ff.

Boulez in his task of constructing form since *Le marteau sans maître.*

All these considerations – to which others could be added, such as the necessity for a high combinative level, already experienced by Mallarmé in his time and felt by Boulez in a much more rational way than his predecessors of the Viennese School – clearly show that the central and most tangible points in the convergence we are trying to demonstrate have the structure of the work as a reference, but that, in both cases, structure was only a means, a springboard to renovate the content of the message in the most profound way possible. In order to achieve this, and having started from an angle of reflexion that immediately led them to want to base their work on their own logical theory[9] – Gide spoke even of 'a priorist literature'[10] referring to Mallarmé – both creators made it their aim to elaborate new poetic systems. 'I am inventing a language', Mallarmé wrote, 'which must necessarily spring from a very new poetic system.'[11] As for Boulez, from the time of his famous 1954 article (above mentioned), he did not cease to devote his musical composition to the same quest. In both cases the concept of 'poetic system' is the same: the concept of 'doing' contained in the etymology of the word, as re-defined by Valéry.

As for the most striking implications of these poetic systems, which have been the most discussed in the last twenty years or so, they are mainly concerned with the concept of the 'livre' and the mobility of the text. Boulez has explained his thoughts on this subject:[12] the idea of the 'livre' came to him very early on, as a result of his reading *Igitur* and *Le coup de dés.* It enabled him not only to imagine very lengthy and highly dense works but also to postulate the unification of his thoughts: the different works are looked upon as 'the different facets of a single one ... of a central concept'. From this point onwards, the paths taken by the composer and the writer begin to diverge. It would indeed be a vain effort to look for a metaphysical basis to the Boulezian concept. The musican, unlike the poet, could not live in the mythical vision of a book reaching out to the world through the word entrusted with expressing it entirely. For the rest, without going so far into the reaches of the imagination, and simply by bringing facts to the level of what individual minds can posit, how can one imagine a man of the twentieth century – and particularly Boulez – assuming an experience as intimate and as tragic as that of emptiness, which was the still mysterious chasm in which Mallarmé slumbered before finding himself? The crisis-situation that Boulez lived

[9] S. Mallarmé, letter to Eugène Lefebure, 20 March 1870, *Correspondance*, op. cit., p.318; P. Boulez, 'Eventuellement' in *Relevés d'Apprenti*, pp.147ff.
[10] Quoted in Scherer, op. cit., p.41
[11] Letter to Henri Cazalis, 1864, *Correspondance*, op. cit., p.137
[12] *Pierre Boulez: conversations with Célestin Deliège*, Eulenburg, 1977, pp.50–2

through around 1950 can be seen as the inverse phenomenon, where man triumphs through mature reflexion and technique over resisting matter; where he makes his own, in the outline of a truly dialectic thought and in the accomplishment of minutely programmed actions, a whole set of data, a universe which imposes itself on him, in order to rebuild it by making its foundations more logical and less rigid. The reason for both these artists attempting to establish, almost at the same age, the plan of their work (and it makes little difference that circumstances might have acted against such a plan in both cases) is very probably because they found themselves faced with a *degré zéro* of expression. But whereas for Boulez this fact, as we have already mentioned, was the result of an inevitable set of historical circumstances (the aftermath of Webern), for Mallarmé it was primarily the voluntary creation of a source, of a vacuum that called out for a new universe to which the French language had not hitherto had access and to which it would never again have access except through the pastiche of less talented emulators.

As for the mobility of the text, the situation is similar. Boulez stated that he had found in the publication of fragments of Mallarmé's *Livre* in 1957 nothing more than a confirmation of what he had just done himself in another way in the published 'formants' of his own Third Piano Sonata.[13] In other words, despite their parallelism the Mallarmé phenomenon and the Boulez phenomenon are independent of each other in this regard. And there is no reason why it should not have been so when Boulez found himself faced with a historical predicament where the message lacked an internal direction imposed by a gravitational centre connected with language, thus implying that the ways of linking the parts of the discourse were becoming optional and introduced from outside, whereas Mallarmé deliberately and *a priori* wanted a mobility that was not directly justified by language itself but which, through typographical artifice and actions directed towards form and context, he had created *ex nihilo*.

In this way the sets of behaviour so far examined have come together to make the syntactical and formal structure the centre of a fundamental transformation of writing and, in both cases – it is important to stress it again – basing it on tradition, something far removed from the wanderings that Boulez often described as 'libertinism' or the journalistic style against which Mallarmé's disdain vehemently defended poetry. But even if this similarity is striking, it remains nevertheless true that the motivations must be understood in the social and psychological contexts of their time, whose options were not at all the same. The notion of 'mobility', for instance, whatever the depth of Mallarmé's intuition, could never again have the same meaning after Joyce or Pound as it had had before.

[13] Ibid., p.51

Even more, its meaning is no longer the same today, after the sometimes too explicit spatial expressions, as when Boulez wrote his Third Piano Sonata. What to make of this, if not that historical trends in art must not be confused, even from the point of view of the approaches that generated them? Being too conspicuous, they incite an over-simple interpretation of their significance.

It is, however, obvious that Boulez cannot be considered apart from Mallarmé without the traits that draw up a common portrait. In the last analysis, would we venture to see, through this common obsession with the perfect work – rejecting the cliché, accomplished at depths that stimulate the faculties of perception to their uttermost limits, untiringly taken up again and elaborated upon – an ultimate fundamental concern: the need to put oneself forward for posterity? No one who has witnessed the philosophical views sometimes expressed by Boulez will fail to recognize him in these lines from Mallarmé to Cazalis:

> I admit that the Science I have acquired, or re-found in the depths of the man that I was, would not be sufficient for me, and that it would not be without a real tightening of the heart that I would enter into the supreme Disappearance if I had not finished my work, which is *The Work*, the Great Work, as our ancestors the alchemists used to say.[14]

But a limit must now be set to this debate. Boulez read Mallarmé as a musician and, through this exemplary reading, the poet's options were taken up again and amplified. Would Mallarmé have agreed with this new accomplishment of his work? The question is now obsolete. The important thing is the undeniable existence of *Pli selon pli*, where the ineluctable conjunction occurs, where the convergences discussed here are evaluated in terms of forms and a content where objects merge. At a time when the historical ground we are dealing with here hardly belongs to us yet, it will be important not to go too far ahead, nor straight into the most complex matters, thus making the analysis too difficult. Basing our reflexion and analysis on *Improvisation I* written on the sonnet *Le Vierge, le vivace et le bel aujourd'hui*, we shall attempt to show how the Mallarméan project of rhythm and of movement of the verse is amplified by the music in the sense in which the poet foresaw the mobility of the alexandrine as desired by those who 'internally loosen the rigid and puerile mechanism of its rhythm'.[15]

---

[14] 14 May 1867, *Correspondance*, op. cit., p.243
[15] S. Mallarmé, *Crise de vers*, Oeuvres complètes, Pléiade, p.362

II

At the end of his life Mallarmé was haunted by an idea, expressed in the preface to *Le coup de dés* and better elucidated in *Crise de vers*. The idea is well known: in his work of constructing free verse and poetry in prose, Mallarmé restored to Letters the original part they have transmitted to music 'heard in concert'. If the 'transposition to the Book of the Symphony' can be worked at and achieved, it is because 'it is undeniably not from basic sonorities on the brass, the strings, the woodwind, but from the intellectual word at its apex, that Music, with fullness and clarity, as the entirety of relationships existing in everything, must result'.[16] This statement is undeniably mythical since it presupposes that Music is necessarily fertilized by the Verb. Nevertheless, Boulez seems to have accepted a part of the challenge contained in this remark by developing Mallarmé's poetic system – or, to put it another way, by safeguarding, through the interplay of musical structures, some aspects of a prerogative of the Verb in the sense of the Mallarméan concepts.

By means of a clear distribution of complementary or contrasted values in the vocal part, by using continuity or discontinuity in the instrumental parts, by the way in which the harmonies within the stanzas are distributed and the sounds of each harmony within the verse are organized, the composer multiplies the possible readings of the rhythms of the stanza and of the verse. Through the metrical extension given to each word, according to whether the treatment is vocalised or not, he modifies its suppleness; through prosody and stress given to certain syllables, he enhances equivalent sonorities.

All these features that emphasize the Mallarméan concept, are they really and rationally related to the structure of the poem? Is it possible for the listener to have a clear perception of it, or is the conjunction too subjacent to be perceived? To the first question one is tempted to reply that, if the relation is clear at certain levels, at others Boulez's interpretation leaves a shadow of mystery. But is it not going too far to seek an over-literal view of the correspondences, and isn't the role of the irrational the necessary safeguard for a margin of non-dependence that must subsist between verbal form and musical form? As for the second question, it raises some delicate points that so far have not been very thoroughly explored in the field of psychology, concerning the perception of the structures of messages in relation to their own origin; *a fortiori*, one may wonder if one is not penetrating into a strictly mythical realm when an osmosis of messages occurs, and if one's powers of perception are capable of going beyond what is merely allusive or subjacent.

The 'reading' now proposed of *Le Vierge, le vivace et le bel aujourd'-*

[16] Ibid., pp.367–8

hui will allow a better understanding of the implications of our observations and queries.

III

Le Vierge, le vivace et le bel aujourd'hui[17]
Relationship between poetry and music

A : major convergences

The form of the sonnet is entirely preserved in the music:
(1) through a very controlled organization of the spaces between the stanzas (structure of the blank spaces) and their surroundings;
(2) through the treatment of the verse in the vocal part.

1a. *Structure of the blank spaces.* The space between the two quatrains is filled by the linear statement, on the vibraphone, of the note-row from which are derived all the morphological structures of the piece.[18]

Ex. 1

[17] Ibid., p.67; P. Boulez, Universal Edition no. 12855 (Chamber version). The reader is advised to consult the score for a clearer understanding of this essay.

[18] The study that follows will not deal with the question of the genesis of the structures. For one thing, this aspect of the analysis does not directly concern our subject, but also, and above all, it is very difficult to submit it to a single hypothesis. In any case, it seems to us that the method of extracting morphological structures from a note-row only provides really relevant information if it coincides unambiguously with the actual structure as it appears in the work. Furthermore, in the case of the piece we are analysing here, the simplest methods seem to have prevailed.

For the benefit of the reader who wishes to undertake a morphological analysis of the piece, we should draw attention to the fact that the row of pitches is divisible into three sets of four notes which provide relative symmetrical relationships between each other. The first two sets have a sort of central axis consisting of the interval of the major 2nd on either side of which the two other sounds form the interval of a minor 2nd presented as a major 7th or a minor 9th; the row can be transformed by moving the chromatic interval of the minor 2nd in relation to the central axis. In the presentation of the row between the quatrains, the third set groups together two major 3rds a semitone apart which, when this presentation is kept to, produces two pairs of minor 2nds in the harmony. In the same way, the two pairs of major 2nds can be brought together through permutation of pitches into pairs of minor 2nds. Moreover, the four last sounds can be grouped together with the sounds 1, 2, 7 and 8, which are their exact reflexion.

107

Symmetrically with this statement, the space between the terzets is characterized by the uttering, still played on the vibraphone and still present in a linear form, of a transformation of the row (Ex. 2). In the space between the quatrains and the terzets – which Boulez apparently has considered the most important, as did Mallarmé, since in the poem it separates the notion of the past (*un cygne d'autrefois*) from that of the future (*Tout son col secouera*) – four syntagms of twelve notes are strung together, forming six harmonies. Timbres are distributed in symmetrical registers in groups of three harmonies (Ex. 3).

Ex. 2

Ex. 3

In response to this harmonic and instrumental arrangement, the singing of the second terzet is followed by the sounding of two harmonies. The instrumental distribution of the first (eight notes) is comparable to harmony no. 1 (of Ex. 3) with an equal number of notes. In the same way, the second harmony (nine notes) is presented in the same register as harmonies nos. 2 and 5, also of nine notes, of the central blank space of the poem (Ex. 4).

Ex. 4

The organization of the percussion reinforces these symmetries, already introduced by the preceding material. In this respect, let us point out that it will be sufficient to note, for the moment, that the distribution of the percussion in the episode corresponding to the central blank space of the poem, and in the coda (the only times that the tam-tam and drums make an appearance), brings home strongly the above-mentioned structural analogies between the two passages. It would be as well to draw attention to the striking asymmetries which dominate these symmetrical arrangements (length of harmonies, internal rhythmic distributions).

1b. *Introductory and concluding harmonies.* Following the same line of thought, it is important to notice certain symmetries between the introductory harmonies of the stanzas. Stanzas I and III are introduced by harmonies containing seven notes, one harmony being an inversion of the other. These harmonies include dual instrumental articulation (detached on the harp, sustained on the vibraphone) (Ex. 5). The less dense harmonies that introduce stanzas II and IV are symmetrical too through one aspect of their morphology, the E flat–D sharp being given an upper or lower minor-9th appoggiatura with the sounding of the bell. The introductory harmony to stanza II is, moreover, symmetrical with the harmony of similar function in stanzas I and III because of the dual articulation (short–long, harp–vibraphone). The introductory harmony of stanza IV also has a dual articulation, but in this case the relationship is between the voice and the instruments. This transformation is most probably due to the particular emphasis that the author wanted to give to the subject of the verse (*Fantôme*) which is isolated by what follows (Ex. 6).

Ex. 5

Ex. 6

As if echoing the introductory harmonies, rhyming harmonies appear at the end of each stanza. They disclose obvious parallels between odd-numbered and even-numbered stanzas. At the end of stanzas I and III it is the harp-writing (arpeggiated harmony plus resonance) that creates the balance (Ex. 7). As for the concluding harmonies of Stanzas II and IV, they initiate the systems outlined in examples 3 and 4.

Ex. 7

2. *Treatment of the verse.* One may also add to all these parasymmetrical relationships the vocal gestures at rhyming moments. The symmetries that can be observed from this point of view provide a complex system of 'cross-rhymings', the arrangement of which is set out approximately in the table opposite. A reading down the table shows up the most immediate correlations; but according to the perspective selected one can distinguish several networks of relationships between the rhymes. At least at the level of one single parameter, there exists a link between each rhyme taken individually and all the others, in the same way that this happens in the poem through the constant presence of the vowel-sound 'i'.

There exists a privileged relationship:

(a) from the point of view of pitches selected, between I–1, III–2, IV–1, IV–2 and I–2; between III–3 and II–4; between IV–1 and IV–3.

(b) from the point of view of the interval, between I–1, III–2, III–3 (descending minor 9th) and III–1, IV–1 (ascending major 7th), relationships to which one can add II–3 (descending major 7th) and III–1 (ascending minor 9th over three notes); between I–4 (descending minor 6th) and I–3 (ascending minor 6th); between II–1 (ascending major 6th), II–2 (ascending major 6th over three notes) and II–4 (descending minor 3rd); between II–4 (descending major 9th over three notes) and IV–3 (ascending major 9th); between II–2 (ascending tritone) and I–2 (descending tritone).

(c) from the point of view of melodic curve, between I–1, III–2, I–4, III–3, II–4 and by inversion of this motion IV–1 and II–2 (also to a certain extent II–1 and III–1); between I–3 and II–2; between IV–1 and IV–3; between I–2 and II–3.

(d) from the point of view of the organization of durations into longs

ble of 'cross-rhymings'

and shorts, between I–1, III–2, IV–1, IV–3, IV–2 $(-+\smile)$[19]; between I–4, III–3, II–4, I–3 and by addition of repeated notes I–2 and II–3 $(\smile+-)$, the two groups being capable of association by inverse symmetry; between II–1 and III–1 $(\smile+\smile)$; between II–2, I–2, and II–3 (series of $\smile$).

(e) from the point of view of intensities, but here the relationships become increasingly blurred.

It would be an exaggeration to consider all the elements of this combinative example to be equally significant: the most important ones are obviously those that are to be found simultaneously on more than one parameter or which show irrefutable evidence of their existence.

However, the whole of the symmetrical forms so far looked at constitute nothing more than a formal framework. While writing them into his work, the composer tries to disguise them. No parallelism is, indeed, real: comparable harmonies do not necessarily have the same morphological structure nor the same duration; degrees of intensity are also subject to variation. As for the musical structure of the rhymes, although present because the composer wished it to be so, it can have nothing more than an allusive function.

Boulez, nevertheless, obviously intended to be as faithful as possible to his model. For example, the rare punctuation-marks indicated by Mallarmé are registered in the music. The most powerful one is the exclamation mark that ends the first stanza and which is translated by a 12/8 value on C sharp in the voice, whereas ordinary punctuation-marks that end other stanzas are given smaller values. Commas in the poem are also marked: the most significant is the one that separates *Le Vierge* from the two other determinants of *aujourd'hui* and which is marked by a substantial caesura in the vocal line (2/8+1/8). On the other hand, the comma that separates lines 2 and 3 of the first terzet coincides with the single D natural of the harmony sung on *nie* and punctuated by the vibraphone. Finally, it is the same D natural – but sung an octave higher and additionally occurring for the first time in the context of the last stanza and also punctuated by the vibraphone – which marks the word *assigne* at the moment where the comma is written in by the poet at this point.[20]

Other structural features reveal a scrupulous fidelity to Mallarméan

---

[19] The notion of short and long here, it should be pointed out, is quite relative. It is simply a question of comparing in a general way the two values that make up the last interval of the rhyme.

[20] It should nonetheless be noted that the composer appears here to have wanted to link line 1 to line 2 of the second terzet, for at this point a new harmony begins which is going to be prolonged into the following line, thus producing, as it were, a syncopated harmony between the two lines.

thought. Without mentioning all of them, we shall deal with some of the most striking.

First of all, it should be noted that before amplifying and diversifying Mallarméan rhythm by musical means, Boulez's intention was to preserve it, mainly by an adequate use of caesuras in the vocal line. One can say, from this point of view, that the music handles the verse, thus respecting Mallarmé's *mot total*. As for the internal caesuras, they appear most frequently at the delineation between two syntagms or tend, but not invariably, to emphasize the order of clauses. In some lines (I. 2, 4; II. 3) they are to be found in the occasional half-line '*é*' rhymes, occurring at points where the syntagms are clearly demarcated; however, this procedure has not been respected in line 3 of the first quatrain, despite the same rhyme. Here, the rhyme has been treated as one block (the quaver-rest of the triplet after *ce lac* cannot be construed as a caesura, but as a simple gesture of articulation between two consonants). We may nevertheless notice that the half-line rhyme has not been totally deleted: it is emphasized by a vocalise and by a C sharp appearing for the first time in the harmonic field in progress.

The rhythm of line I.1 fits very closely with Mallarmé's 3+9 in respecting the function of the comma, as we mentioned earlier; but it would be useful to note how much the rhythm is reinforced by the only appearance of B natural in this line on the conjunction *et*, cancelling out a second comma and demonstrating, on the contrary, the poet's wish to link the second and third determinants of *aujourd'hui*. This B natural carries great weight in this context where the main notes in the harmonic field are, statistically, D natural, A flat, C natural, E flat and G natural, and where the complementary notes F natural, B natural and C sharp only come into play very gradually.

Line II.2 is a remarkable reflexion of the Mallarméan rhythm 3+1+9. Here we have an alexandrine of thirteen syllables, of which there are many examples in Mallarmé because of the presence of the mute 'e' which is not included in the reckoning. The line in question includes two mute 'e's; one of them has to be eliminated in order to obtain a normal alexandrine. Here Boulez has opted for a solution that is not symmetrical compared with similar cases in the same poem (I.2 and 3; II.3; IV.1 and 3): he deletes the mute 'e' of *magnifique* and, by way of compensation, articulates the mute 'e' of *délivre*. In so doing, he considerably isolates *magnifique*, an adjective treated in parenthesis between the subordinate clauses and the conjunction *mais*, a kind of optional link between the clauses. Not only does he bring out the isolation of these two words by rests, but he emphasizes them with a note not yet heard in the harmony in progress (the A flat on the first syllable of *magnifique* and the D natural on *mais*).

The caesura between this line (II.2) and the preceding one is very short

113

$(1/16+\overline{1/16})$, probably in order to protect the overlapping of the clauses. A similar consideration holds good in the very close articulation of III.1 and 2, where the main clause is linked to a subordinate one by the preposition *par*. Line III.2, on the other hand, is musically treated according to the 9+3 rhythm, thus demonstrating the unevenness of the clauses as starting point. In discussing the introductory harmonies to the stanzas, we pointed out in IV.1 the isolation of the subject *fantôme*, linked to the main clause of the following line. Here this is not achieved by a simple caesura but by an interruption of the singing which, by separating the word from both lines, makes it available to both of them. The harmony that includes the word *fantôme* is distinct from that of lines 1 and 2 of the terzet. The isolation of this subject and, consequently, of the subordinate clause that follows it arranges the musical rhythm of the line into 3+9 where there is, once again, interplay between clauses. Is this a memory of the subject at the beginning of the two lines? Their solidarity is marked in the music by a simple 1/16 caesura, which has more the function of a mere taking of breath after the mute 'e' of *assigne* than a separative function. Let us also notice the 10+2 rhythm of IV.3 whose object is clearly to bring to the fore the supreme subject of the poem, *le cygne*, and to give it the full power conferred on it by the inversion that brings it in as a final rhyme.

We have ignored the lines treated as one block from the point of view of organization of caesuras, such as II.1 and 4, and IV.2. Perhaps the reason is because II.4 and IV.2 are made up of a single clause and the composer has not thought it necessary to distinguish the syntagms, perhaps simply because there is no half-line rhyme, unlike certain lines already dealt with and which are divided into 6+6. A similar question possibly arises with regard to II.1, more especially (it would seem) as this line contains two clauses that would, according to the norm usually adopted, lead us to expect an alexandrine with the 9+3 rhythm. However, besides the fact that this kind of question tends to falsify the process of composition in leading one to believe that the system is too rigid, one must hasten to add that the composer has allowed himself many others ways of approaching his model, and not only of approaching it but also of amplifying it and charging it with its full musical potential. It is this point – the most important in this analysis – that we shall now tackle.

B: Opening up verse to mobility

Has Boulez respected Mallarmé's wishes concerning mobility of the verse or has he gone beyond? It is not really important to answer this question, which we have already treated with some caution in our preamble, since the poet's wishes themselves can no longer be a central preoccupation today.

First of all, let us point out, if need be, that by 'mobility' we mean here the multiplicity of possible perceptions of the poem that the music opens up. Using this as a definition, let us now list the main attributes of 'mobility': (1) length of line; (2) internal distribution of durations and intensities; (3) distribution of harmonic fields; (4) distribution of instrumental groups; (5) enhancing of dominant words and syllables marked by phonetics; (6) linking factors between the lines and the musical structures.

1. *Length of lines.* The lines are arranged according to a kind of dyssymmetry which allows for a great suppleness of the whole:

Stanza I   : 18/8 + 13/8 + 19/8 + 30/8
Stanza II : 18/16 + 20/16 + 23/16 + 19/16
Stanza III: (23 + $\overline{2}$)/8 + ($\overline{4}$ + 24)/8 + 31/8
Stanza IV : (4/8+6/8+13/8) + 21/8 + 18/8

Caesuras between lines are included in these figures. Besides the dyssymmetry already noted, the most striking thing is the passage with the semiquaver as the basic pulse, used only in stanza II. Since this stanza is the shortest (the modification of tempo is not very important), apart from its condensed character, perhaps one could consider that the composer intended to turn the presentation of the subject of the drama into an emotional pole in the sonnet by giving it its own special characteristic.

The return to the initial tempo for the first terzet confirms the relative symmetry with the first quatrain, already pointed out, as it will be again later on. We may also notice the comparable length of the last lines of these stanzas, which are also comparable on the grounds of the structure of the rhyme and the instrumental surrounding that emphasizes it. The total length of this terzet is actually greater than that of the quatrain. This unfolding of stanza III is achieved by a more generalized vocalise than in the other stanzas. The first terzet thus contrasts with the concentrated utterance of the second quatrain. It is possible that here again Boulez wanted to indicate a characteristic of the content: perhaps the projection of stanza II towards the past and that of stanza III into the future. However, such observations must remain in the realm of speculation.

Finally, we may notice the equality (18/8) of lines I.1 and IV.4: this might be thought to be fortuitous if it were not for the fact that the distribution of pitches in the harmony produces a correspondence between the two lines. To these global durations one should also add those of the tailpieces, whose proportions contribute to the accentuation of temporal dyssymmetries at various points in the singing.

2. *Internal distribution of durations and intensities.* The main factor of diversification from the point of view of the distribution of durations is the contrast between rational and irrational values. The extremely constricted arithmetical progression of the serialized values gives words an infinite flexibility that allows for homogeneous groups to be formed in turns,

Ex. 8

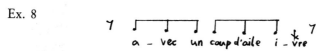

or, on the contrary, that produces successions of completely differentiated values,

Ex. 9

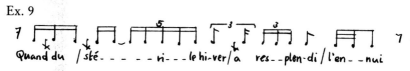

which, through playing off these contrasts, have the effect of dividing a line like this one (II.4) into groups of syllables, thus producing a new syllabic rhythm (2+4+4+2). Many other examples could easily be given.

However, from the point of view of the internal rhythms of the stanza and the line, the system of serialization of intensities is perhaps even more significant than the way in which durations are distributed. Hence there is a noticeable alternation of *f* and *p* zones in the first stanza between odd-numbered and even-numbered lines; and because of this, the curves traced by the fluctuations of intensity within these zones tend to confirm the subdivision of the four lines into their two half-lines. In stanza IV, following the example of the utterance of values, the rhythm of the intensities tightens up. The first verse is clearly divided into its two half-lines by the *piano subito* of the first beat of the 4/8. Line 2, already divided up by the caesuras into 3+1+8, is given a dynamic curve of 3+5+4, whereas, be it noted in passing, the grouping of durations confirms the cutting up by caesuras. Line 3 is divided by the system of intensities into 4+2+1+5, which tends to confirm the distribution of durations and does not go against the half-line division marked by the central caesura. Line 4, interpreted according to the system of intensities, gives a 6+4+2, which allows the subdivision mentioned above, introduced by the grouping of durations. In the whole of this stanza, the curve of intensities is deeper in the odd-numbered lines than in the even-numbered ones.

Stanza III maintains the contracted fluctuations of stanza II, and also the depth of the curve of intensities. These curves divide line 1 into its two half-lines, but the first half-line itself is subdivided into 3+3. Line 2 reproduces the same rhythmic structure with other degrees of intensity, which confirms the already mentioned solidarity between these two lines. The *p* and *f* zones of line 3 cut it into its two half-lines, but admit within each a symmetrical division of 2+4+4+2.

Finally, stanza IV combines the broad curves of stanza I in its lines 1 and 2 and the fluctuating curves of stanzas II and III in its line 3. Line 1, kept in the *p* zone, accepts a cutting up of 3+7+2. Line 2, running over the *f* zone, is rather more prone to being interpreted as a single block because of the feebleness of its fluctuations. Line 3, on the other hand, has a very hollowed-out curve and gives a rhythm of 2+8+2.

Before leaving the subject of intensities, we should notice that the extremes of *ppp* and *fff* are reached on words that emphasize the dramatic intensity:

> *ppp*　*l'horreur du sol*
> *l'exil inutile*　*fff*

3. *Distribution of harmonies.*[21] The harmonic rhythm – or better, the harmonic metre – provides a way of dividing-up that is generally broader than those we have been looking at up to now. It tends to show that by this means the composer wrote into the work a structure with a specific rhythm having no doubt more connection with the overall musical form than with the form of the poem. Whatever the case, the structure pulls a certain weight on the poem and, therefore, cannot be detached from its overall perception.

Stanza I, apart from the introductory and final-rhyme harmonies already mentioned, is built on two central harmonic fields (Ex. 10). The first of these fields supports the first three lines and the second supports the fourth line. In other words, it is still the division of the stanza by lines

Ex. 10

that remains the overriding consideration. Questions may arise concerning this division of the quatrain into 3+1: in fact, as it happens, the looseness of the clauses did not have a bearing on this division, otherwise the harmony would have changed in the middle of verse 3 at the point where the two embedded subordinate clauses follow the main clause. If the harmony changes so suddenly with the appearance of the subject of the main subordinate clause, *le transparent glacier*, occurring within an

---

[21] This distribution is rather a delicate thing. It has been based on the fluctuations of registers. It bears rethinking on the basis of a convincing genetic code.

inversion after the verbal group, it is probably due to a certain concern for the colour, *le transparent glacier* being the second designation (after the subject of the main clause, *aujourd'hui* – symbol of a symbol) of the central subject of the drama, *le cygne*. This assumption can be substantiated by the way in which the vibraphone harmonies fall, in both cases, upon the subject of the main clauses: *aujourd'hui* and *glacier*, as if to give them extra emphasis.

The two central harmonic fields of the quatrain, apart from their own individuality, can be perceived as a global unity at a higher level. They are in fact linked together by six common notes of which two – F and C sharp – undergo a change of register. This higher-level division, which is also found in the other stanzas, is one of the most powerful linking principles (cf. below), marking via the music the autonomy of each stanza as desired by the poet.

In the second quatrain, the harmonic rhythm is contracted in the same way as the durations and the rhythm of the intensities. Eight harmonies (including the introductory and final-rhyme harmonies) follow one another (i.e. twice as many as in the preceding stanza) (Ex. 11). The demarcation of the harmonic fields, particularly as far as the fourth line is concerned, can be questioned on the basis of a genetic code for example (as already mentioned), but also by referring to the common pivot-notes between two consecutive fields. In any case, and as far as the treatment of the poetic stanza is concerned, nothing essentially different would result from using another cutting-up system.

Ex. 11

If we follow what has just been suggested, we can see that lines 1 and 2 each have their own harmony, that line 3 is divided into its two half-lines, as it is in relation to its central caesura, and that line 4 is split up into three pieces according to a cutting-up system that brings forward the two only nouns in the line, *hiver* and *ennui*.

As already said, it is important to notice, however, that this division of harmonic areas also includes a higher level that can be analysed on the basis of the complementarity of the harmonies, a complementarity revealed by the common notes. This new cutting-up gives the following groupings: 1, 2 and 3; 4 and 5; 6, 7 and 8, forming three major harmonic fields that restore the solidarity already pointed out between lines 1 and 2, and give to lines 3 and 4 a homogeneous treatment which individualizes them.

Finally we should notice, as in stanza I, the role played by the vibraphone's entries which corroborate the higher-level harmonic division: the D flat brings together lines 1 and 2, while isolating the central symbolic subject, *un cygne*; the E natural unifies the two half-lines of verse 3; and the absence of the instrument subsequently isolates the whole of line 4.

The harmony remains fairly contracted in the first terzet, where seven fields can be counted. Apart from the introductory aggregate and the harmony of the final rhyme, there are five central harmonies (Ex. 12). It is difficult to discern the reasons that, in the poem, dictated to the composer the places where there should be a transition from one harmonic field to another: in two cases (beginning of line 2, second half-line of verse 3) one may invoke the interplay of clauses (coincidence with the participle clause, line 2, and the second subordinate clause, line 4). However, one cannot exclude a desire to enhance the *cygne* (central subject) designated globally or through one of its attributes. It is to be noticed, indeed, that the first harmonic field isolates *Tout son col*, that the transition from the third to the fourth takes place on the word *oiseau*, and that the fifth field, which appears with the second subordinate clause, emphasizes at the same time *le plumage*.

Ex. 12

The relationship between the harmonies is rather weak at the higher level. The harmonic relationship C natural–C sharp (D flat) is the most significant: it links the central harmonic fields together, but with a change of registers in the transition from field 3 to field 4. Elsewhere one does not find more than two common notes to ensure the link between consecutive harmonies, which implies that it is at the lower level that the cutting-up is most significant.

Finally, the last terzet, like the first quatrain, has four harmonic fields. Besides the introductory harmonies and those of the final rhyme, two central areas mark the singing of the lines (Ex. 13). Six common notes (of

Ex. 13

which two have switched registers) unify these harmonies, and this leads to a second division at a higher level which unifies the entire stanza, except for the first word, which is linked to the rest by a single E flat in common.

The power of the rhyme *assigne* seems to have been of primary importance in the determination of the splitting-up of line 1 on the eleventh syllable, after which no further harmonic disruption occurs.

Apart from this, two symmetrical forms occur in relationship with the first stanza: whereas there the broadest harmony occurs at the beginning and the shortest at the end, here it is the other way round; additionally, all the notes of the second central harmonic field of the last stanza and those of the first central harmonic field of the first stanza (except for C sharp, the eighth note) are the same, taking into account the changes in register for C, G, F and A flat. Furthermore, in both cases the most frequently repeated notes are E flat, D, G and A flat. These factors surely indicate a desire to create in the final lines of the poem an echo of the first lines.

4. Distribution of instrumental groups. Many symmetries can be observed here, certain of which have already been mentioned.

(a) the dual articulation of the introductory harmonies of the stanzas (harp, short articulation – vibraphone or bell, prolonged articulation).

(b) chords on the vibraphone with nouns of primary importance.

(c) linear rows on the vibraphone in the tailpieces of I and III.

(d) the similarity of the plan and the arrangement of the writing in the tailpieces of II and IV, and the precise instrumentation at these points (special entries of tam-tams and drums).

Some of these observations need to be extended and generalized. We therefore need to add, as far as the general plan is concerned:

(e) the existence of rhythmic isomorphism on the metal blocks between stanzas I and III with inversion of registers and transformation of units.

(f) the schema that results from the choice of instruments playing in the course of the stanzas:

Stanza I : metal blocks, crotales, gongs
Stanza II : metal blocks, cymbals
Stanza III: metal blocks, crotales, cymbals followed by gongs at the moment of the harmonic change on *à l'oiseau*, which implies an intention on the part of the composer to integrate harmony and timbre.
Stanza IV: metal blocks, crotales, gongs

One must also add to this general plan of the instrumental distribution the role played by the punctuations on the vibraphone. They have, first and foremost, an equivalent function in all four stanzas – that of pointing out the harmonic development at the broadest level:

Stanza I : the first punctuation is integrated into the introductory harmony and announces the following harmonic field; the second one emphasizes the first central harmony and the third punctuation does the same for the second harmony.

Stanza II : besides the integration into the introductory harmony, we need only recall the unifying function (already mentioned) of the notes D flat and E natural. The D flat underlines the harmonies of the first two lines, strongly related by their common notes; the E natural fulfils the same function for the complementary harmonies of line 3. Line 4 is the only one not to be punctuated.

Stanza III : the first punctuation is linked to the introductory harmony in the same way as for stanza I, after which it is integrated into the harmonic field at the beginning of the stanza. The two following punctuations in turn emphasize the second and third harmonic fields; subsequently the D flat, interrupted for a moment by D natural, dominates the two other central harmonic fields which are strongly related by their common notes.

Stanza IV : after the G natural is integrated into the introductory harmony, the E flat underlines the first central harmonic field by linking it to the second during which the six other notes that make it up are successively played.

Other parallelisms should be mentioned concerning the form of these vibraphone punctuations: those at the onset of stanzas I and III made up of the same notes (C, D, E flat) (cf. above for the inversion of the introductory harmonies of stanzas I and III) which reinforce the other already mentioned parallels between these two moments. The same applies to the second punctuation of stanzas I and III, made up of the same intervals (tritone and perfect 5th), while the rate of vibrato and the intensities are identical.

A parallel can also be drawn between the D flats on the vibraphone that underline (at a different octave) the first two lines of stanza II and the last two lines of stanza III, which is one of the strongest amongst the aforesaid links existing between these two stanzas. Should we see here again a semantic function? It may be, indeed, a way of reinforcing the correspondence between the desperate effort of the swan (stanza II) and the reproduction of the same vision accomplished by the bird denying space while its plumage is irrevocably fixed on the ground.

Finally, one might also consider that the melodic spacing-out of the pitches in the central harmonic fields of stanza IV strengthens the link we have already established with the first central field of stanza I. Here, too, one may perceive a semantic link (assumed for the greater part by the harmony) between the moment of hope (stanza I) and the moment of resignation (stanza IV).

The use of the percussion also gives rise to specific types of organization of the verse-structure. Thus in stanza I, line 1, the metal blocks divide the line into three areas: the first group emphasizes *le vierge*, the second *le bel aujourd'hui*, while in the middle *le vivace et* is marked by a single stroke on the conjunction. At the same moment, the use of the gongs slightly transforms this division by moving the conjunction over to the third area of the line. As for the crotales, they divide the line into two sections in the same way as the harmony, thus isolating *le vierge*.

Every line could be studied, though cautiously, from this point of view. However, we may observe that, in the diversity of the piece, the essential data corroborate each other in order to preserve the line's physiognomy as given mainly by the harmony, the distribution of durations and caesuras in the vocal part, but also by the safeguard of the syntax and the semantics of each line.

5. *Emphasizing words and syllables.* A whole set of features assume primary importance in this respect.

(a) We have already mentioned the way in which sounds are uttered progressively in the successive spreading-out of the notes of the harmony (stanza I, line 1; stanza II, line 2). Many more examples could be given – among others, the F natural reserved for the last note of the harmony (stanza II, line 3) on the second syllable of *chanté*, or the D natural on *hiver* in the following line.

(b) To this aspect of the vocal line should be added the rhythmic function of the vocalises: their rarity only serves to increase their weight, in such a way that the contrast between vocalized and non-vocalized syllables gives rise to great rhythmic suppleness in the line. We shall only give one example (stanza II, line 3) where we can observe the following rhythms per word and per syllable:

Pour | n'a - voir | pas ø | chan - té | ø ‖ la | ré - gi - on | où | vivre ø |

The first half-line is made of an alternation of vocalized and non-vocalized syllables, but two systems of durations divide the syllables into two groups: 4+2. The second half-line includes a vocalized syllable totalling a long value and five non-vocalized syllables giving a succession of shorts: the whole is divided into two systems of durations, whose global perception gives the rhythm 1+5. By repeating this analysis on other lines, and by linking the system of the vocalises to that of the durations, one can find the main source of suppleness given to the line by the music.

(c) As far as the prominence given to certain words of primary importance is concerned, many examples could be cited, at least from the point of view of the composer. Let us limit ourselves to a few striking characteristics:

Stanza I, line 1: *aujourd'hui* is marked by the vibraphone chord on the central syllable, which is also the longest (dotted crotchet) of the line. We should note, at the same point, the interruption in the playing of the blocks and crotales after the accented short syllable has been articulated.

Stanza I, line 4: the noun *glacier* determined, like *aujourd'hui*, by a preceding adjective, is brought forward by the punctuation of the vibraphone and the long note-values in the vocal part. Moreover, it is emphasized by a group of blocks.

Stanza II, line 3: the most striking thing here is the isolation of *chanté*, preceded and followed by short rests and strongly vocalized on three notes with a sudden fall on to a new note in the harmony (cf. above).

Stanza III, line 1: it is probably on account of an analogous semantic consideration that the vibraphone punctuation emphasizes *cette blanche agonie*. As J.P. Richard has rightly remarked,[22] white is the predominant colour of this poem, in which the bird merges with the décor to which it is irremediably bound. Also noteworthy at this point is the entry of the large cymbal, which seems to underline this glacial whiteness of death.

Stanza III, line 2: at the change of harmony on *espace infligée*, it is perhaps the same tragic meaning of the décor that is stressed by the new punctuation on the vibraphone and the substitution of high-pitched cymbals for the low-pitched one.

Stanza III, line 3: *plumage* is given prominence by the vocalises and by its total length of 7/8. At the same moment the gongs enter.

Stanza IV: from the end of the first rhyme onwards, this stanza is dominated by the constant return of the vowel 'i'. It is possibly in the light of this that one should take the change of harmony on the rhyme *assigne*, which is otherwise difficult to understand in relation to the structure of the poem. It is mainly by high intensity, long note-values and three times using the high A flat (the highest note in the vocal line, and only heard twice before) that the composer accentuates the vowel when it is preceded or followed by the consonant 'l': *il s'immobilise inutile*. Only *exil* falls on a D natural of medium length and intensity. We should notice, in particular, the way in which the adjective *inutile* (the moment of the irremediable accomplishment of the drama) is emphasized: two medium note-values (triplet crotchets within a larger triplet) ending with a minim accentuated by a *fff* marking (the longest note-value used in the body of the line – i.e. outside the rhymes – and the strongest dynamic).

[22] *L'Univers imaginaire de Mallarmé*, Seuil, 1961, p.252

6. *Linking structures.* Each stanza of the sonnet is a separate entity, hence Mallarmé's use of the full stop only at the end of each one of them. However, within the stanzas the lines are all linked to one another, by either a pronoun or an adjective, a preposition or a conjunction. Boulez has also used junction-structures to link up the lines, despite the caesuras in the vocal-part. The most powerful means of producing this effect is undoubtedly Boulez's recourse to common notes in the harmony in the cases where an identical harmony is not prolonged as a whole (cf. above). But other junction-structures are provided by the instrumentation. In each case the resonance or the vibrato of at least one instrument effectively fulfils this function. Wherever the common notes of the harmony happen to be the most consistent linking structure, it is naturally the resonance of the vibraphone that best helps the perception of the overlapping.

IV

Having reached the end of this study, the question now arises as to whether it has succeeded in making clear the conjunction between the composer and the poet and between the music and the text, and as to what extent it enables us to grasp the limits of such a conjunction and the necessity for it.

If this study deserves any credit, it must surely be for not having defended *a priori* any one viewpoint throughout the analysis of the piece; however, its major drawback is that of having examined the problem through only one of the *Improvisations sur Mallarmé*. A choice had to be made: either to indicate a certain number of examples having a bearing on various specific and consistent points in the course of an overview of all the *Improvisations*, in which case one would end up with a larger number of facts worthy of attention, but selected from references chosen with the risk of being arbitrary, or to undertake an in-depth analysis within a limited area, but without selecting a perspective. Having to opt for one or the other, for reasons of length, it seemed that the restricted programme would lead to more objectivity and would reveal more of the underlying and less known characteristics of Boulez's work.

In my opinion, one of these characteristics can be interpreted as a fundamental will. All through the analysis we have discovered, at all kinds of levels, parallelisms giving rise to relative symmetries (often, even the word 'symmetry' may have appeared too strong, which is why we talked of para-symmetry). Indeed, in each of the parallels pointed out, the most present and significant elements were all the aspects by which they were disguised. Perhaps we should simply be talking about symmetrical 'gestures' in all these cases where we find equivalent forms in a single parameter, while, although very conspicuous, they are contradicted, denied and destroyed by the other parameters. Boulez always appears to want to assert a form while at the same time concealing it, to reject an immediate datum as something too simple, too self-evident, to search for evidence, but on condition that it is buried, hidden in a dimension that moderates and restrains it. The Boulezian text is as if it was being performed in the course of a form that was merely its envelope, but not the profound substance. Is it not at this very general level that the Mallarméan concept of poetical expression is met by every work of Boulez's? Is it not through this aspect that two languages, in essence different, can confront each other, that the two creators can imprint on the heart of the 'poyétique' a stamp that, just at the point where it brings them together, it distinguishes them from the historical contribution which they so transcend?

(Translation: L.M. Peugniez)

The instrumental and vocal music

Susan Bradshaw

To claim that Pierre Boulez is a neo-romantic at heart might seem perverse, both in view of the evident complexity of his music, and of the fact that he has contributed so much to the theoretical basis of present-day musical thinking. Nevertheless, this apparent contradiction describes the reality of a conflict which is the *raison d'être* of all his best works and which, in itself, is an important clue to the intellectually complex but essentially *sensible* nature of the man and his music. It has to be admitted that the range of musical expression which unconsciously derives from such a conflict has as yet barely been discerned; it remains for future generations of performers, less in awe of the present difficulties of style and idea (and instrumental technique), to uncover the emotional substance behind the often forbidding surface of the music. (Even the composer/conductor himself, too recently involved in its technical organization, is at present unable to reveal much more than its surface structure, or even – dare it be said? – to understand the full expressive potential of his own creativity. It need hardly be pointed out that this assessment intends no denigration of the gifts of Boulez the performer, but confirmation of the imaginative depth of the composer: like all the best music of any period, the best of Boulez's music will continue to expand its ability to communicate as its interpretative challenges are gradually overcome.) Meanwhile, any attempt to penetrate this surface complexity must take account of the fact that the technique of the music is itself a quality of expression as well as of structure, and that it was the requirements of musical expression (as well as of logic) that themselves prompted the initial formation of that technique.

This twofold attitude would seem to be endorsed by the composer's own writings on music, which reveal[1] that it was the formulation of wider technical concepts concerning the interior organization of rhythm and pitch in relation to the exterior qualities of time and space that made it

---

[1] Especially as summarized in *Boulez on Music Today*, Faber, 1971

127

necessary to establish a new means of linguistic expression, just as it was the increasing complexity of linguistic usage that in turn necessitated the formulation of these new concepts. And it should be noted in passing that the musical grammar that Boulez perfected during the 1950s is not only inseparable in significance from the eventual 'style' of his own music, but is, *per se*, a creative achievement that, in effect, has altered the course of musical history: by using his articulate imagination to link the various strands of individual research carried out over the last fifty years, he has at the same time succeeded in establishing the basis of a mid-twentieth century lingua franca.

Although this grammar[2] is evidently no abstract theory, but one that stems from 'a survey of concrete relationships based on existing musical facts', the very nature of its detailed, though broadly-based, reasoning has tended to obscure those musical facts it most seeks to clarify. Which prompts the question: why the need to embark on a detailed verbal classification of processes which could, it would seem, be better and more creatively explained in the music itself? The answer must be sought first in the climate of artistic isolation endured by the generation of post-war composers – a desolation, almost, which did much to provoke those numerous contemporary articles so revealingly, if unwittingly, devoted to self-justification. However, such articles did serve a useful purpose as an international exchange of ideas, if ephemeral ones, for the most part, in the midst of the stylistic upheaval that reached a crisis in the early 1950s. But, while many composers were concerned with the technical innovations of single works, Boulez alone took it upon himself to begin the task of setting the various avant-garde developments of the past fifty years in a true mid-twentieth century perspective. His earliest essays[3] were prompted perhaps partly by scorn for the narrow technical obsessions of so many of his contemporaries, but also by the temporary uncertainty of his own position: on the threshold of an unknown future, the weight of influence inevitably exerted by the historical past was now being challenged by the quasi-instinctive achievements of his own early works. Like the instrumental prodigy's effortless ability to achieve technical perfection, which he is later forced to analyse, Boulez's youthful flair enabled him to produce five powerfully characteristic and mature works almost without pause (the Sonatine for flute and piano, Piano Sonata No. 1 and *Le visage nuptial*, all written during 1946, followed, two years later, by *Le soleil des eaux* and Piano Sonata No. 2), after which he was forced to stop, to draw breath, and to consider what the nature of their existence might imply for the future.

The ultimate aim of any technical system must be to establish a number of stylistic premises, sufficient to liberate the composer from the need to

[2] See p.131ff
[3] Published in book form as *Relevés d'apprenti*, Seuil, 1966

identify himself afresh with each new work and so to free his imagination by removing the burden of absolute choice. Or this is the theory. In practice, it was perhaps inevitable that the effort of shouldering the entire academic responsibility (even if self-imposed) for a new set of linguistic concepts was, for a time, to prove more inhibiting than liberating for Boulez himself. In science, after all, the researcher and classifier of new laws *is* the creative thinker; in music, the musicologist is seldom, if ever, the composer and musicology, however creative, can in no way be equated with creative composition. When the composer turns part-time musicologist, therefore, the dangers are obvious: he who proposes the 'rules' must be prepared to stick by them; and the temptation to demonstrate their academic validity in creative composition is almost unavoidable, especially as, in Boulez's case, their very formulation had early on forced him to assume the position of guide and mentor to his own peers. The remarkable fact, then, is not that the force of his creative energies may have been temporarily weakened by his academic preoccupations, but that – both before and after these periods of (self-)research, not to mention the time and energy later devoted to conducting – his continued output has included music of outstanding originality and vision.

These various essays had a dual purpose. On the one hand, they were an attempt to set the record straight in the face of increasing chaos and misunderstanding: to establish a set of properly musical procedures and considerations, in opposition to the many stylistic fads which came and went with astonishing rapidity during the 1950s. On the other hand, they exhibit a need for self-analysis on the part of a composer whose very brilliance would have enabled him then or later to proceed in any one of a number of directions, but whose intellectual grasp of historical perspective was such that future choice would necessarily have to relate to past achievements – not in any sense of prolonging the past, but of developing from it. Although occasionally arrogant, these writings are also touchingly defensive: aware of a composer's rightful position as a contributing member of society, Boulez's fear of being dismissed as a mere intellectual (a term of condemnation in the minds of a musical public left far behind by composers unwilling to perpetuate the past) is underlined by his continual insistence on the unchanging balance between the rule of heart and head in music, and on the continuing presence of fantasy as a determining element in composition.

Once Schoenberg had cast the musical world into ferment by overthrowing the centuries-old dominance of the tonal system, freedom of choice had seemed frighteningly absolute – even though the full repercussions of this move were not immediately apparent. Indeed, between the wars, Schoenberg's system of composition with 'twelve notes related only to one another' had caused hardly a ripple of unease; although a few isolated composers were reaching towards a similar goal by different means, to the majority, composers and public alike, it was an unimportant, academically-conceived side issue. There were disciples, of course, just as there were those who came under the spell of the other major figures of the time – such unwitting dictators of fashion as Bartók and Stravinsky, for instance. But of these only Webern reacted to the concept of twelve-note composition in a manner that immediately widened its implications for the future: texture (defined by register, dynamics and timbre) began to encompass melody and harmony in the organization of musical space, and duration (especially in terms of sound in relation to silence) began to embrace rhythmic articulation in the organization of musical time. Meanwhile, the young Messiaen, always an isolated figure, was quietly working towards a parallel and equally far-reaching development of his own: just as Schoenberg had revolutionized the field of pitch by denying tonality as the one and only means of sound organization, so Messiaen had begun to transform the field of rhythm, by banishing metrical pulse as the one and only means of articulating duration.

Briefly, then, this was the position (tempered, needless to say, by the influence of both Debussy and Stravinsky) when, as a recent graduate from Messiaen's class, Boulez stormed on to the musical scene.

The overwhelming impact of Schoenberg's twelve-note music (which he heard for the first time in his late teens) is clearly reflected in all of the works dating from the 1940s. However, Boulez's ability to digest information at speed – his conservatoire training lasted only two years, from start to finish – presupposed an equal ability to reject ideas and influences for which he had no further use: with a youthful zest for new discoveries, he quickly denied the Schoenbergian influence as enthusiastically as he had embraced it in the first place. Or so it appeared. In reality, the central thesis of a much publicized, and much misunderstood, article entitled 'Schönberg est mort' (1951) is a just one: it assesses Schoenberg's research as a significant act of dis-establishment (of the classical order), rather than as a significant achievement in itself – and how could it have appeared otherwise to a generation faced by post-revolutionary chaos?

This somewhat over-simplified attitude to the recent past vis-à-vis the present was therefore an essential one: it was this notion of Schoenberg as a one-dimensional composer concerned only with the primarily melodic developments of a harmony derived from the cyclic repetitions of the twelve-note row which itself became the positive spur for the development of those dimensions then judged to be missing.

Yet it is perhaps surprising that the influence of Schoenberg should ever have exerted the kind of hypnotic power that provoked this act of exorcism: it could have been more easily predicted that a young French composer should consider himself the direct heir of Debussy and Messiaen, coloured by his adoptive kinship with Stravinsky, than that he should concern himself with the more specifically harmonic considerations of the Austro-German composers. In the first place, however, it has to be remembered that the true enormity of Schoenberg's revolution had only begun to be understood after the Second World War, when the exclusive nationalism associated with the nineteenth century had shrunk to a European *in*clusiveness characteristic of the twentieth; so that it was not until the mid-1940s that the eyes and ears of the musical world at large began to focus on Vienna – after which nothing could ever be quite the same again, not even for the 'insular' French. Secondly, in this predominantly harmonic atmosphere it was Boulez's growing awareness of himself as a basically harmonic composer (however different in outlook) that eventually compelled him to make a conscious effort to break the spell of an influence still exerted by a composer two generations his senior.

The most striking aspect of his own early works is the manner in which discernible influences are already assimilated into the equally discernible character of the composer himself. There is no evidence of the apprentice composer at work in any of these pieces, whose impact remains as fresh and as overwhelming today as it must have been thirty years ago. Right from the beginning, a startling complexity of texture indicates the abolition of lines and chords as separately identifiable constituents of the whole: the Schoenbergian starting point of melody as extended harmony and harmony as enriched melody thus begins to acquire a new 'diagonal' dimension. The consequent loss of one of the most easily communicable contrasts featured in Western classical music – that of tune and accompaniment – is turned to gain, as unity and cohesion of textural design begins to create its own interior contrasts. This important stylistic development seems to have been partly instinctive, evolved through an imaginative use of articulated gesture, unrelated to the vertical/horizontal priorities of the tonal system – and partly reasoned, according to a logic which concluded that pre-ordained hierarchical concepts had no place in a system of composition with twelve equal pitches. From the evidence of these early works themselves, it gradually became apparent that a new system of priorities (of 'hierarchical determinants') would have to be mapped out if avant-garde composition were not to disintegrate into the indeterminate chaos of free choice.

The musical background, a summary of style and idea[4]

At this stage, rhythmic organization was much less sophisticated. Indeed,

[4] See *Boulez on Music Today*, op. cit.

Schoenberg himself had consciously taken a step backwards in this respect as soon as he had 'invented' the twelve-note row: in order to underline its thematic structure, he set it within the perceptible pulse of familiar classical forms, so sacrificing the more far-reaching potential first envisaged in the asymmetrical phrasing of the last of the Three Piano Pieces, Op. 11. Nevertheless, Webern, with his motivic, rather than thematic, use of the row, had already found a way to dispense with the foreground control of metrical accents dictated by the barline, and to reduce rhythmic pulse to a quasi-imaginary background against which to develop the foreground asymmetries of the rhythmic phrasing. And this phrasing later began to include the duration of silence in relation to sound, so that rhythm had already started to become an ingredient of texture. Later still, Messiaen began to develop the idea of duration as the basis of a rhythmic structure unrelated to metrical pulse. This meant that rhythmic cells (whether symmetrical or asymmetrical, retrogradable or not) could acquire developmental possibilities of their own – since they would be counted outwards from the smallest unit of pulse, not inwards, as divisions of a larger unit.

Faced by these isolated proposals, Boulez set himself the task of discovering the common denominator of a rhythmic organization that would be as coherent as the pitch-organization indicated by the twelve-note row. After all, pitch itself may be said to include duration in terms of the number of vibrations, or beats, per second by which it is defined (though scientific logic can hardly be pursued beyond this point: music, as an art, would disintegrate if forced to consider acoustic proportions – whether of pitch or rhythm – as absolute).

Rhythm and serial duration
The first step in establishing a coherent rhythmic organization was to find a means of marking time-space that would be parallel, if not similar, to the division of pitch-space into semitones. And since, in the tempered system of Western music, the audible range of pitches is divided by the octave, and the octave by the twelve semitones of the chromatic scale, it should be possible to divide a perceptible unit of duration in some similarly convenient, if not equally logical, manner: for instance, if the dotted crotchet is taken as the largest unit (comparable to the octave), the unit of division (comparable to the semitone) would then be the demisemiquaver. But if the pitch-row is numbered from 1–12 throughout its transpositions (that is, according to interval structure), this could only yield a scale of durations augmenting regularly from demisemiquaver to dotted crotchet. A way therefore had to be found to organize the chosen constituents of the duration scale into rhythmic shapes that would balance the melodic shapes selected from the chromatic scale. This was achieved first by relating number directly to pitch, rather than to

intervals, so that successive transpositions of a twelve-note row – transposed now on each degree of its original shape (Ex. 1 – here and in all following examples, notes without accidentals are natural), and not merely step by step, according to the chromatic scale – could be made to yield successive permutations of the duration scale (Ex. 2).

Ex.1

Ex.2

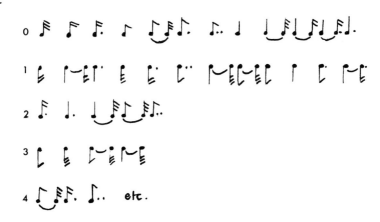

Even so, the durational choice now offered by the four squares of numbers derived from the original row plus its inversion and the two retrograde forms did not, of itself, suggest a means of rhythmic organization other than that of permutation. Moreover, the pitch-row, shorn of its thematic implications, had now become no more than a rotating series of isolated sounds, linked to one another only by the chance of their succession. Nevertheless, it was both possible and necessary to test the abstract validity of the bare essentials described here in actual composition: *Structures Ia* and *Ic* are proof of the practical musical purpose behind these researches. But they also underline a growing awareness of the fact that such limited basic material (even with the additional variety provided by numerically ordered dynamics, attack and registers) could only result in an equally limited range of expression, mainly concerned with texture. It was already obvious that the notion of automatic permutation, whether of pitches or duration, was ultimately to be no more fruitful than the rejected notion of automatic melodic rotation: so that it was the necessary experience of *Structures*, Book I (and also of *Polyphonie X*) that provided the impetus for the development of a true series of more evidently significant relationships.

Once again, Boulez set out from a careful appraisal of historical perspective. Firstly, Schoenberg's pre twelve-note concept of a development based on intervallic, rather than thematic, definition (as, for instance, in the first four of the Five Pieces, Op. 23); then, Webern's concept of a texture defined by register and motivic development; then, Messiaen's concept of independent rhythmic cells, based on duration; and, finally, the extra-musical ideas of John Cage and the early experiments with electronic music – which together suggested a much broader definition of space as a factor in the organization of sound and, indeed, a redefinition of the nature and quality of sound itself.

As an initial step, the very concept and the basic function of the twelve-note row had to be objectively reconsidered, first in its original form of twenty years earlier, and then in terms of what it might become for the future. Schoenberg's idea of the twelve-note row as a unifying chromatic shape which would retain its identity throughout an entire work, and provide the basic material for the harmony as well as the melody, now seemed incapable of further development: the inbuilt notion of repetition on which it was based had become far too restrictive. In any case, a 'system' that had arisen out of the nineteenth-century Austro-German tradition of melody and harmony, tune and accompaniment, could not be expected to remain unaltered in the hands of a twentieth-century Frenchman – especially one whose national inheritance still counts for much, despite his cosmopolitan musical origins.

The Schoenbergian twelve-note row had depended on the rotation of all twelve pitches in recurring order (whether in its original, retrograde, or inverted form) throughout an entire work or for as long as that particular row provided the key to the music. Boulez was quickly aware of what he considered to be a basic anomaly: namely, that the thematic identity of the row was distorted as soon as its interval structure was affected by changing the register of any individual note. This meant that perception of the row as a thematic unit depended on perception of pitch, not of intervals, so that in practice the system tended to destroy that very unity it was meant to achieve.

Perhaps it was this unavoidable contradiction that had led Webern, even if subconsciously, to turn the loss of thematic identity brought about by changes of register to positive advantage – as widely-spaced intervals developed melodic connotations of their own, unrelated to the thematic shape of the row. The fact that his chords came to be identified by their characteristic interval structure, rather than by the relationship of their individual pitches to an original row, indicated that Webern had already begun to regard the twelve-note row as a *series* – as a group of intervals whose conjunction in terms of the symmetries or asymmetries revealed was later to become of paramount importance.

Pitch and duration groups – serial 'objets'

If, then, the twelve-note row could no longer be considered, in a thematic sense, as the basic material in itself, it would have to become the germ from which to derive a chosen number of characteristic 'objects', or objectively chosen groupings, that would themselves become the basis of a truly serial network of relationships. So that, although the shape of the original twelve-note row may have lost its importance as a thematic entity, its structure remains vital in terms of the symmetries or asymmetries that it may contain, and of the number of subdivisions (the characteristic serial objects) that it might usefully yield – usefully, that is, in relation to the needs of a particular composer, a particular piece.

In themselves, these objects would have neither specifically melodic nor specifically harmonic implications, nor would they be considered as motifs: they are, literally, 'objects', neutral in themselves, and characterized only by their pitch/interval structure and by their relationship to one another. But the chosen relationships between one of these serial groupings and another can be made to produce areas of specific melodic or harmonic emphasis, since their in(ter)dependence enables them to create differing overlaps in their order of succession and thus to control the order of transposition (see Ex. 6). Further, these relationships may be widened by building the intervals characteristic of one group upon the pitches of each other group, in turn. Or they may be qualified by the addition of a single interval to each one of a group of original pitches, in turn; equally, each original interval may be tempered by augmentation or diminution. Or, a group may retain its original identity throughout changing registers as a result of one of its pitches being held within a fixed register; conversely, the group itself may be placed within a fixed register, relative to a single movable pitch. All such developmental possibilities

135

can, of course, be applied to more extended relationships, as well as to the original groups; in themselves, the possibilities are limitless – so that the task of the composer must firstly include that of selection.

The ideas outlined above denote the beginnings of an extended serial network, derived from an original twelve-note row. It was then possible to establish a parallel, though not, of course, exactly similar network of durations. Just as an original note-row can be made to yield a chosen number of pitch-groupings whose development will evolve through the ways in which they may be seen to react to one another, so an original scale of durations can be made to yield a number of characteristic duration-groups which cannot, in themselves, be likened to rhythmic cells, any more than the pitch-groups could be defined, in themselves, as motifs. Rather, these groups of durations may then be superimposed, or may overlap or fuse with one another to form such cells. More specifically, the units of duration comprising each group may be regularly or irregularly expanded or contracted, or transformed into irrational values. Or, each may be filled in by repeating pulsation or, conversely, filtered by silences; or a group may be syncopated by silence, or repeated in differing proportions, with or without the intervention of silence; or an original may be mirrored by sounds that replace silences, and vice versa: by these means, silence begins to function as a positive ingredient of rhythmic articulation, in addition to its more negative function of punctuation through absence of sound. And, as with pitch, all such developmental possibilities can again be applied to more extended relationships.

Tempo, dynamics and timbre
But although the serial networks developed for pitch and duration may be usefully considered as parallel organizations, Boulez was soon aware of the one vital difference between the two. Pitch, by its very nature, is an absolute, measurable quality in relation to the space-range of audible sounds: whether it be a single, static pitch, or a complex, fluctuating one, it exists as a more or less definable entity as soon as it is heard. Duration, on the other hand, exists only as a definition of time, and therefore cannot be defined as an absolute, even approximately measurable, quality until it is related to tempo (in itself something of an approximation, except in electronic music). Duration, then, had to be thought of as a constituent of the developing quality of tempo, since tempo alone has the power to clarify or obliterate duration relationships, and thus to achieve rhythmic characterization by virtue of its affective function. For tempo may relate duration to a regular pulse, or it may vary that pulse by means of *accelerando* or *rallentando*; or it may, by indicating an absence of pulse, merely place durations within a period of time. And these interior functions of tempo can, of course, assume exterior functions, relative to form.

Similarly, Boulez then realised that dynamics and timbre (including types of attack) could only function as secondary qualities, since they are inseparable from their expressive roles in relation to pitch and duration: either may be used to affect the quality of a pitch relative to its duration, but they cannot change its existence. In any case, dynamics are scarcely a measurable quality except, again, in electronic music. In theory, the full range of acceptable dynamics could be divided into twelve levels approximating to the semitonal divisions of the octave, or the twelve units of a duration scale and proceeding, step by step, from the just audible to the just bearable. But, in live performance, dynamics will necessarily function within three broadly defined areas: that of an unchanging level (relatively loud or soft), that of gradually changing levels (denoted by *crescendo* or *diminuendo*), and that of abruptly changing levels (denoted by the discontinuity of extreme contrast). Timbre is a more specific quality, which may affect the other qualities by means of its similarity or dissimilarity, continuity or discontinuity; at the same time, it is itself an expression of dynamic level, since the contrasting timbres of different instruments, as well as the differences in weight between single instruments and groups of similar or dissimilar instruments, will themselves include dynamic nuance.

At this stage, the basic serial groupings, seen now in the light of the various networks of extended relationships which may be derived from them, have still to be considered in relation to the space in which they will be placed: that is, the pitch-space of an audible (playable) range, and the time-space (necessarily finite) of a perceptible duration span.

Musical space, pitch and time

Pitch-space remains a useful concept only as an embracing quality, as defined by the tessitura of its changing octave registers – changes which again may be considered in terms of similarity or dissimilarity, continuity or discontinuity. Thought of as an unbroken *glissando* between the outer limits of an available range, which could then be susceptible to similar or dissimilar, continuous or discontinuous divisions by the inclusion of intervals other than the semitone, pitch-space would seem to be scarcely a practical proposition. Like dynamics, which can only be measured as relative, within practical limits, a variable pitch-space (in Western music, at least) can only be measured relative to the semitone – a fact which immediately precludes the use of augmented intervals. Intervals smaller than the semitone have been tried, of course (by Boulez himself in the orchestral version of *Le visage nuptial* where the tritone is made to span a scale of quarter-tones, which reflects, in diminution, the twelve semitones of the octave scale); nevertheless, such intervals are ultimately perceptible only as more or less out-of-tune deviations from the semitone, except when they are used as incidental decorations with trills, *glissandi* and clusters, or as simple passing notes.

On the other hand, the concept of time-space has wider implications, since it already begins to include the notion of form as an organized distribution of events within that space. Pulsed or amorphous rhythmic organizations will contribute to the mobile or static impression of such distributions, whose exterior duration (relative to form) will derive from a proportional extension of the relationships between the original duration groups. In this way, time-space may sometimes be filled by organizations which themselves define duration (pulsed time = mobile space); at others, the space to be filled may itself define the duration of less strictly contoured material (amorphous time = static space). The perception of time-space (and of form) will thus depend on perception of the density or transparency, similarity or dissimilarity, continuity or discontinuity, of the events which mark its progress and on the speed (whether pulsed or not) at which these events unfold. Again, dynamics (including the qualities of attack, suspension and release of sounds) will temper the continuity or discontinuity of the articulation of space.

Form

Form could then result from the succession of a number of events – that is, successive developments, derived from a series of original groups within the space of an allotted time-span. Each of these developments will not only continue to reflect the intrinsic character of an original group, but each may itself evolve into supplementary developments, more distantly related to that original; conversely, a particular development may include a number of related, local developments, so that the function of each original may be understood as quasi-thematic in its relation to the succession of extended events that will eventually make up the form of a work.

It will be obvious that progressive architectural symmetries have no place in a form that is conceived rather as a successive, panoramic view, certain aspects of which will, from time to time, assume more or less importance in relation to certain others, according to the changing emphases put upon them. However, as Boulez himself readily admits, this attitude to musical form demands a complete reversal of the listening habits acquired over three centuries; though, as he also points out, the same could be said of the demands made by pre-classical music. And, in any case, the listener is not expected to become an entirely passive 'observer', since the progressive tensions of classical music, achieved through developments which contradict expectations, are now reflected in the tensions created by the divergence of successive developments in relation to previously-heard material.

However, form, properly speaking, could never derive simply from the automatic permutation of a number of serial groupings and their related networks; for, no matter how well characterized the original groups and however far-reaching the implications of their extended relationships, they are, in themselves, only the preparatory material – the collected ingredients, so to say. It is at this point that the syntax of composition begins.

Texture

The terms of Boulez's syntax – monody, homophony, polyphony and heterophony – would seem to describe different aspects of texture, becoming, in effect, the composed characteristics of the music itself. In any case, their terms of reference constantly overlap, so that each can finally be understood only as a function of the other. Like the basic groups, which are neutral in themselves and therefore able to embrace both horizontal and vertical, monody is an extension of homophony, just as homophony is a contraction of monody. In a context in which chords (whether simultaneously expressed as vertical attacks, or successively as diagonal arpeggiations or grace-notes) are a direct reflection of lines, and vice versa, the concept of harmony expresses the result, not the function, and melody only describes contour. So melody and harmony now relate to form, rather than content. Polyphony retains its original linear connotations, in that it will be used to reflect monody as an overlapping succession of lines, but it can also become indistinguishable from homophony if the composite rhythm revealed by its vertical coincidences is reduced to a horizontal pattern expressed in chords. Heterophony may include monody or homophony, or both, since it indicates only the process whereby the ornamental transformation of a particular structure is superimposed on its own statement (whether simultaneously or successively). But, whereas the horizontal nature of polyphony must include an awareness of the vertical, the vertical alignment of heterophony is incidental. Because each contributory structure (the statement and its transformation) is complete in itself, heterophony can range from the strictest possible simultaneity of a mirrored counterpoint, through the partially-free coincidence of structures distorted by irrational tempo-relationships, to the completely free placing of structures one or other of which may be considered optional.

Evidently, these descriptive terms are useful only if understood as broadly-based indications of technical procedures that determine the nature of the music itself, not as definitions of its analytical content: their hierarchical dependence, interdependence or independence will ultimately relate to the expression of a creative composition, not to its organization.

The reasons for this long introductory digression – in reality, only a brief survey of the aims, formation and expressive purpose of a then entirely new linguistic usage[5] – are best explained by the composer himself, when he writes: 'To seek to analyse a piece by Bach in terms of its pitches and registers would be as absurd as to attempt a literal comparison between the formal structures of, say, Webern and Beethoven.' If, then, a work is only to be understood on its own terms, how vital to explore something of what those terms might be – especially when, as in the case of Boulez himself, they happen to be so complex, yet undidactic in conception, so creatively far-reaching in implication. Indeed, in his case, by charting the progress of a musical journey from post-Schoenberg serialism to the verge of the unconfined spatial preoccupations of today, he has already said all that needs to be said about the objective character of his own music – the more so, since the details of his 'grammar' are clearly intended as a musical manifesto, as well as a technical statement of intent.

But, of course, like all generalizations, these are only half-truths. For one thing, the bias dictated by the personal experience of a particular listener will inevitably temper his musical (mis-)interpretation of a composer's verbal philosophy, however clearly expressed; it is only when he and the composer meet on the common ground of the music itself that individual terms of reference can become mutual experience. (After all, to someone who had never actually heard a piece by Bach, the reasons for *not* regarding it purely in terms of its pitches and registers might seem obscure.) As an introduction to this common ground, an examination of the more subjective evidence of the music itself may help to bring this experience nearer.

Sonatine for flute and piano
   – the development of the interval characteristics of the twelve-note row; the fusion of melody and harmony in relation to classical motivic techniques; the beginnings of an independent rhythmic structure based on proportional duration.

One of the most remarkable aspects of Boulez's extraordinarily influential and successful career is the fact that he was able to establish his linguistic identity so early on. The Sonatine for flute and piano (1946) is a breathtakingly confident indication of musical character, and of the power to communicate within the complexities of a language then scarcely dreamt of. A tremendous sense of urgency – of suppressed violence, almost – invades the expressive gestures of the opening bars and, with gathering momentum, propels the music into the thick of the contrapuntal debate that forms the central thesis of the work. Neverthe-

---

[5] The material for *Boulez on Music Today* derives from a series of lectures given at the Darmstadt Summer School in the late 1950s

140

less, the stunning originality of the Sonatine is securely founded in historical tradition and its underlying influences are as diverse as they are inevitable. In addition to adopting the formal model of Schoenberg's tonal Chamber Symphony No. 1, the mainly motivic structure of the piece is clearly an extension of classical twelve-note writing; then there are the wide-ranging contrapuntal imitations and intervallically-characterized chords suggested by Webern; the Debussyan overtones of its static, impressionistic interludes; taut, rhythmic developments reminiscent of Stravinsky, and even a brief episode based on the permutation of rhythmic cells first outlined by Messiaen – and which were later to form the basis of Boulez's own development of duration-networks.

Although these various influences give the work a classical foundation – discernible in the precision of its imitative detail, as well as in its recapitulatory form – there is astonishingly little sense of incongruity between its tumultuous modernity of expression and the means used to achieve it. This is because of an instinctive compromise, which led Boulez to use the row not only as a self-contained melody but also as a series of characteristic intervals and to superpose characteristic duration-patterns (which may expand or contract, but which retain their original proportions) without necessarily stressing their imitative rhythmic significance. And this compromise is further expressed in the conflict between exact mirror-images at the one extreme, distorted reflections at the other.

The suppressed tension of the introductory bars gives no hint of the jagged explosion that marks the main *Allegro* section of the work. Nevertheless, the quiet menace of the recitative-like outline of these bars contains the material for the entire piece: intentionally ambiguous at this stage, they seem poised like a coiled spring, waiting to be set free. Thus, while the first two bars evidently span the chromatic contents of a twelve-note row (Ex. 3), such is the prevailing atmosphere of suspense that

Ex. 3

confirmation of the opening gesture as the material of an actual note-row is delayed until the ensuing *Allegro* – where it is triumphantly displayed as a true first-subject theme (Ex. 4).

The first two bars present the succession of pitches that will character-

Ex. 4

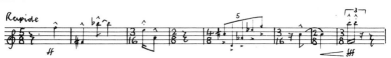

ize the melodic structure of the entire work; they also underline the characteristic intervals – major 7th/minor 2nd, minor 6th/major 3rd, augmented 4th, perfect 5th/4th – that will define the main harmonic pull of its quasi-tonic centre. Stated first as a five-note chord on the piano, this material is immediately confirmed in horizontal form (with the intervals re-ordered) by a quintuplet on the flute – whose two-note cadence already hints at the role of extended intervals (here, from minor 2nd to minor 9th) in relation to texture. The tensely-rising curve of bars 1 and 2 is then answered by the mainly falling curve of bars 3 and 4, as a sextuplet (the first note replaced by a rest) on the flute subsides on to a six-note chord on the piano. And the downward curve of the flute melody is now reflected in a harmonic relaxation which introduces the softer, secondary intervals of a quasi-subdominant area – major 2nd/minor 7th, minor 3rd/major 6th – from which the opening phrase then tapers off into harmonically neutral semitones. The curve of these opening bars from tension to relaxation is reversed in the following phrase: here, the two halves of the original row are superposed to reveal a succession of minor thirds, whose extended sub-dominant relationship is used to effect a modulation back to the tenser, tonic surroundings of the opening (Ex. 5).

Ex. 5

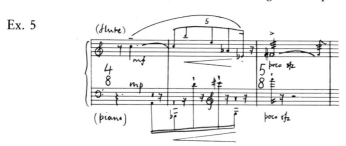

These preliminary indications of the harmonic role of minor thirds (relative to the major 3rds that characterize the row itself) are endorsed in the melodic shift of the bass-line across the opening phrase – from C to E flat. And the significance of this particular minor 3rd (which is to recur throughout the work as a pivotal *idée fixe*) is confirmed when it is echoed in diminution in the closing bars of the introduction – where it quickly assumes a rhythmic purpose from which the whole motivic impulse of the succeeding developments is to derive.

Right from the beginning, it is clear that melody and harmony are no longer thought of in terms of their separate functions, but that the one includes evidence of the other, and vice versa. That is to say, the vertical function of chords (whether simultaneous, successive or arpeggiated) is related to the horizontal succession of their characteristic intervals, just as a horizontal succession of intervals implies a vertical relationship; because of this, the evidence of bars 1 and 2 as harmony + melody is more apparent than real, since the two functions are complementary. Even at this stage, it is clear that melody has relinquished its once dominant position in the hierarchy of a musical structure, and that it has already become a linear definition of an implied harmony.

This early evidence of what was later to become a complete fusion of vertical and horizontal purpose was, of course, a direct result of the abandonment of tonality. Since the melodic/harmonic tensions arising from the fixed hierarchies of the diatonic system could no longer be taken for granted, it was natural to think of the basic material of a particular work as responsible for its own contrasts and its own tensions between 'lines' and 'blocks' of sounds. It was because of this that the twelve-note row was gradually to lose its dictatorial powers as a melodic entity in the Schoenbergian sense, eventually re-forming itself into the neutral objects described earlier.

Even here, in the opening bars of the Sonatine, intervals are evidently defined not by their size but by their quality (which remains the same whether within or beyond the octave) – so that a given interval can be considered interchangeable with its inversion or extension, without in any way weakening perception of this quality. And, since it is now the quality of the intervals that defines the character of the row, the distribution of individual pitches may safely be widened in range to include the entire gamut of available sounds. It is at this point that register becomes an important consideration: not only as the expression of contrasts between high, medium and low, but as a means of identifying chords (as well as sections); as a means of clarifying the individual movement of lines; and as a means of expanding or contracting the contours of both lines and chords, through altering the placing of individual pitches. And, since register influences not only the expressive impact of the pitch distribution itself, but also its textural surroundings (widely-spaced intervals are perceived as points rather than lines, as texture rather than counterpoint), it thus begins to include the enveloping quality of tessitura.

Yet, in spite of these various shifts in stylistic emphasis, the Sonatine clearly develops from within the Schoenbergian tradition in its treatment of the twelve-note row, since the overlapping conjunction of its various formations is made to yield a natural and, at this stage, ·traditional, continuity (Ex. 6). Thus, the change of one note between the quintuplet in bar 2 and the flute figure in bar 5 gives a directional twist to the harmony by underlining the relationship between the initial statement of

143

Ex. 6

Ex. 7

the row and its inversion. And the harmonic shift in bar 4 is achieved not only by the change in register of four of its notes (E flat, C, B flat, E) but also by the change of emphasis that it gives to the three pitches (C, B, G) that it retains in common with the opening bar – even though the C is now placed in a different register.

However, the overlapping continuity of the row-formation used here already indicates a measure of independence between its characteristic interval groupings. So that the ambiguity suggested by partial likenesses (such as that between bars 2 and 3) already includes the notion of the sort of independent, and therefore interchangeable, existence that will later be entrusted to such groupings when they come to be regarded as neutral objects. These (inter)relationships define progressive developments as related differences, and recapitulatory evidence, of which there is plenty, as recurring likenesses: bars 14 (with the up-beat) to 19, for instance, communicate a sense of homecoming by their retrograde relationship to bars 3–5, so that the altered position of the underlying chord in bar 14 is heard as a true inversion (in a quasi-diatonic sense) of the chord in bar 4 (Ex. 7).

Later in the work, the difference between lines and chords begins to be more sharply defined in terms of what Boulez was afterwards to classify as monody versus homophony: that is, vertical chords become a direct reflection of horizontal lines no longer related, in themselves, to the continuity of the twelve-note row (Ex. 8). Moreover, such chords can already be understood as an embryo indication of the process of multiplying the intervals of one chord upon the successive pitches of another. Still other chord formations indicate the possibility of creating more neutral harmonic zones by the successive addition of the same interval or intervals.

Ex. 8

In all these ways, the Sonatine confirms the basis of an essentially intervallic development that would, from now on, replace the essentially thematic development of the classical era. Rhythmically, too, it confidently replaces the regular continuity of a measured pulse essential to the definition of diatonic harmony with the irregular discontinuity of a pulse measured only from point to point across a succession of asymmetrical durations. Moreover, because rhythmic organization is no longer directly linked to pitch as an expression of the relationships between strong and weak harmony, it is free to develop independently of the new intervallic hierarchy, as well as side by side with it – and free, too, to accept or reject a countable pulse as one among many possible contrasts.

As with its pitch structure, the introduction is intentionally ambiguous in its presentation of rhythmic formations that are later to be given motivic shape; at this stage, the various units of 2, 3, 5 and 7 (of no matter what relative duration) permeate every level of the rhythmic organization without committing themselves to any motivic significance. Just as the characteristic intervals of the opening bars are not actually revealed as a twelve-note row until the succeeding *Allegro*, so the characteristic durations mask their multiple implications until they too are given a basic shape to which to relate successive distortions. These multiple implications result from the layers of conflicting evidence brought about by the virtual disappearance of the bar-line (except as a visual convenience) so that rhythmic relationships may be perceived simultaneously as

Ex. 9

expansions on one level, contractions on another (Ex. 9). In spite of the background symmetries which may be revealed by the phrase structure, no single rhythmic grouping is the same as any other throughout the introduction; even when imitation is implied, it is never exactly parallel. And although the development of these groups later becomes more specific in relation to the first-subject rhythm associated with the main statement of the twelve-note row, the unpredictability of their various proportional relationships is to remain an essential and positive feature of the work. Like the pitch organization, which remains coherent through the strongly-characterized intervals of its basic material, the rhythmic organization continues to be understood in terms of its duple, triple, quintuple or septuple groupings, whatever the context – and whether or not it coincides with, or deviates from the intervallic emphasis (Ex. 10).

Ex. 10

Even when the rhythmic structure settles into the quasi-automatic permutation of two triple-duration groups, each with its reverse image (at the climax of the central development section), the complex coincidences that result are still understood as part of an asymmetrical ostinato derived from variants of the same triple rhythm (Ex. 11).

Ex. 11

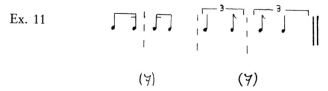

The many hidden meanings that pervade this work – the imitations that are apparent rather than real, as well as the multi-layered implications of both the pitch and the rhythmic structure – create the impression of a dream-world, where nothing is quite what it seems, and where everything is continually changing in its relationship to everything else. But this is no nightmare vision of a distorted future; indeed, the very strength of the work, and its continuing fascination, lies in its refusal to be pinned down. Whether this richly imaginative quality of will-o'-the-wisp evasiveness was later to have a detrimental influence on some of the succeeding works is open to question; certainly, for a time, the ability to disguise musical intentions – to leave them open to as many different interpretations as the listener cares to put upon them – came dangerously close to uncommittedness. But that was much later. The Sonatine itself shows a firm grasp of its place in history as a basis for future explorations. Such stylistic inconsistencies as might betray the youth of the composer (the central scherzo, for instance, relies rather more heavily on canonic superposition of fixed motivic shapes than the introduction would suggest) are handled with such disarming brilliance and unpredictable originality that they are readily absorbed into the virtuoso fabric of the piece. In any case, such obvious classical influences were short-lived; only a few months later, it is noticeable that Piano Sonata 1 had already adapted these received images to its own linguistic expression.

Le visage nuptial; Le soleil des eaux
– the last extended use of melodic development and the beginnings of harmony as a means of defining musical space; the first attempt to define form as a continuous development based on the equality and interdependence of melody, harmony and rhythm.

At this stage, the validity of pre-determined architectural structures was not yet in doubt, in spite of the fact that Boulez had already begun to evolve a concept of musical form as the continuous development of a number of characteristic objects, rather than as their statement, development and restatement. So the ready-made structural framework of the Sonatine was an essential curb in delimiting its developments, just as the framework of classical sonata form was to exercise a similar, if less binding, control over the design of the two early piano sonatas. The advantage of some such control, however loosely applied, is seen in Piano Sonata No. 2, whose far-reaching and texturally complex developments are held in check by a much stricter sectional definition of sonata form than was necessary in the context of the more constrained, local procedures that characterize Piano Sonata No. 1.

However, since poetry can be made to reflect something of its own form when placed in a musical setting, words themselves can be used as an alternative formal framework. And such is the case in the two vocal works of this period – *Le visage nuptial* and *Le soleil des eaux*.

Each of these works (which originally date from 1946 and 1948 respectively) has undergone more than one radical transformation, so

147

tending to obscure its chronological relationship with the other works of the period. The original version of *Le visage nuptial*, scored for soprano, contralto and chamber orchestra, was never performed; its present full orchestral version dates from 1951, but this in turn is soon [in 1985 this still applies – see p. 224] to be revised in order to eradicate some of the difficulties that stand in the way of regular performance. Nevertheless, the 1951 version is clearly contemporary with the early works in its zestful exploration of an expanding technique that in no way detracts from its innate romanticism; if the sometimes aggressive expression of the Sonatine suggests an impatience that seeks to compress what has to be said into the shortest possible space of time, *Le visage nuptial* redresses the balance in favour of a relaxed unfolding of much more expansive contours. In this work, Boulez seems to be examining the opposite side of his personality to that displayed in the more violent gestures of the Sonatine, so that the often frenzied tumult that characterized many of his works in the 1950s and '60s can now be understood as a violence that has absorbed romanticism – that is, in a way, an expression of its continuing ardour.

Le visage nuptial, a cycle of five songs with words by René Char, centres around the setting of the title poem; this, the third song, is scored for soprano and alto soloists, SA chorus, and a large orchestra consisting of quadruple woodwind and brass, a vast percussion section (including xylophone, vibraphone and glockenspiel), celesta, two harps and strings. The opening song, 'Conduite', dispenses with the chorus and reduces the orchestra to triple wind; the second, 'Gravité', reduces yet again – to double wind and no harps; the fourth, 'Evadne', matches the first, and the final 'Post-scriptum' is for voices, strings and unpitched percussion alone.

While the twelve-note row continues to function as the source material for a number of characteristic interval groupings, the quasi-motivic use of such fixed groups – as in the Sonatine – has now given way to a much freer exchange of pitches in the make-up of the groups themselves, so that melodic recurrences in the motivic sense are no longer a structural concern. Instead, the freely-changing internal contours of the note row (stated in its entirety by the voice at the beginning of the setting of 'Le visage nuptial' itself – Ex. 12), together with the overlapping conjunction of its four basic versions, allow for the harmony to be centred around recurring intervals. The opening bars of 'Conduite', for instance, indicate a harmonic ambience characterized by a succession of intervals (stretch-

Ex.12

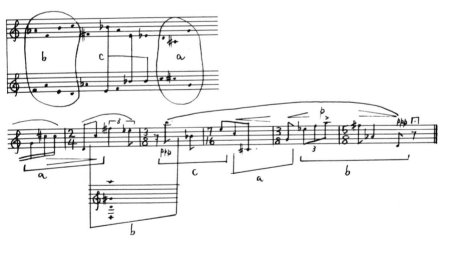

ing outwards from minor 3rd, to major 3rd, diminished 5th, perfect 5th, to minor 6th/major 3rd) not themselves drawn from the intervals of the original twelve-note row, but from the overlapping superposition of its retrograde inversion (Ex. 13). And this kind of harmonic definition, with its recurring reference points, gives a similar security to the melodic contours of the wide-ranging vocal line of the composite voice part (soprano + alto – Ex. 14).

Rhythmically, the whole work floats on the lilting asymmetry of the proportional relationships that arise from the central shape of the twelve-note row itself (in 'Le visage nuptial', see Ex. 12). This 3/2 formation offers the utmost freedom: in itself, it dictates nothing, yet influences everything, while disguising as much as it reveals of its developmental intentions. Although the textural detail is often obscured by its structural complexity, the musical intentions are outlined with a strikingly vivid immediacy; indeed, it could hardly be otherwise in a work that is spell-bound throughout by the complex sensuality of the words to which it gives musical expression.

It was perhaps inevitable at this stage that a growing preoccupation with contrasting registers as a means of defining tessitura should lead to the notion of musical space as an enveloping quality to which all internal divisions – whether of duration or pitch – would relate. And this in turn led Boulez to consider if equality – whether equality of pulse with regard to duration, or the equality of the tempered scale with regard to pitch – was necessarily the sole means of dividing such space. But, while it was simple to imagine a scale of durations related only to one another, it was humanly impossible to conceive of, let alone to execute, a similar scale of pitches, unrelated to a given norm. The compromise solution was, of course, to make use of a scale of equal pitches other than – though related to – the semitone; but, since augmentation of the semitone would effectively destroy this relationship, such a scale would necessarily have to derive from its diminution. This reasoning resulted in the idea of dividing the twelve-note semitone scale into two twelve-note quarter-tone reflections of itself, as a counterbalance, roughly speaking, to the proportional augmentation or diminution of the units in the duration-scale.

In this way, strict canonic writing temporarily acquired a new lease of life, both as a means of reflecting a single line with its own distorted mirror-image (Ex. 15) and of fragmenting the outlines of canonic superposition in layer upon layer of additional distortions giving the blurred effect of a fluctuating harmonic mass. Further textural nuances resulted from setting a melodic line on a polyphonic tracing of its outline harmony – an idea that was to have a significant effect on the harmonic organization of many of the later works, long after the dream of a variable pitch-space had been abandoned as unworkable in practice. In another direction, this same idea was to suggest that the dependence of polypho-

Ex. 15

nic lines might develop into the independence of heterophonic blocks
(whether of lines or chords), since the kind of polyphony described above
is based on the notion of simultaneous variation that was later to be
extended as a definition of heterophony.

With all its evidence of an expanding technique, and its continuing
search for ways to broaden the horizons of musical choice, *Le visage
nuptial* is nevertheless a farewell to large-scale gestures and to the use of
musical climax as a means of defining architectural form. The gentle
reminiscence of 'Conduite' is set as an unbroken aria for voice(s) and
orchestra, whose one moment of dynamic intensity is silenced as
suddenly as it began. 'Gravité', on the other hand, uses its microtonal
counterpoints to propel the music towards a climax which draws all the
voices (solo and chorus) into a momentary *fortissimo* unison. The central
setting of 'Le visage nuptial' alternates the rapid, mainly staccato
articulation of a *Sprechstimme* recitative (A) with the more relaxed,
mainly *legato* contours of an aria (B). This alternation eventually subsides
into a still slower episode (C), whose static harmony derives from the
sostenuto rotations of single chords, punctuated by the asymmetrical
continuity of unpitched percussion and by unpitched speech alternating
with song. The form of this movement – by far the longest and most
substantial of the cycle – derives its overall symmetry from the alternation
of these three developments: ABAB C BABA C-coda. The fourth song,
'Evadne', presents another kind of symmetry, this time the result of a
form whose opening and closing gestures (the last mirroring the first as a
falling inversion of the rising original) enclose a spoken recitative whose
continuity is measured against the discontinuity of three separate orchestral variations. The last song, 'Post-scriptum', is a concluding *envoi* – not
only to the cycle itself, but (or so it would appear, in retrospect) to the
world of a musical tradition that had already come to seem too self-
indulgent because by now too easily reproduced. The microtonal
bleakness of this conclusion is reflected in the monotone colours of divisi
strings. Here, the sectional form is defined by contrasts in register
between low, medium, high and 'mixed' pitches, separated by passages of
zero range scored for spoken voices and unpitched percussion, until the
final cadence chord is sustained over the entire compass (including the
unpitched zero).

151

Le soleil des eaux was originally a collection of musical interludes – including an unaccompanied setting of the poem 'Complainte du lézard amoureux' – for a poetic drama for radio by René Char. These interludes afterwards formed the basis of a cantata for three solo voices and chamber orchestra, first performed in Paris in 1950. In 1958, the cantata itself was re-scored for soprano, tenor and bass soloists, SAB chorus and symphony orchestra (double woodwind, three horns, two trumpets, trombone, tuba, percussion, harp and strings); a decade later it was again re-scored, and this final version (1965) is for soprano solo, SATB chorus and orchestra – with the addition of a second harp. These last two versions provide a fascinating study in comparative orchestration. The first is purely idealistic, and ultimately self-defeating in its fragmented instrumentation in the tradition of *Klangfarbenmelodie*; the second, absolutely practical, is enriched with the depth of texture resulting from a clearer and more pliable differentiation of the available orchestral colours. But this transformation is not entirely due to the practical experience gained through years of orchestral rehearsal and performance: the second movement, 'La sorgue', has been largely re-composed in terms of the much more flexible techniques evolved during the decade separating the two versions.

The stylistic compression of *Le soleil des eaux* places it closer to the Flute Sonatine than to *Le visage nuptial*, in spite of its later date. However, there is now no vestige of the toccata-like rhythmic ostinatos that featured prominently in the Sonatine and, to a lesser extent, in Piano Sonata No. 1. In *Le visage nuptial*, such procedures had already begun to seem at variance with the idea of a continuously developing interval structure, thus provoking the need to evolve a rhythmic structure that would be equally independent of symmetrical imitations, the more so since contrapuntal conventions had already been stretched to a point where the use of widely contrasting registers (in the final pages of the Flute Sonatine, and throughout long sections of Piano Sonata No. 2) had made the traditional concept of voice-leading largely irrelevant – so removing the need for rhythmic coincidence as a means of contrapuntal definition.

Just as the abandonment of tonality had involved the loss of modulation as a vital ingredient of form (a loss which had made it necessary to establish harmonic networks characterized by intervals, and to include register as a definition of pitch), so the abandonment of regular rhythmic coincidence in relation to the bar-line involved the loss of metrical pulse-accentuation as an equally vital ingredient. Moreover, now that the concept of principal and secondary material had been superseded by that of continuous development, it gradually became clear that form itself could no longer be considered as a sectional hierarchy (as Schoenberg had already discovered in the context of his atonal works – notably, the last of the Three Piano Pieces, Op. 11).

The first movement of *Le soleil des eaux*, 'Complainte du lézard amoureux', is dependent on the sectional contrasts of an unaccompanied vocal recitative, interrupted and sometimes overlapped by orchestral interludes. Nevertheless, it suggests the basis of a form defined by evolutionary development, expressed in terms of texture and articulation (as definitions of rhythm) and of register and dynamics (as descriptions of pitch). Here, smooth lines explode into jagged blocks, which in turn resolve on to static chords. And sustained chords are 'revealed' through the changing emphases put upon the lines that they can be made to yield, so that textural continuity is inflected by the discontinuity of its interior organization – as if a microscopic examination had uncovered a teeming life beneath its apparently unruffled surface. Put another way, the exterior polyphonic decoration of a single line (see *Le visage nuptial*) is here translated into the interior polyphonic elaboration of a single chord (see fig. 6 in the score of *Le soleil des eaux*).

The compressed introductory bars are heard first as a tangled thread, later to be unravelled by the voice. The tension expressed here derives from an absence of strong beats in relation to the bar-line (Ex. 16) – a

Ex. 16

tension that is markedly relaxed when the bar accents do eventually coincide with the pulse accents of the inflected chord and are finally released in the hectic discontinuity of a climactic *Vif*. Outwardly characterized once and for all by the detailed accentuation of its phrasing, the opening of 'Complainte' is nevertheless constructed in a way that allows the balance of its foreground asymmetries (like those of the Flute Sonatine) to remain freely suggestive of a number of different interpretations, even of including unexpected symmetries. As in the two previous works, the harmonic ambience of *Le soleil des eaux* is defined initially by the characteristic intervals contained within an original twelve-note row (and, in this case, its transposition a semitone higher – Ex. 17). But even in the opening bars, the actual row-structure is quickly confirmed as no more than the source material for its characteristic intervals.

In 'La sorgue', these intervallic cross-references are much more tightly entwined, as the formal clarity supplied by the linking vocal recitatives in 'Complainte' is relinquished in favour of a more rhapsodic design. The

153

Ex. 17

characteristic features of the harmony now seem to explode inwards into a densely-packed mass of overlapping events, matched by a greater textural density resulting from the introduction of the chorus. However, the 1948 version of 'La sorgue' seems dangerously uneventful, in spite of – or because of? – the underlying continuity of its hectic textural activity. So, the attempt to define form by means of the contrasts offered by the inter-changeability of vertical and horizontal (melody and harmony) is ultimately hindered by a lack of perspective of both depth and distance. Twenty years later, the revised version allowed harmonic implications to become audible facts, and the spacing of events in time then became crucial to its form.

Even at this stage of Boulez's career (he was still only twenty-three), there is ample evidence that an individual harmonic language was already well on the way to being achieved and that the communicative intentions of that language (as well as many of the means by which they would continue to be expressed) had already become recognizably characteristic of the composer. It will be equally evident that form was as yet dependent on a development of inherited designs. Nevertheless, the clear-cut discontinuity of the rondo form of 'Complainte du lézard amoureux' already begins to seem strangely at odds with a rhythmic structure arising out of the continuous variation of asymmetrical rhythmic units. The very unease of its interim compromise would now seem to have pointed to the eventual necessity of relating form to a succession of continuous developments rather than deriving it from the balance of discontinuous contrasts. In this respect, and with all its initial defects, 'La sorgue' is much more radical.

Livre pour quatuor[6]
    – the beginning of rhythmic duration as an ingredient of texture, and of tempo as a means of phrasing.

At about this time (1947–8), Boulez undertook a considerably more

---

[6] This work also exists in a version for string orchestra

searching exploration of form as the continual permutation of related developments in the abstract, instrumental *Livre pour quatuor*. Without the figurative connotations of words or the motivic associations of sonata form, *Livre* is by far the most forward-looking of the early works, both in the integrated nature of its formal design, and in the abstracted Webernianism of its structural detail. But, although Webern was to prove the strongest and most discernible influence on almost the entire generation of post-war composers, Boulez not least (emotionally, as well as technically, Webern's idealism was seen as an attractive antidote to a lingering romanticism), this is the only work in which he takes overtly Webernian detail as his starting point.

However, *Livre* pays homage to the more complex Webern of Op. 18 and Op. 20, where figurative detail is obscured by the texture it creates. In the quartet, duration-cells serve to articulate harmony, not melody, and achieve rhythmic status only within the textures to which they contribute. And texture is paramount, both as a means of spacing and giving impetus to the harmony and as a means of defining the various formal divisions (phrases, sentences, paragraphs, chapters) at all levels of its interlocked sextuple design:

$$\text{I--II} \mid \text{III} \mid \text{IV} \mid \text{V} \parallel \text{VI}$$

Such a texturized harmonic fabric is created by a maximum dispersal of all elements within it – above all, by a dispersal of register, so that the four instrumental voices lose their separate linear identities within a fourfold textural unity. This unity is reinforced by a dispersal of dynamics over the widest possible range, and by a similar dispersal of attack (which includes the notion of timbre) over the whole gamut of possibilities offered by normal string techniques. These various means are used to achieve textures that contrast complete smoothness – of unchanging register, dynamics and attack – at the one extreme, with maximum 'striation' (to adopt the composer's term) at the other.

Here, for the first time, the quality of tempo is made to assume much wider responsibilities in relation to expression, and so eventually to form, than those involved in its earlier definition as an indication of speed. Tempo now becomes a focusing agent, able to clarify or obliterate the other qualities by the creation of conjunct or disjunct movement, or by the expansion or contraction of the space in which the other qualities unfold, as well as by confirming or contradicting the smoothness or striation of the textures it expresses. This notion of tempo is based on a compound relationship between tempo *rubato* and tempo *giusto*, stemming from its use as a means of structural phrasing, first explored in the late works of Webern. But, whereas Webern used tempo as a means of shaping a phrase in relation to the rhythmic pulse which frames it (in other words, as a superimposed means of expression, able to affect the emphasis or de-emphasis of a phrase, but not its content), Boulez employs it as an exterior reflection of the musical structures themselves. Just as the continual expansion and contraction of overlapping duration-cells obliterates pulse in favour of a pulsating texture, so the continual ebb and flow of tempo is a reflection of the activity within these textures, rather than of speed of movement.

Yet the apparently new direction taken here – into the controlled disorder of an organized unpredictability – is, in reality, no more than a logical extension of the classical techniques employed in the Flute Sonatine: as it were, a composed appraisal of the ways in which such techniques might evolve if *not* allowed to develop imitative implications in the foreground of a musical structure. The closely-reasoned framework for the textural foreground of *Livre* evolves from the changing alignment of partial likenesses (quasi-imitative distortions within the duration-cells) which are prevented from acquiring motivic significance by their independence from their melodic surroundings; any threads of

Ex. 18

Ex. 19

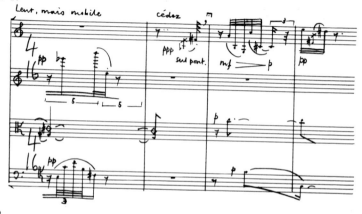

figurative melody that do momentarily emerge (as at the opening of movements III and V, Exx. 18 and 19) are quickly reabsorbed into their harmonic background. The quicksilver motion of the rhythmic particles which give rise to this texture could only have succeeded within the bounds of a relatively stable harmonic frame. For this reason, the work proceeds on two different levels, at two different speeds: the rate of development of the rhythmic texture is extremely fast, exhibiting a maximum dissimilarity of contrast; while the rate of the harmonic development is, by comparison, extremely slow, underlining the similarities in its step-by-step progress so that each area is carefully re-confirmed before moving on to the next (Ex. 20).

Ex. 20

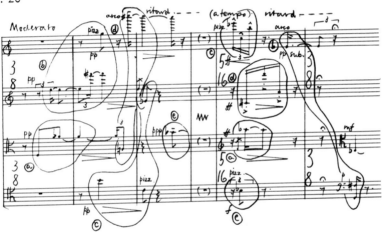

Written during a period when the composer was immersed in the much more luxuriant harmonic and textural environment of *Le visage nuptial* and *Le soleil des eaux*, *Livre pour quatuor* provides an early indication of the kind of many-faceted stylistic explorations that have continued to mark the progress of Boulez's development – notably, during the decade following the completion of *Le marteau sans maître*. Although the quartet may lack something of the definitive character that so strongly informs the other works of these early years, it remains remarkable for the sheer scope and variety of its abstract invention; moreover, as a study into the possibilities of an independent rhythmic development, no longer subservient to the pitch curves of melody or harmony, its implications for the future were to prove of considerable importance.

Nevertheless, the already tottering edifice of architectural form (as explored in all the early works, with the notable exception of *Livre*) had still to be tested to structural breaking-point before its validity as a contemporary concept could finally be discounted – just as the richness of nineteenth-century harmony had earlier been sacrificed to the clean palette of the twentieth. It was typical of Boulez that he should arrive at the annihilation of sonata form not by an intellectual decision, but by an emotional exploration of its extreme limits as a perceptible (and workable) frame. The compositional and pianistic virtuosity of Piano Sonata No. 2 exposes both the frustration of a creative energy supremely aware of its own power, but as yet uncertain how best to direct and control it, and the subconscious determination that demolition, however painful, was a necessary prelude to rebuilding.

The finality and completeness of the formal explosion achieved in Piano Sonata No. 2 was confirmed by the years of 'silent' research that followed. This was surely the point of no return, and relief at breaking free from a received tradition must have been tinged with horror at the remaining void, and at the immensity of the task that lay ahead if new aims and ideals were to evolve into a system. With the advantage of hindsight, it is easy to assess the position in which Boulez found himself in the late 1940s, and to predict the decisive actions that would later determine the whole course of his development as a composer. But the fact that the twenty-three-year-old composer (already on the threshold of what would undoubtedly have been a successful career in any circumstances) should himself have possessed the visionary self-awareness to understand the necessity for objective decision, let alone the determination to pursue such a lonely endeavour, once embarked on, remains astonishing. For this was a course that was to result in much heartache and, it can be imagined, near despair; inevitably, it involved a calculated suppression of the instinctive originality of the early pieces, in order to extract from their analysis the elements of a new technique which, ironically, was temporarily to stifle the very creativity that inspired them.

The years 1948–52 were devoted entirely to research into the future via a minute and wide-ranging examination of the past[7] and any works, or portions of works, that did emerge were in the nature of interim theses on one technical facet or another, and were quickly withdrawn. Apart from two studies in *musique concrète*, only one piece dating from these years – *Polyphonie X*,[8] for eighteen solo instruments – was actually performed. It was not until 1952 that these researches were co-ordinated in a work which showed the new technical priorities being joined to the beginnings of a new musical expression. *Structures*, Book I, for two pianos, is a technical treatise that was to prove the turning-point not only for Boulez's own future, but in relation to the whole course of mid-twentieth-century musical thinking: there can be few composers who have remained untouched by its influence, if only in their reactions

---

[7] See the essays dating from this period in *Relevés d'apprenti*, op. cit.
[8] This work is currently being revised

against the neo-academicism of its fundamental restraints. Moreover, the coldly mechanical procedures of *Ia* are already the basis of future technical achievement, even though they insist on the development of what was later seen to be a fallacy: namely, the notion that dynamics and attack could be made to function independently of pitch and duration and of one another. And the more vivid musical expression of *Ib* and *Ic* already provides ample evidence that new technical considerations had started to become a malleable ingredient of composition.

The technical basis of *Structures* sprang primarily from the notion of a rhythmical development dependent on a series of durations 'related only to one another' (see Ex. 2) within an enveloping tempo. If this now seems to have been a step backwards from the more sophisticated concept of proportionally-related rhythmic cells characteristic of the earlier works, it was nevertheless an essential move if such cells were to be purged of their associations with classical counterpoint – associations still evident even in the partial likenesses of *Livre pour quatuor*. In the first set of *Structures*, the duration of sounds and of silences, their negative image, is used as the connecting thread which binds one isolated pitch (isolated by register, as well as by differences in dynamics and attack) to another. The success of such point-to-point movement as even an interim means of virtuoso expression can best be gauged from the second piece (written some time later than the other two) of Book I: in it, less obsessional controls are already being moulded into an extension of the florid brilliance characteristic of Piano Sonata No. 2.

But it was not until *Le marteau sans maître* (1952–4) that the true rewards of these researches became apparent. By then, the proposals outlined in *Structures* had developed into a set of expressive facts – a secure means of procedure, which obviated the need for models and so allowed the music to recapture something of the zestful confidence of the previous decade: the demolition complete, and the plans drawn up, rebuilding could now begin.

Le marteau sans maître
– the twelve-note row expands into related networks of pitch and duration, and tempo begins to be used as a means of defining form.

This is not only a triumphant justification of the four years of technical research and patient classification but, as was immediately evident, a masterpiece by any standards. The title of the work (taken from that of a collection of poems by René Char, published in 1934) immediately suggests something of its extraordinarily hypnotic, almost oriental quality, achieved through the setting in motion of a number of musical gestures which are then allowed, as it were, to develop their own momentum. The poems themselves (three of which are woven into the

159

fabric of the music), although obscure in detail, would appear to evoke the eternal struggle of Everyman and his efforts to escape from the enclosing circle of material existence, from a civilization that marches inexorably towards its doom, regardless of the individual ... hence 'the hammer without a master'. Boulez's musical evocation of artistic endeavour as the struggle to master, rather than to be mastered by, the machinery of its own technical creation, is equally vivid.

The work is centred around the settings of the three poems: 'l'artisanat furieux', 'bel édifice et les pressentiments' and 'bourreaux de solitude' (movements III, V and VI). These vocal expositions are linked to instrumental movements which act as prelude or postlude ('before' and 'after' 'l'artisanat furieux'), as recapitulatory coda (the 'double' of 'bel édifice ...'), or as interludes (the three 'commentaries' on 'bourreaux de solitude'). However, these developmental connexions – 3, 3, III; V, 5; VI, 6, 6, 6 – are at least partially severed by the eventual form of the piece, which re-orders its tripartite structure into nine movements, separated by short, medium or long pauses: 3, 6, III, 6, V, VI, 3, 6, 5.

The scoring of the work is contained by the middle-register range and mellow tone-quality of alto voice, alto flute, guitar and viola: that is, two melodic 'instruments' (voice and flute), with a sound production dependent on breath, and two melodic/harmonic stringed instruments (guitar and viola), the one plucked, the other alternately plucked and bowed. These are set against the pitched percussiveness of vibraphone and xylophone – the first alternately sustained or not, the second producing only short, *pizzicato* attacks – and against the unpitched contrasts offered by the short, dry sounds (sometimes sustained by trills) of skin and wood and the enveloping resonance of metal. From this, it is evident that timbre had already become a conscious, if secondary, ingredient of expression; each of the nine movements is scored for a different combination of timbres, the full range of instrumental contrast being reserved (as in *Pierrot Lunaire*) for the last.

The restraint shown by the muted colours of the chosen instrumentation is matched by that of the technical limits which characterize each group of movements; there is no trace here of the occasionally self-indulgent virtuosity and consequent textural overcrowding which, six years earlier, had brought the composer of Piano Sonata No. 2 to a standstill.

The pitch structure of the work fans outwards from the melodic tracery of the central fifth movement, 'bel édifice ...'. Here, the chromatic outline of a twelve-note row is shaped into a melody on the viola (Ex. 21). Together with its flute counterpoint, this melodic shape represents the gentle undulations of the *rubato* argument (between viola, flute and guitar) from which the main part of the movement will develop, as well as

Ex. 21

Ex. 22

suggesting the basis of the more relaxed harmonic environment of the episodic vocal entries (Ex. 22). These two thematic characters (the melodic and the harmonic) alternate to form a rondo-like centre-piece to the work as a whole: A, B, A, B (+A), A, B.

Pitchwise, then, the basic material of *Le marteau sans maître* derives from the germ of a traditional twelve-note row. But this is a row chosen not for its melodic characteristics, but rather for its ability to generate harmonic offshoots, from which melodic characteristics may then emerge. So the quality of intervals – instinctively emphasized as long ago as the Flute Sonatine – is finally confirmed as the central generating force behind the new harmony. Each interval, or group of intervals, that the row may be made to yield as a definition of the harmonic area for a particular movement or section of a work can, in turn, be made to dominate by being superimposed on, or absorbed by, each of the others. In this way, a whole network of extended harmonic relationships begins to be brought into play – a network which retains an audible relationship with the interval-structure of an original row and its derivations (Ex. 23, see also p. 135).

The rhythmic tracery of the work has its origins in a parallel network. This rhythmic network derives from a fusion of the arithmetical duration-row which gave rise to *Structures Ia* and *Ic*, and the recognizably imitative rhythmic cells which gave impulse to the earlier works (imitations that quickly began to include the notion of a textural counterpoint, deriving from the superposition and permutation of asym-

Ex. 23

Ex. 24

metrical groupings – see bars 296–339 of the Flute Sonatine, and *Livre pour quatuor*). The reconstituted rhythmic cells therefore might more logically be referred to as duration-blocks, since they form rhythmic phrases that relate to tempo, in its broadest sense, rather than to pulse, to the passing of time, rather than to its metrical division (although, of course, regular pulsation remains one of the possible ways of marking the passage of time).

162

In 'bel édifice . . .', these duration-blocks underline their indebtedness to more classical procedures by allowing the perceptible recurrence of rhythmic groupings (3 and 5 at the outset, later including 7 and 9). However, such recurrences now have no motivic significance, since they are no longer attached to recurring melodic shapes. Instead, they become an expression of tempo – of a rubato (crochet = 66→80→120) that is, in turn, a reflection of their ambiguity, and vice versa. Throughout the work as a whole, then, it is clear that motivic likenesses are not intended to be heard as such, but rather as the changing coincidence of related particles whether of pitch or duration, within textures characterized by contrasting timbres, tessitura, dynamics, attack and, above all, by tempo (fast or slow, static or fluctuating, continuous or discontinuous) as the one quality that envelops and 'interprets' all the others.

Just as the fifth movement presents the pitch material in its simplest form as a twelve-note row, so the sixth – 'bourreaux de solitude' – develops its rhythmic structure from a row of twelve durations counted in semiquavers (Ex. 24).[9] The missing semiquavers between the initial sounding of each overlapping pitch of the row (now revealed in a different guise – see Ex. 23) are filled in by a percussive tapping that later acquires a quasi-independent life of its own through a development of the negative/positive (sound/silence) relationships suggested in the opening bars. The semiquaver-based durations retain their chronometric identity throughout a pulsed *Andante*, which gives way only at the cadence-points outlining the shape of the whole – so that the movement attains a formal symmetry through the asymmetrical tempo relationship (rit.→ meno mosso; accel.→ più mosso) of its episodes:

tempo 1 – rit. – tempo 1 – rit. – meno mosso;
tempo 1 – accel. – tempo 1 – accel. – più mosso;
accel. – tempo 1.

In the third movement – 'l'artisanat furieux' – the rubato tempo of 'bel édifice . . .' is translated into a rubato phrasing pulsed by irrational values

---

[9] The actual placing of these durations (i.e. the initial sounding of each pitch) is dictated by a method derived arithmetically from the original row. Although an important structural device at the time (and evidently more complex than would at first appear since it is not made any less obscure by Ex. 4 from *Boulez on Music Today*, op. cit.), not even the composer can now explain the means by which such a procedure was arrived at.
Since the completion of the main part of this chapter (1975), musicological research has provided several interesting solutions to this and other problems: in particular, the reader is referred to Robert Piencikowsky, *René Char et Pierre Boulez*, an analytical study of *Le marteau sans maître* (Schweizer Beiträge zur Musikwissenschaft, Verlag Paul Paupt, Berne and Stuttgart, 1980), and to L. Koblyakov, P. Boulez 'Le marteau sans maître', analysis of pitch structure, in *Zeitschrift für Musiktheorie 77–1*, ed. P. Rummenhöller (Musikverlag Döring, Horrenberg), pp. 24–39.

and set within a controlling tempo (minim = 52/crotchet = 104). Here, four variations span the four lines of the poem, separated by pauses. Just as the rhythmic outlines are blurred by more complex proportional relationships than those of the duration-row, so the pitch-material relinquishes its hold on the original note-row in favour of the overlapping melodic derivations offered by an enlarged serial network (whose basis is shown in Ex. 23). Although such serial offshoots were already beginning to inform the harmony as far back as *Livre pour quatuor*, it was not until *Le marteau sans maître* that theory was turned to a properly coherent and audible harmonic practice. This harmonic practice is greatly strengthened by the re-admission of register (the actual pitch of a note, relative to others) as a quality of harmonic definition, as well as of texture; in addition, grace-notes begin to function as harmonic modulators as well as rhythmic ones – so that apparent shifts in the harmony may be effected by a subtle shading of the melodic emphasis (compare the opening flute solo with the first entry of the voice – Exx. 25 and 26, also Ex. 23).

Ex. 25

Ex. 26

At this point, the basic pitch-material of the work (as stated at the opening of the central fifth movement) begins to be understood not so much as an initial twelve-note row which is then varied – that is, differently ordered – to form the basis of the third and sixth movements, but as the foundation of the tripartite serial network responsible for the three groups of related movements: III = I and VII; V = IX; VI = II, IV and VIII.

The gently curving melismas of 'l'artisanat furieux' are split into more impulsive rhythmic particles in movements I and VII, with the pulse of the music now at double the speed. In the first movement, two composite instrumental lines (drawn from the pairing of flute and vibraphone, guitar and viola) weave a muscular counterpoint that balances the symmetry of true rhythmic canons (Ex. 27) and short-lived palindromic designs (Ex. 28) against the asymmetry of distorted likenesses (Ex. 29), coloured by the whole tones, major and minor thirds and the fifths characteristic of

Ex. 27

Ex. 28

Ex. 29

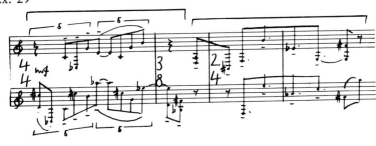

Ex. 30

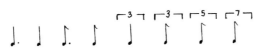

'l'artisanat furieux'. The overlapping phrase-lengths are articulated by permutations of the changing relationships between groups of 2 and 3 – an argument which underlies the entire movement, no matter what the (variable) unit of definition (Ex. 30). Even though these relationships are now the result of a systematic planning (relating to the asymmetrical super-position of duration-blocks, as opposed to the imitative augmentation or diminution of thematic motifs), they retain all the vitality of the more instinctive ambiguities that typified the earlier works. So that, in spite of the systematic scrutiny to which rhythmic procedures had been submitted during the intervening years, they re-emerge here as a pliable means of organization – and communication. At this point, then, the development of rhythm (duration) can be considered equal to that of pitch, though independent of it. For, just as the pitch organization is no longer thematic, but still clearly dependent on characteristic intervals as the basis of both melody and harmony, so the rhythmic organization, no longer motivic, still evidently depends on characteristic duration-groups.

The sectional form of 'avant l'artisanat furieux' (ABABA) unfolds within the hectic continuity of a regularly-pulsed tempo, interrupted only by the pauses which punctuate the sections and by the momentary hesitations or forward surges (*presser/poco rit.*) which underline the tension or relaxation of the interim cadence-points. This introduces the expressive potential of tempo in its simplest form: as a means of cadential emphasis. Later, the function of variable tempo in the first movement can be understood as having prepared the way for the disguised pulsation that underlies the apparent fluctuations of 'l'artisanat furieux' itself. Later still, 'après l'artisanat furieux' (for flute, vibraphone and guitar) presents the reverse image: that of tempo as a distorting factor. This, in turn, relates to 'l'artisanat furieux' in the sense that a regular pulse, divided by irrational values, has now widened to the level of an irrational tempo; by stretching pulse to the limits of its elasticity, it can only be understood in terms of tempo, so that, in the seventh movement, the 2:3 relationships of the first are torn apart by the accelerating or decelerating twists of a telescoped development (A-BAB-A).

The four versions of 'bourreaux de solitude' – movement VI and its three 'commentaries' (II, IV and VIII) – act as quasi-static interludes between the more impassioned developments associated with 'l'artisanat furieux' and 'bel édifice ...'. The second movement (scored for flute, xylophone, pizzicato viola and drum – replaced by two pairs of bongos in the central episode) is a *sotto voce* exploration of a regular pulse, irregularly punctuated by asymmetrically-grouped durations. Its narrow dynamic range (*pp–mf*) is matched by the relatively narrow confines of a six-unit duration scale (semiquaver → dotted-crotchet), and by the textural restraint of an unyielding *pizzicato* – against which the *legato* flute explores a soaring *espressivo*. The narrowly-bounded harmony characteristic of 'bourreaux de solitude' is heard here as a fragmented pre-echo, stretched across wide intervals, and the negative/positive (sound/silence) aspect of its accompanying rhythmic pulsation is now suggested by the least possible resonance ('almost on the frame of the drum'). The harmonic overtones of the *legato* flute are replaced in the central episode by a harmonic thickening achieved by the addition of recurring intervals to the more linear outlines of the opening, and underlined by an additional percussive resonance deriving from the change to bongos. At first, this thickening is characterized by minor 3rds/major 6ths, later by 2nds, 7ths and 9ths, which then relax into 4ths and 5ths; as these intervals are extended beyond the octave, they begin to lose their identity, finally evaporating in the entanglements of a development which includes them all. The re-entry of the flute (and a return to the drier articulation of the drum) denotes the reappearance of the opening material: still under the influence of the greater harmonic density of the central episode, this is now heard in a condensed version that creates its own thickening by the harmonic contraction of phrases first stated as extended melodic lines.

If the second movement can be said to employ tempo as an extension of pulse, the two remaining commentaries can be thought of as exploring tempo in its role as an enveloping quality which affects perception of all the other expressive qualities. The fourth movement falls into two distinct sections: the first within a mainly fast tempo, the second relaxing into a pre-echo of the mainly slow tempo, though not the style, of the eighth (which, in turn, is to include a brief reference to the tempo character of the previous commentary). The opening section of the fourth movement itself is pulverized by the shock tactics of a tempo that employs both unprepared silence and abrupt cessation of movement as sharply disruptive elements of expression: each phrase is separated from each succeeding phrase either by the door-slamming effect of a sudden silence, or by the equally sudden 'freezing' of all activity, as time is suspended on a pause. The timbre, too, is given a more cutting edge, both by the absence of the softening influence of the flute, and by the use of harshly-articulated double-stopping on guitar and *pizzicato* viola, xylophone and vibraphone, each pair of instruments being forged into an entity productive of plucked or hammered sounds. The syncopation of tempo which underlines the harmonic relationship between phrases by interrupting their succession is mirrored by a rhythmic syncopation in the structure of the phrases themselves (Ex. 31). Throughout the movement, this fragmentation of tempo is intensified by the composed *rubato* of its accelerating or decelerating *espressivo*, so that time itself becomes temporarily cheated of any constant against which to measure its passing.

But compensation for this disorientation of the time-space is provided by a re-orientation of the pitch-space. Harmony here takes over from tempo as the constant element: each phrase is solely concerned with the

Ex. 31

interval relationships that evolve between individual pitches (fixed in register for the duration of each phrase) of a single chord. The recurring emphasis given to these relationships forces each chord to uncover its complementary melodic connotations – a process that is reversed in the concluding *meno mosso* section, where the mainly harmonic emphasis of the opening becomes a mainly melodic one.

In the eighth movement, this duality of the pitch function is reflected in reverse, as chords emerge through the emphasis of melodic repetition (Exx. 32 and 33). And the opposite images of tempo as expressive of conjunct or disjunct motion in the first two commentaries here meet on the common ground of an undulating *rubato*.

Ex. 32

Ex. 33

Because 'bel édifice ...' acts as a central pivot, around which the other movements revolve, its own quasi-thematic outlines are themselves reflected in subsidiary developments only insofar as they permeate the entire work. Not until the last movement do its characteristics underline their radial influence on the rest of the work by absorbing quotations from the previous movements. In this way, through its emphasis on the threefold unity of the contrasts evolved in movements III, V, VI and their related developments, the *double* of 'bel édifice ...' is also a recapitulatory coda to the work as a whole. This second setting of the poem establishes its conclusive function by rotating the harmony of each line around a single note (E flat), that is fixed in register for the duration of each 'verse', so acting as a quasi-tonic pedal (Ex. 34). The four lines of the poem are interspersed with direct quotations from the other song settings; after this, the music branches out into further references to III, V and VI, but now adapted to the style of the original instrumental

Ex. 34

developments. The final coda translates the vocal melismas of 'l'artisanat furieux' into a long aria for solo flute, enclosed in a haze of resonating metal which includes the ceremonial sound of gongs, silent until this moment.

The sense of recapitulation is further endorsed throughout the movement by the changes of speed characteristic of each of its quotations – and these, in turn, create an overall flexibility of tempo, reflecting the *rubato* role played by contrasting tempi throughout the work. In this way, the quotations themselves are made to act as a function of tempo, stopping time, as it were, by the use of flashback, and finally dissolving it in the echo resonance of gongs and cymbals suggestive of timelessness extended into infinity.

The variety, intensity and vitality of *Le marteau sans maître* could only have been achieved by a composer gifted with apparently inexhaustible powers of invention, and inspired by the challenge to seek the greatest diversity of expression within a seemingly restricted range of contrasts. Nevertheless, the enclosed nature of the short-term developments so characteristic of this work was to signify the end of a period, rather than a new beginning. Just as the ultra-virtuoso textures of Piano Sonata No. 2 had led to the virtual extinction of just those contrapuntal premises on which they were based, so the equally virtuoso containment of *Le marteau sans maître* had, by its very economy, been temporarily drained of further possibilities.

It now seems almost as if the effort involved in writing this crucial work had meant the sacrifice of several years'-worth of creative energy and, just as the composition of Piano Sonata No. 2 had led to a period of introspective analysis, so the completion of *Le marteau sans maître* was followed by a similar period of compositional soul-searching. But, whereas the years 1948–52 had been devoted to strengthening the organization of the two basic elements of musical composition, pitch and duration, in relation to the secondary, affective qualities of dynamics and attack, the years 1954–6 were concerned with the enveloping qualities of time and space (relationships already touched on in *Le marteau sans maître* itself) and with tempo as a functional element in relation to musical form.

But the nature and function of form as a quality of musical expression had yet to be explored. While the earliest works had tested the viability of sonata form by inflating its proportions almost to bursting point (as, finally, in Piano Sonata No. 2), and while *Structures*, Book I, had largely evaded the issue by employing the 'uncommitted' format of sectional variations, *Le marteau sans maître* returned to the small-scale symmetry of classical song-forms, set within the frame of its larger, tripartite design. Successful though these adaptations had proved as interim solutions, it was inevitable that the concept of form as both finite and symmetrical, however loosely applied, must come to seem irrelevant in the context of the infinite possibilities offered by the concept of asymmetrical serial hierarchies established from work to work. This growing unease as to the incompatibility of form and content afflicted many composers during the early 1950s and was only temporarily stilled, for Boulez, in *Le marteau sans maître*. Elsewhere it resulted in the prevalence of non-form works in which several European composers (first, and most notably, Stockhausen, in his Piano Piece XI) handed over responsibility for form, and even duration, to chance, or the performer, or both. Typically, Boulez reacted against a trend which he saw as an abdication in the face of difficulty, rather than as a properly considered attempt to find a cure for what was fast becoming a widespread compositional malaise. For himself, he found it impossible to imagine form, however 'infinite', as anything other than a logical summation of the various strictly-controlled elements (pitch, duration, dynamics, attack – and tempo) that contribute to it; once again, he felt himself forced to adopt a more positive position vis-à-vis the negative attitude of many of his contemporaries. And it was a logical extension of the reasoning applied earlier to the interrelated developments of pitch and duration that he should now begin to envisage form as the expression of the proportions already in existence between the various serial networks – a form that would then be finite only by virtue of the limits imposed on the number of events that compose it.

Although arising out of its contextual need to fulfil the function of a recapitulatory coda, the last movement of *Le marteau sans maître* had already suggested several of the basic premises from which this new attitude towards form would evolve; once again, analysis of the 'facts' contained in his own music was eventually to provide Boulez with a way forward. Through its use of inserted quotations, the *double* of 'bel édifice . . .' had instinctively proposed the notion of form deriving from the overlap or interruption of proportionately-related developments and, if indirectly, that certain aspects of such developments could be freely re-ordered without destroying the sense of their relationships to each other or to the whole. Hence the concept of heterophony as a counterpoint of developments. The coincidence of such developments could be then either freely chosen (by the performer) or strictly controlled (by the composer); they could even be made to include the notion of alternatives, to be played or not – as in the third Improvisation from *Pli selon pli* and in Piano Sonata No. 3. However, such an evidently conscious effort to include freedom of choice in performance as a calculated ingredient of form seems to have been an offshoot of Boulez's reaction against the more sloppy miscalculations in the use of such freedoms shown in the works of others, rather than the result of any permanent personal conviction. Such an open format as applied to a large-scale work is strangely untypical of a composer whose best music is characterized by an unusually detailed decisiveness, far removed from the haphazard.

The testing of these freedoms, however, was yet another vital interlude in Boulez's development and was, in itself, to play an important part in determining the future function of time and space in the interpretation of musical form. Above all, these experiments were to have the effect of finally exploding any nostalgic notion that the space in which music unfolds must necessarily be related to tempo solely as a definition or a distortion of chronometric time (as in the classical period of Western European music). But they were also pertinent to the growing conviction that form as a reflection of serial thought must eventually be defined as an expanding panorama, no longer dependent on the gravitational attractions of tonal architecture. In other words, form would result from a manipulation of the relationships between internal structural moments, and not primarily from the relationship of these moments to the totality of a preplanned design. Even so, it is once again a question not of jettisoning the past but of expanding its horizons to fit the future – so that certain aspects of architectural form (notably, that of the balancing element of restatement or recapitulation) remain amongst the many means of mapping this expanding panorama. Tempo could now be made to reflect durations (whether rational or irrational) by marking periods of time either with a regularity related to pulse, or with a static irregularity related only to the overall duration of such periods. In the same way, form could reflect either the predictability of finite periods marked by recurrences of whatever kind or the amorphous unpredictability of non-recurring developments that could be continued into infinity. And as tempo may be used to blur the outlines between chronometric and amorphous time by means of *accelerando* or *ritardando*, which likens the first to the second – or by means of regular pulsations placed within an undefined period of time, which likens the second to the first, so form may include references to the architectural within the panoramic, and vice versa. Moreover, melody may also reflect harmony, and harmony reveal melody (so that polyphony may be fused into homophony) just as rhythmic duration may be used to inform both lines and chords and to underpin the connection between horizontal and vertical by suggesting a third, diagonal dimension.

The strength of this reasoning – which aims at ensuring the utmost cohesion between the motivic elements characteristic of the two main parameters (pitch and duration) of a composition and its eventual form – is obvious. So, too, is the weakness inherent in such inter-related structures, the danger of a sort of musical inbreeding that could end in the de-characterization of those very qualities it seeks to enhance. But, as Boulez himself has stressed, this is the point at which the act of composition must involve the process of selection, of choosing from among the infinite number of possibilities and permutations of possibilities which such an expanding network of intricate relationships could be made to offer. At this stage, therefore, the composer's first task is to determine the limits within which a particular piece will unfold – limits that will, so to speak, define its field of action within the vast landscape of the possible. Only then will the comprehensiveness of the system itself emerge as a means of characterizing all the facets of a work, from the smallest element in its design to the finished form.

In this sense, then, and from now on, the problem of form – as the product of a set of framing decisions, related to but separable from the other ingredients of a composition – no longer exists. Quite simply, it has resolved into a natural evolution of related developments which may be either successive (as, for instance, in *Figures–Doubles–Prismes* or *Éclat/Multiples*) or cyclic, branching outwards from a central point (as in '... *explosante-fixe* ...' or *Rituel*). At last, the earlier vision of form as the process of expansion rather than of containment seems on the verge of becoming a convincing reality.

However, such dreams of a future untrammelled by the demands of architecturally stylized forms could not in themselves either promote or obstruct the flow of strictly musical inspiration that would give them practical reality. And, as Boulez slowly emerged from the bleak surroundings of the years following the completion of *Le marteau sans maître*, it was the two smallest, most conventionally-structured pieces (*Improvisations I* and *II*, later incorporated into *Pli selon pli*) that were to give rise to the least self-conscious music of the rest of the decade. Perhaps even longer; for the remaining years of the '50s, and almost all of the '60s, can now be understood as a period of musical trial – fanning outwards in all directions in a search for the best means of relating style to idea, content to form.

It was also a period marked by an increasing conviction that timbre was to become of paramount importance as a descriptive quality – a quality which could, of itself, be made to express dynamics, attack and tessitura through differing weights of instruments or instrumental groups, differing articulative characters and registers, and which could also be thought of as qualifying harmonic meaning in a quasi-adjectival sense, particularly when large and diverse forces are involved. Primarily, its new role arose from the need to find a means of altering the focus of sounds in relation to the space in which they are heard. Again, this was an exploratory development that seems almost to have been pre-ordained by the character of the early works themselves. There, a barely disguised, if subconscious frustration with the limits of instrumental technique (that of the flute, the piano, the string quartet – even that of the normally-constituted symphony orchestra) was already prompting an urgent review of the nature of sound itself. More recently, a prevalent interest in non-European cultures, as well as the results of early experiments in electronic music, has led to a reconsideration of the function and specific quality of timbre as a constituent of musical expression.

If, at the beginning of Boulez's development as a composer, it had been true to say that he had inherited the fruits of a harmonic revolution considerably in advance of that of rhythm, by now the reverse was the case. The evolution of a rhythmic concept based on duration and no longer necessarily related to pulse had made way for the creation of textures of previously unthinkable complexity – textures in which the explanatory, motivic, function of duration-groups had already become subservient to that of their contributory role (as in the a-rhythmic intricacies of *Livre pour quatuor*, for instance). Meanwhile, in spite of intermittent experiments with the quarter-tone scale the concept of pitch remained absolute and largely unaltered and it was only now, with timbre being made to yield new combinations of sounds, that the musical distinction between pitch and noise came to be understood as no more than a description of the extreme limits of a wide range of richly expressive sound-mixtures.

These acoustic theories were explored in three large-scale orchestral works, all begun during the last two years of the 1950s: *Figures–Doubles–Prismes* (1958–64, still incomplete), *Poésie pour pouvoir* (1958 – originally planned as a work in several movements, of which only the first is extant), and *Tombeau* (1959–61, now the final section of *Pli selon pli*).

Figures–Doubles–Prismes
– the idea of form as the continuous development of overlapping harmonic areas related to contrasting textures.

Figures–Doubles–Prismes (Boulez's first purely orchestral work) started life as an eight-minute piece entitled simply *Doubles*, in which form it

173

was first performed in Paris in 1958; since then, it has grown to more than four times its original length, and still remains open-ended. The work is scored for a large array of chamber ensembles: three each of woodwind, four of brass and six of strings, disposed by the seating arrangements into three chamber orchestras – the first of which also contains harp and percussion, the second (without brass) harp and timpani, and the third harp, vibraphone, xylophone and celesta. This fragmentation of his symphonic forces allows the composer to promote antiphonal relationships between the three chamber orchestral groups, as well as to explore the characteristic timbres of the various chamber ensembles within the *tutti* orchestra. Boulez has said that the work resulted from a conscious attempt to create a large-scale work without reference to formal landmarks, so that the form of the piece stems entirely from the initial impetus of its opening bars. Once set in motion, the music gathers momentum through the snowballing effect of increasing complexity as each successive group of interleaved developments builds on the foundations of the last. On a metaphysical plane, the work could be thought of as able to continue its expansion into a timeless infinity; on a more down-to-earth level, such a form must eventually burn itself out in relation to the size and scope of the forces involved. But, since there are no inherent expectations in a self-perpetuating, evolutionary design of this kind, its end, though inevitable, can afford to be merely a stopping point . . . without the need to pave the way for a predictable finality. This means, of course, that the work (any work, written from a similar standpoint) can enjoy a perfectly valid existence even though its eventual 'end' is still not in sight.

In terms of its musical style, *Figures–Doubles–Prismes* is more relaxed in its willingness to absorb freely-associated influences than any work since the early Flute Sonatine. In fact, the influence of the Sonatine itself – with its emphasis on recurring chord formations and motivic figuration – is much in evidence here, as is the Stravinskian one of block developments based on quasi-ostinato chording. The piece owes much, too, to *Le marteau sans maître*, particularly in its extended development of the relationship between rhythm and tempo, duration and metrical time. With the exception of sections of the polyglot *Pli selon pli*, it is, moreover, the last work to evolve against a 'classical' background of a chronometric pulse until the recent *Rituel* . . . still more than sixteen years in the future.

In spite of its open-ended format, *Figures–Doubles–Prismes* also adopts limitations of a classical nature in the ternary succession of its interlocking developments – a threefold character that may be loosely defined as static and sustained, vertical and *non legato*, horizontal and *legato*. The first of these thematic characters is linked to a slow pulse, which may include scattered figuration derived from the regular or irregular subdivision of that pulse; the second to a much faster pulse, which translates irregular divisions of the beat into irregular bar divisions; and the third to a very fast pulse, characterized by extended groups of regularly-pulsed figurations spaced at irregular intervals. From this, it will be evident that the work as a whole marks a temporary retreat from further investigation of time in relation to space in spite of its concern with a spatial orchestration; also that, certain elements of *rubato* emphasis apart, it is content to explore its own particular means of setting up an on-going formal momentum *within* the bounds imposed by a chronometric beat.

Ex. 35

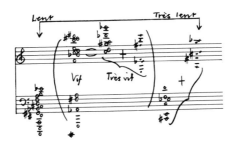

The slow first section also has an introductory function, since the exposition (and, indeed, later development) of the harmonic area(s) defined as *Lent – Très lent* includes, in parentheses, as it were, a passing reference to those later defined as *Vif* and *Très vif* (Ex. 35). The shape of this first section therefore acquires a ternary aspect of its own – *Lent→ (Vif→ Très vif)→ Très lent* – which thus anticipates the threefold nature, though not the proportions, of the work as a whole:

Lent – Très lent:	introduction (parallel + vertical/horizontal)
Vif:	theme 1 (vertical)
Lent – Très lent:	expansion of theme 1, gradually evolving into –
Très vif:	theme 2 (horizontal)
Lent – Très lent:	extended expansion of introduction
Très vif:	extended expansion of theme 2 – unfinished

For the first time in Boulez's career, the harmonic statement with which the work opens gives no hint of its melodic (row) origins. It is clear from the outset that any such thread has already been invisibly woven into the fabric of its harmonic derivations, and that the fundamental character of each of these harmonic areas and their relationship to one another is to provide the sole impulse for the logical progress of the entire work; moreover, that these harmonic characters are to retain their separate identities throughout, even though the extent and complexity of their expanding development is such as intentionally to blur these very distinctions – as the character originally specific to one harmonic area is allowed to infect that of another. The musical (and orchestral) design of the work as a whole accordingly traces a progression from extreme diversity to the all-embracing unity that would appear to be its eventual destiny.

The relatively confined range of the twelve-note chord with which the work opens (see Ex. 35) is itself an indication of an intrinsic aspect of its character – a character that is reflected in a similarly close-positioned spacing throughout the ensuing developments of its particular harmonic area. This area is a dense and mainly static one, whether the harmony is presented as a sustained chord (as for the duration of the opening *Lent*) or fragmented into ostinato repetitions; in either case, it continues to be phrased by canonic emphases that dictate the re-articulation of certain notes or groups of notes, as well as by its dynamic shaping. The more transparent basis of the complementary *Très lent* attracts reflected extensions of itself both vertically, in the form of overlapping chords, and horizontally, as disjunct fragments of a melodic recitative later to achieve conjunct expression through the increasing ornamentation of its development. The first brief reference to the pitch outlines of the *Vif* and *Très vif* areas (the specifically vertical/horizontal material) already touches on the particular identity of each: the first widely-spaced across the *tutti* orchestral register, the second contracted in both content and range (see Ex. 35). It also suggests the elasticity of a *rubato* that will allow successive expansions of the introductory *Lent – Très lent* to absorb more and more of the contrasting characteristics associated with the decorative developments of the *Vif* and *Très vif* (Themes 1 and 2).

A similar cross-fertilization of ideas is to affect both the expansion and the interaction of these two thematic characters themselves. Initially stated as absolute in their vertical or horizontal formation (as block chords or superimposed lines – Exx. 36 and 37), and couched in rhythmic terms that underline the separateness of their thematic identities, the later course of the work directs the development of each towards the influence of the other.

The symmetrically-tiered tempo changes (crotchet = 126/112/144/112/126) of the vertical material – Theme 1 – endorse the quasi-symmetrical curve suggested by the ternary shape of the introduction (crotchet = 96 → (112 → 144) → 84) and so confirm the arithmetical relationships on which the whole pulse of the work is to depend. Once

176

Ex. 36

Ex. 37

stated, the vertical theme is developed within the mean tempo of crotchet = 112, expanding its original phrase-lengths into paragraphs punctuated by pauses. The extended registration of the initial chord denoting its particular harmonic area (see Ex. 35) presupposes the continuing *tutti* nature of its instrumentation – whether in terms of the full symphony orchestra (as in its expositionary statement – Ex. 36) or of the antiphony later developed between the three chamber orchestras.

Just as the extended harmonic registration of the original vertical material – Theme 1 – had presupposed its continuing association with the full gamut of the tutti orchestral register (of both pitch and timbre), so now the narrow range of the original horizontal statement (see Ex. 35) is expressed within the limitations (of both pitch and timbre) imposed by one or more of the various chamber ensembles. Thus, the first, long-delayed intrusion of the winding ostinato figuration characteristic of the horizontal material – Theme 2 – is confined to the middle-register placing and uniform timbre of a trio for violins (Ex. 37). Spanning outwards from this point, and gathering further instrumental support with each developing appearance, the horizontal Theme 2 completes its invasion of the vertical Theme 1 when the mass of chamber ensembles eventually includes all sections of the *tutti* orchestra.

Figures–Doubles–Prismes would seem to mark a cross-roads on the long journey of self-(re)discovery that was to lie ahead for Boulez. Although perhaps too slow to unfold to rank among his best works even presuming its eventual completion, the piece will continue to fascinate for the sheer virtuosity of its invention, as well as for its explanatory position on the threshold of a future still haunted by a fading echo of the past.

Indeed, the very scale of its development makes it reminiscent of an orchestral study in the traditional grand manner, and the generosity of its expressive gestures certainly makes for closer comparison with the climactic developments of Piano Sonata No. 2 than with *Le marteau sans maître*. Nevertheless, its importance for the future is obvious: by virtue of its existence, *Figures–Doubles–Prismes* is proof of the previously untested possibility of maintaining the progress of a large-scale work without recourse to melodic characterisation.

Poésie pour pouvoir
– *the testing of variable tempos and instrumental timbres as a means of creating more flexible forms.*

Having established the vast ground plan for *Figures–Doubles–Prismes* (whose actual composition was to span the next six years), Boulez was free to adopt a much more specific attitude towards the contemporary *Poésie pour pouvoir*. This was originally planned as the first movement of a much longer work for orchestra and an electronic tape derived from the words of poems by Henri Michaux, hence the title. As it now stands, *Poésie pour pouvoir* is a single short piece for orchestra alone, or rather, for three differently-weighted orchestras. But the fragmented orchestration of *Figures–Doubles–Prismes* had been devised as a means of modulating the space (defined by pitch, dynamics and articulation, as well as by timbre) occupied by each of its harmonic characters. The tripartite division of the instrumental forces in *Poésie pour pouvoir*, on the other hand, is used to emphasize the complex durational relationships that result from the successive, overlapping or simultaneous encounter of a number of differently-paced events, relative to the space of time in which they occur.

This denotes a return to the notion of tempo as the controlling element of musical form – as already asserted in *Le marteau sans maître*, but largely ignored (except in terms of a more conventionally-paced *rubato*) in the arithmetically-related pulsations of *Figures–Doubles–Prismes*. But, whereas *Le marteau sans maître* had explored the modulatory possibilities of tempo as an expressive quality, *Poésie pour pouvoir* takes the fact of variable tempos as its central thesis. Visually, this fact might best be described in terms of the relationships between two 'travelators' or walkways, moving in opposite directions, at speeds which may be similar or dissimilar, variable or constant – and between the pedestrians who move on and off those walkways and who, meanwhile, may stand still, or walk forward at a regular or variable pace and who may, in addition, vary the length and duration of each stride in relation to the surrounding speeds of movement. In musical terms, such a situation is explored by means of the relationships between an accelerating or decelerating division of the unit of pulse (♩=♪, ♪♪♪, ♪♪♪♪, ♪♪♪♪♪ etc.) and the acceleration or deceleration of the tempo that controls that pulse.

Of the three orchestras involved here, the first and second are complementary in their solo/tutti formations: the first is a chamber orchestra of woodwind quartet, brass trio, string nonet (including a five-stringed bass), vibraphone and electric guitar, while the second includes the main woodwind (minus flutes) and brass groups, violas, double-basses, xylophone, timpani and percussion. The third orchestra – containing flutes, saxophones, two harps, celesta, strings and percussion – performs independently, with the assistance of a second conductor, falling in or out of step with the other two according to whether their relative speeds are diverging or converging, momentarily dependent or independent.

The concentrated *pianissimo* explosion of the opening bar consists of three superposed horizontal statements, which are immediatly contracted into a vertical chord, and the phrase is completed by a suggestion of the diagonal dimension arising from their combination (Ex. 38). This

Ex. 38

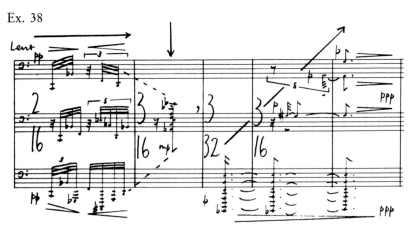

threefold proposition is in itself an exposition of the three aspects of tempo which form the subject of the piece: the horizontal being indicative of events moving forward in time, simultaneously, but independently of one another; the vertical relating to the marking of time in a rhythmic unison which may or may not involve forward movement; the diagonal suggesting the annihilation of time as a perceptible unit of measurement, so cheating time through the aural illusion of simultaneous acceleration and deceleration.

As a musical thesis on the nature of form expressed entirely in terms of the relationship between changing tempos, *Poésie pour pouvoir* has a particular interest; above all, perhaps, for the insight it gives into the character of a composer not only willing but eager to confine himself to such cramped conditions in order to explore a specific technique. As evidence of such a thesis being elaborated into a genuine means of musical communication, the piece is less successful. A concentrated de-characterization in the development of the basic material set out in the opening bars ultimately leaves the surface of the music too smooth as a meaningful expression of those very relationships it seeks to define; too smooth and, at the same time, too emphatic in the foreground detail of procedures (mirror-phrases and small-scale canonic distortions) that are too enclosed and complete in themselves to allow their wider relationship to the background structure of the piece to become an audible reality. Perhaps this is because the middle distance seems strangely unfocused in relation to a minute attention to foreground detail on the one hand, to background structure on the other. This blurred area was of no particular significance as it affected *Poésie pour pouvoir* itself – which now stands as an interim study on a specific and limited subject. Much more serious in implication were the signs of an increasingly introverted attitude to composition which seems, perhaps coincidentally, to have stemmed from about this point in time – an attitude that was to result in a widening of the communicative gap between background and foreground, form and content, and to drive the composer into an at times almost untenable position over the course of the next ten years.

Pli selon pli
   – contrasts in form: from the continuous evolution of melody, harmony and rhythm, to the composed 'splicing' of separate developments and the use of heterophony as a means of allowing for the free alignment of sections.

The five pieces for voice and orchestra, later collectively entitled *Pli selon pli – hommage à Mallarmé*, date variously from both before and after the two orchestral works discussed above. Two short settings for voice and chamber ensemble of sonnets by Mallarmé – *Improvisations sur Mallarmé I* and *II* – were the starting point for a much wider consideration of the linguistic innovations of Mallarmé's poetry, and of their possible implications in relation to the linguistics of new music. *Tombeau* for orchestra takes its title from another of Mallarmé's sonnets – that of the poet's own homage to Verlaine, whose death had taken place a year earlier; in Boulez's orchestral 'transcription', the actual words appear only retrospectively in a vocal recitative which forms the coda to the piece. While still engaged on the composition of *Tombeau*, it began to occur to him that its poetic derivations might be thought of as a commentary on the two earlier pieces and, with this in mind, he interrupted work on *Tombeau* in order to write a third *Improvisation*. *Improvisation III* extends the scoring of *Improvisations I* and *II* from single instruments to groups of similar instruments and, instead of the music setting the words, the form of the sonnet itself becomes a framework for the music. After this, *Tombeau* was completed in the knowledge that it was to form the mainly orchestral conclusion to the predominantly vocal *Improvisations* – by which time, it was evident that an introduction would be needed to balance the whole. The resulting *Don* (originally conceived for piano alone) was thus the only movement of the five to be composed specifically within the context of:

Pli selon pli – hommage à Mallarmé

> *Don* (1961–2)
> *Improvisation I* (1957)
> *Improvisation II* (1957)
> *Improvisation III* (1960)
> *Tombeau* (1959–61)

From this brief account of the history and origins of *Pli selon pli*, it is clear that it is a continuing development of the various styles that reflect Boulez's musical progress over the years 1957–62. For this reason, it would seem most logical to consider the five separate movements in order of their composition, rather than as they appear in the eventual context of the work.

The earliest of the five pieces – *Improvisations I* and *II* – seem to have been written at unusual speed, and with an unusually direct inspirational response to the poetic imagery of the words. Thus, the image of 'une dentelle s'abolit . . . enfui contre la vitre blême' (lace, blown by the wind, casts its whiteness in a window-pane) finds its musical counterpart in the choice of instruments for *Improvisation II*: harp, bells, vibraphone, piano and celesta were chosen for their twofold ability to produce the brittle 'glassiness' of short, damped sounds, and of allowing the harmony to suggest receding reflections of itself if the resonance is left to fade unchecked. And this visual image is enhanced by the 'lacy' melismas of both instrumental and vocal writing – just as the structural image (the strict rhyme-formation) of the sonnet itself is mirrored in the structure of the music. The less opulent surroundings of *Improvisation I* (harp, vibraphone and metal percussion) are infused with a similar imagery but now the whiteness is that of a winter landscape reflected in ice, with the passing vision of a phantom swan seeming to become the symbol of regret and, finally, of resignation. The haunting bleakness of this scene is captured in music that is almost entirely monodic and without harmonic colour. In the original, chamber music version, the soaring vocal line winds around the restricted number of pitches allotted to each melodic phrase, supported by no more than a ghostly shadow of its own

181

Ex. 39

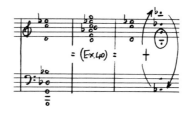

= (Ex.40) =   +

Ex. 40

Pas trop lent, très souple

A

Ex. 41

Très modéré

B

harmony; in the later orchestral version,[10] these harmonies are substantiated to the extent that their shadow takes on the reality of a continuous inflection of the melody.

At the opening of *Improvisation I*, the vocal line derives from the vertical statement of a seven-note chord (Ex. 39 – in itself a derivation of the now suppressed twelve-note row) which is immediately turned on its side to become a horizontal melody (Ex. 40). It is clear from the outset that the slow-moving harmony (whether vertically or horizontally exposed) is to progress through a series of evolutionary 'dissolves' as one seven-note chord fades into the next, closely related in interval structure. The mainly horizontal orientation of this (vocal) harmony necessarily places it mostly within the soprano register, so that each verse of the sonnet gives the impression of being set within the confines of a composed harmonic series from which the bass has been cut away; it is left to the instrumental interludes to re-confirm the missing area below the treble stave.

The harmonic character of the verse settings thus depends on an entirely melodic emphasis: it derives either from the relative dominance of each pitch in relation to a chosen root (A, Ex. 40 – see also Ex. 33, from *Le marteau sans maître*), or from repeating intervals which gradually explain themselves in terms of the chord of which they form a part (B, Ex. 41). Verses 1, 3 and 4 outline the harmony by the melodic

[10] For 3 harps, celesta, 2 vibraphones, glockenspiel, xylophone, mandoline, guitar, 2 flutes, 2 clarinets, 2 saxophones, 4 horns, violas, double-basses, and metal percussion

182

rotation relating to A; verse 2 (in the sonnet form, the developmental restatement of verse 1) develops it through the intervallic succession characteristic of B. The instrumental interludes re-define the essential duality of the basic material in terms of melody (X) which may 'acquire' harmony, and harmony (Y) which may imply melody (Ex. 42). The

Ex. 42

overall succession of verses and interludes gives the piece the form of an asymmetrical rondo (A, X, B, Y; A, X, [AB], A, Y), pulsed by an underlying percussive articulation which links the verse settings through the overlap of its independently recurring sequences (A,B,A,B).

Improvisation II develops this interdependence of melody and harmony into a much more complex set of relationships. Just as in *Improvisation I* the harmonic hierarchy of each chord was defined in terms of the proportional relationship (frequency of occurrence and duration) of each of its individual pitches, so now in *Improvisation II* the form of the piece itself derives from the fragmented proportions of its four main sections. Perhaps the cinematic analogy used to describe the harmonic 'dissolves' of *Improvisation I* will again provide the closest equivalent to the musical technique of 'cutting' from the interrupted development of one sectional character to that of another in *Improvisation II*.

The initial statements of each of these four sections defines them as different expressions of the relationship between tempo and harmonic content (or between time-space and pitch-space). At the opening, the regular pulsation of the instrumental A (Ex. 43) is given rhythmic shape through the irregular placing of the lines laid across it – lines whose imitative influences (Ex. 44) alternately expand into chords as a result of

Ex. 43

Ex. 44

Ex. 45

Ex. 46

Ex. 47

the resonance that envelops them, and contract into decorative punctuation (Ex. 45). The slower and more flexible metric outlines of B, verse 1, are clouded by grace-note inflections of the instrumental harmonies that mirror the melismatic contours of the vocal melody (Ex. 46). The percussive interlude, C (Ex. 47), reflects the hollow of musical zero ('aux creux néant musicien') so vividly evoked by the poet, in terms of the 'zero' harmony of left-over resonance – articulated by the zero rhythm of a repeated pulsation that is related to metrical pulse only by the continual distortion of its tempo through *accelerando/ritardando*. D hardly exists at this point, but finds its place later as a single extended cadence, confirming the complementary qualities of A and B. Verse 2 is set within the zero-tempo definition (*senza tempo*) of E which fractures verbal rhythm into syllabic duration so that the harmony is reduced to a static affirmation of the pitches contained by the indefinite time-span of the melody (Ex. 48). And grace-notes, always ambiguous in their relationship to both duration and tempo, now reject both, becoming merely a

Ex. 48

function of time. The main development of the piece is concerned with the gradual reconciliation of the two most extreme elements in its formal design: the pulsed time and impulsive harmony of A, and the zero time and static harmony of E. As the syllabic pronouncements of E become ever more widely spaced, they are overtaken by the greater momentum of the instrumental A – so that the bare melodic outlines of E begin to acquire decorative elements increasingly suggestive of the melismatic contours of B. This evolutionary development makes way for the final section (verses 3 and 4), which links the contrasting vocal styles of B and E by juxtaposing the two – a juxtaposition somewhat obscurely dictated by the feminine (B) or masculine (E) word endings of the sonnet rhyme formation.

The interaction of the various characters involved in the musical argument of *Improvisation II* is of such complexity (owing to the frequency of cutting from one to another) that the form of the piece can best be understood in terms of a retrospective summary of its evolution:

Introduction (verse 1): ABC(D)C
Development (verse 2): EA . . . . AC
Conclusion (verses 3 and 4): B(D)CEC – ABAE . . . . ACEBAC

In contrast with the entirely mellifluous harmonic environment of

Improvisation I, that of *Improvisation II* promotes sharper divisions between areas of greater or lesser consonance or dissonance: whole tones and minor 3rds, semitones and tritones are the predominantly formative intervals. In *Improvisation III*, the harmonic field is less explicitly defined. This is because the form of the piece depends on an extensive use of heterophonic alternatives needing to be more freely linked harmonically, as emphasized by the introduction of quarter-tones: these are precisely fixed in tuning on two of the three harps, conveyed as an expressive sharpening or flattening of the semitonal norm on wind, strings and by the soprano voice. And this, in turn, allows for semi(quarter)tonal clusters to function as pitch-complexes, whose harmonic role is defined (as with single pitches) by the interval(s) separating one from another – as well as, now, by the interval spanning their size. Nevertheless, the gradually emerging evidence of 4ths and 5ths as the strongest and most frequently recurring interval(s) – obvious because of their effectiveness as antidotes to the semitone – later gives the harmony a quasi-tonic centre around which to revolve its mainly static permutations.

There is now no attempt to reflect verbal images in musical ones, or even to 'set' the words themselves: only the first three lines of the poem appear at all and, even then, so distorted by syllabic extension as to be virtually sapped of meaning. Boulez has said that his aim was rather to make the sonnet *become* the music. This transformation of the words into music takes place at three different levels, in three different ways.

First, and most obviously, in terms of external shape: the four main sections of the piece correspond to the four verses of the sonnet, and the number of musical 'sequences' within each section to its characteristic fourteen-line (4433) formation. Secondly, in terms of mood: in 'A la nue accablante tu', the poet portrays nature as menacing and oppressive – the overwhelming pressure of clouds and rocks gives rise to the nightmare image of falling into a bottomless abyss, of drowning in 'the trailing whiteness of a siren's hair'. This oppression pervades the music through its unyielding harmonic succession, as well as through the choice of orchestral colour – which sets the hard, bright sounds of xylophones, harps, mandoline, guitar and percussion against the alluring entanglements of flutes, cellos, basses and trombone, linked by the intermediary chiming of celesta and bells. In this way timbre takes on a quasi-structural role as a means of suggesting initial conflict (the diverse solo material presented by the plucked and hammered instruments) and eventual resolution (the blown and bowed instruments of the *tutti* orchestra).

Thirdly, and most significantly, in terms of grammatical structure: Mallarmé's highly original use of language in relation to poetic form was to have a direct influence on Boulez's attitude to musical form during this whole period. In the poet's terms, once a word has been selected for its associative meaning within a particular context, it becomes a composed object, freely transposable, within the limits of communicable sense, in relation to other such verbal objects and to the overall structure of a poem. The composer, on the other hand, has to create his own 'words' – to identify the contextual meaning of his material – before reaching the poet's starting point. But, having done so, he may reasonably hope to promote a similar ambivalence in the relationship between musical language and form.

Boulez had already started to explore the possibilities of such structural transpositions in Piano Sonata No. 3, both by means of the alternative routes offered in *Formant 3, Constellation*, and by the transposable order of sections in *Formant 2, Trope*. And he was to pursue the verbal analogy still further in the free succession of formal components in *Domaines*, for clarinet and ensemble. But, however interesting these experiments may have been, and however necessary, as a staging-post during the search for new approaches to musical form, they were to have only an indirect influence on future developments. Unlike a word, a musical structure can evoke no associations until it is placed in the context of other such structures; so, neither can its contextual transposition in any way affect such associations, unless they have already been established ... in a previous performance, for instance? It is obvious that a single performance of any piece of music, however freely-routed, can only be understood as the definitive version of that piece – except by a listener who knows the work well enough to be able to recognize when his expectations are contradicted. Hence, the hoped-for freedom ends by becoming a burden to the composer – a message that can only be communicated to the performer. In any case, practical considerations brought about by the near impossibility of producing orchestral material that would allow for every alternative seem already to have dictated a definitive shape for *Improvisation III*.[11]

In spite of its origins in the essentially clear-cut form of the sonnet, the musical preoccupations of *Improvisation III* seem to include thematic implications too numerous and wide-ranging for the prescribed limits of a single short piece. These implications derive from four *Indicative* statements, first heard in succession, and then expanded into a series of overlapping sequences. At the outset, they are vividly contrasted, both in terms of musical syntax and of the formal consequences likely to derive from their very different attitudes to the measurement of time. The three harps are evidently to be 'indicative' of a homophony expressing the vertical division of pitch-space that will relate to tempo only through the bands of time spanning each of the ensuing sequences; the voice is necessarily concerned with the horizontal divisions indicative of

---

[11] As in the revised version, 1983 – see pp. 223–4

Ex. 49

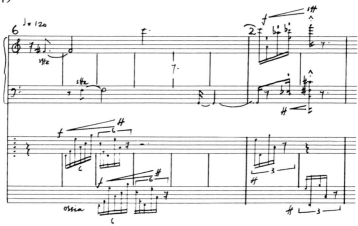

Ex. 50

monody, and this is expressed in durations that are clearly related to tempo though not to a metrical pulse. Mandoline, guitar and percussion, on the other hand, promote the strictly metrical definition of a tempo that underlines the contrapuntal associations of their linear dependence (Ex. 49), while the two xylophones are indicative of the interdependent harmony and metrically divergent tempo relationships characteristic of heterophony (Ex. 50). Thus, the contrast between time articulated by unspecified durations, and durations expressed within an unspecified time, could be described as overlapping characteristics of the variable articulation of time-space – just as the contrast between absolute monody, absolute homophony, could be defined in terms of the variable depth of pitch-space. Moreover, these *Indicatives* are themselves indications of tempo and, eventually, of time, since it is their rhythmic (and metronomic) characters that determine the time-spans of the various structural alternatives in relation to the eventual form of the piece. The contrasting characters of these *Indicatives* are upheld throughout the following sequences. Here, they are expanded at some length, now freely placed within periods of time measured by the whistling inflection of variable-pitch chord clusters placed high on piccolos, flutes and cellos in the upper register (Ex. 51). This time-measuring device introduces the

Ex. 51

suggestion of a quasi-harmonic dimension that links unequal divisions of pitch (through the curve of its slow *glissandi*) with unequal divisions of time (through the inaudible pulsation which 'counts' the span of its durations). And it is this harmonic dimension that emerges as the pivotal connection between the contrasts established during the first half of the piece and the increasing unity of the second. From this moment on, the music begins to turn its back on the diverse characters of the opening *Indicatives*, transforming their differences into the likenesses that derive from their mutual origins when they are later related to melody and harmony. Counterpoint and heterophony then start to coalesce into a percussive homophony (including the plucked instruments) which in turn articulates the progressive, metrical development of an orchestral polyphony (dominated by flutes and cellos) that eventually involves all the wind, all the strings.

Whether or not the dependent structural freedoms envisaged here are (could ever be?) a communicable factor in actual performance, they denote a reaction against the intensely concentrated development of the two preceding orchestral works that is real enough. They also represent an orchestral consolidation of the alternative routes followed by a single instrument in Piano Sonata No. 3 – a consolidation that is in itself a continuation of the search for a logical and final means of escape from the finite forms of the eighteenth century whose preliminary demolition had begun a decade earlier, in Piano Sonata No. 2. Other composers, less troubled by an intellectual conscience, may have reached this point sooner and with less effort; but to deny the known achievements of the past merely to grope haphazardly into an unknown future would have seemed to Boulez like a childishly misplaced courage, and certainly a waste of time. For him, the persistent pronouncements of John Cage served only to intensify the urgency of the need to find a means whereby the abstract notion of freedom dictated by chance could be made to influence the logical facts of a composition – in the search for which he was never content to rely on simple trial-and-error.

But the free-form achievements of *Improvisation III* and the preceding Piano Sonata had, perhaps inevitably, involved a temporary loss of freedom in the expressive development of the music. In order to prove that musical structures need not always be contained by a rigid frame, so long as each alternative is fully composed in terms of its possible conjunction with every other, the on-going development of both rhythm and harmony was, so to speak, held in abeyance, in favour of the development of form. In retrospect, the musico-social trends of the '50s and early '60s can be seen as having led to the weakening of a composer's traditional role – giving way to the establishment of an uneasy democracy based on an attempt at power-sharing between composer and performer (and even, in a few extreme cases, the audience). This atmosphere was certainly responsible for depriving Boulez of the means to express that aggressive commitment that is so basic a characteristic of his musical personality; so that he was, for a time, forced into the more and more fragmentary expression of material whose structural significance was to become increasingly veiled.

Less negatively, however, this whole period (from 1958 or so, until well into the '60s) can be viewed both as a logical outcome of earlier developments and as a necessary stage in the continuing quest for a twentieth-century renaissance. In this respect, it was inevitable that formal structure should now have to be considered on its own terms. Just as terms of reference had been evolved earlier on in relation to pitch and duration, form at last becomes a third dimension in its own right – the ultimate result of relating all aspects of serial organization to the wider perspective of time and space. The emphasis given to this third dimension in *Improvisation III* allows the wider time/space relationships of its 'indicative' characters to emerge as the narrative thread of the music, while the detailed internal development of rhythm and harmony is allotted a mainly static, descriptive role – giving the piece a feeling of suspended animation.

Tombeau, on the other hand, constitutes a much more detailed exploration of a correspondingly restricted area of research; in this respect, it has more in common with the stylistic unity and evolutionary progress of *Figures–Doubles–Prismes* than with the sectional developments of the three *Improvisations*. But, whereas the previous orchestral work branched outwards from a series of initiating chords, the branching developments of *Tombeau* are controlled from the central trunk of the harmony laid down in turn by each of the orchestral groups (excluding the brass) during its quintuple exposition – a harmony which continues to underpin the extended *tutti* development of its central section. As in *Figures–Doubles–Prismes*, the orchestra is again an ensemble of ensembles, but now on a much smaller scale (only thirty-eight players in all) and without the spatial emphasis of the earlier work. The six ensembles here consist of piano (an 'ensemble' of colour and register on its own); a mixed group of plucked and hammered instruments (two harps, celesta, vibraphone 1 and guitar); brass (horn, two trumpets and three trombones); woodwind (two flutes, cor anglais, three clarinets and bassoon); a hammered group of wood, skin and metal percussion (xylophone, timpani, bass drum, vibraphone 2, bells and gongs); and a group of solo strings (4.4.2.2.).

The poetic images of the sonnet are again concerned with the inevitability of fate: with the timeless indestructibility of wind-blasted rocks and crushing clouds, in whose embrace man must forever struggle to 'besilver the crowd' with his ephemeral creations. But, says the poet, hope revives in the works of such men as Verlaine, whose more enduring achievements are able to cheat the bleak finality of death by their vision of 'the peaceful oasis of a shallow stream' – as depicted by Boulez in the extended melismatic setting of 'un peu profond ruisseau calomnie la mort' (the last line of the poem and the only one actually quoted) in the vocal coda to the otherwise orchestral *Tombeau*.

Insofar as any verbal image can be said to influence the musical expression of *Tombeau*, it is reflected in the rock-like harmonic structure, and in the effectively contrapuntal developments that strive to free themselves in flights of creative fantasy. *Tombeau* is evidently a one-dimensional study of the self-perpetuating reflections of a single chord, and the monothematic character of the piece is underlined by the fact that the frenzied events that propel it are determinedly self-effacing in motivic significance (except insofar as they contribute to the character of contrasting textures). This agitated detail explodes against the background of an unyielding metrical pulse, which sinks through a prolonged *rallentando* from slow to very slow, following the gradual expansion of the controlling harmonic periods. The underlying tensions of the piece thus evolve between the regular pulse of a broadly-based harmonic succession and the impulsive nature and splintered rhythmic definition of its decorative derivations. Nevertheless, this is a debate which hinges on the certainty of its unruffled harmonic purpose – however elaborate the discontinuity of contrapuntal discussion that it provokes (Ex. 52).

The fact that all linear movement is here expressed in terms of the relationships between composite harmonic blocks defined by the particular timbre of each instrumental ensemble would seem to presuppose that each of the constituent ensembles should be 'equal' in relation to each other and to the *tutti* orchestra – and that differences in timbre should be sufficient, *per se*, to identify them. Ideally, timbre can be considered as a

Ex. 52

quality separable from considerations of instrumental weight, penetration and resonance; in practice, differences in timbre are often obliterated by the unavoidable dominance of certain instruments, or instrumental ensembles, over certain others. Neither can such imbalance be entirely compensated for by dynamics and articulation: it is obvious that the cutting *sffz* attack and relatively powerful resonance of vibraphone, piano or brass, for instance, cannot be equated with that of woodwind, harps, celesta and guitar, or with that of the 12 solo strings – at least, not by 'natural' means. However, while the limitations of the instruments themselves may temper the clarity of contrapuntal balance that is a *sine qua non* for the very existence of *Tombeau*, it is typical of Boulez that he should never have been content with the merely possible. In attempting to realize a dream (in *Tombeau*), he had sown the seeds of a future reality and, by 1972, the partial (electronic) solution to similar problems of balance – between instruments of similarly diverse character, though within a small group of soloists – had already begun to emerge (in '. . . *explosante-fixe* . . .' – see pp. 209ff.). In any case, the chordal theme of *Tombeau* remains untarnished throughout its progressive ramifications – even though its glittering textures may lose some of their virtuoso sheen in performance.

In shape, the piece divides into two balancing sections, plus the coda, which is evidently not only a conclusion to *Tombeau* itself, but an *envoi* to the cycle of *Pli selon pli* as a whole. The first of these sections is further subdivided into five statements of the chordal theme (see Exx. 53 and 54a), each defined by its particular instrumentation and rhythmic articulation, and each becoming progressively longer, more complex, and more emphatic. These five variations explore the harmonic personality of the chord by means of its characteristic interval structure. Beginning with the simplest possible unfolding of its harmonic content as a series of absolute pitches (such as might be likened to a traditional twelve-note row, though no longer bound by a fixed melodic rotation), it quickly becomes clear that the reason for the changing coincidence and register of these pitches is to establish the identity of the chord through a 'composed' analysis of its bias in favour of certain intervals (Ex. 53). The first variation, then, is outlined by the shadowy harmony stated by the

Ex. 53

Ex. 54

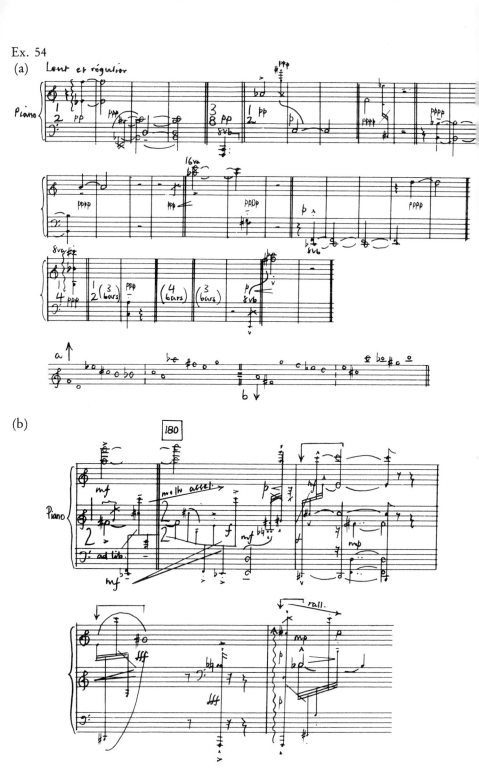

piano, with its corresponding echo sustained by each of the other orchestral ensembles in turn (Ex. 54a). The register and range of each succeeding variation is similarly dictated by a particular ensemble, which not only initiates the shape of each variant of the original chord (by fixing each of its pitches within a given register), but also controls its duration. This ordering of the control-groups (first the hammered percussion ensemble, then the woodwind, followed by the strings) gradually increases the range of each harmonic proposition, matching the increasing length and textural complexity of each succeeding variation until, in variation 5, the mixed ensemble of harps, vibraphone, celesta and guitar achieves the sense of climax foreshadowing the end of the first section by transposing the harmony up a major 3rd (Ex. 54b).

Not until the second section does this ostinato harmony start to incorporate remote reflections of itself in an extended *tutti* development. This subsists in a shimmering web of trills and tremolos which sustain an unbroken continuity by functioning as pedal-point focuses for the surrounding deviations (Ex. 55). The entire second section is an extended

Ex. 55

variation + restatement of the five variations that form the first section – not only in terms of its continuing (and continuous) harmonic development, but in terms of the various textural rhythms occurring earlier as a succession of events, and which are now developed simultaneously within the tutti ensemble of ensembles.

The unmeasured recitative of the coda seems a strangely alien, even incidental, conclusion to the canonically-inspired rhythms and articulative detail of the main body of the piece. But its recapitulatory function in relation to the cycle as a whole is obvious: it not only completes the circle of *Pli selon pli* (literally, the last chord of *Tombeau* = the first chord of *Don* – Exx. 56 and 57), but suggests the epitome of the stylistic conflict between durational control and quasi-improvisatory freedom that is the essence of the work.

Don reveals its introductory function in the fluid presentation of its anticipatory material as well as in its instrumental character. It is the only one of the five movements to be scored for full symphony orchestra of

Ex. 56

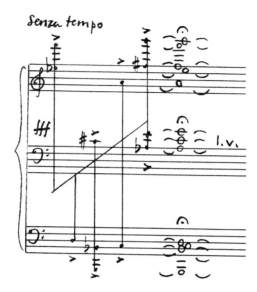

Ex. 57

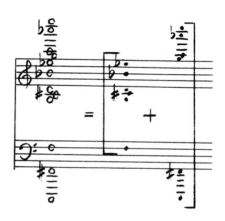

more or less normal proportions, [12] as the tutti scoring of the opening bars at once shows. Nevertheless, it soon becomes clear that its purpose is to forecast the orchestral timbres characteristic of the succeeding movements by allowing the solo qualities of the 'percussive' instruments used in the three *Improvisations* gradually to surface from the continual realignment of the instrumental forces within this tutti orchestra. It is as if the *sffz* attack of the opening chord had effectively shattered the orchestra into as many isolated fragments as it has instrumental constituents –

[12] Woodwind 4.1.3.1; brass 4.3.2; strings 4.4.5.3; 3 harps, celesta, mandoline, guitar, 2 vibraphones, timpani, bells, glockenspiel – together with a large percussion section requiring 7 players in all

fragments which then coalesce into small groups, only to drift apart and re-form into other such groups. This kaleidoscopic permutation of orchestral colour is matched by an equal mobility in the permutation of harmonic blocks, which float freely in relation to one another until fixed in place by the decision of a particular performance – at which moment they may emerge as conjunct or disjunct, as overlapping in succession or superposed. Such permutational mobility is, of course, an extension of the antiphony explored earlier in relation to timbre (*Figures–Doubles–Prismes*) and to tempo (*Poésie pour pouvoir*), recast from the experience of the heterophonic relationships of Piano Sonata No. 3 and the third *Improvisation* from *Pli selon pli* itself. But the actual structure of *Don* is more classically orientated – even though its character derives from relationships between harmonic duration and tempo, presented as an atmospheric study in timbre.

At first, very slow-moving, widely-spaced harmonies are dispersed irregularly across the changing orchestral spectrum, sustained at the lowest possible dynamic level, and gently impelled by occasional shimmers of movement induced by *pizzicati*, trills, tremolos and arpeggiated chords. A new paragraph introduces a suggestion of urgency by contracting these harmonic blocks, thus accelerating their rate of succession, and by subdividing the orchestra into smaller, more soloistic units. Later still, the hint of an underlying pulsation is evoked by the barely perceptible attacks and slow-fading resonances of the piano. This leads to the introduction of quotations from *Improvisation III* (characterized in turn by xylophones, harps, celesta and bells, mandoline and guitar, flutes and strings), which are flashed like still pictures against the moving screen of time measured by the continuity of harmonic succession outlined on the keyboard.

These defiant contradictions of the rarified atmosphere of the opening, and of the continuing serenity of the background harmonies, are themselves abruptly silenced by the brutal intervention of two up-beat chords, which cancel the wayward perorations of the previous section with a return to the *tutti* scoring (woodwind, brass, percussion and strings) and unison rhythm suggested in the opening bars. The whole central chapter of the piece is concerned with the development-by-disintegration of this unison, now confirmed as the destined outcome of the opening recitative. As the rhythmic grip gradually loosens its hold, the orchestral colours re-dissolve, and the close succession of short blocks characteristic of the first section now alternates with their tutti superposition. The suspended harmonies previously outlined on the piano are here focused on the strings, blended with the sympathetic resonance of unpitched percussion, and the solo interruptions are transferred to the soprano voice, so allowing for the rhapsodic intervention of reminiscences from *Improvisations III, II* and *I*. The coda translates the unmeasured tempo of the opening into a measured *rubato* derived from contrasting the unattached durations of the first section with the tighter, properly rhythmic formations of the central unison – a thematic character that is finally recast in terms of the antiphonal relationships arising from the free alternation of two stable orchestral groups: woodwind and horns (plus xylophones, harp and bells), strings, trumpets and trombones (plus piano, vibraphones and gongs).

Don, then, owes its existence to its particular place in the context of *Pli selon pli* as a whole, so that its consciously stylised, quasi-symmetrical format would seem to be an instinctive reflection of its contextual function as the beginning of a work which also has a middle and an end. It is therefore as dependent on its surroundings as the other movements are self-contained and independent of each other, and it is this dependence that permits (or cannot prevent?) a last, nostalgic appraisal of recapitulation as a means of structural reference.

Domaines
 – a new approach to the variation of rhythmic motifs, combining quasi-classical techniques with a free ordering of the related elements.

As an interim work of polyglot origins and varying objectives, *Pli selon pli* could not, of itself, point to any one stylistic direction. On the contrary: the latter stages of its composition show an increasingly subjective turmoil – particularly so in the 'withdrawn' personality and uncharacteristic rhythmic inertia of sections of both *Improvisation III* and *Don*. At this point, Boulez took what was, for him, an unprecedented decision. Instead of embarking on another large-scale work, or returning to wrestle with the unfinished *Figures–Doubles–Prismes*, he decided on the dangerously revealing step of preparing to open his compositional notebooks to public view – in the compendium of thumbnail sketches that constitute *Domaines*, for clarinet and ensemble (1961–66).

Like the earlier *Structures*, Book I, this is a composed realization of a number of intellectually-calculated procedural possibilities. But, whereas *Structures* had been mainly concerned with the ordered (serial) permutation of pitch and duration, together with an equivalent ordering of the secondary, expressive qualities of dynamics and attack, *Domaines* is a series of studies in rhythmic development. Like that of *Le marteau sans maître*, the compositional continuity of *Domaines* is disguised in the discontinuity of its performance. A discontinuity which now depends on the choice of route made firstly by the clarinettist (in presenting the original material), secondly by the conductor (in connection with its mirrored recapitulation) – with additional choices to be made within each section, or *cahier*.

The eventual form of the piece, no matter what the chosen route, is that of variations of variations. All its essential material is contained in the six *cahiers* (A–F) of music for solo clarinet, reflected, in reverse, in six corresponding mirror versions. Since this material is complete in itself, as a fragmented set of developing variants, the piece can evidently exist as a clarinet solo, even though a somewhat cryptic one. Additionally, each *cahier* may be reinforced by an instrumental group of from one to six players: bass clarinet; marimba and double bass; oboe, horn and guitar; four trombones; flute, trumpet, saxophone, bassoon and harp; string sextet. These groups initially react to each of the solo originals, and later take the initiative which prompts the mirrored reply; each ensemble presents a considerably more expanded and continuous variation on one or more of the variants suggested by the clarinet, and each has its corresponding version of its own original – not now a mirror image, but a continuation, or mirrored development.

Detailed cross-references abound throughout, both within the clarinet part itself, and between it and the instrumental responses. The various possibilities of rhythmical development summarized on p. 136 are nowhere more clearly illustrated than in *Domaines*. Take, for instance, the randomly-chosen example of *cahier* E, in which the clarinet is linked with the trio of oboe, horn and guitar. Developmental processes are at first disguised by their fragmentary disposition in the clarinet part: telescoped into the shortest possible space of time, they are heard as a tantalising succession of asymmetrical likenesses (Exx. 58 and 59) which can only be understood as a catalogue of events yet to unfold or in the mirrored recapitulation, as a reminder of events just past. It is left to the instrumental sections to develop the multiplicity of implied relationships, and to explain the purpose of their asymmetrical distortions (derived from the regular or irregular expansion or contraction of phrase-lengths by the addition or subtraction of dots, by the translation of rational into irrational values, sound into silence, and vice versa – see Ex. 58) within the balanced symmetry of a wider sentence structure (Exx. 60, 61 and 62).

Without pretensions to any overall formal design, these miniature inventions achieve a spontaneous characterization that had recently seemed in danger of disappearing from the large-scale pieces. In many ways, they represent an act of real courage on the part of a composer previously noted for his extreme reluctance to explain the steps taken to arrive at the completion of any of his own works – although the fact that this collection of subjectively-inspired musical jottings, made over five years or more, was eventually allowed to see the light of day was probably occasioned more by external pressures (to prove that the years of silence had not been entirely unproductive) than by any specific intention on Boulez's part. Whatever the reason, its presentation as a definitive work seems to have started a revival of that explosive necessity

Ex. 58

Ex. 59

to compose that had generated the enthusiasm and passionate intensity of the earlier works – a necessity that had seemed during the intervening years to have become something of an onerous duty.

Éclat; Éclat/Multiples
  – the extension of variation technique, with motivic procedures now used to define different aspects of time.

The origins of *Éclat* would seem to have been equally sporadic, although more evidently related to an eventual context from the outset (if not at first foreseen in the entirety of *Éclat/Multiples* – 1965–9, unfinished). Indeed, a very similar approach to the process of composition would appear to have been the starting point: ideas are allowed to proliferate, seemingly by free association and as if a new confidence enabled Boulez to admit that first thoughts should not automatically have to account for their existence in relation to every aspect of an overall plan. But, if the attitudes that inform the two works are similar in this respect, the end results are very different. *Domaines* achieves its breakthrough from an application of 'academic' disciplines, imposed from without, as a spark to its particular inventiveness; *Éclat*, without such models to lean on, derives its disciplines from within. If the former may be compared to a line-drawing in black and white the latter becomes an impressionistic study in colour, the former as detailed in its rhythmic derivations as the

. 60

. 61

x. 62

latter is fluid and boldly-gestured. Both, however, derive from small-scale variations whose cumulative effect *is* the eventual form – that of *Domaines* centering freely around its 'set' pieces, that of *Éclat* resulting from the predetermined succession of its events (though not of its structural details).

When speaking of *Éclat*, however, there are at least two separate works to be considered. The first – *Éclat* itself – is a ten-minute piece for the much favoured ensemble of piano, celesta, harp, glockenspiel, vibraphone, mandoline, guitar, bells and, for the first time, cimbalom; the additional presence of a sextet of wind and strings (alto flute, cor anglais, trumpet, trombone, viola and cello), used briefly to colour the harmony at the opening, and to more obvious motivic purpose in the coda, is only fully explained in the context of the second, larger work: *Éclat/Multiples*. This is a vast work-in-progress, planned as a hugely-detailed orchestral development of the chamber ensemble variations of *Éclat* – a development in which each instrument of the original sextet will, in turn, call on support from a whole section of such instruments. However, the existence of the orchestral work in no way invalidates that of the chamber music piece as a separate entity; in any case, *Éclat/Multiples* will itself consist of a number of separable entities, each characterized by one of the orchestral groups in question (of which only the first is so far complete).

Éclat opens with an unashamedly dramatic gesture, whose initial ascent is founded on chords matched in pairs by their characteristic intervals (Ex. 63), and whose torrential descent uncovers the intervals additionally

Ex. 63

to be found within their paired superposition. These same chords are then given a properly harmonic identity in an improvisatory piano cadenza of unprecedented rhythmic simplicity: a single unit of pulse (♩.♪♪), together with a single articulative contrast (between the extremes of *legato* and *staccato*) allows for each harmonic feature to express the natural curve of its internal structure in terms of dynamics and tempo (Ex. 64). This irregular surging gradually subsides as the intervals extracted from the chord are restored to their rightful place in the harmonic spectrum. The keyboard preamble is then thrown open to the rest of the ensemble – a composite timbre which effectively suggests a heightening of the already complex timbres of the piano itself – and the improvisatory pulse-control of the opening yields to the time-control of improvised durations. In

Ex. 64

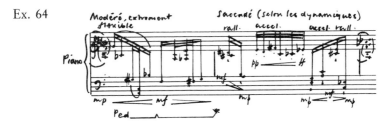

other words, the durational passage of time is now determined solely by the space required for each particular chord formation, according to the subjective judgement of the performers – a subjectivity that is not perceptibly affected when, in the harmonic nadir of the note-by-note central section, durations are governed only by their relative proportions. The pulsed tempo initiated in the piano cadenza does not recur until the re-entry of the orchestral sextet (Ex. 65) in a passage leading to the final cadence of *Éclat* itself, when it reflects the shape of the opening bars in reverse, and so abruptly revives the argument that is to become central to the continuing orchestral development of *Éclat/Multiples*.

This is an argument that revolves around contrasting bands of time: strict time, controlled by pulse, free time, outlined by improvised durations, and time that is proportionately free within periods measured by surrounding pulsation. In addition, all these bands of time continue to be affected by the elasticity of tempo that is an integral expression of the harmony described in the opening cadenza. At first clearly separate in function, each of these time bands gradually absorbs more and more of the features of the others until, at the height of its development, their differences are all but obliterated as the music starts to make its way backwards. The various steps are now retraced in reverse order, but in the greatly altered circumstances of a continuing development in which the argument of extreme contrast has relaxed into a more continuous discourse.

Once past the jagged scenery and bright colours of the original *Éclat*, the vast panorama of its 'multiples' casts more flickering shadows, blending the sharp contrasts characteristic of the percussive ensemble into the mellower environment provided by the soft-spoken violas, coupled with the matching tone-quality of a single basset horn. Each new tutti group is likewise to be partnered by a member of the single reed clarinet family (omitted from the original sextet for this purpose) chosen, for its similarity of range and tone colour, to act as instrumental liaison between each *tutti* section and the solo sextet.

The essential character of *Éclat/Multiples* derives its intense energy from self-perpetuating rhythmic cells that continually reproduce their own likenesses in the changing circumstances of their environment, and the sinewy strength of the music lies in the very circumscription of its

Ex. 65

Ex. 66

Ex. 67

Ex. 68

developments – in its refusal to admit the intrusion of any expression extraneous to its central purpose. Even in its present incomplete state, it is evident that *Éclat/Multiples* is to be a detailed survey of the technical means used to derive the widest possible implications from a 'multiplication' of the smallest motif. Perhaps the almost superhuman size and scope of such a project makes it doomed to remain open-ended, although it is certain that designs for its eventual completion already exist. But composers of Boulez's calibre do not stand still, and it may be that plans for various unfinished projects have even now been superseded by the developments of more recent works. Even if that should prove to be the case, the imaginative scope of this already vast canvas, and the sheer inventiveness that enables each limited development to sustain its logical impetus throughout such long paragraphs, is indeed extraordinary – the more so, since there is no suggestion here of the recurring foundation harmony that underpinned the implied counterpoints of *Tombeau*. Instead, the progress of the music depends on a quasi-baroque decoration of its almost entirely linear structure: that is, the rhythmic contours characteristic of a particular section are thickened by unison chording derived from the prevailing harmonic intervals (Exx. 65 and 66) which in turn are decorated by splintered linear reflections of themselves (Exx. 67 and 68).

The present form of *Éclat/Multiples* is clearly an evolutionary one; nevertheless, each of its 'variations' is independent of the others and complete in itself, so that the design of each tutti section and of the work as a whole is evidently to evolve from the sum of its individual parts. Ultimately, this loose-knit structure may prove an obstacle to the understanding of its broader intentions, especially over such considerable periods of time (the piece already lasts more than half an hour); even so, during the testing years following *Pli selon pli*, this marking time in relation to exterior form was the best possible means of sustaining the flow of ideas stemming from a more detailed, interior organization, particularly that of rhythm. In any case, it had the positive effect of allowing rhythmic processes to re-occupy the foreground of the music and of re-admitting the notion of figurative rhythm as a life-giving force with its own separable existence. (The parlour-game test, involving the recognition of rhythmic shapes divorced from pitch, would immediately prove the point.) Once again, and not only in Boulez's case, rhythmic evolution would seem to have lagged behind that of harmony, to have taken longer to re-establish a functional identity in the 'non-hierarchical distribution of space'. Certainly, the free-form obsessions of the late 1950s and early '60s precluded anything approaching motivic development, so that rhythm was content to hide behind duration – with differently-paced textures then the sole means of harmonic propulsion.

Inevitably, this led to a featureless impasse, and to withdraw from it necessarily implied admission of defeat; so that the stand taken by *Domaines* was to prove all-important in preparing the ground for the more positive assertions of *Éclat/Multiples*.

This rhythmic renewal was absolutely vital to Boulez at a time when his very survival as a composer had seemed threatened by an increasing suppression of personality, which amounted, almost, to a denial of his own rhythmic identity – the result of a progressive ironing-out of all traces of that compulsive energy earlier seen as the vital force of his inspiration. But the removal of successive layers of character-disguising camouflage, applied over the years since *Le marteau sans maître*, was not to be completed during the course of a single work, not even of a work as comprehensive in the scope of its developments as *Éclat/Multiples*.

e.e. cummings ist der Dichter
– *the reintroduction of harmony as a quasi-thematic basis for development.*

Meanwhile, a brief work for voices and instruments was less concerned with taut, rhythmic developments than with the placing of harmonic developments in relation to time and space. Like the two *Improvisations* of a decade earlier, *e.e. cummings ist der Dichter* (1968) was conceived and completed within a relatively short period and, as with the Mallarmé pieces, the words themselves would appear to have fired an unusually immediate musical response. Not, in this case, so much a response to verbal imagery (although the idea of 'birds . . . inventing air' and of 'twilight's vastness' does infect the music) as to typographical design and to the use of split syllables as expressive sonic entities, separable from their verbal context. In this sense, Cummings is evidently heir to Mallarmé's verbal transpositions, and his syllabic imagination is in exact accord with Boulez's own use of severed syllables to abstract the meaning from Mallarmé's poems in *Improvisation III* and in the quotations at the end of *Don*.

However, *e.e. cummings ist der Dichter* stems initially from a classical melodic emphasis quite foreign to either of the above; it takes up the thread of an evolutionary phrase-development, as in *Domaines*, but now set within a finite form which enlarges on the structural implications of *Improvisation II*. Like *Improvisation II*, *e.e. cummings ist der Dichter*[13] is cast in a single movement, which nevertheless reflects the four divisions indicated by the typographical design of a poem whose syllabic elements

[13] Scored for woodwind (flute, 2 oboes, 2 cors anglais and bassoon), brass (2 trumpets, 3 horns and 2 trombones), 3 harps, strings (1.3.3.1) and a mixed chorus, of which the female voices are used in the opening paragraph

206

become more and more dispersed until, in the last 'verse', sense can be gleaned only from the context of the whole.

So, too, with the music, which proceeds from the harmonic cohesion of its opening section, to the harmonic dispersal of its conclusion. And, just as the various verbal elements which make up the poem derive continuity from the words of which they form a part, so the diversity of the music derives its meaningful unity from the 'theme' of its central harmonic core (literally, in the final section, where the harmony is sustained throughout as a high flying pedal).

An evenly-paced exposition of the *legato* melodic contours revealed by the opening harmony (Ex. 69) quickly evaporates into a scattering of harmonic syllables, as the men's chorus lapse from the unison chording of the opening into a *staccato* utterance that includes the percussive punctuation of unpitched speech. However, just as the syllabic discontinuity of the poem is more apparent to the eye than real, so with the apparent disorientation of the dispersed harmony. In fact, this free, rhapsodic development (now phrased in terms of the greater or lesser degree of regularity with which events are spaced in time) is spliced on to the continuity of the melodically-shaped opening. This creates the illusion of two simultaneous developments, each of which, in turn, is cut away to reveal the other (in a manner evidently related to the 'cutting' technique employed in *Improvisation II*). A similar duality of expression is carried over into the third section. Here, harmonic connections are restored in the form of sustained *tutti* chords, whose *pianissimo* duration is determined by the movement of individual vocal lines within each constituent two- or three-note group (Ex. 70), and the now *fortissimo* interruptive element develops a quasi-rhythmic ostinato patter, comprising the 'percussive' pitch of rapid, *staccatissimo* chording and syllabic speech. In the final section, the various time-measuring characteristics of the piece are co-ordinated within the overall duration of a single sustained chord (voices and strings), whose internal rotations are so widely spaced as to have abandoned the original pulsed emphasis of Ex. 70, and whose pedal-point function now reflects the opposite, static image of the paced harmony of the opening bars. The *legato* melodic shapes initially revealed by this harmony are here entwined (on the wind) with their more rapid, *staccato* development, and freely placed within the shorter time spans defined, as earlier, by the greater or lesser degree of regularity in the spacing of the events (on the harps) which mark such periods.

This conglomerate layering of differently-paced events, each of which has now succumbed, as it were, to the influence of the others (see also, though in a very different context, the last movement of *Le marteau sans maître*), gives rise to a textural rhythm that creates its own impulsion, entirely without reference to chronometric time. The musical progress of *e.e. cummings ist der Dichter* is thus immediately concerned with the

Ex. 69

Ex. 70

progressive transformation of pulse into the eventual 'polyphony' of variously characterized time measurements. At a distance, it can be seen as an almost autobiographical reflection of the progressive developments in Boulez's musical thinking during this period: developments that were soon to explode in the creative revival of the 1970s.

'... explosante-fixe ...'
– the achievement of a network of audible derivations.

This revival seems to have been sparked off by a commission from *Tempo* magazine, when Boulez was asked to write a brief musical tribute (as one of a series of such tributes by sixteen composers) to the memory of Stravinsky on the anniversary of his death. Instead of contributing a short piece, he submitted the matrix for such a piece, entitled (after a half-remembered quotation from André Breton – '... la beauté sera explosante-fixe, ou ne sera pas ...') '... *explosante-fixe* ...'. This consisted of a seven-note 'row' and six variants, or *transitions* (numbered II–VII), which pursued a gradual development, via inversion and transposition, from the single line of the original to the seven lines of Transition VII. These lines were characterized by a scale of dynamics which offered a choice of from one to seven alternative levels (ranging from *pppp* to *f*) and by seven different types of *rubato*, linked to changes in articulation. At this stage, the rhythmic character of the material was outlined in unattached motivic fragments expressing the relationship 1:2:3, the notation and actual duration of which would be determined by the tempo indicated by four different speeds (ranging from very fast to moderately slow):

This sevenfold description of the matrix was to be realized by seven instruments (or instrumental groups), first proposed to consist of two flutes, two clarinets, two violins and harp. Using these instruments, a ten-minute realization of the piece was performed for the first and only time shortly after publication of its matrix in 1972 – a preliminary version that was quickly superseded by the composition of the definitive '... *explosante-fixe* ...' (1972–4). This is scored for a mixed sextet of flute, clarinet, trumpet, violin, viola, cello and the composite pair, vibraphone/harp. These instrumental sounds are then qualified by electronically-induced distortions of timbre (including the quantity-control of dynamic balance), calculated in advance and reproduced by computer during each performance.

'... *explosante-fixe* ...' shows such a startling advance in compositional freedom from the creative bondage and partial stalemate of the previous ten years that its achievement must have seemed more than sufficient recompense for the struggles of the 1960s. For, with the exception of the

209

first two *Improvisations* from *Pli selon pli* (and discounting the works known to have been partly completed before being withdrawn), all the music written since *Le marteau sans maître* would seem to form part of a quest: each work directs its explorations towards a different place on the same horizon, but none, until now, had attained that long-sought vantage point of a truly panoramic view. All the visionary ideas on expanding networks of harmonic and rhythmic relationships, as well as on the articulative purpose of dynamics, timbre, and, above all, tempo, as the eventual ingredients of an 'exploding' form – all these ideas are here triumphantly included in a true network of expressive relationships, whose individual parameters are no longer separable.

Whatever the changes that have taken place during the thirty years of Boulez's career as a composer, the one factor that has remained constant as a characteristic feature of the music is his treatment of harmony, which has remained largely unaltered in kind, however marked the differences in its application or derivation. This reflects a single-minded confidence lacking in many of his European contemporaries, a number of whom have succumbed to the comforting lure of harmonic *objets trouvés* gleaned from the past. However, the fact that Boulez has never betrayed his own harmonic character is evidence not only of strength of purpose, but of the fact that, for him, this particular temptation has never existed (even though the instant, if ephemeral public acclaim enjoyed by the more obvious novelties of this latter day neo-classicism may perhaps have made him wish that it had).

This harmonic security derives from an ability to create a seemingly endless proliferation of ideas within a clearly defined field of action, so that the intervallic character of an original harmonic area remains an audible reality, however remote its derivations. And this reality is the one constant feature underlying the temporary uncertainties of the '60s, even when he did not entirely avoid the temptation to expand harmonic implications to the verge of 'clustered' obscurity. So it is that harmony is the single force that finally absorbs all parameters as an extension of itself in '... *explosante-fixe* ...', a work whose textural fantasy is inspired by a free amalgam of all the procedural devices developed during the preceding years, not excluding the element of chance.

In fact, chance is allotted a major role as an expressive determinant in '... *explosante-fixe* ...', but now in the more subtle guise of the 'hazard' of true interpretation. Gone is the notion of choice (of dynamics, articulation, even structural route) as a means of attempting to create the fantasy of the unforeseeable through the medium of the performer who, in any case, is embarrassed, more often than not, by such unsought creative responsibility. In its place, the much more telling fantasy of interpretative expression is a natural consequence of the restoration of functions proper to creative composer and recreative performer.

Each of the seven instrumental parts that contribute to the free-flowing texture of '*... explosante-fixe ...*' is a virtuoso solo, played independently, and linked to the other six only through the relative placing in time of each of its 'transitional' variants (a placing determined by the director of each performance in relation to his control of the computerized timbral *espressivo*). Thus, while the tempi which characterize these sections are themselves variable within bands of metronomic definition (from the *Très lent* of the *Originel* to the *Très rapide* of Transition VII), their actual speeds become the ultimate responsibility of each performer in relation only to his own part. And it is the interaction of these individual decisions which makes chance a formative element in the creation of an overall interpretative *rubato*, itself a reflection of the composed *rubato* pervading all levels of the musical structure – from the elasticity of phrasing that characterizes the harmony of each section, to the structural elasticity deriving from the eventual *mélange* of these sectional characteristics themselves.

Such free (horizontal) alignment between the seven solo instrumental parts is made possible by their mutual (vertical) attachment to the actual pitches of the original seven-note row (Ex. 71a). Each instrumental part takes the 'key' of its transposed harmonic area from a different one of the seven original pitches (Ex. 71b), and the ostinato harmony of each area is underlined by a progressive increase in the number of pitches that act as recurring pivots: from the single pitch of each *Originel*, to the seven pitches – the complete chord – of each Transition VII (Ex. 71c). In this way, the recurring foundation pitch of each area – the bass of each original chord (E flat, before transposition) – adopts the function of a tonic. And since the foundation pitch of each transposed chord sustains a different degree of the same original chord, the effect is something akin to a neo-tonality, rooted in the tonic harmony of the initiating seven-note row.

Ex. 71
(a)

(b)

(c)

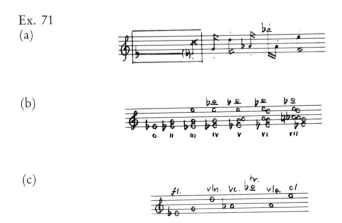

Ex. 72

(a)

(b)

Although the form of ' ...*explosante-fixe* ...' derives its expressive detail from the *rubato* interpretation that is an inbuilt ingredient of each performance, its structure is inviolable as to the ordering of the 'transitional' routes allocated to each instrument. This composed structure is not only essential as a frame for the multi-layered *rubato* expression of the music, but essentially pertinent to the recreative art of the performer since it allows for relationships that are immediately communicable in performance: each instrumental entry (or exit) will be heard as a contribution to the structure of the work as a whole, as well as in terms of its own structural continuity. The focus of these instrumental strands is identified primarily by differences in timbre, and further differentiated by contrasts in musical characterization: from the mainly melodic development of the basic material on flute and cello, to the mainly decorative, grace-note emphasis of clarinet and violin – with trumpet and viola drawing their inflections from each in turn, and the centrally-placed vibraphone/harp underlining the *sostenuto* aspect of the otherwise linear harmony.

The rhythmic structure of the piece is equally clear in its attachment to the 1:2:3 of the original matrix – a relationship that is now translated into the quasi-thematic shapes characteristic of each particular Transition (Ex. 72a). It also retains the idea of an increasing variety of motivic figuration (and of dynamics) originally to be derived from a 'scanning' of the increasing number of lines in the matrix but now transposed to the 'transitional' level. Each successive Transition (from II–VII) thus includes an increasing number of thematic references originally characteristic of another, achieved by scanning the contents of its neighbours; for instance, the 'transitional' content of a particular instrumental part could be graphically transcribed as:

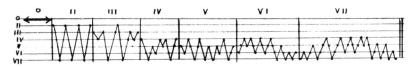

Only the *Originel* – which acts as a coda to each instrumental part – is immune from the scanned influence of the Transitions; together with its thirteen introductory variants, or 'Emprunts', dispersed throughout the work, it pursues an independent and noticeably more stable development of the 1:2:3 relationship at its simplest, that is, without derived rhythmic implications. This relative simplicity allows each appearance of the *Originel* to underline its function as the source material for the entire piece, and to guard this source from the more remote derivations of successive Transitions (Ex. 72b).

Through the permutational disorder of the transitional routes allocated to each instrument, the design of the work as a whole emerges as an enlargement of the disordered contents of the Transitions themselves – in which sense the scanning process is seen to be transposed to the ultimate level of structure. It is as if every segment of the sevenfold material of the piece were thought to proceed simultaneously, and continuously, in forty-nine soundproof rooms (one for each section, for each instrument), so that the music would then have to be 'revealed' by opening the doors to each of these rooms in turn, to a maximum of seven at any one time; no door could be re-opened once closed (on a particular Transition), except for that leading to the various 'Emprunts' of the *Originel*, and the end of the work would then be signified by the closing of the door to the room containing the last instrumental version of the *Originel* itself.

Because of its origins in the relatively uncomplicated surroundings of a published matrix, '... *explosante-fixe* ...' provides fascinating insight into the way in which ideas are compositionally processed from their crude, undeveloped state, to their eventual 'composed' refinement. More importantly, the finished work would seem to realize the goal of being able to characterize musical objects in relation to their total environment in such a way that their essential meaning is assured, whatever the context: like the words of Mallarmé's sonnets, they become transposable at will. The excitement generated by this discovery permeates the invention of '... *explosante-fixe* ...' at every level, so that, however elaborate the texture, its characteristic profusion of ideas transmits an irresistible exuberance.

There is, of course, nothing new, *per se*, in the idea of defining musical objects in terms of their interval structure and motivic formation; it is their context that has undergone such a radical reconstruction. In itself the establishment of independent objects in this piece is clearly a derivation of the independent rhythmic cells that were first projected in the early Flute Sonatine, but fell into gradual disuse as they were superseded by other considerations. The prolonged suppression of overt rhythmic characterization had perhaps arisen from an instinctive fear that even such partly inherited procedures could in turn become too facile in their relationships; so that their contemporary validity had first to be proved by obliterating all traces of their origins, before they could re-emerge in a context where likenesses are now freely aligned but equally coherent and purposeful in characterization.

Their contextual purpose is, of course, very different. The classically-influenced Sonatine was concerned with the progressive development (from phrases, to sentences, to paragraphs, to sections) of its basically thematic structure, underpinned by broad harmonic arches, and shaped by a metronomic pulse. The same could be said of all the other works dating from the 1940s, although inherited procedures quickly fade as the harmony becomes less reliant on the traditional consequences of a twelve-note row. While many of the same features evidently pervade *Le marteau sans maître*, their context was by then so different that their expressive aims had altered almost beyond recognition. The notion of a progressive harmonic development, allied to figurative rhythm, had already given way to that of a static permutation of closely-related harmonic blocks, propelled by the compressed energy of a rhythmic pulse that no longer needed a motivic life of its own; the objects had then become primarily chordal. It was these self-sufficient harmonic blocks that were to remain a constant preoccupation of succeeding works as, later in the same decade, rhythmic structures began to drift towards periods of time owing little or no allegiance to a chronometric pulse – just as, almost twenty years later, they were to blossom into the polyphonic textures of '... *explosante-fixe ...*'.

This textural 'explosion' is itself a product of preceding works: of the diverging tempos in *Poésie pour pouvoir*, of the differently-articulated group counterpoints in *Tombeau*, and of the scattered recapitulation at the end of *e.e. cummings ist der Dichter*. But, in all these works, texture is predominantly subservient to the underlying harmony on which it depends and, since these two parameters were then parallel and dependent, tension could only be brought into play at the secondary, expressive level of contrasting dynamics and articulation, and of contrasts in timbre, register and degree of density (both horizontal and vertical). Almost by chance, the figurative jottings of *Domaines* (begun at a time when the compositional flow was at its lowest ebb) were to mark the turning point: the seemingly casual re-introduction of characterized, independently-recognizable rhythm was at last to break the spell of an unarguable harmonic supremacy.

The revitalizing argument of '... *explosante-fixe ...*' springs from a true equality between its various parameters – parameters that are no longer only parallel and dependent, but also (and equally) divergent, independent and interchangeable in their relative dominance or subservience. Background and foreground evolve as relative descriptions of a shifting perspective, whose differing emphases are provoked by the changing course of events in the middle distance. Sometimes, rhythmic emphasis may overshadow harmonic perception; at other times, harmony will obliterate rhythmic definition – and both are affected by differences (whether naturally or electronically induced) in timbre and textural density. But, whatever the changes in musical perspective resulting from alterations in focus on this aspect or that (much as dramatic perspective can change according to the focus of a revolving stage), the underlying tensions of the musical drama itself concern the actions and reactions of a *dramatis persona* whose characteristics are sufficiently distinctive for expectation once again to be countered by surprise.

This re-establishment of perspective as a setting for the interplay of

215

recognizable musical objects was fundamental if the concept of form as necessarily a set of pre-announced intentions were to be superseded. Of course, such an achievement had long since been foreshadowed, and its final realization owes much to the more consciously-structured earlier pieces: to the spliced developments of *Improvisation II* and *e.e. cummings ist der Dichter*, for instance, as also to the 'inset' sections of *Structures*, Book II and to the freely-related fragments of *Domaines*. Nevertheless, '... *explosante-fixe* ...' is the first work to assert the convincing reality of a formal ideal that originated in the re-disposal of the related movements in *Le marteau sans maître*: that is, the ideal of form as a panoramic succession of related events, whose interactions pervade every level of a musical structure. And it is in this respect that the means of re-introducing a perceptible tension was so vital a discovery: without it, permutation of structural elements can have no real significance in relation to the development of large-scale forms.

More subjectively, the achievement of '... *explosante-fixe* ...' seems to signify an escape from the composer's own constraining objectives: the self-imposed pilgrimage of the '60s would appear at last to have ended in a new and visionary freedom of expression.

Rituel, in memoriam Maderna
 – form as a progressive and equal development of all related elements.

As if to confirm this new-found freedom, Boulez's next work, *Rituel* (1975), transforms the same basic material into a means of expression further removed from that of '... *explosante-fixe* ...' than could possibly have been imagined from any of the previous works. Not only is it conceived almost entirely in terms of the alternation of unadulterated monody and homophony, but the central theme of the piece, because now inseparable from the rhythmic scheme that supports and surrounds it, would seem to qualify as true melody. Certainly, this is a melody that submits to continuing development through the continual multiplication of both its vertical and its horizontal aspects (the one through the addition of instrumental lines to an original line, the other through the extension of the decorative up-beats attached to each main note) as well as through the inversion, transposition and permutation of its pitches and durations. Nevertheless, it remains melodically identifiable through its recurring proportions – of its intervals, as well as its durations – as a continuation of one and the same tune.

Written in memory of the composer's friend and near contemporary, Bruno Maderna, the timeless, ritualistic allusions of this melodic processional are endorsed by the increasing affirmation of its harmonized responses. The work is extraordinarily concentrated in its almost Messiaenic simplicity (without the least hint of sentimentality); more remarkable still, the technical basis of the original matrix is now brought into the structural foreground in a manner and to an extent that would previously have seemed inconceivable.

Shorn of many of its more complex implications, the matrix is now revealed in its pristine state as the quintessence of seven-ness from which *Rituel* derives in its entirety (see Ex. 71). In fact, so absolute is the Rule of Seven that it permeates every level of the organization: from the smallest particular detail of pitch and duration, including the number of instruments and instrumental groups, to the number and length of the sections whose sum is the eventual form of the work. Furthermore, this form describes an asymmetrical curve that is constructed entirely by means of simple arithmetic: the gradual augmentation of all elements forming the main body of the work is achieved by addition (from one element, to one-plus-six such elements), while the more rapidly-effected diminution of the coda (from seven elements, to seven-minus-six such elements) is the result of subtraction. A similar curve is traced by the increasing or decreasing weight of the instrumentation just as the prevailing septuple influence is mirrored in the septuple disposition of an orchestration that alternates *tutti* homophony with solo monody. The conducted *tutti* section consists of fourteen brass (four trumpets, six horns and four trombones) plus the independently-aligned percussion of seven nipple-gongs, while the seven unconducted solo groups of increasing range and timbral density comprise from one to seven instruments: one oboe; two clarinets; three flutes; four violins; a mixed quintet of oboe, clarinet, alto saxophone and two bassoons; a string sextet of two violins, two violas and two cellos, and a mixed septet of alto flute, oboe, cor anglais, E-flat clarinet, bass clarinet and two bassoons. The corporate independence of each of these groups is ensured by the co-ordinating influence of a particular percussionist, who plays seven different instruments (one for each of the seven sections denoting the main body of the work and, in reverse, the coda). Additionally, the asymmetrical distribution of these solo groups provokes a ternary emphasis within the binary curve of the piece as a whole: 1, 1 2 3, 1 2 3 4, 1 2; 1 2 3 4 5 6, 1 2 3 4 5 6 7, 1 2 3 4 5; (coda) 7 6 5 4 3 2 1, 6 5 4 3 2 1, etc, 3 2 1, 2 1, 1.

Within the general curve described by the *crescendo/diminuendo* of its orchestration, *Rituel* is shaped by asymmetrical duration curves arising from different permutations of the numbers 1 to 7. The most symmetrical of these curves is that described by the 'responsory' brass chords. These cadential affirmations become regularly more emphatic as a result of their arithmetical prolongation (+1, +2, +3, and so on) from the single chord of the opening statement (Ex. 73), to the seven chords of the seventh. The melodic processionals follow a curve that is likewise regular in its arithmetical phrase extensions: +1, +2, +3, etc., quavers to the one-bar phrases of the initiating oboe melody, reaching a maximum of +6 quavers

Ex. 73

in the sixth section, together with a maximum orchestral density.

The contrasting functions of these alternating tuttis and solos are further differentiated by the nature of their rhythmic articulation as evidence of the overlapping relationships between pulsed and unpulsed time. Thus, the uncounted durations of the *tutti* chords are linked to measured after-beats of from one to seven demisemiquavers, while the measured durations of the main notes of each solo phrase are preceded by up-beats whose demisemiquaver durations are 'counted' only in terms of their numerical quantity. The number and relative duration of both fore- and after-beats is dictated by augmentation of the ruling duration scale (1 3 5 4 7 6 2), and these figures are applied by regular addition, though in reverse order, to each of the seven paired *tutti*/solo sections (1; 31; 531; etc.). Meanwhile, the main melody-notes of each solo group are pulsed by a regularly increasing number of punctuating quavers – so that the duration shape of the opening oboe solo becomes 2 4 6 5 1 7 3 + 1 (Ex. 74), and the seven-group section will read 8 10 12 11 7 13 9 + 6 (plus, by then, additional permutations of the same scale). However, the internal distribution of these figures differs in application to each solo phrase, so that, although beginning simultaneously, and moving at a similar speed, each group is quickly thrown out of alignment with each other group. While this results in an independence of horizontal movement that can be considered as a simplification of the non-aligned textural polyphony of '...*explosante-fixe* ...', *Rituel* introduces a further fundamental dimension: that of the unpredictable rhythmic counterpoints which may emerge from the non-aligned, yet similar pulsation of its various strands.

Meanwhile, the rhythmic relationships between *tutti* and solo are reinforced by instrumental ones. Each succeeding *tutti* response absorbs the instrument or instrumental group(s) from the preceding solo section. This anticipates the full orchestral *tutti* of the coda, where the phrase structure of the solo groups is mirrored in reverse on the percussion – and in which the instruments retreat in the same order, beginning with the oboe, until only the original *tutti* group remains to sound the final unison E flat.

Even from this brief analysis, it will be evident that clarity of communication is the single outstanding feature that sets *Rituel* apart from the rest of Boulez's *oeuvre* – including its immediate predecessor, '... *explosante-fixe* ...'. All rhythmic disguise has been dropped, and

218

even the pitch structure is content to remain closely in touch with its harmonic origins: throughout, the inverted chords characterizing the *tutti* responses trace a melodic curve that outlines the pitches of the original seven-note row (until, in the coda, chords based on the original are built upwards from a bass line that traces the pitches of the inversion), with the obsessive E flat cadentially placed as a recurring unison.

Whatever the particular nature of *Rituel* itself may predict for the future, Boulez's own future as a developing composer would seem to be once again as certain as is the fact of his established place in history. For one who has successfully survived the long years bridging the instinctive genius of youth with the secure self-awareness of maturity, and whose exploratory energy has never slackened, no matter how great the effort involved in this survival – for such a composer, there can surely be no turning back.

(1975)

And what of the ten years since *Rituel*? If the whole of Boulez's career can be seen in one sense as a quest to discover freedom within the discipline of a precisely detailed set of technical aspirations, then the last decade has been a period both of consolidation and of continued development of the new expressive potential first revealed in the definitive version of '. . . *explosante-fixe* . . .', later confirmed and enhanced in *Rituel*. Hindsight now lends weight to the suggestion that the composition of these two works was to mark a major turning-point for Boulez, for together they led him to devise a means of widening the range of his technique to include the kind of audible relationships that have since enabled him to give his characteristically complex textures a more easily perceptible focus. Taken on their own, the works of the 1950s and '60s would be likely to lead to an assessment of his development solely in terms of a quintessentially French composer for whom a chord is a chord – sufficient unto itself and without implications of greater or lesser dominance in relation to other chords. But any narrowing of the pitch field from which such chords are chosen immediately creates its own priorities, and the music of the 1970s and '80s owes its distinctive profile to a harmonic selectivity that shows a quite different influence.

The seeds of this apparent contradiction were sown much earlier – perhaps even in the twelve-note *Notations* for piano, where there is plentiful evidence of ostinato piches being used to suggest tonal reference points. Certainly by 1946 the concept of a functional bass line harmony had seemed to be the driving force behind the inspiration that led him to construct the formal arch of the astonishingly mature Sonatine for flute and piano. But even here, the ideal of an independent rhythm had already

219

begun to confuse the issue – with long stretches of development made to float in a harmonic limbo that reached its point of no return in Piano Sonata No. 2 a couple of years later. The Sonatine remains the only work apparently to acknowledge the harmonic functions of a pitch-anchored bass, and there is no further instance of pitch being used even as a stabilising factor until the recurring E flat in the recapitulatory final movement of *Le marteau sans maître*. While the concept of chords as neutral objects that could be displayed horizontally as well as vertically was by this time securely established (see Exx. 32 and 33), it was only in *Tombeau* from *Pli selon pli* that fixed chords were extended to underpin the decorative derivations of longer sections (see Exx. 53 and 54).

Nevertheless, it would seem that the emergence of a new harmonic stability of the kind noted in *Tombeau* was more concerned to define the structural background than to clarify the moment by moment progress of the music, since its influence on foreground events is minimal in terms of perceivable effect: the harmony is functional only in the sense that each succeeding chord denotes the interval structure, range, and often the pitch register of the linear detail imposed upon it. At this stage, Boulez's chordal polyphony (many voices derived from and related to a single chord) would seem scarcely distinguishable from his definition of heterophony (the superposition of different versions of the same line), since all lines are chord-based and all chords can unfold into lines. The fact that each part of the chordal landscape reflects the same scene viewed from a different vantage point inevitably led to a negation of harmonic priority – even of perceptible emphasis. And since there is no observable basis for the chords themselves, there is nothing to which to relate the decorations they inspire; so that *Tombeau* and all the works of the 1960s (particularly the still unfinished *Éclat/Multiples*) read like novels from which all evidence of plot has been excised to leave only the evocative colour. For a time, it seemed that the sheer brilliance of musical description had become an end in itself.

With '... *explosante-fixe* ...' and *Rituel* all this was to change: the basis of the musical plot is clearly stated, and the loosely organized heterophony of the first and the ornamented homophony of the second define themselves in relation to the same easily memorizable seven-note row. Moreover, although the chords in *Rituel* still function as static objects in themselves, they derive harmonic momentum from their relationship to the fixed pitches of a serial refrain defined as an ordered hierarchy stemming from and always returning to its initial E flat and, for the first time in more than twenty years, from their association with the continuity of a rhythmic pulse.

Produced under pressure to meet the deadline of a magazine tribute to the memory of Stravinsky, the matrix for '... *explosante-fixe* ...' was to provide Boulez with sufficient material for the work of the next four

years. Another occasional offering – written as a tribute to Paul Sacher on his seventieth birthday – has in turn become the matrix for the following generation of works. Unlike the original '... *explosante-fixe* ...', which was no more than an outline plan, *Messagesquisse* (1976) is a short piece, complete in itself and unchanged since it first appeared. The fact that he for once resists the temptation to elaborate makes it uniquely self-explanatory. Scored for solo cello (the commission came from Rostropovich) and cello sextet, it sets out to re-examine the essentials of serial writing at the simplest level, in such a way as to give rare insight into the thought processes of a composer for whom the process of imaginative composition generally begins only after the laying down of a ground plan of the kind exposed here – by which time the basic format has become buried beneath the surrounding complexities of a finished work.

Messagesquisse is like a birthday telegram written in an easily decipherable musical code that relates everything to the single cell of an initiating series drawn from the letters of its dedicatee's name (Ex. 75). This six-note row is extended to form an unbroken circle by transposing its interval structure back onto the E flat with which it began – a procedure which, incidentally, not only illustrates the fundamental interchangeability of melody and harmony (see Ex. 79) but also the connection between row transposition and chord multiplication. It also underlines the growing need for a tonic reference point first suggested in '... *explosante-fixe* ...' and strongly endorsed as a formal anchor in *Rituel*. In *Messagesquisse* an initial note (by chance the same E flat) is again used to define harmonic areas, pinning down the outer sections of its symmetrical form (ABA coda) by its obsessive presence (Exx. 76 and 77) and effecting a sense of modulation by its omission from the repeated notes that shape the course of the central episode (see Ex. 78). Meanwhile, the complementary need for pulse as a definition of rhythm is again, as in *Rituel*, a reflection of number: that is to say, pulse remains rhythmically neutral, since pitch and duration relate to each other only through number – numbers of grace notes, as in *Rituel*, but also the placing of accents within a pulse which is now not only regular but metrical in emphasis (see Exx. 77 and 78). But *Messagesquisse* also includes a coded rhythmic element (a series of long/short motifs derived from the translation of its pitch names into morse code) which, while of little importance in the context of this piece, was to have far reaching motivic consequences for the work of the 1980s.

While *Messagesquisse* is a mainly linear exploration of an implied harmony, another short piece, dating from 1984, investigates the harmonic potential of the same basic material. In *Dérive*, for flute, clarinet, violin, cello, vibraphone and piano, written for Sir William Glock, the non-repeating intervals of the Sacher row (semitone, whole tone, minor 3rd, 4th, tritone) compose a permutating series of six fixed-pitch chords

Ex. 79

(Ex. 79). These rotate throughout on the piano, outlining a simple binary form in which the chords at first drift slowly past, immersed in multiple grace notes and trills, later to emerge as a canon of long melodic lines. The uninhibited expressiveness of *Dérive* (Drift) reflects something of the musical freedom gained from the almost wilfully cast-iron technical preoccupations of *Messagesquisse*: was the latter perhaps Boulez's way of taking stock of the (for him) unprecedented implications of *Rituel* and in musical terms – as twenty years earlier he had done in words – setting out his priorities for the future? In any event, the years 1971–6 would seem to have been a time of homing in on ever more clearly defined thematic objects, essentially neutral though they may still be, and of devising a sharper, more specific means of rhythmic articulation. It would also seem to have been a time of fining down, of focusing attention on musical characters, and of allowing his avowedly labyrinthine textures to reveal features particular to themselves before embarking on *Répons*, the major undertaking of the 1980s.

Meanwhile, he began work on a series of orchestral studies based on the twelve *Notations* he had written as exercises in twelve-note composition when a student. Only four of the *Notations* are so far complete in their recomposed form (1980), but it is already clear that they are to be supreme examples of the orchestrator's art. They are also an object lesson on the ways in which relatively simple material can be made to acquire layers of sophistication without losing sight of its origins, as well as on altering time scales without destroying perception of shape (a process which lies at the heart of *Répons* – compare, for instance, the first two and a half bars of Ex. 80 with the first two and a half pages of the full score). A more straightforward re-orchestration in fulfilment of a long-standing

Ex. 80   Assez lent

intent to give definitive orchestral form to *Improvisation III* from *Pli selon pli* was to follow in 1983. The somewhat clangorous soloistic contrasts of the original have now been shaded into the surrounding orchestral colours and the result is much more coherent in its textural unity, despite the continuing violence of its dynamic contrasts. It is also gentler and more decorative in overall effect, matching the earlier orchestration of *Improvisation I* and perfecting the symmetrical balance of *Pli selon pli* as a whole. Yet a third re-orchestration, of *Le visage nuptial*, is still under way.

During the compositional hiatus that lasted from the spring of 1976 until he began work on *Répons*, Boulez directed his creative energies first to the setting up and preliminary organisation of IRCAM itself and then to the need to learn the language and explore the potential of the techniques offered by its computers – a lesson which he is now using to brilliant effect, just as he had previously used his acquired knowledge of the orchestra to clarify and enrich his orchestral palette in the inspired recomposition of the first four *Notations*.

This whole period was in every respect one of preparation for *Répons* (1981–), a work-in-progress which, on completion, is destined to fill an entire concert programme on its own. It is the first and so far the only product of the composer's co-operation with the IRCAM 4X computer (the pre- IRCAM use of computerized electronic effects in '. . . *explosante-fixe* . . .' was never wholly successful and this aspect of the work awaits reorganization). Scored for chamber orchestra[14] and six electronically modified solo instruments (two pianos, harp, vibraphone, glockenspiel/xylophone and cimbalom), *Répons* is a hugely wide-ranging investigation of the proliferating reflections of a single aural image – a succession of spiralling echoes that sometimes follow one another, almost like classical imitation (as at the start, see Ex. 81*a*/*b*); are sometimes simultaneous in the vertical sense (as at the first entry of the solo instruments, where a single chord is multiplied by reflections of itself – 81*c*); and are often superimposed horizontally in heterophonic layers.

It is in all these respects – of imitation, multiplication and superimposition – that the computer proves itself so well adapted to compositional needs, or rather, it is in these respects that the composer has succeeded in programming it to be so precise an extension of his own mind. It would seem that, at last, the computer has provided the answer to the various abortive attempts – on the part of Boulez himself and others before him – to invent new instruments or to squeeze new sounds out of old ones: Boulez's own dream of a mobile space (dividing the octave by intervals other than the semitone) is fulfilled not by purely instrumental means but by the computer's ability to produce image reflections of a supra-instrumental kind. It also acts as an expressive modulator of dynamics (by

[14] 2 flutes, 2 oboes, 2 clarinets, bass clarinet, 2 bassoons, 2 horns, 2 trumpets, 2 trombones, tuba, 3 violins, 2 violas, 2 cellos and double-bass

Ex. 81 (a)

(b)

sustaining sounds that would otherwise fade) and of timbre (by absorbing diverse sounds within the envelope of its electronically induced echoes), just as it extends perception of time by prolonging sound way beyond the active physical movement that initiates it.

The very title of *Répons* (literally, response, in the ecclesiastical sense), like those of all Boulez's works since the early sonatas, would appear to mirror the sort of *doubles entendres* which abound in the music itself. Apart from suggesting the ritualistic element of the musical responses themselves, it could also be a response to a *message(esquisse)* as well as a series of *dérive(ations)* from it – or even a response to the challenge of the computer. In any case, it is evident that both *Messagesquisse* and *Dérive* have in some way been absorbed into the much more complex procedures of variation and development underlying the vast proportions of *Répons* (whose ground plan already exists in its entirety).

Between *Le marteau sans maître* and *Rituel*, form had seemed largely irrelevant to music in which procedure took precedence over outcome. But although the works of the later 1950s and '60s mirrored many of the youthful obsessions described in *Boulez on Music Today*, their tendency to focus on background chord structures expressed in terms of duration meant that the notion of an independent rhythm was temporarily held in abeyance: the outstanding inventiveness of Boulez's characteristically ornate harmonic style had for a time threatened to accept rhythm as an elusive by-product. At this stage, the sought-after formal contrasts

225

between pulsed and amorphous time (the mobile and static distributions of time space[15]) had become largely dependent on the smooth, one-dimensional continuity of a harmonic background that refused to reveal them. So that the undeveloped suggestion of a newly independent rhythmic purpose sketched out in *Messagesquisse* can now be seen as the start of a long build-up towards the multi-dimensional rhythmic emphases of *Répons*.

Répons achieves its formal purpose above all by allowing duration to develop rhythmic character. It is here that the fixed-pitch chords newly characteristic of *Rituel* are for the first time given a sense of harmonic perspective that depends not only on timbre, texture and duration (whether perceptibly pulsed or not), but on a parallel rhythmic organization with its own set of long- or short-term, dependent or independent priorities. This organization derives its entire network from just two units of proportion – long/short, strong/weak – which, right from the outset, are given evidently thematic connotations. Heard first as a memorable shape whose motivic implications soon become apparent (compare Ex. 81a, the opening bars of the work, with Exx. 83a and 85), it later dissolves into a series of ostinato pulsations – opening out from a unison A to uncover a not too remote relationship with the opening motif (Ex. 84). These sort of likenesses are not of course strictly motivic in the classical sense, since their development remains independent of recurring thematic shapes, just as the thematic shapes stress recurring intervals unrelated to particular rhythmic patterns. Nevertheless, the purpose of their independent articulation is clearly a motivic one, evidently related to the long/short, strong/weak emphasis that inflects the music at all levels of its ensuing development. With harmonic stability already (since *Rituel*) measured in terms of a chordal hierarchy specific to a particular piece and audibly pivotal to its structure, the new and equally specific rhythmic focus proposed in *Répons* is free to explore the kind of long-term contrasts crucial to the definition of form.

The harmonic basis of *Répons* is again that of the row devised for *Messagesquisse* – or rather, that of the related chords outlined in *Dérive* (see Exx. 75 and 79). But this is at first veiled by the energetic rhythmic unison of an orchestral prelude that only gradually reveals its harmonic indebtedness to the pitches of the opening phrase, as these are in turn sustained (as in Ex. 82a[2]) to form a slow moving pedal-point melody of their own. This harmonic theme describes a curve that contours the entire first section of the work, up to the entry of the solo instruments: from the impulsive rhythmic momentum of the opening (B–F sharp), through the almost stationary repose of a period of amorphous time where rhythm serves only to inflect sustained chords (F sharp–B flat–E), to arrive at a

[15] See p. 138

Ex. 82

point where the long/short focus of the motivic rhythm yields to the strong/weak emphasis of static pulsation (see Ex. 84) and the harmony begins to acquire a rhythmicized momentum of its own (B/A). Boulez's harmony is now effectively controlled from the top, with the bass-line emphasis of the Flute Sonatine at last confidently up-ended to focus on the treble.

The introductory nature of these carefully structured paragraphs is endorsed by the relatively narrow pitch range within which they define and unfold their proposals. With the entry of the soloists, not only is the whole computer-enhanced register of available pitches unveiled at the stroke of a single chord, but so too is the central core of a harmonic character till now revealed only piecemeal (Ex. 81c). As this reverberating harmonic statement continues to expand, encased in echoing fragments of the pulsating rhythm, it emerges that successive chord transformations are again drawing attention to the melodic shape of the opening bars (Ex. 82a²), working backwards (B–A–-F sharp–B flat–E) to reach a long held *tremolando* on its final chord (Ex. 82*b*); with the total harmonic spectrum now confirmed in relation to its melodic origins, this same cadence chord remains to support a free contrapuntal development (a sort of rhythmic heterophony) of the long/short motif. Beginning simultaneously, freely aligned permutations of the original phrase rhythm (Ex. 83a) gradually contract into the pulsating *ostinati* of their *alter ego* (Ex. 83b – see also Exx. 84 and 85). And as this developmental section in turn draws to a close, so the supporting chord is left sounding to introduce a *moto perpetuo* variation of the opening rhythmic unison, this time punctuated by the soloists (Ex. 85).

This recapitulatory variation concludes the first chapter (14 minutes) of a work which at present comprises about half its projected length (45 minutes of a planned 90 minutes). From now on, it would seem that the sort of proportional relationships observed between the pitches of the opening phrase and the melodic contours of the introduction as a whole are to be extended over the still longer term: certainly the scale of the music alters radically at this point – with a slow movement and an *ostinato* scherzo together equal in duration to the whole of the opening chapter. This change of time scale immediately affects perception of the rate at which events unfold, not only because the pacing of the music is at first very slow, but because it has a still centre based on a protracted harmonization of the same treble clef E.

The slow movement begins as the preceding rhythmic variation arrives at an E-topped chord (Ex. 82*d*) which both concludes the opening chapter and, through a long *diminuendo*, leads into the next. The speed

Ex. 83 (a)

(b)

Ex. 84

Ex. 85

of the music is now noticeably relaxed, slowing down still further as the texture fills out, the register expands, and the dynamic range increases; in addition, the shifts of emphasis within the harmony itself, as it searches out and eventually finds its resolution in the chord that marks the opening of *Dérive* (see Ex. 78, though now with an added B flat) are so gradual as to pass almost unnoticed. With the harmonic background almost at a standstill, a new sense of rhythmic perspective is introduced, allowing the intricate details of a wave-like foreground (rhythmic and melodic derivations now closely entwined) to appear to be moving at a different speed – as the shadowy canonic implications of the solo parts drift across the regularity of a quietly insistent pulse that increasingly highlights elements of the background chord.

Here too, the breadth of the music is evidently adapting to its considerable length: like a scale drawing, the contents of the introductory chapter are being developed and expanded to fit the proportions of a much larger design. Just as the original small-scale elements acquired characteristics that were carried forward from one paragraph to the next, so the slow movement chord becomes the subject for development in the following *ostinato*, and its multiple grace-note decorations in turn become the central feature of the section that opens chapter three. Moreover, although the surface configuration of the music is often very complex, there are seldom more than two strains of development operating at any one time, and it is the relative dependence of one upon the other, as in the haunting slow movement, that enables their evolution to be understood not only in terms of differing harmonic emphasis, but also of contrasting speeds. This kind of articulation – which relates rhythmic movement to harmony and thence to form – is paramount in *Répons*, where rhythm is not merely pulsed or amorphous, but may itself be relatively dependent or independent, creating states of action, inaction or reaction that define character as well as degrees of mobility.

If the speed of Boulez's revolutionary first period development for a time slowed down in the second, it has noticeably quickened in this third period of his musical life: each new work shows an evolutionary zeal that marks a new burst of creative energy. *Répons* is in every way a culmination of the work of the last fifteen years, of which it is also a vast and still continuing development. Perhaps its title is, above all, a response to the challenge imposed by its composer's own visionary techniques: even in its unfinished state, it stands as a monument to the many-faceted freedoms he has always insisted were ultimately to be found only through discipline.

(1985)

229

With Boulez at the BBC

William Glock

It was in 1963 that I first asked Pierre Boulez if he would conduct the BBC Symphony Orchestra, and when the concerts came, in March 1964, they were a revelation. Within a year or two he had led the orchestra to some of its greatest triumphs since Toscanini in the 1930s. The performances had been of works that were still fresh to him as a conductor, just as his readings of them were still fresh to the orchestra. But overlapping with this period in which he achieved a new realization of some of the music that lay closest to him – by Debussy, Stravinsky, Berg and Webern in particular – there also stirred the beginnings of a policy that was to lead later on to an attempt to change, by his own example, the patterns of orchestral concert-giving in London.

Here it might be helpful to try and define some of the different strands which came together when Boulez associated himself with the BBC. He must have been keenly aware that in working with the BBC he would have a far greater chance of pursuing an enterprising policy than with any orchestra run on a commercial basis. Of course any institution, however liberal in its basic ideals, has periods of drabness as well as of brilliance. The broadcasting of contemporary music had been a vital ingredient of programmes in the 1930s, had become cautious and middle-of-the-road in the 1950s, but since 1960 had begun to revive, especially in the so-called Thursday Invitation Concerts broadcast by the Third Programme, and in the Henry Wood Promenade Concerts.

The Invitation Concerts covered a wide historical range of music from Machaut to Boulez himself. Indeed the first concert in January 1960 included *Le marteau sans maître* – though the early programmes as a whole were not avant-garde; they had too much ground to make up in introducing, or re-introducing, some of the fundamental works of the present century that had hardly been heard in the 1950s. The patterns of the individual concerts varied a good deal, sometimes including only twentieth-century works (one evening consisted of Janáček's *Diary of a man who disappeared* and Berg's Chamber Concerto), but more often combining the old and the new, as for example with Webern's Chamber Concerto, Beethoven's Septet and Schoenberg's *Serenade*, or again, the Goldberg Variations and Schoenberg's *Pierrot Lunaire*. Sometimes the

231

pattern was like a switchback, as with one particular concert of Byrd, Boulez, Machaut, Boulez, Byrd. These were not schemes that aroused very much enthusiasm with Boulez himself later on. If a concert did begin with a work of the past, he often preferred to follow it with a twentieth-century classic and then with something of the present day – to plan the programme in an ascending line, as it were, rather than as an arch or a semi-circle. Nevertheless, the Invitation Concerts did mark a revival in BBC music broadcasting and were greeted with an extraordinary fervour which suggested that the listening public had been waiting for something exactly of this kind.

Where the radio audience for each Invitation Concert was about 150,000, the Henry Wood Promenade Concerts (which run from July to September every year) are on another scale altogether, with an audience in the Royal Albert Hall itself of sometimes 5,000 or more and – by the time the new television channel, BBC2, opened in 1964 – a total number of listeners and viewers of about one hundred million over each season as a whole. The influence of the Proms – as they are called – is therefore very powerful; and these concerts have other attractions, amongst which are their atmosphere of informality, and the fact that through the enterprise of Sir Henry Wood, who conducted the Proms for fifty years, those who come to the concerts are potentially the most receptive and open-minded of all London audiences. Again, the planning of the Proms had been safe and repetitive during the 1950s, and the great tasks that seemed to lie ahead from 1960 onwards were to expand the repertory in every dimension possible, to make sure that performances were of the highest quality, and to venture a few yards out to sea where contemporary music was concerned.

All this was well in train when Boulez first appeared at the Proms in 1965. Three years later, when I asked him to become the next Chief Conductor of the BBC Symphony Orchestra, I was influenced not only by the outstanding performances he had given in London and by his many exciting and boldly planned concerts with the Orchestra in New York, Moscow and Leningrad; but also by my admiration for him both as a composer and as a man of brilliance and imagination, and by our long association which, in one way or another, went back for more than fifteen years. In 1951 he had written a famous article, 'Schoenberg is Dead', for a magazine I was then editing called *The Score*; in 1955 I had met him briefly at Baden-Baden and had heard the first performance of *Le marteau sans maître* under Hans Rosbaud; in 1956 we had met again several times during his visit to London with Jean-Louis Barrault and his company; in 1957 he had given two concerts for the musical section of the Institute of Contemporary Arts of which I was then chairman – one of them in which he played in a masterly way with Yvonne Loriod at the Wigmore Hall, in a programme including *En blanc et noir* and his own first book of *Structures*, the other at the BBC with the ensemble of the Domaine Musical, when he conducted *Le marteau sans maître*, Webern's Chamber Concerto, Stockhausen's *Zeitmasse* and Nono's *Incontri*. That was a black evening for some of the BBC music staff of those days, as can be imagined, but the effect on many young members of the audience was exhilarating, though it was to be another three years before any consistent sequel to such a concert would be provided by the BBC itself.

Since 1954, Pierre Boulez had also sent me advance programmes each year of his Domaine Musical concerts in Paris, with comments of various kinds of which two are worth recalling in the context of this chapter. In one of them, written in 1956, he says that to have to play or conduct one's own works and to face their difficulties of execution is the best possible training for a composer. (And he added a footnote on this subject in a talk given in London in November 1981, when he spoke of the 'utopianism' of some of his earliest works which he now finds hard to decipher easily, and then of how through the experience of actual performances he gradually came to combine utopianism with practicality.)

The other comment that seemed relevant to our future work together was on the projected series of four Domaine Musical concerts for 1956/57, which Boulez summarized as follows:

(1) Antecedents: Stravinsky and Webern

(2) Exploration of new sounds, by traditional means (works for prepared piano by Christian Wolff and John Cage; Stockhausen's *Zeitmasse*) and non-traditional (electronic music, including Stockhausen's *Gesang der Jünglinge*)

(3) Chamber music past and present: Dowland (*Lachrimae*), Webern, Maderna, Schoenberg

(4) The balance sheet of a single year's new works: by Bo Nilsson, Michel Philippot, Luciano Berio, Pierre Boulez (Third Sonata for piano), Olivier Messiaen.

Here, from quite early days, one sees Boulez's urge towards 'thematic' planning rather than for freely varied programmes, however integrated. One could say, in fact, that whilst we were both of us dedicated to a policy of adventure, he was the theorist and thinker, I had always felt my way, one move at a time. Yet, interestingly enough, the two different approaches were happily reconciled.

In planning individual programmes Boulez seemed to rely to some extent on a process of suggestion and counter-suggestion; on a game of tennis, so to speak, which can't be played by one person alone. I myself have always looked on the planning of a good programme as a small work of art, though one may not produce very many that deserve that name. And I think Boulez had something of the same attitude. We usually began with an 'ideal' choice of works, but then came revision and second and third thoughts. Problems of rehearsal had to be taken into account and, of equal importance, the need to balance enterprise and attractiveness. However challenging our plans might be, we also wanted to carry the public with us.

On the subject of rehearsal, I think it would be true to say that Boulez sometimes displayed a streak of optimism that could stretch the resources even of the BBC Symphony Orchestra, which as a result of undertaking by far the largest and most varied repertory of any orchestra in Britain had developed sight-reading skills and an ability to grasp new difficulties that had astonished many conductors, including Hans Rosbaud during his visit of 1961. Where his own works were concerned, Boulez seemed to take it for granted that the players would do their homework thoroughly between one rehearsal and another, and always showed his pleasure when this had happened. But an occasion could arise when plans had to be changed at the last moment. As originally conceived, the concert at the Festival Hall on 16 March 1966 was devoted to Mallarmé, and consisted of Ravel's and Debussy's *Trois Poèmes* and the first London performance of *Pli selon pli*, for which Boulez had set aside six rehearsals. Then came an urgent letter to say that he thought he had been 'excessively imprudent' in estimating the rehearsals needed, and suggesting that it would be far better to play three of the five movements of *Pli selon pli*, preferably I, III and IV, than to attempt all five and achieve hardly more than a piece of public sight-reading. On such questions there was never any argument . . .

A very different reason lay behind one other important change of plan in these years. A long-advertised performance of *Éclat/Multiples* was abandoned because Boulez had not quite been able to finish the scoring of it, and did not want to fall back on yet another performance of the original *Éclat*. 'I am struggling to compose, and become more and more impatient about the fact that I have so many ideas unfulfilled and unrealized when life is passing so quickly.' That was a refrain that rang out more than once at this time; and it was impossible not to feel involved in the burden that Boulez had imposed on himself in taking on two simultaneous lives, as composer and deeply-committed conductor. But it was a burden that only he could resolve.

In the meantime, the privilege of working with him was something never to be forgotten. We planned programmes at each other's flats, during lunches or dinners, during orchestral tours abroad, everywhere but in an office. And the 'need to balance enterprise and attractiveness' remained a constant guide. There are a few twentieth-century works that have taken on a mythical quality, but outside this small circle of pieces such as *Pierrot Lunaire* and *The Rite of Spring* it is difficult to find compelling choices that will ensure large audiences for adventurous programmes. Nevertheless, nearly all the concerts given by Pierre Boulez at the Festival Hall and at the Proms from 1964 to 1972 were entirely of contemporary music, most of them consisting of twentieth-century classics, it is true, but with notable exceptions. Of course he had won an incomparable reputation as a conductor of most of this repertory; but he was also infinitely patient about repeating certain favourite works, when his artistic impulse was to innovate and not to repeat *ad nauseam*. It was a compromise about which I often had an uneasy conscience, but from time to time it made possible an astonishing response to programmes that included major novelties.

One example in Boulez's earlier years was the Prom of 5 September 1967. The programme consisted of Berg's Three Fragments from *Wozzeck* and the *Altenberglieder*, Stockhausen's *Gruppen*, and *The Rite of Spring*. As part of the preparation for the Stockhausen, Boulez and the two other conductors of *Gruppen* had spent hour after hour together in silent rehearsal in a small room at the BBC's Maida Vale Studios. When the concert came there was an audience of 4,000, as large as that of the night before for Covent Garden's Prom performance of *Fidelio*. I sent a note about this to Boulez who had gone to Provence immediately after the *Gruppen* evening, and he wrote back saying 'Thank you for the marvels of the box office. I think both of us can be proud, and also Stockhausen! Well, we must continue! and next year give some Proms with more new things.'

The Proms had aroused Boulez's enthusiasm from the beginning. They were unique in the fact that the most prominent part of the audience consisted of young concertgoers who stood throughout the evening in the arena, where seats would have been installed on more conventional occasions; they were unique, too, in the rapt quality of attention that these concertgoers paid to each performance, and in the tumultuous reception that would follow if all had gone well. Boulez is certainly not one of those artists who invite and prolong applause by bestowing an endless series of papal benedictions on the audience; but the warm response to programmes that were anything but traditional must have heartened him greatly. Here are just three of his remarkable concerts at the Proms in 1968 and 1969: (1) Bartók's Music for Strings, Percussion and Celesta, and *Pli selon pli*; (2) Varèse's *Arcana* and *Ionisation*, Stravinsky's *Le Roi des Étoiles*, *Requiem Canticles* and *The Rite of Spring*; (3) Messiaen's *Chronochromie*, *Le marteau sans maître*, Stockhausen's Piano Piece No. 10 and Berg's Three Orchestral Pieces, Op. 6. There one sees the leavening of chamber music that Boulez had first tried out with the Schoenberg *Serenade* in the previous year at the Festival Hall, and which was to become characteristic from then onwards, especially at the Proms.

Much later, in December 1972 and January 1973, we put on a short season of Winter Proms, which began with an evening of Stravinsky. I mention this only in order to give an example of Boulez's attention to the artistic and dramatic ingredients of every programme. No documents seem to exist that would show all the services and returns in this particular game of tennis, and I can only guess after so many years that the succession of pieces I may have suggested to him was as thoughtless as follows: *Le Roi des Étoiles*, *Renard*, the *Symphony of Psalms*, and the by then almost totally forbidden *Rite of Spring*. At all events, a letter arrived from Cleveland, sadly accepting *The Rite of Spring* but pointing out that between *Le Roi des Étoiles* and the *Symphony of Psalms*, *Renard*, with its burlesque story, seemed somewhat out of place; and that *Le Roi des Étoiles* itself would be completely lost if it came at the beginning of the concert. Boulez's alternative programme consisted of *Le Chant du Rossignol*, *Symphony of Psalms*, and in the second half *Le Roi des Étoiles* and *The Rite of Spring*, with perhaps the *Symphonies of Wind Instruments* between *Rossignol* and *Symphony of Psalms* if the concert seemed otherwise too short. For whatever reason, this was not the final form of the programme, but the main points about *Renard* and *Le Roi des Étoiles* were happily observed. I like to think, however, that sometimes our suggestions and counter-suggestions were more evenly balanced!

On the larger issue of orchestral concert-giving in London, Boulez's conviction grew from 1968 onwards that reforms were needed, and as time went on letters would arrive from Boston, Provence, Baden-Baden – wherever he happened to be working at the moment – with a call to arms. He had been much impressed by the fact that in Boston in 1969 his performance of Berg's Three Orchestral Pieces, Op. 6, was the first ever heard there, and by the growing opinion amongst intelligent musicians he had met in the United States that changes were more than overdue. 'What is needed', he said, 'is a new approach to concert life that will bring it into touch with what composers are doing to-day'; and in our only full season together after he had become Chief Conductor of the BBC Symphony Orchestra he did try to provide a model which others might or might not follow.

For many years he had been educating British audiences in the music of the twentieth-century classics, and in performances – especially of Webern – such as they had never heard before. But he was no longer satisfied with giving a series of isolated concerts, or individual 'menus', as he called them; and now that he had the opportunity, he wanted to plan for each season coherent patterns that would be clearly remembered, and in which different categories of music would be heard in the surroundings that suited them best. One aspect of his policy was to concentrate each year on two 'retrospectives' – one of a particular twentieth-century classic, the other of a famous but relatively neglected composer of the seventeenth to nineteenth century; while at the other end of the spectrum he wanted to introduce in the right informal setting a number of contemporary concerts ('prospectives') that would set out to discover 'new works, new media, new composers, new means of expression ...'

In February 1970 we made a journey of exploration around London, and found in the Round House (where railway engines were once housed and turntabled) and in the baroque church of St John's in Westminster (where the BBC already ran a successful series of lunchtime concerts) the ambience, the adaptability and the lively and informal attitudes of those in charge that promised to make these venues ideal for the purposes that Boulez had in mind. By now, despite my British unease about 'categories', I was fully in support of Boulez's general aims; and it must certainly have been through his influence that in planning the Proms of Summer 1971 I moved some of the concerts away from the Albert Hall for the first time – to Westminster Cathedral; to Covent Garden for a full-dress performance of *Boris Godunov* (with the stalls removed for the promenaders); and to the Round House itself for a late-night concert of contemporary music which Boulez conducted and also introduced.

The idea of moving from the Albert Hall was to be able to offer in each case a more authentic or immediate experience than would otherwise have been possible; and these principles were also an important element in Boulez's reforms. The two 'retrospectives' for his 1971–2 season were of Haydn and Stravinsky (the Stravinsky 'not just as an act of homage, but to try to get a general view of his music and see what he really means in the music of our time'). Haydn found a perfect setting at St John's, Smith Square; Stravinsky was heard both at St John's, in works like the Mass and the Cantata, and in the Festival Hall, where, with one exception, Boulez himself concentrated on his favourite period of Stravinsky up to *Les Noces*, Colin Davis conducted a performance of *Threni*, and nine or ten of the chamber works were included in two pre-concerts, making twenty-five works in all. It was a substantial review, especially of the earlier Stravinsky; and the season as a whole showed every sign of exuberant planning, including, as it did, Ligeti's Requiem, Ives's Symphony No. 4 and, in a Boulez concert which needed sixteen rehearsals of one kind or another, *e.e. cummings ist der Dichter* and Schoenberg's *Jacob's Ladder*.

At the 'other end of the spectrum', the evenings at the Round House were much more informal, with Boulez and the musicians dressed as casually as the audience. In an interview with Peter Heyworth of *The Observer* before the concerts began, Boulez had said that 'we must try to rid ourselves of the idea that when we listen to new music we are searching for the masterpieces of the future'; and that what he wanted at the Round House was 'to create a feeling that we are all, audience, players, and myself, taking part in an act of exploration ... and if something valid or valuable turns up, then we can be pleased'.

The programmes of this first season in 1972 included works by Maderna, Stockhausen and Ligeti, but it is difficult now to remember how some of the more controversial new pieces were chosen. Some were commissioned, and so were unpredictable. Once or twice, it has to be admitted, we came close to banality (not with Boulez's help, one may be sure!); and where such misjudgments were made I suspect that they arose from looking perhaps not so much for 'well written' pieces as for those which seemed to contain a spark of vitality or a hint of new directions. It seemed a risk well worth taking at the time.

In his own concerts, Pierre Boulez threw all his energy into an effort to provoke some discussion with the audience; and though this did not quite succeed as he would have wished, his magnetic presence, his stimulating introductions to the various works, the high standards of performance, and the setting of the Round House itself, all combined to make a memorable experience.

In the end, Boulez's grander strategies did not change the routine of London's orchestral concert-giving. He says that if he had been a conductor and nothing else he might have persevered for longer and succeeded; on the other hand, he would surely never have been fired with the same ambitions that he wanted to realize. What he left was the memory of a crusade for contemporary music and of inspired performances that will remain unique in Britain's musical life in the twentieth century.

Reprinted, by permission, from the Boulez-Festschrift, issued jointly by Südwestfunk, Baden-Baden and Universal Edition, Vienna, 1985.

IRCAM

Jonathan Harvey

If the man of talent, as Schopenhauer said, hits the target every time, the man of genius hits a target that no one else even sees. Boulez's early writing about the necessity for a collaboration between technology and musical creativity is revealed to be more and more important as time passes; what seemed outlandish a few years ago is now without doubt crucial. Boulez saw the point with sufficient clarity in November 1970 to convince the President of the Republic that many millions should be invested in the idea for an indefinite period. By 1973 a staff was picked to work out goals – goals which were announced at a press conference in the Théâtre de la Ville in March 1974: and so was born the *Institut de Recherche et Coordination Acoustique/Musique*, perhaps the most positive gift of its size ever made to the art of musical composition anywhere.

The time was historically right. Boulez perceived musical culture to be a 'museum' culture, essentially conservative. Performers, intensively trained from early years to acquire a certain traditional repertoire, lacked the breadth of education to question the validity of this ever-repeated round of classics. (They still do.) Their specialization often precluded such an education. The general tendency of historicism in musical life was perhaps itself a defence reflex, he argued, against the ever-increasing power of technology. This wondrous new beast was used only to perfect the presentation and conservation of the museum: to make ever higher quality recordings, transmissions and so on. It was not used to develop many new instruments. Instrument makers plied their trade much as they had done for decades, centuries even. What inventions there were succumbed often to the temptation of fulfilling the immediate needs of one creator rather than deeply-researched more general needs. The uninhibited pop world alone showed how learning to love technology could open up new vistas within an imaginative world.

Boulez felt that the quests of the adventurous few to find new sonic media for a struggling new language were somewhat ill-coordinated. Equipment meant for other purposes was adapted; what new equipment there was was designed by scientists insufficiently aware of the workings of composers' minds. For instance, pioneer computer music research was conducted not in music centres but on the side at Bell Telephone

239

Laboratories, New York and at Stanford Artificial Intelligence Laboratory, California.

What was crucial was to see that, first, new music was under severe strain because new instruments and sonic media scarcely existed to carry the visions of the new post-atonal acoustic language; secondly, the repressive stagnation of our musical culture was unlikely to move from within; and that, thirdly, the explosive progress of technology, which would soon pervade all our lives so completely, was the very source from which an answer could be drawn. In particular, computers were sufficiently generalized in nature to be developed into something more than the toy of an individual maverick.

For this to happen would entail research. Research would have to be in the form of a dialogue between the musicians and the scientists, the former learning to master the new sound sources, the latter learning to understand the true nature of musical problems. Fully cognizant of the fact that composing is the work of solitary individuals, Boulez yet saw clearly that composing is not a miraculous creation *ex nihilo*: it rests on others' endeavours. To bring the 'solitary' creative individuals together with scientists and, equally important, to have them share their technical needs and solutions with each other in pooled research became the aim of IRCAM.

If Boulez's conducting mission has been to create a taste, a climate, for contemporary music, his IRCAM mission has been to create the means for its further development.

The development of IRCAM itself has been rapid and colourful. The team chosen in 1972–3 to define the aims of IRCAM included Berio, Vinko Globokar, Jean-Claude Risset and Gerald Bennett. Nicholas Snowman was artistic director and Brigitte Marger director of external relations. One of their tasks was to advise on the nature of the building to house this enterprise. A budget of 59.2 million francs was fixed in 1974, and three years later the extraordinary building was complete. For sound insulation it was decided to site it underground, and across the square from the Centre Pompidou itself, with which it has high-level administrative connections. There are several large studios, a computer room for the main 'brain', an anechoic chamber, laboratories, a conference room, technical areas and thirty-two offices, many of them with terminals. But the most luxurious feature of all is the concert hall, the *Espace de Projection*, which has the task of exposing the fruits of IRCAM and elsewhere to public light – an essential adjunct to the philosophy of research, and one of its most important tests. It is the only hall of its kind in the world: its reverberation time can be changed from half a second (very dry) to 4.5 seconds (quite echoey). Any part of the hall can be either dry or reverberant according to the settings of 513 wall panels which can each be electronically rotated to show either an absorbent or diffusing (angled) or reflecting surface. In addition, the ceiling can be lowered in three separate parts: one can have intimacy at one end of the hall and spaciousness at the other, or any setting the composer requires. Composers adjust the overall settings for their pieces in some detail with the technical staff during rehearsals, and the possibilities for music theatre have been interestingly explored by Kagel, Holliger, Maurice Béjart and others. The hall floor is level, allowing for complete freedom in the placing of seating podia for the audience and performers. The hall is itself used for research, by architects and acousticians and also by recording engineers.

In addition, there is a connected adjoining building where administrative offices, a well-documented library and more studios are situated.

The distinguished team lasted for seven years. Berio's relations with the computer were ambivalent, and his one attempt at a piece is still a 'work in progress'. He had, with the true researcher's vision, requested IRCAM's principal electronics engineer Pepipo di Giugno to build a synthesizer with 1000 oscillators. It was duly built, and Berio never used it. Globokar likewise did little computer work, and his work on extended instrumental techniques now seems (however valuable in itself) slightly peripheral to IRCAM's technological thrust.

Thus, at the end of 1979, the stars left, and IRCAM's original departments of computer, electro-acoustic instrument, extended instrument and voice, diagonal (which cut across these) and so on were re-organized. The new arrangements fell under two committees, Scientific and Artistic.

A research department was created, with Tod Machover in charge, also a pedagogy department, with the psycho-acoustician David Wessel in charge, a production/creation department, and an information department. These changes meant, for one thing, that a democratic atmosphere of helpfulness and co-operation greeted the visiting composer or researcher: the new staff were never so engrossed in their own work that they could not devote long hours to the projects of others. IRCAM became more truly a co-operative venture, with a total staff, eventually, of about fifty-four.

An autonomous control of its budget has given IRCAM the flexibility to change and adjust to the rapid developments in information technology and to the demands for new projects inevitable with so many creative minds, resident and visiting, in one building. Choosing priorities within a budget is a constant subject of lively debate, sustained by the sense that almost anything is possible. The budget comes from public money, and also from a Swiss foundation run by Paul Sacher. Commissions given by IRCAM to composers are supported by a group of private donors headed by Boulez's friend, Mme Georges Pompidou. Such commissions are handsome.

Let us examine in more detail the functions of each of these new departments.

The research department is at the heart of Boulez's vision, it supports everything else, it is the thrust of evolution, technical and imaginative. Work is carefully documented with manuals, papers and sound examples so that it is generally accessible and can be built upon by the next in the field. There is no private property, although many break-throughs are, of course, the result of very private thought and highly personal composition.

The research can for convenience be split into two types (which interact constantly): musical research and scientific research. Here are a few examples of musical research. A high-priority topic is the development of machines and programs to effect live transformations of the sound. *Répons* is a good example of the fruit of such research. The 4X synthesizer receives live instrumental figures and instantly plays them back in varied forms of transformation, according to one of several programs Boulez and his assistant Andrew Gerzso have worked out and stored inside it. Such machines have pre-programming and live manual control available simultaneously. This is much the same situation as in non-electronic music where the score represents a structure which is the fruit of months of labour, and the performance is the fruit of split-second intuition. (The danger of losing spontaneity and intuition in difficult technological work has been one of the guiding caveats since the beginning at IRCAM, and the constant concern is to exploit technique to the full whilst never losing natural musical intuition. It is important to note that more and more 'intuitive composers' are coming to IRCAM and feeling at ease.)

More easy to manage is the new Yamaha Frequency Modulation system run with IRCAM software co-ordinated by David Wessel. IRCAM's co-operation with Yamaha for mutual benefit and progress is a heartening augury of the breakdown of barriers between commercial and non-commercial worlds.

In other areas computer programs are developed which synthesize sound, often in radically different ways to those developed before in the USA. For example, CHANT is a programme developed by a team under Xavier Rodet which synthesizes sound by pushing impulses through a simulated model of an 'instrument' (such as the vocal tract or any pipe or body) shaped by highly flexible areas of resonance called formants. Thus this method encourages a detailed attention to the profile of the required sound in terms of the width and placing of these resonating 'hollows' of which the artificial instrument is built. It is like designing an instrument without having to go through the tedium of sticking together bits of wood or metal.

The way most instruments sound is a result as much of the fact that a human being is 'exciting' them as of their own structure. Humans are complex: our sounds are full of unpredictable irregularities. CHANT's study and analysis of these emblems of liveliness is basic to an escape from the dehumanized dullness characteristic of earlier electronic music. The JITTER parameter in the program, for instance, modifies the frequency of the voice's or instrument's fundamental pitch by the quasi-random interaction of three number generators, the fastest perhaps set to operate about fifty times a second (but that is determined by the user). The vibrato width and speed are also set by the user to give both minute, scarcely perceptible fluctuations and fairly large ones simultaneously. The ear is very sensitive to these variations. As an upper partial vibrates with the performer's vibrato, it moves up and down, into and out of a formant region. In other words, as it goes up it gets rapidly louder, and as it comes down it gets softer again (or vice-versa). This oscillating amplitude-allied-to-glissando is perhaps the most important factor in our perception of timbre. The flexible formants basic to CHANT synthesis lay out, for the composer's manipulation, the timbral field as seen from just this angle.

This is only the beginning of what such a program can do: its further consequences lie at the limits of our ability to perceive and imagine. The same team has also invented FORMES in 1983, a program of great sophistication deriving from American Artificial Intelligence research and its principal language, LISP. It 'drives' a synthesizer or a synthesizing program. It manipulates structures, whether small (so many per second) or large (figures, cells, phrases) with facility, and is particularly attractive for the building of forms which involve repetitions or varied repetitions, or repetition within repetition, etc. Such things sound dry on paper, but once the music they facilitate is hovering in the imagination their extraordinary potential becomes clear.

Much research is done by computer on timbre. A four-day seminar on timbre was held in April 1985 at Boulez's instigation to review progress. The relation of timbre and musical structure, of fusion and fission (when is a sound two sounds?) are fascinating new areas never open to such precise modelling and examination before.

A large portion of research has been directed towards semi-automatic generation of structure. Boulez has been exploring LISP-like methods derived from artificial intelligence to generate structures in *Répons*. (Patrick Greussay gave an influential series of seminars on artificial intelligence in 1980–1.) Other composers (analysts, rather?) have made attempts to automate by rule their own compositional styles or predilections, and then produce whole works automatically. Others have attempted to analyze existing languages, the better to understand compositional processes.

On the scientific side there are also many topics of research. Berio's demand for a synthesizer of 1000 oscillators (4A) though of no immediate use to Berio has led, as is typical of research at its best, to targets way beyond those originally envisaged. The 4B synthesizer was developed two years later using frequency modulation principles, but proved to have too noisy a filtering process. The 4C was a great improvement, but was difficult for composers to use. Finally, the 4X Real-time Digital Signal Processor (to give it its full name) made its début in October 1981 in *Répons*, and has been used by a great many composers since. It has now been reduplicated and marketed. Some of the possibilities of this flexible and formidably fast machine are over a thousand oscillators, additive and subtractive synthesis, non-linear distortion (wave shaping), frequency and ring modulation, many types of filtering, linear prediction, fast Fourier transforms, phasing, 'harmonizer' effects, reverberation and delay.

A very important side of scientific research is psycho-acoustics – the study of how we perceive sounds. David Wessel and Steve McAdams, for example, have found the various synthesis programs invaluable for designing experiments in perception charting the borders of how rhythm, pitch and timbre define one sort of pattern or another: how the same sequence of notes can be heard completely differently if the timbre, for example, is changed just 'so much'. This has been fascinating for composers and has brought them a salutary realism.

Another important scientific area is acoustics. Instrumental acoustics are studied. Methods of mechanical extension are invented. New mutes for brass instruments have been developed, and Robert Dick and later Pierre-Yves Artaud (now in charge of this department) have studied flute transformations. Also, digital sound-processing techniques are constantly being created. If a computer is to react instantaneously and 'intelligently' to a sound or phrase it hears, it must have very discriminating 'ears' and much successful research has gone into how a machine can analyze what it receives fast enough to make a response. One recent program is so fast that the live player complained it was unreal in effect – accompanying without the usual accompanist's split-second inertia. (The computer is thinking in millionths of a second.)

Room acoustics are researched into by means of the adjustable concert hall, the *Espace de Projection*. Computer analysis of the way sound is reflected and how sound is changed by such reflections is paving the way for the concert halls of the future.

Tod Machover, who as well as composing, made an enormous contribution as head of research from 1980–4, organizing (amongst other things) large conferences on 'The composer and the computer' and 'The concept of musical research' has been succeeded by Jean-Baptiste Barrière, also a man of unusual vision, and the incumbent of the post will change every two years.

The pedagogy department, like that of research, receives applications and invites considerable numbers to come to IRCAM, some with IRCAM commissions. Over six-week periods the visitors are taught by tutors the foundations of sound processing, acoustics, psycho-acoustics and programming. No previous experience is necessary.

The production/creation department takes over from pedagogy and invites the new initiates to take part in research or the realization of a composition. Many distinguished composers have of course been invited to work at IRCAM without needing pedagogical initiation; no one would deem it necessary (or politic) to put Stockhausen, Cage or Steve Reich through this process in order to realize their projects. Each year, with the exception of 1984 – a difficult year in which the main computers were changed – fifteen to twenty composers have been invited. They work with tutors who teach them the programs, etc., necessary for their work. They are greeted by a spirit of enthusiasm and helpfulness which must surely be the unwritten philosophy of IRCAM. Anybody who is approached is ready to explain patiently his discoveries, his specialities, if they can be of use to the composer. He will only demand in return information on what new things the composer sees and demands.

The final link in the chain is the department of public information. This department presents the finished work together with an educational programme about music of our century in general and IRCAM's news in particular.

This brings us to a very important part of Boulez's plan which has not yet been mentioned: the Ensemble Intercontemporain. This group of contemporary music specialists was created in December 1976 to go hand-in-glove with IRCAM. It is not only the vehicle for commissions which involve electronic-live interaction (which is most commissions), it is also available for research and experiment. The players are well-salaried with sufficient time on their hands to explore link-ups with computers or acousticians. But, of course, their main activity is to give concerts, not just in Paris, but all over the world.

Twice each year a changing international panel sits to read the many hundred scores sent to IRCAM and decide who should be kept an eye on, who should be invited to take the pedagogy course, who should be commissioned to write a new work at IRCAM or who should simply have his score (whether involving electro-acoustic techniques or not) performed by the Ensemble. The principle of anonymous scores (all names taped over) is rigorously applied. Boulez aims to discover the best living composers and to make them known, a parallel policy to his more familiar quest of popularizing the Second Viennese School and other still-misunderstood masters of the century. Finally IRCAM's Public Information department produces cassettes and, more recently, records and videos to go with the recondite research papers. The record *IRCAM: un portrait* gives a host of research examples, all carefully explained in the sleeve notes and eight extracts of compositions realized at IRCAM. The series *Points de repère: collection dirigée par Pierre Boulez* gives a wide selection of new works, many of them not using electro-acoustic media at all, but carefully conducted by Boulez with the Ensemble Intercontemporain and recorded in the *Espace de Projection* to show the works' acoustic and timbral finesses to full advantage.

It is a firm policy that IRCAM should not exist in splendid isolation. IRCAM is part of the *Centre Pompidou* and contributes to the cultural perspective of the *Centre*'s huge international exhibitions such as *Paris/Moscow* or *Vienna* with performances of unusual works and musicological documentation. IRCAM tries to get its works performed by other ensembles. For instance 'IRCAM in London' (1985) was a BBC collaboration consisting of nine works performed by British players. This makes sound economics, as it is cheaper to exchange compositions than orchestras, and is better for the composer. IRCAM also seeks creative collaboration with other performing groups, as in the case of Birtwistle's and Höller's operas, where there is, as it were, an IRCAM element in a larger commission.

Sometimes one may find it difficult to remember that all that has been described is the result of the vision of one man. Yet his role is not that of a dictator. Instigator, certainly. But his hand is not oppressive and IRCAM gives the impression of an institution that is being encouraged to evolve naturally now it has been set on its course. Like a new composition, IRCAM must increasingly make its own way in the world, and that it is certainly doing. Nevertheless, one has to admire it as the outpouring of an exceptionally creative individual. It is a unique institution.

Biography

1925–   Born at Montbrison (Loire) on 26 March. Went to the grammar school at Montbrison, and then to the Catholic school at Saint-Étienne.

1941   Left school, and for a year attended a class in higher mathematics at Lyons as a prelude to gaining admission to the École Polytechnique in Paris. At the same time he studied piano and harmony with Lionel de Pachmann, son of the famous Chopin player.

1942   Left for Paris, and decided to try not for the École Polytechnique but for the Paris Conservatoire.

1944   Joined Messiaen's harmony class at the Paris Conservatoire, and also attended his renowned class in analysis held privately in a friend's house.

1944–6   Took weekly lessons in counterpoint from Honegger's wife, Andrée Vaurabourg, in Montmartre.

1945   First prize in harmony at the Conservatoire. Studied serial techniques with René Leibowitz.

1946   Boulez becomes musical director of the Compagnie Renaud-Barrault, and continues in this post until 1956.

1947   Première of the Sonatine for flute and piano (Van Botterdael, Mercenier) in Brussels.

1950   First performances in Paris of the Second Piano Sonata (Yvonne Loriod) and *Le soleil des eaux* (under Roger Désormière).

1951   First performance of *Polyphonie X* under Hans Rosbaud at Donaueschingen.

1952   Première of part of the first book of *Structures* given by Olivier Messiaen and Pierre Boulez in Paris.

1954	Foundation of the Petit-Marigny concerts under the patronage of the Compagnie Renaud-Barrault.
1955	The Petit-Marigny concerts are re-named Domaine Musical. Première of *Le marteau sans maître* under Hans Rosbaud at Baden-Baden, and of part of the *Livre pour quatuor* by the Marschner Quartet at Donaueschingen.
1957	Boulez gives first performance of his Third Piano Sonata at Darmstadt, and conducts première of *Le visage nuptial* (2nd version) in Cologne.
1958	Première of *Deux improvisations sur Mallarmé* (afterwards included in *Pli selon pli*) under Hans Rosbaud in Hamburg. First performance of *Poésie pour pouvoir* under Hans Rosbaud and Pierre Boulez at Donaueschingen.
1959	Settles in Baden-Baden at the invitation of the Südwestfunk and of Heinrich Strobel. Conducts *Tombeau* (afterwards included in *Pli selon pli*) at Donaueschingen.
1960	Conducts première of *Pli selon pli* in Cologne. Gives lectures at the Darmstadt Summer School that were later published as *Boulez on Music Today*.
1960–3	Takes classes in analysis and composition at Basle.
1961	First performance of second book of *Structures* (Yvonne Loriod, Pierre Boulez) at Donaueschingen.
1963	Visiting professor at Harvard University. Conducts in Paris the French première of *Wozzeck* and the first performance of Messiaen's *Sept haïkaï*.
1964	Conducts première of *Figures–Doubles–Prismes* in Brussels. First concert with the BBC Symphony Orchestra at the Royal Festival Hall in London.
1965	Conducts première of *Éclat* in Los Angeles. Takes conducting class in Basle.
1966	Conducts *Parsifal* at Bayreuth at the invitation of Wieland Wagner, and *Tristan und Isolde* in Japan.
1967	Hands over the direction of the Domaine Musical to Gilbert Amy. Is invited by Georg Szell to conduct the Cleveland Orchestra, and makes regular visits as guest conductor until 1972. Conducts the BBC Symphony Orchestra in Moscow and Leningrad in concerts of contemporary music including *Éclat* and Webern's Op. 30.

| 1968 | Premières of *Livre pour cordes* in London and of *Domaines* in Brussels, both with Boulez conducting. |

1969   Appointed Chief Conductor of the BBC Symphony Orchestra. First period as guest conductor of the New York Philharmonic. Conducts Debussy's *Pelléas et Mélisande* at Covent Garden.

1970   Première at Stuttgart of *e.e. cummings ist der Dichter*, under Pierre Boulez and Clytus Gottwald. Boulez himself conducts the première of *Éclat/Multiples* in London. Appointed Chief Conductor of the New York Philharmonic in succession to Leonard Bernstein. Is asked by President Georges Pompidou to plan and establish IRCAM.

1973   First performance of '*... explosante-fixe ...*' by the Lincoln Chamber Society, New York.

1974   Première of Jean-Louis Barrault's play, *Ainsi parla Zarathoustra*, based on Nietzsche, with music for voice and instrumental ensemble by Boulez.

1975   Première of *Rituel* by the BBC Symphony Orchestra under Boulez in London. Founding of the Ensemble InterContemporain, a Parisian counterpart to the London Sinfonietta. Boulez ends his period as Chief Conductor of the BBC Symphony Orchestra.

1976   Is made a professor at the Collège de France. Wolfgang Wagner invites Boulez to conduct the *Ring* at Bayreuth for the hundredth anniversary of its first performance, with Patrice Chéreau as producer. Further performances each year until 1980.

1977   Opening of IRCAM. Boulez leaves the New York Philharmonic. Conducts première of *Messagesquisse* at La Rochelle.

1977–8 Resplendent series of concerts of contemporary music – *Passage du XX Siècle* – at IRCAM.

1979   Conducts the première of Berg's *Lulu* with Friedrich Cerha's completion of the score, at the Paris Opéra.

1980   Première of *Notations* for orchestra, transformations of four of the 1945 piano *Notations*, under Daniel Barenboim in Paris.

1981   Publication of *Points de Repère*, collected essays on music since 1945.

1981–4	Boulez conducts successive premières of *Répons* 1 (Donaueschingen 1981), *Répons* 2 (London 1982) and *Répons* 3 (Turin 1984).
1984	Première of revised version of *Improvisation sur Mallarmé III* (from *Pli selon pli*) by the BBC Symphony Orchestra under Pierre Boulez in London.
1985	First performance of *Dérive* under Oliver Knussen in London.

Index

Index